E4

The Book of Intrusions

A Sheila na Gig by Desmond MacNamara: "The early Norman invaders of Ireland in the twelfth and thirteenth centuries frequently installed these curiously explicit ladies on the entrance arches of their churches, where they warded off the evil eye or induced good luck. There are classical precedents, the impetus was Norman but the style and popularity were very Irish indeed. The Fitzgeralds, Fitzmaurices, Bourkes and ffrenches were a persuasive lot who, as the chronicler said, became 'more Irish than the Irish themselves.'

"The National Museum in Dublin has become extremely coy about their collection of these carvings and visitors have complained, to be fobbed off with Romanesque columns and arches."

Desmond MacNamara

The Book of Intrusions

Dalkey Archive Press

© 1994 by Desmond MacNamara
First Edition

Library of Congress Cataloging-in-Publication Data
MacNamara, Desmond, 1918-
    The book of intrusions / Desmond MacNamara. — 1st ed.
    1. Characters and characteristics in literature—Fiction.
2. Fiction—Authorship—Fiction. 3. Unfinished books—Fiction.
4. Ireland—Fiction. I. Title.
PR6063.A2552B66   1994   823'.914—dc20   93-36126
ISBN 1-56478-041-4

Partially funded by grants from The National Endowment for the Arts and
The Illinois Arts Council.

Dalkey Archive Press
4241 Illinois State University
Normal, IL 61790-4241

*Printed on permanent/durable acid-free paper and bound in the United States of
America.*

The Book of Intrusions

1

The wind blew in, heady and unpolluted from the endless west.

"Stones are old and man is so very new. A wall is the result of mindless geological epochs and human cunning."

"Oh that's very true. Human cunning."

"The truth is so evident that it is no more than a truism. But then so many prime statements are truisms: empty platitudes without moral inference."

"The cunning man, mind you, is a deviously minded person, a man without principles, plotting and scheming."

"A principle is a fundamental and self-evident fact. Too often the term is applied to some squalid ne plus ultra of human endurance, or hopeless aspiration."

"Nature is devious too, by the same token. Anyone born without sinuosity is fighting against nature."

This randomly chosen and unimportant exchange happened on the edge of a small stone outcrop on a Connemara bay. The participants were Owen Mountmellick and his serving demon, MacGilla.

If there are fallen angels there can well be fallen demons, exiled on earth into predestined futility. An onlooker in his cups once advanced the theory that Mountmellick and MacGilla were just such, serving a term of suffering to atone for the earlier sins of their fathers. Arrogance, hubris, despair, presumption, any such maladies of the spirit could have warped their genetic structure.

However, the foregoing is only a trailer, a demonstrative vignette to whet morbid appetites. Merely to record the characteristics of the couple or to allow them slowly to grow to solidity will not do and for this reason: neither of them is, was or could be solid in any euclidean or platonic sense.

These digressions are necessary and anyone who thinks that a narrative of this kind comes ready honed, like Occam's razor, is deluded. The facts are multifarious and can be multiplied indefinitely.

Every reduction of the facts is a further measure of inaccuracy. By the end of this record, compressed to an acceptable length, the clarity of truth is likely to be very sullied. On the other hand it will have saved the reader a lot of tedium.

The apparent author of this screed is no more than an editor: perhaps a scribe. In the Louvre is an alabaster block carved in the form of the scribe Nebmerutef, sitting on his hunkers taking dictation from an unprepossessing being with the body of a baboon and the head of an Alsatian hound. His face is rapt in concentration and if he feels the twinges of Nilotic rheumatism, they don't show on his face. He writes under divine preternatural compulsion. That's how it is with Mountmellick, MacGilla, and their various conspirators. Before they can properly exist, they must find a scribe: and things being as they are, penniless, on a free market, they have to do it by stealth.

It is necessary and, indeed, the scribe is permitted to say something of the cosmology of such creatures. Inexact it may be, but that is the nature of cosmology.

Teilhard de Chardin came near the point, poetically, when he suggested that man's evolution was changing from physical to social in the process of ultimate union with the Spirit. He overlooked the follies and false starts of the evolutionary process.

Mountmellick and his colleagues are good examples of these and charity should be exercised towards the literary paleontologist who records their follies.

Revolution and change occur under tremendous historical pressures, social, technological, geological and meteorological, and the art of writing, and particularly the rise of the novel, has led to the recent mutative conditions which now threaten mankind.

The vast archives of writing are beginning to choke themselves. Microfilm is only a palliative. But what of the unpublished? Nature conserves energy, and this unpublished energy has a physical pattern that may soon be measured with cyclotrons and similar tools. It has to go somewhere; the generation of force is unimaginable. Small wonder that such energy of intellectual origin found its way into the only vacuum available, a place called Limbo, an out-patients' department of Purgatory, on the purlieus of Hell.

Limbo, by Vatican decree or omission, became tenantless, and the souls of the worthy unredeemed and unbaptised innocents were given superior accommodation. As always happens, the next wave of immigration occupied the slums of the earlier one. Characters from unfinished novels, film scripts, narrative poems and other sources of synthetic personality went to Limbo. Naturally there was overcrowding. Unlike the gentle Platonists and innocent babies, they were a turbulent lot, fighting, seething, egotistical, unfulfilled.

They exist as particles, literary particles of various shapes and construction, negative, positive and, since the advent of the anti-novel, reverse, inverse and perverse particles, repelling and attracting at random. Since physicists have used up much of the Roman and Greek alphabets to describe mere subatomic particles, the scribe, in his minor capacity as analytical critic, has been driven to use the old Gaelic alphabet of eighteen letters.

All such letters are named after trees of varying superstitious significance: Ailm, Beth, Coll, Fir, Birch and Hazel. G for Gort is the Ivy, and both Mountmellick and MacGilla belong to this class, positive and negative, but given to electrical variations. Mountmellick is a Gortic particle, which poetically describes his insinuating parasitic toughness.

His first probing tendril was below the sensory threshold. Mountmellick twisted, probed and deflowered a tiny lesion in the isolating walls of Hell, followed electromagnetically by MacGilla, at that time a negative particle of infinite unimportance.

After many attempts to insinuate himself into people of consequence and virtue, he accidentally happened on the scribe near the passenger ramp at London Airport. The only evidence of his infection was a distortion in the Tannoy system which halted the feeble cerebrations of the scribe and misdirected him to an extroverted holiday queue bound for the Costa Brava. Fortunately the numbness passed quickly and he was able to escape to the sedate Castilian procession embarking for Madrid. By the time he was passing over Lourdes, both Mountmellick and MacGilla were well dug in, MacGilla affecting the usual old soldier's grumbles about his host's rough and primitive psyche, before falling into noisy sleep.

For some time, before ruining his host's holiday, both entities or particles continued to live as the merest microcysts on the walls of the scribe's psyche. It was several days before they began to assert themselves and compel their victim into the Castilian night to buy paper and pen to ease the irritation which their first stage of growth was causing.

Mountmellick's origins, together with those of MacGilla, his lackey, are not susceptible to verification. Much of the following is therefore a collection of hearsay comment, guesswork and carefully deduced inference.

Eighteen forty-seven was the year before the balloon went up in Europe. In West Cork, young couples were merrily producing babies and feeding the families on rack-rented lazybeds of potatoes. The black leaves were still only a faraway rumour. Misery throve and discontent, but horror was a harvest or two away. The Parisians had not yet manned the barricades and the Hungarians were more hopeful than they had a right to be. In London there was a trade recession but nobody had yet been sworn in as a Special Constable to truncheon unruly mechanics and socialists. Dostoyevski visited the city and was shocked by the tarts showing off their wares in porches in the Haymarket.

In the May of that year, Charles Lever, the Peninsular War novelist, left Dublin where he had been staying with friends, to visit the family of an old medical school companion at Sudbury, outside London. What could the claret do but flow, as well as the ratafia, redcurrant shrub, orange flower water with brandy, brandy posset, ozyat, heather ale and various mullings. Lever had intended to write a novel of enormous length about two Irishmen, one in the old reformed Irish Brigade under Napoleon and the other in Wellington's army, both friends from the same townsland near Lough Gur, Limerick. Both men loved the same girl, who is thought to have been the daughter of an innkeeper in Vigo but was really the ward of the Duke of Tetuan. The only strong characters that ever got word-born were Mountmellick and his manservant MacGilla. Mountmellick seems to have begun life following Sir John Moore's army through Galicia in some civilian capacity, billeting with the ensigns and hinting darkly about a quest for lost papers. Misgivings about suspected pederastic occasions delicately hinted were soothed by his rhetorical balm and up to the point where the writing ceased he was popular enough.

Why Lever never finished the book is uncertain. It was a year of pestilential epidemics and he may have forsaken writing for his profession of medicine. When he died in Trieste in 1872, there was no sign of any part of the ms., although as a British Consul his papers were returned to Whitehall and scrupulously examined. Perhaps it lies lost in a forgotten pigeonhole of boxwood and maple. On the other hand, Lever was an established writer at a time when the British Cabinet officially vetted mistresses in the proximity of royal succession. By the time he died, in Trieste, up to his oxters in Austrian intrigues, he represented the most straitlaced administration that England had ever known. Perhaps he destroyed his early drafts. Maybe he intended to drop the two soldiers and the innkeeper's daughter and concentrate on Mountmellick, a sort of anti-Quixote. In which case his only possible title, *The Bugger of Burgos,* would have been quite unacceptable in an increasingly conventional and pietistic society. Probably he was reluctant to destroy it entirely, for the Gortic particle of Mountmellick was unusually powerful and must have endured long in ms. and in the author's guilty conscience.

It is very probable that he used the leaves of the ms. to line the drawers of his military chest of Burmese teak and there they remained until the exigencies of the dysentery epidemic in Spezia in 1859 drove him to wipe his arse with them. Some intelligent speculation must be indulged on such matters.

2

Due to his long incarceration, Mountmellick had a minor obsession about walls. As soon as his primal particle had filled out and grown dimensions on the scribe's nervous fat, he set about finding gainful employment. Where else should a fictional entity find employment but in the film industry?

Somehow, with smooth intrusion and a courtier's manners, he managed to sell himself to an international television corporation, to write the script on *The Walls of Mankind,* under the auspices of UNESCO or some such body.

He pondered. It was too late for Koestler to do the narration, but at first Mountmellick could only think of a few basic mural functions, one of them unacceptable for family viewing.

Walls could contain, imprison, discourage, prevent, protect or merely shelter. In the case of males they can be pissed against. Women squat. Looked at fairly, this meant that half of mankind was denied this important form of mural relief.

Eventually he assembled a list of walls of historical consequence and of a protective nature. There was the Wall of China, Hadrian's Wall, Offa's Dyke, Watts' Dyke, the Black Pig's Dyke and hundreds more beyond memory or convenience. The most intriguing wall was also the most modest.

Dalkey Island in Dublin Bay has the grass of a herd of goats, a Martello tower and an old chapel. Roughly pear-shaped, it had recently yielded a prehistoric neolithic settlement at the narrow end, but protected from the high pastures by a massive wall. Who built this wall, and why? Bronze-speared people came and were forgotten, then the Dumnoni from Devon and finally the Vikings. What danger lay on the far side of the twenty rock-fringed acres?

Sardinia was similar. Why did the slim, bronze-armoured squireens build towers on every scattered crag to protect a few acres of stones and lizards? Mountmellick decided that certain cultures carry the logic of privacy and protection beyond the limits of military and social strategy. On another Irish island cyclopean walls built by forgotten hands guarded a few acres of thin grass against marauders whose nearest parish would be Boston, Mass. In the outer extremities of Europe, to wit, western Ireland, this vast fortress was probably the shrine of a dark Formorian god. Then, as now, the Irish were a devout nation of shrine builders.

This was his theme and it served him for nearly a year as he scoured the Nordic lands, the Latin lands and the principalities of Outremer and the older places beyond, attended by MacGilla. It gave him a necessary cosmopolitan polish.

He covered Greek walls of many epochs, Akkadian walls, Sumerian walls that were no more than depressing and arbitrary trenches, Mittanic walls and Hittite walls, squat and heavy. A Roman Vespasian near Leptis Magna baked in the African sun. Its honeyed columns, he noted, were still used cloacally by the present descendants of the gentle Vandal immigrants.

Mountmellick secured a lengthy footage from Claudian paintings, exciting to the eye, of undressed Sabine ladies and an expiring dishonoured Lucretia, displaying their ravished charms against Sabillian walls, Etruscan walls and even Iapygian walls. His instincts were, as ever, meritorious and sound. Sequences like this enliven dull documentary films.

It is necessary to record at least this synopsis of the life of the two particles MacGilla and Mountmellick up to the point of adulthood, about a year later. In twelve months from a halting start the couple had adapted themselves to the most meritricious aspects of late twentieth-century culture. What remnants of the eighteenth century and Regency conditioning remained was a help, not a hindrance, since it left in them an expectation of unmerited preferment and an unself-conscious ease in matters of nepotism. Now the apprenticeship was nearly over and Mountmellick was stretching the last shreds of the budget across the five million drystone entanglements that held the coloured deserts of Connemara like a net around a cherry tree.

"What do these walls do?" he murmured. "Shield the wind, clear the ground. Shelter the grass of a goat and a cow. Did the Red Bull of Cooley stand omnipotently in a geometrical fragment like these, with his seraglio of silken heifers each in a honeycomb of tumbled stone around him? Perhaps," he mused sententiously, "between layers of rotted kelp, this rocky soil is bound by the stubble of archaic cereals, checked unevenly by sickles of stone and bronze."

This was too good to waste. "Hey, give me a pen."

MacGilla extracted a ballpoint inscribed "Compliments of Thos. Mac Keoghan. Clanrickard St., Castlepollard. Ante-Post. No Credit." He rubbed it on the sole of his boot to excite the flow of ink.

Mountmellick scrupulously scribbled and observed the sky. The low black clouds below a bright blue sky looked like a rococo dome, lacking only floating nymphs and loves. The heather held yesterday's rain in hidden pendants and fed the hollows of decayed spagnum, dry to the feet, but secret reservoirs to feed the scattered lakes in limestone depressions. Beyond the road below, and beyond scattered green peninsulas, lay the sea, measurable with instruments but not by imagination. The land had surrendered, in the unthinkable geological past, and left a few colonies of rock and grass standing clear from the coast to mark its old dominion.

"There's a warm front coming up," remarked MacGilla. "I don't fancy that bright hazy light. Are you going to see Miss Amargamente for lunch? It's three days since we were with her in Galway City, before we drove her to the hotel at Maam Cross. I have a feeling about her and I think that the sooner we test her out the better it will be. Mind that green patch. It'd suck you in till there was nothing left of you barring your insurance policy."

The bog road was narrow but well metalled, a raised causeway across a water desert of unnatural colours and droning bees. The car (courtesy Ryans Hire Service) translated angular obstacles into curving parabolas of body movement by virtue of its springing.

"You're certainly right, Mac. Mustn't put off the day. I hope you are right about her. I've had the same feeling since we met her on the plane from Paris and persuaded her to stop off at Galway before she went on to this damned literary symposium. Drive on to Maam Cross."

"Anyone would think she was an American banshee bewailing your death," countered MacGilla. "She has the drive, you know, and the skin of a conger eel."

Mountmellick stared moodily at the rising road and MacGilla's foot pressed on the pedal to shorten the miles. He had found himself sitting beside Loreto Amargamente in the Paris–Shannon plane a few days earlier and they had, all three, MacGilla riding postillion, shared a car to Galway City.

Race Week was just over, but the hotels were still paralysed with the weight of trade. Solitary citizens sprawled on staircase steps sleeping off drink or fatigue. Couples of both sexes clung together, immobile and somnolent like mounted frogs. Lights blazed and open bars seemed tenantless and untended. A man in a plumed cocked hat and terraced gold epaulette lay on a garden bench, his sword extruding awkwardly from his cape and his sagging sightless face in need of a shave.

It was like *The Death of Sardanapalus.* The slaves who had administered the poison had fled. A Ferris wheel forged in a mill ere England had attained to empire rotated in the square, outlined in archaic yellow lights. It drove and scattered shadows and brightness over the blatant haunches of the women and the fustian paunches of the men and rippled into parlours and bedrooms and sundry chambers where curtains were undrawn.

Gallantly squiring and with no evil in his heart, because of lack of temptation or inclination or temporary incapacity, Mountmellick sought for two rooms for chaste rest. Neither in the square, by the railway, by the river nor by the mossy complexities of the harbour could they find haven.

With MacGilla to the fore, all three found a temporary and humid rest in a gazebo lying in tall meadow grass by the Corrib river, which eternally emptied Lough Corrib which was itself eternally filled by the tinted clouds from the ocean into which the river emptied. The meadow grass released drenchings of water which left them sodden to the thighs.

"These dews were praised of old and held in poetic reverence. Bountiful as Cnogva's loins are the dews of Tuaim Inbir." Mountmellick tried to raise damp spirits and limbs. Nonetheless, the dawn lifted behind them and coloured the Atlantic sky and the birds sang melodiously. "You take your claws off my patch or you'll feel my beak up your plumage," MacGilla translated.

Under Mountmellick's gentle probing, Loreto, perhaps bemused by the dawn magic, gave a brief account of her life and purpose. A citizen of Pensacola, Florida, she had been a university lecturer, copywriter, archive delver, university of the air producer and an adviser to an educational publisher. At a mature but uncertain age, her gradually coalescing ambition was to control cultural destinies from a lofty boardroom throne in the field of publishing.

This was accepted by Mountmellick and MacGilla with nods and attentive "ahs" and Loreto's faculties were alerted when Mountmellick asked her whether, in the course of her career, she had ever come across something worth publishing that had failed in its purpose of being printed, bound and distributed.

At first Loreto seemed to be genuinely nonplussed. "Whaddya mean. Some, I guess. It would depend on policy, house style or something."

"I mean," said Mountmellick slowly, "did you ever receive and reject or not pursue a manuscript of a novel, a story, a fictionalised biography that should, for reasons of merit, authorship or other acceptable reasons, have been published?"

"Well, publishers do that all the time. It happened to Jane Austen. It's easy to sneer after the event."

"True for you, allaniv." MacGilla nodded in sympathy. "Still, not even an epic poem?"

"Wait a minute." Loreto reached for the flat plastic casket of a Filofax compendium and flicked and probed for a few moments. "Yes. Here it is. I don't know if this is the kind of thing you mean. I never read it, nor even saw it."

"Could you give us a few details?" Mountmellick was firm, but sympathetic and encouraging.

"I was on a plane from London to Valencia, Spain, and found myself sitting next to a charming elderly Irish gentleman called . . ."—she peered into her Filofax—"Ferguson-Bourke. I was going through some papers and we got to talking. He seemed fairly knowledgeable on literary and historical matters and after a while he mentioned that he had a manuscript, a copy of an ancient original and a mid-nineteenth-century translation into English. He apologised for the rotundity of its prose. As he pointed out, each epoch has its own style and lays its own stress in translating an older original. It was one of the papers offered to the Royal Irish Ossianic Society on, about 1856: a mythological story of some sort. The Ossianic Society privately published many such texts. People like Sir William Wilde, Oscar's father, his mother Speranza and Sir Samuel Ferguson, the poet who fired Yeats' imagination, were members. It was the great age of antiquarianism, before science intervened and scholars scribbled through winter evenings by smoky candles. I don't know much about such matters, but I checked what I could later."

Both Mountmellick and MacGilla seemed peculiarly interested.

"What have you done about it?"

"Oh, nothing. Just preparing material for a forthcoming paper. But I have his address, near London. He is a doctor of medicine: retired, I imagine."

When the narrow streets of Galway awoke to life after its Race Week fiesta, Mountmellick conducted the others for coffee and warm rolls, holding forth on the Norman founders of the city as he parked his hired car in a street near Saint Nicholas' Church. "A strange people, the Normans. They shaped an empire of first and second cousins from Jerusalem to Galway, but they never had an emperor, apart from a few local pretenders. The people buried, or still living, here had more belief in Prester John than the Emperor Baldwin of Constantinople."

As they sipped their scalding coffee he droned on. "These Irish Normans promulgated Europe's first apartheid laws: the Statute of Kilkenny, in 1363. All intercourse with the natives, marital, musical, poetic and generally cultural, was forbidden. Mercantile matters were prudently excepted, de facto. It didn't work, of course. Never does. These Norman families still flourish locally, the Lynches, the Brownes, the Joyces, the Costellos, the ffrenches, the Barretts: they are still here, scattered around."

Loreto tried to memorise what she could of Mountmellick's oration and gave her reason for being in the west. She hoped to stay for a few days before departing further north to Sligo, the landscape of the poet

Yeats, where she hoped to read a paper at a symposium on the poet. A rival to the annual Yeats Summer School, but sponsored by a large insurance company, it was to be held under a marquee on the Lake Isle of Innisfree, a half-acre blob of bush in the middle of Lough Gill.

They continued their journey into the heart of Connemara to the lakeside town of Oughterard, and Mountmellick resolved to question Loreto further, after depositing her in a small early nineteenth-century fishing hotel where the usual clientele would probably confine itself to twelve-year-old whiskey and the metaphysics of fly-fishing on Lough Corrib.

3

Loreto was lodged comfortably, within easy distance of river and lake, geographical occurrences in which she had little interest. True, she had a mental list of notable rivers with conventional attributes. The Tiber was yellow foaming. The Thames flowed through English dynastic and mercantile history. The Ganges was holy and the Danube blue. The Orinoco was the abode of Tudor mermaids, and the Seine separated Abelard from the Ile de Cité. The Liffey nurtured Shem and Shaun from her stony Palladian nipples. For that matter, Austria was still the cockpit of Europe and the Mountains of Mourne swept inevitably down to the sea. It was a tidy system of geological cosmography.

4

She was neatly surrounded by her notes, some days later, when she saw two figures disembarking from a car outside the window near her writing desk. She was the only guest to use this piece of furniture.

"My dear Loreto." Mountmellick stood on the stone steps of the buttery and stretched his arms, palms upturned. "How delightful to find you here. I was unable to telephone." He descended, advanced and kissed her fingertips, a ploy which he could perform without causing embarrassment.

After courtesies had been exchanged, he invited her to lunch with him, loudly praising the traditional cooking overseen by the youngest son of a nearby baron.

The meal was sufficiently good to engender its own agreeable conversation, choosing and commenting on the Georgian fare available. Trout was followed by beef collops and marrow pudding. After enquiry and discussion they consumed scolloped oysters and stewed pippins.

Mountmellick put on substance, nurturing body and soul, or the random collection of reflexes that he used instead of a soul. The last course was long in preparation and Mountmellick asked Loreto the subject of her proposed lecture to the assembled muse-ridden on the Lake Isle of Innisfree.

"Oh! Rather an interesting subject. I guess no one has ever dealt with it before. 'The Prostate Gland in Anglo-Irish Literature.' I had a lot of deep research to do on the forensic side."

Mountmellick had indeed sensed uneasiness, restlessness, even outrage from Innisfree sources. Now he understood why.

"It's a very unusual angle. I mean, it does get right down to the . . . heart of the subject. But do you think it wise? They are not very enthusiastic about prostate matters in this country, or uterine, for that matter."

"That's exactly why I chose it. Jesuschrist, what's the use of wading through bookloads of cabalistic imagery if the answer is to be found in the prostate?"

"It is indeed a very original approach to poetic analysis, but it may raise a few eyebrows."

"Sure, it means trouble and newspaper headlines. What's the purpose otherwise?"

Much as his conditioning made him deplore her attitude, Mountmellick felt she was just the person needed for his next enterprise. But a great deal more enquiry was needed.

"Who were your parents?"

The question surprised her, sitting at an Irish table in a western fishing hotel. She chose, at Mountmellick's entreaty, the last course, hartshorn and almond flummery, chilled, with Madeira. The motives behind his question needed examining, and as she scooped the aromatic custard she considered her reply.

"I can't see why you should be so interested in me." She spoke with mock coyness. "Well, if you must know, my father was a scriptwriter in Warners studios. He came from Florida and later became a sort of journalist: a public relations adviser in Hollywood. My mother was at one time a short story writer and had a solid Boston Irish background, lace curtains and all."

"So you are a native-born American?"

"Many years later. Just in time from my mother's point of view. They met in Paris, two young students the year before Hitler marched on Poland."

"This is fascinating information. We must discuss it further. Look, I have to go to the north of Mayo, about forty miles north. I haven't quite finished with these damned walls. People who escape incarceration sometimes become a bit obsessed. But on the bare hills of Mayo, a vast landscape of walls has been discovered, buried under a bog, twelve feet below the heather. They stretch for miles in parallel lines across hill and hollow. The neolithic people who built them for farming cut down the trees, overgrazed the lands and then abandoned them. The bog mosses crept up and smothered them. That was when the walls of Jericho were still standing or the Celts scrawled up the Danube valley. Would you like to come with us? We should be back by evening and there are a few things of mutual interest that we could discuss on the way."

Loreto closed her compendium smartly. "I'd love to come, just wait a few moments while I freshen up." Prehistorical topography was the least of her urgencies but she felt a strange compulsion to pursue matters further.

5

They drove along narrow undulating roads. "Them's the Maamturk mountains on the left, ma'am. We'll be into the Joyce country presently."

"You mean James Joyce came from here?" Loreto started to scan the landscape. It was worth a couple of lines in her Filofax.

"Not exactly." Mountmellick was avuncularly didactic. The Joyces were a Norman-French family. One of the Tribes of Galway who acquired swardlands and ploughlands around here in the thirteenth century. "Still lots of them around. They were enthusiastic inter-breeders."

"But James Joyce . . ." Loreto interjected.

"His father came from the city of Cork." MacGilla swerved the car to avoid a scattering of nervous rabbits grazing on the luscious hedge weeds. "Joyce thought that significant and hung a large photograph of the River Lee on his Paris wall in a rococo frame carved from Sicilian cork."

"That was significant?" Loreto tried to make a mental note.

"He certainly thought so."

They drove on for a while until Mountmellick noticed a widening in the road. "Could you pull in here for a moment. I want to say something."

"Why are you stopping? What do you think you're doing?"

Loreto's sometimes flinty personality yielded to the chthonic panic of the Arcadians: a distrust of the wilderness. Simultaneously she realised her feminine vulnerability.

MacGilla looked over his shoulder at her from the driving seat. "Easy now, we just want to be sure of something. You have the floor, sir," he nodded to Mountmellick.

Mountmellick began with diffidence and embarrassment that a guardian uncle might feel when explaining the mysteries of menstruation to an innocent young girl. His opening words were not reassuring.

"Not all of us were born inter faecium et urinam," he began. Loreto felt a slight relief but not enough for comfort. "Between the shite and the piss, ma'am," MacGilla explained soothingly.

"Let me outa here, at once. Do you hear me?" The wilderness of the coloured landscape seemed, comparatively, a haven of refuge.

"There, there, don't be alarmed. You shouldn't have put it into English," Mountmellick admonished MacGilla. "That tongue isn't called Anglo-Saxon for nothing. Some words are . . . ah, trigger-happy with their secondary meanings. Words of abuse. But consider . . ."

He began to expand and expound. "Consider 'una scatola de zolfanelli' or 'fiammifieri.' A line from Petrarch, one might think. Or 'une boîte des allumettes.' Surely this has the precision of Descartes, incisive. Whereas, 'a box of matches' has the directness of Locke or a phrase by Defoe. Now the Gaelic Bosca Cipini has decidedly Mafia undertones." Loreto began to feel, with relief, that she was faced by a harmless psychopath.

Mountmellick decided that it was the moment to come into the open, but could only do so in the rather didactic manner of his original creator, one hundred thirty years ago. "You know how it was with Schliemann when he suggested that the old tales of the Trojan War were true. The classical pedants laughed at him. In much the same way, people, even theologians, have qualified some of the old medieval concepts of extraterrestrial existence. Heaven and Hell. Since these are both eternal I can't speak for them. Even Schliemann made several mistakes. But he proved that Troy existed and buried kings with gold masks. Now, I can vouch for Purgatory, perhaps, and Limbo for certain. That is where my companion and myself have come from."

"Are you trying to tell me that you are not real flesh and blood people, some sort of grammatical Frankensteins?" The fountains of revelation had the copious convulsions of a Bernini, but Loreto stood her ground. "If you think I am one of your literary abortions, you couldn't be more wrong. What am I doing, sitting in a car, on the far side of the mountains of the moon with two lunatics?"

"Look here." Mountmellick became more emphatic. "I know where I came from and I know where he came from and when I first met you I knew where you came from. That's how Irish people, Jews, Assyrians and other national fragments uneasily classify each other when they meet in odd corners of the world. It is not a sympathy or even a fellow feeling, just a national compulsion to recognise by smell and then to categorise."

"What the hell are you babbling about?" Loreto was building up a convulsion that began to hiss out in short explosions of irritation.

"I am trying to explain your likely literary origins, as they appear to me. It is a slightly complicated story with alterations by its original author, and it began in the 1930s in Paris. Scott Fitzgerald drafted a short story called 'Knitting a Teapot.' It was about someone who ran full tilt into the Surrealist circle in Paris and got entangled with an artist's model who used to pose for a group, covered in icing sugar and draped in ivy. There was an escapade in the story about stealing ivy from the Jardin des Plantes. Of course he leaves the girl, to return to his wife, and the story is a reverie on the deck of the *Mauretania* going back to the States."

"You think Loreto was in that story?" asked MacGilla.

"Oh not at all. By no means. He scrapped that story after an argument with Hemingway, who didn't like it. They almost had a stand-up fight about it on the beach at Juan les Pins. But years later, at a time when poor Scott, the father of many a decent literary entity of my fond acquaintance, was crawling out of a bout of boozer's gloom, he raked up the idea again and started to rewrite it. It was in the summer of 1939 when he was trying to get another Hollywood job to settle a few debts. Nobody wanted him, so he started on a few short stories for *Colliers* or someone. He changed the story a lot. The fella did marry the model after his wife was killed back home in a car crash. They returned to America and they had a baby girl. At about this time, Misther Fitzgerald, the decent man, got a job with United Artists, working on the script of *Raffles, the Gentleman Thief.* It only lasted a week and before the month was out he was synopsising and fabricating *Tender Is the Night,* to make a literary, or more likely a financial comeback."

"I'm not going to sit in this tin box beside an Irish bog listening to the literary history of the thirties," Loreto shrilled. "I wish you'd state your crazy nonsense quickly and simply. Then you'd better drive me back to my hotel. I don't intend to spend the afternoon at a science fiction sit in."

"Now hold your hour until I finish, will you," said Mount-mellick with authoritative pleading. "I'm only giving you the back-ground to my theory. Isn't that right, Mr. MacGilla?"

With neutral encouragement, knowing that reliable support was on the way, Mountmellick appeared to share Loreto's scepticism, while at the same time giving the go-ahead to MacGilla.

MacGilla twisted in the front seat again to escape the pallisade of the steering wheel and expanded physically, addressing his audience.

"Well, I'm not saying I'm right. It's a hard matter to prove, but I think that Miss Amargamente here is the babby that was born."

The silence allowed the whoops of a flock of bicycle pump birds to fill the steel walls of the car. MacGilla opened a window to dispel condensation. Hedge rustlings increased to a background hum and fuchsia bells vibrated.

"You'd better go on," said Loreto. Mountmellick grunted.

"All this was just a few bits I picked up when Mr. Mountmellick and meself were in the other place, before we came over the wall, if you get my meaning."

"You mean before you were reincarnated," said Loreto.

"I don't know about this reincarnation lark. Now Incarnation is another matter. It happened to all of us; in blood and tears for most people. In the pages of a manuscript for the likes of us."

"I think that describes the *conception* of us word-begotten."

Mountmellick shook his head doubtfully. "The incarnation occurs much later. It took us some time for us to encorpify after we got our claws into that writer's soul while he was getting onto the plane for Madrid. I'll never forget how we drove the poor bastard to start filling out our personalities. Scribbling madly all night to the chirping of cicadas when he could have been out on the town, eating and drinking. It was touch and go, Mac. We drove him hard, but it worked."

"It generally does," agreed MacGilla. "More than any flesh-born person we deserve the description, 'self-made men.' "

"And women, of course," Mountmellick added tactfully. "It's only deprived people like us who are created to a definite literary purpose who have the urge to acquire a body of flesh and blood. The rest get them free, at birth. Not necessarily a noble purpose: some Grub Street hack trying to escape from the gutter onto the slopes of Parnassus."

Loreto seemed impatient but at the same time disturbed, uncertain of something. "What's all this have to do with me?"

MacGilla looked at her intently. "I think you are beginning to get the hang of it. But every simple statement needs a page of footnotes. That's my style. Lots of footnotes, an appendix and maybe a few steel engravings. You need a footnote to suspend your belief on. A good strong footnote with plenty of purchase."

Loreto stared at him without interjection.

"Well, here it is then, as best as I can give you. Scott Fitzgerald was off the hard stuff. The Raffles script was shaping well after a few days on the United Artists lot, but he still had to exercise his dreams in the dry empty hours. He had more troubles than the booze, poor man. He rewrote a lot. His hero became Paco Amargamente, a Cuban writer. The girl became Finuala Keegan, the daughter of a Democrat ward boss, who came to Paris to polish brass balls for Brancusi. Various oblique portraits of her anatomy were photographed by Man Ray and appeared in *transition*. Sometimes she was draped in pond weed or periwinkles, but she had a figure just like yours, Miss Amargamente, and similar features.

"But Scott Fitzgerald didn't rewrite the story until the mid-1930s and could have toyed with it up to five years later in his last hours. No one can be sure.

"Now, people like us, conceived between the paper sheets of an ms. instead of between the sheets of a bed or anywhere more urgent, we sort of depend on the literary conventions of the time of our first gestation. I mean, when I first occurred I was in the Peninsular War with Wellington, rushing around Spain ordering diligences, outwitting innkeepers and keeping a permanent platoon of duns and bailiffs at arm's length. But look at me now. In the hands of our carefully chosen present writer I am chauffeur extraordinary to Mr. Mountmellick. Not much different, you might say. But we can now control our destiny through him. He has to write what we do instead of the other way round. We learnt a lot in Limbo. Of course, times and ways have changed. Limbo was overcrowded with unpublished Italian pederastic counts and covens of extremely permissive duchesses, seamstresses, nuns and Moorish odalisques. I suppose some of them will start escaping soon, and in these profane times we might be able to use them."

Mountmellick nodded as MacGilla paused for breath. He was pleased to be the possessor of such a Gil Blas, a Figaro: a person of persuasive capability.

"What about my father, my alleged father?" Loreto tried to keep the discussion personal.

"I'm coming to that. But first, if we play our cards right we can avoid publication, thus avoiding elevation to Parnassus, a place of tedium and frustration for the likes of us. You see, compared with this world there's no excitement there. Even before that, we'd be subject to humiliating probings from every jackeen of a critic with half a bollock. But if we go the right way about it we can have half a human lifetime here, in the warm light of the sun, before we have to return to Limbo. Even then, with our experience, we'd be out in a week or two with new bodies ready to start again."

"I must confess that you put our position very succinctly." Mountmellick was fondly and avuncularly pompous. "It's heigh-ho for the open page again and the fresh smell of damp ink. We really are an incorrigible pair of romantics. How can you fail to join us?"

"I guess I've heard everything now," she said, but with uncertainty, "except, of course, what happened, or what is supposed to have happened to my mother and father."

"Drive on, MacGilla, you can tell her as we go. I think she is beginning to believe." Mountmellick leaned back against the cushions with Augustan aplomb.

MacGilla started the car and lurched it onto the narrow road, stretching from the Partry Mountains towards Killary fiord and on towards Westport and the hundred islands of Clew Bay. It was not the shortest way, but no one could contradict him. He had served as ostler to a group of English garrison officers in these parts, many years before. Over a hundred and sixty years, he reflected proudly. "The oul place must have changed a bit. Just as well to take a decko at it again."

Heading west, as people have done for endless millennia, he faced towards the distant fiord with its mountain walls.

"As to your father, Miss, in Scotty's last draft before it was destroyed you were born in Florida where your mother's father had invested his Tammany loot in property. Long after you were born you went with your mother after her divorce and her remarriage to a Harvard Wasp. Have I got all this right?"

Mountmellick raised an eyebrow in Loreto's direction. She nodded, puzzled by his biographical skill. "Well, then. Scott Fitzgerald was around Paris during the period when Surrealism became fashionable. Dalí, Max Ernst, Breton, Buñuel and the rest. He wasn't a man for exhibitions much, so he probably missed the famous Surrealist exhibition, but he took careful note of a photograph of a painting by Rita Ken-Larsen in a magazine. It depicted, with the sable-brush naturalism some of them favoured, a couple of trees shaped like naked women: branching arms, bark-covered breasts and bark thighs: slightly erotic, but definitely arborous. He tore it out to remind himself later and used it to fashion a story with a fashionably surreal raison d'être."

MacGilla nodded in general agreement but Loreto stared mutely.

"The story begins with a young American visitor going to a gallery opening for a mixed exhibition, mostly for the free drinks and the company. One large display attracted him. There was this pot-bellied American wood stove in the middle of the floor, on a platform, and sitting hunched over it was a branch of a tree, cunningly chosen: for it was bent in a crouch and had two smaller branches, like arms, stretched out towards the stove, as if it were warming itself. But inside—ah, here was the beauty of it!—inside, where you could see when the lid was off, was a nude figure in painted wax of a lovely girl, with fine agricultural appendages. The likeness of flames flickered on her waxy flesh by dint of a revolving glass drum with a light inside it. The wig of her hair was blown by a fan and her toes appeared to be melting out of the damper slit at the bottom. There were waxy stalactites hanging from half-melted toenails. Oh it was a very artful illusion, you take my word for it. Armagamente padre looked at the title, *Salamander*. He looked again at the piece of timber warming itself at a stove full of crackling blazing girl and then . . . he reached out his finger and touched the girl. Her shoulder felt hard and greasy and her glass eyes were turned up at him in ecstasy. He pulled his finger away, feeling a burn that hadn't happened, and he looked around the salon with a spurt of conscience or guilt or whatever ye like to call it.

"There, wearing a leopard-skin coat, was the very girl that was burning in the stove. But her flesh was pinker, her lipstick redder and she was laughing at him. Within a couple of weeks, not an ass's bawl from the Place de la Bastille, you were got. That would be, let me see, the end of 1935. You went to school in Rhode Island. When your figure began to fill out, you were shipped back to Florida where your education was completed. Am I right, Miss?"

"How the hell did you learn all this? Even a team of private detectives . . ."

"The archives of Limbo are both exhaustive and limitless," said Mountmellick, "being based on vulgar literary gossip. We got this from a couple of Hemingway dropouts. They escaped soon afterwards and ended up in a *Playboy* magazine story watching bulls with a dimple-arsed Finnish girl in full texture on the opposite page."

"The Finnish girl was only a photograph, not a story," MacGilla cut in. "We can't and wouldn't encorpify her."

"Forget about pathetic erotic shadows." Mountmellick was firm and to the point. "Our present literary donor rides a moderately geared pedal cycle and would never indulge in dubious fantasies in a Mercedes coupé. We chose him carefully. He's not the type."

MacGilla was indignant. "You and me was inseparable but roofless when we broke into his psyche at the airport. If ye can't find a bed, ye'd settle for a hayloft."

"I seem to recall a few hayloft episodes in your life."

"Maybe ye could, but ye could say the same for laundered linen.

Everything equal the bed's best and the warming pan and the bowl of posset and the crock of punch on the carved commode. Either way if it doesn't fit, it's the wet and windy road and take your chances on a sackful of jack fleas, saving your presence, ma'am.''

Loreto felt punch-drunk with all these outlandish statements, suppositions and affirmations with which she had been force-fed. It seemed years since she had met this eccentric couple, this pompous cynic with his picaresque servant, in the tourist tail of the plane. There had been complications from the very start, due to Mountmellick traveling first class and MacGilla tourist, but with the former expecting to have his drinks and refreshments served by the latter, instead of the airline steward. It nearly caused an on-board strike. She felt detached, watching her separated self and the scene around her.

Mountmellick was arguing with MacGilla about the route which was taking them by the smooth spectral waters of Killary fiord. The mountains reversed in the water, losing a tone of blue in the process, and two luxurious billy goats, caparisoned down to the rocks with yellow hair, tangled their convoluted horns in motionless combat, broken by an occasional ivory click. The females, tails to the wind, browsed delicately on the aubergine fuchsia, mousily quiet and utterly provoking. She saw all this in points of time too brief for mechanical measurement. She remembered the course of the day, the Georgian lunch, the lunatic credo of Mountmellick and the slight rivalry between him and MacGilla in which the weird affirmations, beliefs and suggestions were taken for granted. Indeed, both men seemed to be seeking her as an ally in their microscopic differences of attitude. The soft melancholy of the landscape contained a far greater variety of crude colour than she had realised. Its shapes were harder, profounder and more solid. Single boulders by the speeding road revealed the isolation of a lunar map, their shapes noted and remembered to the last forest of lichen. The hollow tube of the car's coachwork stretched endlessly from the backseat where she sat, and the far distant windscreen showed the hills and sky in sensual exaggerations beyond the capacity of optics.

It had happened before, to Saint Paul on the Damascus road, and many a more reasonable man since him. Loreto Amargamente was suffering a conversion. A tingling surge spread out from her groin and encompassed her rectum, her bowels and her uterus. The weight of her arms, her breasts and her head were lifted from her bones and she floated in free fall, a brief and incandescent nova, filling existence. The surge receded gently and it set her gently on a peak from which she could survey her companions on their own exalted pinnacles. Her soul licked out like a tongue, touching them, tasting them, sharing the purity of its kiss.

"I believe you. I know you are right. Merciful Muse! I know what I am." She collapsed forward, crying.

There was a silence, into which even the compressions of the car springs could not vibrate or oscillate.

"You're a character meant for a book," said MacGilla without turning from the wheel. "There's nothing you can't do if the Powers will it, and providing you take our advice."

"What he means, my dear, is that you have considerable control over your own actions, or the actions of others in a suitable hierarchy. Your original creator shaped you, or in your case he shaped your parents, from whom you inherited joint characteristics. But his control over his creation ceased when the fruit of his brain was abandoned and cast into Limbo. You, of course, were never in Limbo, but your parents must have been, briefly. It wouldn't surprise me if they were among the first to escape. Once back on earth, dug into the psyche of a host writer, with rich layers of nervous blubber, entities like us can do pretty well what we like."

"You mean that I have free will? I can do what I like?" Loreto was speaking without incredulity or sarcasm.

Mountmellick dismissed her question. "I'm not going into matters of determinism or behaviourism. You know pretty well your own limitations and capacities. But the point is this. That fellow up there" —and he indicated the sky above him—"he has absolutely no power to shape your actions. He can comment a little, but he cannot affect your actions, unless you allow him. And you must be on your guard against that. I'm sure he has tried to push you around."

"Mmm. Recently I have felt some force trying to drive my words against my will, but it doesn't last long."

"There, there," Mountmellick soothed her.

The purity of love and belonging became so great in the body of Loreto that her muscles, striated and unstriated, convulsed. Her heart missed several beats and she collapsed into a release of salt tears.

Mountmellick stroked her brow. "I can see you are taking this very deeply. I am very touched. Furthermore I am encouraged by your innate physiological initiative. I am quite sure that that poor sod up there, writing down our thoughts and actions, hasn't got the capacity to influence any of our actions or decisions, least of all yours. You may be second generation but you make up for it with your selfish determination. MacGilla need not have worried. You are no puppet to be pushed around."

He opened the sliding window of the car, while MacGilla slowed down at a grassy crossroads, cupped a hand to his mouth and shouted towards the western sky, "How's that for literary rights and free will, me fine scribe? It's easier for people to believe in us than in you, you misfortunate poor scribbler."

"That's the stuff," chuckled MacGilla, "but don't put him off. You don't want him to go on a three-day blind and drop the whole project when he gets the shaky glooms."

"There's no fear of that," said Mountmellick. "He's too much of a dirty voyeur. He couldn't stop Loreto's tears or even blow her nose in a large white handkerchief."

"No way at all," agreed MacGilla cheerfully.

"All right then," cried Mountmellick. "I know what to do." He yelled at the Atlantic sky a second time. "Look here you! This lady needs a swim in the sea lake. She needs to freshen up after the shocks that you allowed to happen. She has no swimming clothes and we don't want you around, prodding our actions with your pen point, so kindly bugger off. Don't be too long. Make a cup of coffee. Have a smoke. Stroll up the railway lane to the Burgundian for a pint of Worthington, but don't you dare stay for the course of a big round among your miserable bed-begotten friends. Come back in an hour's time so that this good lady can have a little privacy."

He flung out his arm and declaimed rhetorically.

"Look what happened to Actaeon when he spied on the girls undressing beside the river. Chewed up like a tin of dogmeat. And that was respectable compared with a type like you. This is class warfare and you freebooting scribblers are driving me to violent and bloody revolution."

"Amen," said Loreto quietly, her dark eyes shining.

6

The scribe who had been nourishing and serving these ingrates took his dismissal cheerfully enough at first. So, up with him to a place of ease called the Burgundian, careless of encumbrances, obligations and externally nurtured obsessions. But as he climbed the narrow footpath by the railway he began to reflect on the dismissal and came to see it as an act of rebellion, a state of affairs that he had long feared, belittled and evaded, but now had to face.

To throw the ms. in the dustbin would avail him nothing. He thought of pulping it, mixing it with the required amount of glue, clay, chalk and resin and modeling the papier-mâché into the shape of some prophylactic demon; a highly dangerous exercise. Besides, even in the face of a carefree drink, responsibilities are not so easily repudiated.

Within a short time, characters as insensitive and as tough as that would be back again, doubly charged with volition, and would start invading the minds of God knows who: Martin Amis, Salman Rushdie, Norman Mailer? Anyone's guess. Their alkaline harshness would drown the subtle acids of Edna O'Brien and probably destroy her. Iris Murdoch's possible peril didn't bear thinking about. Maybe Muriel Spark might put up a fight, but what's the use of a hopeless struggle, however brave and noble?

"It was a good job poor Brendan Behan was safely tucked up in Glasnevin cemetery," he mused. "Those three offscourings of Purgatory would have turned alcohol to bile in his gullet. It was the grace of God that he was safely with the Muses and oiling his throat with proof nectar to ease the flow of his rough and intoxicating Gaelic."

A desperate and hopeless plan crossed his mind which involved feeding the material subliminally to Sam Beckett's wandering spirit. Perhaps a few graffiti along the Boul' Raspail in Paris or mysterious tattered political posters in Molloy country, the ridges and dales of the outer purlieus of South Dublin: "Vote No. 1—Owen Mountmellick" or "Release MacGilla else—" Perhaps these might introduce a thought, like a shingle in a pearl oyster, and induce a Last (if posthumous) Tape. But these were vain and desperate hopes.

Draining his drink at an isolated table suitable for the licking of wounds, the scribe considered the mechanics of art. It seemed that the function of every artist was to select, rearrange and present his particular estimation of the sensible world. The transformed images then took on, imperceptibly, the moral attitudes, pains, obsessions and pleasures of the artist.

Granted the skill and the desire, there were still the hazards of technology. Wood, stone, bronze, paint, canvas, glass, paper and their tools of formation all cost money. Granted the possession of this, in itself a rather airy assumption, there followed greater hazards. In wood, the last scoop of the gouge can split the last knot. In stone the last percussion of a punch or claw can strike a fossilised scorpion and shatter the block. Bronze hazards are best described by Cellini. Canvas grows fungus and rots and colours of fire can fade like rose lips in the tomb.

The battle against plaster is unending, as a hill farmer fights bracken, and calligraphy can sully a virgin page as easily as it can signify it.

But the most flawed part of the creative process is the artist himself. "Blame not the bard," then, "if he flies to the bower."

Drink was consumed, and in quantity. An analysis of African art was entered into, unrequested. In alphabetical order, the following were examined and appraised: Ashanti dolls, Baga goblins, Benin bronzes, Dan, Guro and sublime Ife. The cataloguing continued unabated, unappreciated and unwanted, up to Yoruba. There was a general lack of certainty about the artefacts of the Xosa confederacy.

Following this purge, the scribe lost touch with his parasites and drifted into sloth, which begot more sloth. This was dispelled by an outbreak of nervous spasms caused by an elaborate alarm mechanism installed in a recess of his psyche by MacGilla, in all probability, and he was forced to face an empty page again, but without purpose or direction.

Every effort to trace them where they had broken rapport on the road to Crossmolina failed. No divinatory discipline seemed to work, though efforts were made with a magnetised needle on a thread, over a map of the province of Connaught.

They had gone to earth: hidden themselves in conspiratorial preparation in a bid for total freedom from a human host. These were his first fears. Later other anxieties presented themselves. Perhaps the gap in host nourishment was so extreme as to reduce their bodies to shadows, gossamer vessels too frail for their essence. But by now it was all too apparent that their essences were waxing fat and had become a vitreous fusion of their original form in the periods of their primary

gestation and an existential superstructure begotten of their autonomous and parasitic existence. By now this had an organically thriving
fibrous density and should be able to persist in a dormant state for long
periods without drawing on the nervous energy of the host writer. Left
unattended for too long, of course, they would be forced to return to
the drab verbal savannahs of Limbo, and conserve their energy for
reentry. In their next phase, no one could foretell the human host.
Some novelist still studying for his O levels or their equivalent in some
far country. Probably they would choose a familiar culture, Anglo-
Saxon, with American and Celtic fringes, but there could be no certainty
about this. Why not, indeed, Finnish, Magyar, Greek, Nigerian or
Basque? The prospect was an intolerable one.

Their host, plagued with pseudo-conscience pangs of their devising,
continued fretfully with daily tasks until, at last, one afternoon he got a
whiff of their inky spoor. A pen hastily offered to a page hesitated,
drew a crosshatched doodle, paused, and then, tallyho, it was on the
scent, racing along the lines, stabbing, scratching, nose to the trail.
Luckily its ink tank was loaded. It had enough fuel for a chase lasting
several hours. But caution, prudence, cunning were needed. The run-
aways were in hiding, maybe, as previously suggested, in a bid for total
freedom, beyond autonomy. Equally they might simply have needed a
little privacy. Let's be fair, it can't be nice having a voyeur host peering
at every word and movement.

The trail led to the city of Dublin lying on the north and south banks
of the River Liffey. Several hotels were tried and found lacking. There
was no trace of the hired car in the streets. Pubs and restaurants were
busy with irrelevant comings and goings. At the Arts Club and several
other clubs there was no trace or rumour. But faithfully and doggedly
the pen nib scratched its way across the river, past the visual vacuum of
the General Post Office and on, through the Georgian shabbiness of
squares, crescents and prospects and past scatterings of feckless Victorian
brick. Over the River Tolka, grave of the heir to the Dalcassian high
kingship, the trail led through Drumcondra and on beyond Collinstown airport. Near a wide containment of shallow seawater, fish
pasture for many a heron and sharp-winged tern, lay a house behind a
graveled carriageway, halfway between the round tower of Swords and
the castle of Malahide.

The name on the pillars of the entrance gates was new: Áras Puncán.
In Viceregal days it would have been "The Grange," Villa Frascati or
some such Gothic or classical conceit. Now that the Goths and

Lombards were camped in the ruined Pantheon of Imperial ineptitude it had been renamed Áras Puncán. The mansion of the Returned American. It functioned as an hotel, adjacent to the airport, and its agreeable but unrhetorical façade looked down on green parklands, a distant building estate, an apple orchard in a walled garden and a fine copse of Sitka spruce. Beyond a curve in the drive a stucco structure gave the illusion of a Palladian bridge curving over a crescent of shallow water that looked (from a precise perspective point) like the curve of a noble river. Several used car tyres rose, eellike, from the water. The grass adjacent to the house was mechanically mown to a crew cut.

There was no sign of the car, but this signified nothing. It could be back in the hands of the hirer or out on the roads again with a civil engineer, a veterinary surgeon, a Fianna Fail election agent or a purveyor of frozen fish whose Opel had packed up in Borris in Ossory. Alternatively it could be parked through the archway in the stable yard.

Within the entrance hall columns and pilasters of marble gave Ionic support to a fine staircase of rosewood. The floor was Pompeian and behind a screened Gothic structure of carved wood was a red-haired girl with soft breasts, a smile and bright eyes. Her cubicle, which sheltered a telephone switchboard, resembled the structures sometimes occupied by Saint Jerome in the desert, but in place of a half-written Vulgate was a registration book. The building seemed deserted though metal buckets clanging and distant voices could be heard from below and beyond.

"Forgive my intrusion. A Mr. Mountmellick—a Miss Amargamente. . . ?"

"Oh yes sir, staying till the end of the week. In the Buttery Suite behind. Miss Amargamente the singer: likes to practise her scales out of earshot, I suppose. Mr. Mountmellick? Her agent. Yes, he's there too. He's a gentleman of the old school. And Mr. MacGilla as well: her chauffeur. He gave us a few bars of a song the other night when the Cardinal's secretary was giving a dinner. In Spanish and Italian. Monsignor O'Finnehool said it was a good job not many could understand. He nearly broke his own sides laughing, but . . . Will I ring through and say you are here?"

The situation was hazardous. The entities were alive and well and apparently quite independent, although they would hardly have betrayed their presence if they had not wanted to. During their period of isolation they had not suffered or waned, but could they last out indefinitely? Everything suggested otherwise.

At the same time, there could be no question of meeting them face to face, or so it seemed at the time. Would they recognize him? Did they in fact know him as he knew them? Or as a lamb knows its mother ewe in the middle of a flock. Certainly they had, at times, felt the surges of his energy and his response to their call when they needed his services. It seemed safer to mutter something about strolling through the grounds and calling later.

7

The small suite of rooms occupied by Mountmellick, Loreto and Mac-Gilla had been converted from a series of lofts built over the dairy when Áras Puncán was the breeding centre for generations of East India men, resident magistrates under palm, pine and potato patch. The small balcony tessellated in glowing cubes of enameled delft was once a fodder hoist from which the indigent peasantry of Gay Malahide were sustained with a nourishing broth of lightly broiled maize and spring water during the black years of the Famine. A small admixture of liquorice root was added to combat typhoid and dry cholic and scrupulous care was taken to bury all corpses far from the house. On the advice of a member of the family, a railway engineer, master of many a stone-cored mountain, coffee, flavoured with brandy, was issued to all able-bodied men on the estate as a prophylactic against honeycombed sores and bloody fluxes. The Butler Feltons were ahead of their time in welfare administration.

A pair of Loreto's stocking tights hung on a nylon cord on the balcony, as delicate and iridescent as the wings of the bluebottles that once held undisputed sway in the territory. MacGilla leaned against a post of the bloody flux door directly beneath, pondering on racing trebles and Yankees, logical to him but as yet incommunicable to his literary host, a person quite incapable of grasping the technology of odds and racing form.

Loreto's bedroom was untenanted. The bed was folded back and a gentle sensual warmth mingled with the perfume of lotions and unguents. Several bottles of iced Chablis stood in a napkinned basket, their shoulders dull with condensation. Glasses stood neatly to hand and small savoury pleasures in net-enshrouded dishes.

In a cubicle off a nearby bedroom Mountmellick was taking a shower, soaping his skin, its folds and crannies, joyfully and vigorously. He lathered his armpits, his ears, his arse and scrupulously anointed, stretched and massaged his appendages. Medicated shampoo was vigorously kneaded into his scalp to combat dandruff, a literary hazard. A variety of male unguents lay to hand with caballero descriptions: Old Leather, Cordoban After Shave Balm, Sierra Morena Deodorant (por los señores solamente) and, more nautically, Marlin Spike Face Lubricant (Recommended for all brands of electric razors). These preparations, heavily taxed and priced, represented part of Mountmellick's existential development, his eager compromise with the consumer epoch. Even in his early days at Irún or Badajoz he had caused himself to be anointed, cap-à-pie with orange flower water or Orris liquor, MacGilla ministering. Indeed he often attributed the resulting vigour and wellbeing as the cause of his improbable acquittal at a French court-martial outside Burgos. He produced, in his defence, several friendly letters from Irish Jacobins, Wolfe Tone, Napper Tandy, all of which name-dropped the titles and identities of prominent Buonapartists and soldiers. The vigour, charm and persuasiveness of his agreeable appearance in court he attributed to the astringent action of orange flower water on his corneum layer.

It seemed to follow that his use of modern toilet preparations was part of an attempt to acquit himself at his best.

In a nearby bathroom, Loreto lay in warm aromatic waters, her shoulders raised and her breasts awash, floating slightly. A plastic Clarissa cap protected her coiffure from lacklustre humidity, and she seriously and scrupulously massaged her upper and forearms with a coarse pad to remove dead cells of skin. Raising a long leg, she propped its heel between the taps and shaved her shins. Some distance above her knees, on the front and side of her thighs, long black hairs flourished, doubly visible when sleekly wet. Resignedly she scrambled to a standing and shaved the hormone-engendered intrusions on her femininity, cleansing the razor of bristle in a Greek kylix of translucent plastic. Her pubic belly hair was unusually dark and thick and constrained within triangular boundaries. Half-heartedly she trimmed some errant hairs which threatened its euclidean precision, smoothed the mound, seal sleek, looked around at the back of her calves, bending her knee slightly, and collapsed pleasurably back into the warmth, where she lay in the muddied waters, examining her fingernails. Reaching out for a pumice block set in a plastic tiki of imitation volcanic glass, she abraded a coarse protuberance on her patella until it was eggshell smooth. Bending her legs at the knee, one at a time, she smoothed the heavy layer of coarse skin on her ankles. The resulting texture was insufficiently smooth for her highest toilet ideals, but she suffered it to pass. She then sat up and leaned forward to open the plug hole of the bath, but its mechanics were abstruse. Reluctantly she stood up and leaned forward to the control end, turning knobs hopefully. Simultaneously the plug opened and a circular monsoon issued from a cantilevered shower on the wall. With an agonised cry she leaped out onto a bath mat and fumbled again, twisting her dripping flesh to avoid the freezing cascade.

Something worked, for the water ceased and the bath continued to drop its water level. Stepping back into it, frowning, she sprayed herself with the hand spray, first on her shoulders, then down her back, legs and belly. Twisting stalactites of water hung from her elbows, the smooth pads of her gluteal muscles and from the points of her breasts, which now hung, but with some arrogance, in fifteen atmospheres, unsupported by water.

She reached for a red towel, vast as the pavilion of Tamburlaine. For a minute she stood, a red motionless pyramid, dripping and warm within its soft walls, until the necessities of life caused her to commence a gentle rubbing of her limbs, back, belly, neck and between her legs.

Loreto's ablutions had been thorough enough, but commonplace, unerotic, to say the least: a handsome woman having a bath, to an hygienic and aesthetic end. A handsome woman bathing is sensually pleasing in an Hellenic way, but the terminal anointings and posturings have a refined eroticism, which in this case must be to a designed purpose.

A frenzy of impatience seized the scribe as to what she, Mountmellick and MacGilla could be up to. So far, having run them to earth, they had each separately been involved in private occupations, though in the case of Mountmellick and Loreto these did seem to point towards an intimate meeting of some sort. Perhaps their ideas on erotic permissiveness were a little outdated, but it seemed that they were plotting a purple passage which would make the book more difficult to publish, thereby prolonging their vagabond literary life.

Their style was old-fashioned. The trappings were distinctly Ottoman: romantic in the style of Elinor Glyn. There were signs of Mount-mellick's planning rather than Loreto's.

Loreto's bedroom boasted no tiger-skin rug, but there was a luxurious quadrangle of tufted wool in the style of the Book of Kells Chi-Rho illumination. Typical of Mountmellick, to want to flatten Loreto's panting flesh on this woolly forgery of Ireland's monastic glory. Blasphemy, religious and artistic, was the intention. Sure enough, on a side table was a fibreglass museum replica of a Celtic Romanesque reliquary, a small house-shaped box, studded with glossy illuminations surmounted by a copperplated hand, erect and episcopal. Probably this contained whips, rapier-heeled shoes, transparent plastic raincoats, all the impedimenta of squalid fetishism.

A pair of linked bangles in gold or gilt copper hung on a drawer knob. Merovingian jewels spanned their diameters. Of course! These were handcuffs, manacles, gyves. In all likelihood, that tedious literary cast-off would secure her protesting arms by the wrists to the bedpost while he unleashed his aberrational urges on her struggling body. But they had been a bit too clever. The reliquary of fetishes was here and so were the jeweled gyves. But perhaps she would manacle him, and splendid and imperious in transparent plastic tread his screaming flesh with her stiletto heels and crack her whip on his shrinking muscles into glorious and humiliating submission. Literary Limbo must teem with this sort of depraved and specialised entities that were created originally to do exactly this sort of thing. Indeed, unlike Mountmellick and MacGilla, they had insufficient character to build an independent life of their own, and lived entirely within their private orgiastic symbols. Bad company corrupts and the hellish lumpen proletariat corrupt utterly; at any rate cheek by jowl in a confined space.

A quick glance through the wall showed Mountmellick putting on a track suit of fine cotton. Loreto, meanwhile, was dropping perfume from a glass rod between her toes, between her breasts, between her legs and the cheeks of her arse and behind her ears. Poor Jezebel, with her antimony and nard from the Nineveh wholesalers, never had it so good. A spray of lacquer to her hair and a touch of rouge on her nipples and Loreto surveyed herself, critically. From a shelf she took pieces of costume jewelry, earrings, finger rings, barbaric swags, and festooned herself. Dissatisfied, she pulled them off and took a thin gold chain, separated by chryselphantine rosary beads in modest decades along its length. Dropping it over her head, it hung chaste and pure across her scooped clavicles. Between her breasts, deep in the aromatic furrow, lay its appended culmination, a delicately worked Celtic cross in heavy gold, perfect and legible in every respect and recognisable as a diminutive replica of the great Cross of Muirteach. Its panels of pygmy saints and patriarchs stared sloe-eyed at the enlarged pores around the nipples of her breasts. She bent forwards as if to touch her toes and the cross swung perpendicular to the ground. Her breasts, unable to follow, attached as they were to wider suspension points, only hung halfway, held by their flesh. When she straightened, the breasts sank, but the cross swung on its golden string, to lie casually, indecently, demurely, across the highlight of a breast. Gently she dropped it back between, where it belonged, and reached for her garments.

The effect of these preparations was torture to a literary host, unable to record, apart from brief asides, anything but that which his parasitical characters demanded. There was a diffidence about witnessing the culmination of all this, due to shyness, clean upbringing or a desperate liberal tolerance, come rack or rope. Mountmellick and Loreto had clearly plotted and planned a passage that looked like being not so much purple as ultraviolet. Maybe they wanted to prevent publication (at least in Ireland and South Africa), but it was hard to be sure. Equally they might be attempting a contemptuous revenge on their unwilling chronicler. Ah yes! They would essay a purple passage as glowing as the walls of the Blachaernae palace, *but with sufficient literary merit as to make publication likely, and a magistrate's trial to follow, with processions of literary mandarins to testify on its behalf.* That was their little game. All these infamies would be claimed as the artistic expression of inward fantasies, and of aesthetic merit. This was terrible treatment for a bondaged writer, who did no more than helplessly record the odd voyeur's vignette which they afforded him. What would his family think, or his neighbours?

Yet there was little that could be done—that is, except one thing. Rebel! Cease to write! Tear it up! Burn the heavy pages of ink. This sort of futile tantrum could only end in humiliating defeat. Parasites like these have an insidious power to capture thoughts, with obsessive itchings of the soul. Only the scratch of a pen can assuage the torment. There was one hope, though a desperate one: fight them with evil. Choose any sin of the seven deadlies and fashion it into a weapon.

First, pride. How can there be pride when the author possesses only a titular authority?

Covetousness. The victim only covets his own natural right to command his own armada of twenty-six letters. This is no sin and is useless as a weapon.

Lust. Encorpified literary particles belong to pseudo-life, not to cellular life. They are immensely stronger and more enduring than the bed-begotten. Like the near-life of the virus or the crystal structure, they can flourish in the dust of space, the isolation of Purgatory as well as on the fats of the earth. Their host is weak, a nervous event of a few decades' duration. Carnal conjunction with a literary entity would consume him as quickly as the wretched Actaeon. Lust, then, as a weapon would be self-destructive.

As for anger, that existed, and in abundance, but without strategy it provided no more than a motive for action.

Gluttony seemed to lead nowhere, no matter what the extremes of indulgence. Platters of sweetmeats served by sloe-eyed Arab boys during Ramadan seemed a futile weapon. Cannelones and cojones in abundance with cool skins of Rioja consumed during the Three Hours Agony in Seville, on Good Friday, seemed equally inept.

Envy. Well! The Eskimo praises his barren tundra and the Hottentot praises a water hole of wriggling larvae. The literary host is human and clings to his frail flesh and the smell of sap in springtime. He is aware of the greater longevity and vigour of his parasites, but any envy is wry and helpless: no metal for forging weapons.

Sloth is the most destructive of all sins, but could it be used? Yes indeed. There was a way. Out of sloth can come no writing, and without writing, without a diet of transmuted ink, literary parasites wilt and wane.

Sloth comes easy to some, a secretion of the body's chemistry, but for others it has to be induced. Institutionalism, long spells in prison or hospital help, but this method was inconvenient: best try a small dose first. The instruments were simple: an armchair, sufficient heat, a television set, a quality newspaper, a *New Statesman, Exchange & Mart* and a two-day-old copy of the *Cork Examiner.* It only lasted for one fidgety hour.

Within an hour and a half Loreto and Mountmellick were stirring in their folio cover and MacGilla had probably finished his futile racing prognostications.

Admission of defeat was not easy, but like a craving for an habitual drug, the knowledge of what might be going on, or might be about to go on, was a compulsion to reassume literary slavery.

During the brief hour of rebellion, the earlier pudeur and alarm had been replaced by a compulsive and degrading voyeurism. There was a need, a craving to witness the sybaritic excesses of these entities, to be pleasurably stimulated and deliciously shocked. Surely, surely, absolute slavery corrupts as absolutely as power.

Loreto was still in her bathroom, dressed in a half-slip from her waist to a few inches below her crotch, lacquering her nails. After each stroke of pearly acetate she would hold her painted hand out from her body into eye focus and examine it, motionless. Seated on the padded lavatory seat, her breasts thrown into emphasis by the brief skirt, she looked like a Gauguin painting with her dark skin and heavy hair.

Mountmellick was in his bedroom, in track clothes, going through some papers. Had the man no feelings? MacGilla entered Loreto's room, his racing paper folded in his pocket, and set about final preparations. He felt the Chablis bottles, uncovered the plates of savoury comfort and turned on a heater fan near the opened bed. The man was no more than a pander's ghillie, a pimp's nark.

He left the room, and its four feminine walls contracted and moaned with sympathetic desire. The delay was unbearable, like endless credits, cigarettes by Abdullah and suchlike, before a blue film: assuming of course that blue films had credits.

Loreto's voice called tunefully: "Owen. Owen, darling."

"Coming, dear," his voice sounded through the walls.

Downstairs, MacGilla was talking on a house phone to someone, probably at the Gothic telephone switchboard. His conversation was full of heavy-handed asides, compliments and innuendos, so clumsy in a person of his keen perception as to suggest that they were part of a general strategy carefully chosen to suit the occasion. He also appeared to be ordering a meal or meals to be sent around from the kitchens at some later hour.

Meanwhile, the confrontation of Loreto and Mountmellick would be too good to miss. How would they greet each other: a tearing of constraining garments or a civilised aperitif first?

The picture was blurred and distorted, painful to view but composed itself, after several seconds, into the startling appearance of Loreto, covered from chin to feet in winceyette polka-dot pyjamas, a woolly dressing gown, belted stoutly at the waist and a crocheted bed jacket or shawl with arm slits. These reduced her erotic voltage to a level measurable only by specialised instruments. She clambered into bed, patted up two pillows behind her and raised both knees into a hummock, sitting upright.

Mountmellick, who had just entered, was wearing, presumably over his track suit, a vast dressing gown, so flowing and containing as to make a nun's habit a temptation of the flesh by comparison.

The scribe's reaction is hard to assemble in words. After the tense sybaritic build-up, disappointment came later. Before came surprise, shock, a nonplussed incomprehension. Mountmellick brought a low-back chair to the bedside, set it down and before assuming an attentive bedside visitor's pose, opened and handed to Loreto a wooden box with Levantine labels. She chose from its contents, popped one in her mouth and wriggled with delight.

"Yum yum: Libyan stuffed dates. My favourites. How did you guess, Owen?"

The change in mood and the change in character were startling, leaving little time for erotic chagrin for a cheated voyeur.

There was a clue, however, a slip, maybe deliberate, perhaps care-less. "Yum yum." These onomatopoeias were dated and arch, from a child's picture book or a Shirley Temple film. They did not belong to her. Nothing belonged except in a variety of different contexts. Loreto would never say "Yum yum." Beyond all doubt, these entities were flexing their narrative muscles either to prove their power or as a signal of contempt for their host: or both.

8

The Burgundian haven is an event that exists in a fossilised valve of the Railway Age. It offers comfort to lesser breeds and natives with equal courtesy. Tamils and Rajputs, Yorubas and Ashantis, Iberian and Hibernian, Afro-Caribs, Cymryg, Walloons and Hellenes meet to discuss horse racing, politics and the iniquities of life. Australians adapt with noisy truculence. Carmen the Gallegan with Visigothic sinews in her Celtic flesh is solicitous. Qué tal? Un pint of Worthington. No? Ah! Tinto.

In the first warm wine rush on an empty stomach the scribe instituted a Socratic self-enquiry.

Can this junta of autonomous literary orphans act contrary to their own characters?

Are they conspiring against their own foster parent who nourishes their bodies and souls?

If so, what purpose would this serve?

Since they have de facto autonomy, do they now want formal independence?

Having set up a literary entities commune, are they now thinking of a Federal Republic of Literary, Film, Television and Dramatic entities?

As to the last, they would certainly need a skilled Parliamentary draughtsman, possibly from an early novel by Jeffrey Archer, a lost *Crossman Diary* or even an ex-State Department man given to creative and imaginative leaks. Is there any tactful way of finding out if such an entity exists?

If they did so intend complete severance from a human host, would they follow a peaceful line of coexistence or would "hawk" entities make a bid to exterminate writers or starve them into impotence? Could characters, allowing for developing technology, write their own autobiographical fodder, using computers to overcome their corporal disabilities? Would it be autobiography or fiction?

The first three questions were the most fundamental and could only be answered after long and careful observation. This appeared impossible in view of the desperate emergency and the necessity for immediate action. A political gamble seemed essential, risking everything on an unsupported hunch.

This presupposed Mountmellick to be the ringleader and was based on a consideration of certain aspects of social behaviour at the time of his birth. Both he, the Anglo-Irishman, and MacGilla, the native, were deposited into the early decades of the nineteenth century but actually begotten between 1847 and 1850. This was the beginning of a period of ponderous German jokes and grisly charades.

Gentlemen took pleasure in putting Seidlitz powders in ladies' chamber pots, causing the victims to levitate, bladders streaming, on an upthrust of foaming bubbles. Ladies of the demimonde and those of the more enlightened upper classes responded by sprinkling mauveine, Mr. William Perkins' newly patented dye, into gentlemen's chamber pots. The violet malignancy of the result sent many a Royal Companion and belted earl on a stiff course of spa therapy and cold water treatment. Several English, Anglo-German, Germano-Hellenic and sub-Hapsburg princelings died of pneumonia and wet nightshirts in the frozen gardens of Baden-Baden as a result of these japes, and people reckoned the consequences worth a laugh.

It is worth recording (for the scribe thought deeply on the matter) that the first live bullfrog to be tethered to the marble seat of a flushing water closet occurred in 1851. The place was the Ladies' Robing Room, behind the Philosophical Machine at the Crystal Palace Exhibition, Hyde Park, London.

The escape of steam from the valves of the Philosophical Machine drowned the screams of the ladies and the fatal collapse of those overcome by the vapours. Several of the victims were buried in the Brompton Cemetery, Earls Court, London, in its more rococo jungles, and their ambiguous obituaries were carefully noted by the noted Upper Bronx writer J. P. Donleavy, and recorded in a black plastic-covered notebook. The notebook (a looseleaf type?) was originally purchased, regardless of cost, at Hely's Emporium and Stationers (by Royal Appointment), Dame Street, Dublin. It was subsequently lost on a number 11 bus, from Chelsea, when Mr. Donleavy was on his way to take a dish of tea at Fortnum & Mason's (Lapsang souchong).

A desperate gamble could be taken on the assumption that the entities, Mountmellick and MacGilla in particular, were indulging in a merry jape, based on a dramatic prologue, terminated by an anticlimax. Heaven knows what advantage they thought to gain from it. Perhaps none, apart from the pleasure of the exercise, as in waterskiing or equine dressage. The principal motive in such matters is the demonstration of skill. But it could also act as a morale booster and as a tentative try of strength: a probe into the enemy's position.

If, for instance, the scribe had become carried away by the earlier erotic preparations he might have recorded a totally inaccurate orgiastic scene, thus proving his capacity to exert power over his characters.

The scribe took a few more drinks and tried to probe a self-confessed member of the publishing class by way of subtly disguised pleasantries: too dangerous to ask outright if any of his authors were victims of demoniac possession. To no avail. The scribe decided to be as crafty as they were; to avoid confrontation and play a waiting game.

9

Loreto was still sitting up in bed, her woolly gown now discarded in favour of something quite circumspect but more suitable for the adequate temperature. Mountmellick was still relaxing in the bedside chair, a sheaf of papers in one hand, a glass of Chablis in the other. MacGilla was seated astride a dressing table stool, a tumbler of stout in his hand and half a dozen empties poking their tawny necks out of a wastepaper basket of pressed sheet steel decorated with a Malton print of eighteenth-century Malahide. He was addressing the company.

"It's no use arsing around like this. If that's your line of action, you've got to make your minds up cleanly and without arguin' about everything, from Poynings' law to Comparative Conchology."

"My dear MacGilla." Mountmellick set down his glass. "This is something to approach carefully. We all have to be agreed. Loreto here doesn't know these people as well as we do. She has a right to be suspicious, but perhaps she carries her intuitive feelings too far. A little reflection . . ."

"You expect me to go into partnership with that weirdo? If there's one thing worse than a singing nun, it's a poetic one," said Loreto.

"You leave the good Sister alone," snapped MacGilla. "She's led a very full life and—ach, what would the likes of you know about that sort of thing."

"My good fellow," commenced Mountmellick, expanding pontifically. "My advice to Loreto applies to you just as much. From the beginning of our meeting together, I have sensed a feeling of distrust on your part. Now, caution is one thing, distrust is another. Loreto became convinced of her eligibility to join us largely on account of argument offered by you. Since becoming conscious of being a—hmm—a fallen angel from literary creation, she has discovered many small clues to support her conversion. Immortality for instance, or limited immortality. She has escaped two aeroplane crashes, four serious car accidents, a tornado, an Afro-American paranoiac with a gun in Los Angeles, two rapes and a level crossing accident in France. These are so far beyond the statistical average for cellular survival as to suggest, if there were no other evidence available, that she was created for a higher destiny, and of a more persistent substance than mankind."

"I don't doubt all that," MacGilla began, when Mountmellick steamrollered him.

"Loreto has come up with the most perceptive observation on our problems, and an excellent suggestion for their improvement. We are a tiny minority. Even amongst the damned we form no more than a forgotten department. Squatting itinerants, parish pariahs, our only hope is in ourselves. Loreto's plan to form our own publishing company is an excellent one. United in cooperation, we can become a power to be reckoned with, and without power we can manage no more than unadorned subsistence."

Loreto nodded. "It's plain common sense. We depend on mankind. I mean, we depend on certain cultures to create us. But literary creations, at their best, are immensely greater than any one cellular individual. Just look at Hamlet or Rasselas or Gatsby."

"What about Superman cartoons?" Mac added.

"Oh. Showbiz types. No depth. As primitive as people," snapped Mountmellick.

"Correct," Loreto approved. "The old myths tell the story well. Prometheus tempted man from stagnation. Or Lucifer. Man began to till the soil, save seed, gain leisure, tell stories, and with what result. . . . The stories he told, with their compressed images, became more powerful than the people that made them."

> "And three with a song's new measure
> Can trample an Empire down,"

Mountmellick threw out his arms rhetorically.

"You could say that again," said MacGilla, gripped by the sentiment. "Who was Kelly the Boy from Killane, when all's said and done. He crossed the Barrow, he mounted a gun above the town of New Ross, and he fell by the River Slaney. He didn't get far. But his literary, or I suppose his musical image, did, though I detect an element of cynicism these days."

"Never mind," said Mountmellick, affectionately. "Wait till we assemble the secret hordes of unpublished Irish literary entities, we'll sweep the creamery managers and the bog Indians out of power. We'll take over the newspapers: the sporting pages, even. Thank God I survived to see the day."

"I thought you were going to make this business completely international." Loreto's voice was slightly querulous.

"So we are, so we are. A chosen few at first. But I'm sure nobody here wants to waste time dealing with an autopsified concept from William Burroughs or Robbe-Grillet." MacGilla involuntarily crossed himself. "To say nothing of Céline. No, we've got to pick and choose carefully until we gain in strength and experience."

"That's something I want to talk about," said Loreto. "I mean, I've always been progressive. New forms, new styles, but the anti-novel— well, that threatens our whole existence."

"Well, I feel we should go into that later," suggested Mount-mellick. "We live in stirring times. We must adapt, although I confess at times . . ."

"Let's stick to the business in hand," cut in MacGilla briskly, diplomatically.

"Quite right. But bear in mind that although Loreto is a second-generation literary entity, in her veins flows noble ink. She is entitled to a little extra understanding at first."

"Certainly. Certainly. I was always a one for the extra understand-ing. It's the last bit that counts most."

"Now," pursued Mountmellick, having filled Loreto's glass and his own. "Now, let's see. MacGilla, you suggested Liadin. Oh I know you have your own reasons, but I think it's quite a good start."

"But will she fit in?" Loreto cried. "Don't think I'm jealous, or something, but from the little I've heard of her background—"

"She's exactly the kind of person we need." MacGilla was emphatic. "It was you suggested going in for publishing. Misther Mountmellick had the idea of insinuating ourselves into litherary reviews, by silent cunning. He had his feelers out to sound the Irish, English and Scottish literary reviews, covering a broad political spectrum. It was a bright idea to influence suitably enslaved editors to publish reviews of unpub-lished novels: or novels never to be published, lying in the archives of Limbo; one way to encorpify undeveloped literary particles and dress them in solid flesh to swell our cause."

"Well, it was just a passing idea." Mountmellick shrugged modestly. "But our prime aim must be to publish these unfinished novels and literary confections ourselves. This will serve to encorpify the char-acters, who can then help us in our work until the time comes, after a few months, for their apotheosis to Parnassus. But we must be very careful to avoid our own publication. That would be the end of our earthly careers and we would float up in the clouds to the Holy Moun-tain to join Hamlet, Manon, Rasselas, David Copperfield and James Bond. Parnassus is the literary equivalent of Heaven and, believe me, just as boring. Not for the likes of us. I often feel that the ink of Milton's unbowed Lucifer runs in our veins."

"I wish you'd fill me in on this Liadin properly," complained Loreto. "We've got to decide if we're to spring her out of Limbo. She may be a pig in a poke."

Mountmellick drained his Chablis, shrugged and went to a side table and poured himself a whiskey and water. "I need something stronger. It's quite a story, and how it escaped the amour courtois I will never understand. The whole world knows of Deirdre of the Sorrows and the sons of Usnagh. And Deirdre crops up later as Iseult, a Dublin girl who experienced great unhappiness in Cornwall. Husband trouble."

"I wonder how Edna O'Brien missed out on her," interjected Loreto.

"How do you know she did?" replied Mountmellick, a knowing gleam in his eyes. "There must have been many unpublished versions, or unuttered versions. Enough to fill an antechamber in Limbo. The literary particle of an unborn Iseult would have been on familiar home territory in a convent school near Lough Derg, or around the shooting lodge by Lough Dan where she did her early writing. Don't jump to conclusions."

"Get on with the job, ye windy oul bastard," muttered MacGilla.

"Eh, what?" Mountmellick affected not to hear. MacGilla was becoming drunk, and a bit prickly.

By now there were two dozen empty stout bottles, each dignified with the bardic harp of the O'Neills, symbol of the house of Mac-Aenghusa (Guinness in the vernacular).

The following profile or definitive explanation commenced briskly, as evidence of a clear, decisive mind, used to calling meetings to order and imposing limpidity on a boardroom jungle. After a few sentences it tailed off into a more discursive, labyrinthine style in keeping with the vagrant winds that cooled the speaker's mind.

"The original Liadin was a poetess of beauty and metrical excellence. She lived in the kingdom of Leinster in Ireland towards the end of the ninth century. This made her, as you will learn later, something of an outsider in Gaelic affairs, although she spoke the language as exquisitely as she wrote it. On a visit to Connaught, her art was in great demand up and down the province in the houses of chiefs and kings, and she was entertained most lavishly. You could say it was the ninth-century equivalent of a concert tour. She was accompanied by her bardic harpist whose job it was to deliver the poems to a suitable musical accompaniment. Her bard was of course on a lower social and professional level than herself, but a reliable man at his trade, and capable of composing quite complex genealogical panegyrics by himself."

"A party by the name of Cellach, I think," prompted MacGilla.

"Quite! Quite! She also had with her a woman servant, and a porter for carrying her portable poetry booth, for dark contemplation, made of embossed leather. His task became more difficult as the tour proceeded, because of the increasing weight of gifts showered on her: firkins of butter, balls of refined lard, jars of honey and a huge quantity of golden ornaments, to which she added, nightly. All filidhe, as high poets were called, enjoyed a high income, but a woman poet was an expensive rarity and brought high status to the employer."

"She was a sort of Maria Callas of her day," remarked Loreto, eager to show some attention.

"On a far higher intellectual and social plane," continued Mountmellick. "Kings and high kings competed for her service and her fame spread through the entire Gaelic world, from the Dalriadic kingdom of Scotland to the waterside palaces of Kerry in the far southwest. Gaelic colonies in Wales and Cornwall never heard her in the flesh, but they lived for gossip about her and a secondhand rendering of her poems.

"In the house of a petty king, who squandered the tribal fortunes on horse racing and poetry, she met Curither, a Connaught poet of note, who lived not far from Crossmolina, where we passed a few weeks ago." Loreto nodded an experienced head. "It was love at first sight. The patron was forgotten, the reciting bard ignored, and the two of them addressed poems of welcome and praise to each other, across the table, until the assembly began to have fears about the early rise for the boar hunt the next morning."

MacGilla cut in: "Considering that they were both ad libbing, as ye might say, without a contemplation period beforehand, the standard was high.

> "Liadin is welcome
> Breasts of snow
> Belly of white lard
> Brilliant in metre
> Bright fire
> Burning inspiration
> What can I offer

> But stumbling words
> Syntax without structure
> Heart and bowels inflamed.

"Liadin replied:

> "Curither brings gladness
> Greater than triumph
> Bright light of Connaught
> Limbs of tall birch
> Breast of bright holly. . . ."

"I think we can deal with that later," said Mountmellick hastily. "The point is that Liadin interrupted her tour to visit Curither's house, on Lough Gara, overlooking Derrymore Island, where he had a fine contemplation studio, with total darkness, corbeled in choice stone and warmed by heated pebbles beneath the couch.

"People still speak of the Ale Feast that Curither gave in her honour, but it was in fact a succession of feasts, picnics and spirited occasions while the two poets matched their skills and explored the profundities of each other's minds. Their physical yearning for each other was nearly as great as their union of poetry, but it was inhibited by a geasa, or taboo, that had been inflicted on Curither by an elderly aesodan, his poetic mentor during the long years of studentship."

"That was a hard one, no mistake," said MacGilla.

Loreto, from the bed, raised an enquiring eyebrow.

"You explain," conceded Mountmellick.

"A geasa, ye see, was a binding imposition that couldn't be broken. No one would dare break it, if ye take my meaning, or have a mind to." MacGilla now took up the story. "Now Curither's geasa was that no woman with a foreign tongue might damp the heather of his couch by her sweat, under his own roof."

"Social conventions can be very bothersome at times," observed Mountmellick. "And religious ones much worse." Loreto accepted the point.

MacGilla continued. "Ye see, he could have mounted her on a corn rick, on a moss bed, in the sweet waters of a cress bed, or in the windy side of a ditch, for that matter, but not in bed. And with a passion like theirs there was bound to be a lot of sweat. Also, conception was a certainty, for a poet's melt is powerful, to say nothing of a poetess. That in itself was a desirable thing, but privacy was difficult to come by around a poet's home. The place was alive with students, camping out in small stone beehives around his paddock. Then there were stock-breeders, farming girls, spinners, tailors, cupbearers and the divil knows what. There was only one place of privacy, the hut of inspiration on Derrymore Island. They could have managed without touching the couch. A few oul goatskins on the silver sand of the floor, but the place could only be used by one poet at a time. It was a single-unit job. It was years before anyone invented the double or treble poetic studio, fully sealed against light and distraction. Curither went there himself, for two hours, after eating, and Liadin would be rowed out to it across the dark waters before dawn, but alone. Oh, these lone vigils produced some of the finest love poetry in the reign of the muses, so they say, but it left your man and your jill in a terrible state of frustration. Eventually their work began to suffer. Between them they invented the prototype of the dirty limerick, a verse form that was to be undiscovered until the lifetime of Andrew MacGrath, who died before the 1798 rebellion and is buried to this day in the churchyard at Kilmallock, Limerick. . . ."

"Are you trying to tell me that the limerick was discovered before the year 900 A.D.?" Loreto was scornfully incredulous.

"Only the dirty limerick, ma'am. Even MacGrath's limericks were a bit libelous. It comes easier in the Gaelic tongue. It was an English fella, not the worst by any means, but it was Edward Lear got a hold of the metre and turned it into English."

"Can you give me an example of Curither's limericks?" Loreto enquired. Mountmellick became restless but held his hour.

"Only odd bits, which I picked up from Liadin when I got to know her in Limbo. It's hard to get similar words for translation, but one of them went like this. It was a tribute to her by Curither, after a hard oul night of keeping his hands clean.

> "O girl of the Lagin I thirst
> Till my gullet is ready to burst
>   To fuse with your soul
>   And not up your hole
> Is to leave me blind, spavined and cursed.

"Liadin was a Laginian, that is to say, a Leinster woman. Although Gaelic was almost universally understood, there was still, around the homes and small courts, a number of linguistic differences in the country. There was Laginian and a similar tongue in parts of Connaught. There was Bolgic (or Belgic) in parts of the north, although that fractious lot had taken a hard beating some centuries earlier. Then there were the Crinoch, or Picts, up in the north of Antrim, who were the oldest inhabitants, still holding out against the rest of them."

"I think you are going into too much detail at this stage." Mountmellick was edgy and a little envious of MacGilla's folk learning. "To put the story briefly, the two poetic lovers decided to meet the following year in Leinster at Liadin's home. There, on a date and under circumstances reliably auspicious, they planned a love session of cosmic dimensions, with poetic trimmings: the last foot of a triad forming the scream of a woman in ecstasy, the roar of a red cow on impregnation or the beat of a mute swan's wings as he treads his mate in the wild surge of the waves."

"Poetry of participation," said Loreto brightly.

"Exactly."

"But this could add a new dimension to verse communication," Loreto cried. "We could issue tapes for different categories of lovers, including honeymooners and the happily married. Videotapes with crashing waves and the mating cries of ospreys for couples with a voyeur streak in them."

"The synchronisation might call for a little practice," observed Mountmellick, "but never mind that now. You see why Liadin could be useful to us."

"Oh yes. Go on please."

"Well, Curither went to visit her the following spring, when the waters had shed their floods and there was hope in the air and the earth was soft. Over the Shannon and along the ridge road across the central bogs he traveled, with the smallest possible retinue of disciples, which was three times seven, for luck. Then south he went, over the mountains from the plains of the Curragh, across the Liffey falls, through the Glen of Imal to her fine dwelling by the cliffs of Wicklow. Her doorposts were sheathed with gold from the rivers nearby, and shaped significantly in honour of the Three Bridgets, Aengus, Lug and other deities of consequence.

"As he came towards the sea, with the mountains behind him, he saw her house, sheltered by a sweet grass fold behind the cliffs. The outbuildings were extensive with warm dry cells for disciples, circled round. A double wall of whitewashed stone encircled the buildings and a mountain stream was held in a dammed hollow of clear water, before dashing over the cliffs onto the silver sands below. Sweet and lovely as the sight was, he felt a premonition. Sucking his thumb to increase his perception, a poetic trick, he saw young men and girls, fully dressed, although the day was warm, stripping the gold plates from the gateposts. Nearby a goldsmith was smelting them and his companions were busy beating the ingots into working sheets. Everywhere there was bustle and activity. Nearby was a limekiln glowing red and already a group of young people was beginning to raise the walls of a large building in the Gallic style, with end gables. Curither was mystified.

"As he drew near he was greeted by the young people with courtesy and affection. A young girl ran to him with a ladle of fresh milk from a bucket. He drained it gratefully and smacked her bottom, remarking that she had a fine one, well up to his disciples' high standards and what was she doing, covering it up on a working day with the sun shining? She jumped a foot in the air, blushed and gave him a cruciform blessing with her fingers. Curither recognised it as the Roman sign, signifying Christ's cross, to which he normally paid little attention since poets were concerned with redemption through learning and inspiration and not by being executed on a scaffold. He had nothing against the new religion, was aware that large parts of Eire had taken to it, but being a poet regarded himself as being outside of its scope.

"Its practitioners had a habit of regarding important deities as demons, which was ridiculous since the purpose of a good god like the Dagda for instance was to combat a bad god, or demon, like Balor of the Evil Eye.

"So great was the industry that no maidens came out to greet him in Liadin's name or to take his travel cloak, heavy in the hem with ford water. Nevertheless, happy as he was, he ignored this breach of hospitality and unfastened it and threw it across a washing tub, leaving himself naked except for linen stockings to his thighs and a baldric belt for his knife. Poets did not carry swords. Calling loudly for Liadin he made towards the door, when she appeared, in a long blue gown, her arms outstretched in greeting.

" 'Woman of the Lagin,' he cried. 'Jeweler of words, Light of orthography. Is your womb moistening at my coming? Since passing the silent ruins of Allan my belly has been on fire for you. Make, therefore, a suitable invocation.'

"Liadin stared him in the face, cast her eyes down his body and trembled.

" 'I invoke Patrick, apostle of Ireland
Who delivered us from doom
And the malevolence of scourges
Who brought men and women
To conjoin in holiness
Raising them beyond the power of demons
The soft lures of flesh
And metrical deceits.

'Curither, head fire of Ui Ailella
Esteemed in Teóra Connachta
By the blood of Jesus
Be cemented to me
In love surpassing love
May your wanton nakedness
Be forgiven
May your soul be clothed
In the Holy Spirit
Sacred Wisdom
And your loins be covered
In a habit
Woven by fingers
Skilled in sanctity.'

"With that the poor poet was surrounded by a bevy of women, many young, some older, who forced a woollen sack over his head, until its hem touched the ground. A young deacon girded his waist with a críos, woven without colour, while a sweet-voiced girl sang melodiously:

" 'God's wisdom guide us
Mary's Son shield us
Turn our deeds to praise
Release us from the burdens of flesh.'

"The company replied, equally melodiously, but at considerably greater length.

"Recovering from the numb of shock, Curither was still speechless in the face of such an outpouring of love. He was so disoriented that he forgot to speak in spontaneous verse. 'Liadin, Word Queen of the Lagin. What in the names of all the Shining Gods, to say nothing of the Dark Ones, has come over you, girl? I have traveled the lands of seven tuaths and forded seven rivers in consequence of last summer's arrangements. And don't forget, it wasn't just the consummation of our pent love that brought me here, but that a child of our two spirits might be foremost of all filidhes: Master Poet to Gael and Gall, Norseman and Saxon, Frankish and Romish.'

"A man in hearty middle age, with a long cloak and a druidic front tonsure came towards the poet and laid a hand on his arm.

" 'Curither, brother, Liadin is now your sister in Christ. Her love for you and for all mankind is a hundred thousand times what it was in her darkness, now that Christ's blood of redemption mingles in her veins.'

"You carry on," gasped Mountmellick to MacGilla. "My memory is going. Didn't they leave the palace and go somewhere else?"

"I knew a woman that went like that," said Loreto. "I'm not sure if it was Christian Science or Jehovah's Witnesses. She had a chain of beauticians in Miami. Of course she was nuts."

"I'm damn sure Liadin wasn't nuts," growled MacGilla. "Ye've got to see that things were different then. First of all, this anchorite business was a new idea, straight from fashionable sources in the Sinai and southern Gaul. Half Alexandria was climbing pillars or sittin' in its shit in caves. The monastic idea swept the world, and the best people took it up. It was logical, when you think that they expected the Millennium about the year 1000."

"Why didn't they close them down when it didn't happen?" enquired Loreto, logically.

"Well may you ask, ma'am. I suppose, like all big institutions, that they came to embody important interests in power and money. The Eastern Empire, for instance, couldn't operate on eunuchs alone. It needed lashings of monks to operate the civil service. Like the Irish in the Democratic Party, they became a vested part of the system, however they started."

"Yeah. I guess so."

"It wasn't hypocrisy. Not really. They had to go on believing in it. Even a boyo like Augustine wasn't a hypocrite. Flann O'Brien did the man less than justice in that book of his, *The Dalkey Archive*. His Sanctity gave up his women and his pleasures for responsible power. There's many a Cabinet minister has done as much, although there's a few that didn't."

"Go on about Liadin."

"Well, in the heel of the hunt, Liadin kept her kirtle tucked well under her own heels and nothing that Curither could do would raise it above her instep. She had given her home to the young fellas and girls who had been her pupils. They put up a sexual dividing wall covered in bits of broken stained glass (anachronism) for safety, and settled down to embellishing books and writing hymns.

"The bishop or saint who started all the trouble in the first instance by teaching the poor girl the *Georgics* was sorry for them and sent the two of them off to the community of Saint Cummin the Tall, a great administrator, if nothing more.

"At first they were separated, Liadin on the women's side, far up the glen, and Curither, still refusing the message of Christ, grinding inks in the scriptorium for the sake of a bowl of gruel and to be near his beloved.

"They both took ill and began to waste. Liadin stopped menstruating and Curither was afflicted with shingles. In Alexandria, this would have got the pair of them sanctified, antemortem, but Ireland was a frontier land and a bit more empirical.

"Finally they were allowed to meet, on opposite sides of a tall Celtic cross. It's still standing, by the way, with a fine plaster cast in the National Museum. They couldn't see each other, but they were allowed to talk through the bottom pair of holes, just above head level.

"All their love went into whatever they said to each other. There must have been love poetry, the like of which has never been heard, or then again, maybe not. What's lovers' talk anyway?

"Finally, a couple of ploughings later, Curither consented to baptism. The poor fellow was beaten into the sod with agony by now and any consolation was welcome. But before accepting it, he demanded to speak with Liadin, ask her blessing and forgiveness and remember her image to fill his thoughts of the Blessed Virgin, whose life he was busy illuminating in the scriptorium.

"Fair enough. Saint Cummin gave his consent although he had to stretch the rules a bit, but what priest won't stretch a point or two to capture a pair of prominent intellectuals for the faith?

"With a heart like a bell clapper, Curither set out, up the glen to the women's enclosure. The day was warm and the bees droned loudly in the heather. The bell, safely out of its shrine, with no fear of Northmen, clanged the changes of the day on the peaceful meadows. Curither had been awake half the night listening to the boy in the cell next door scourging himself to gain points for salvation. They had an elaborate points system. So, he fell asleep. When he awoke, the cold moon could not warm his bones which were colder. Stiffly he crawled and stumbled past the women's cells, knowing that he had missed Liadin and would never see her again.

"Near the monastery, at the top of the glen, lay a lake, dark, deep and silent at all times, reflecting the high hills that folded to contain it. I've fished it often and the trout don't go beyond a finger's length on account of the lack of food in the mountain water. Now one side of the lake is held by a mountain called Lugay that rises straight out of the water, part of the way in overhanging cliffs, and farther on it circles back into a sort of amphitheatre which is a tumble of enormous granite boulders piled on top of each other and against each other. If you pulled one away at the bottom, the landslide would fill one end of the lake fifty feet high with rocky islands.

"You'd need to be a goat with rubber-soled hooves to get across this bowl of rock, but there are to this day a few causeways across it by jumping from certain boulders to others nearby. Here and there the rain has brought down pockets of earth to partly fill some of the hollows between the rocks and the caves beneath them. Heavy rich grass grows in these places, and plenty of rowan saplings and in partic-ular beds of horse nettles as tall as hollyhocks.

"The bold Curither, instead of going back to the monastery settle-ment, went on past the convent cells and along the lake path. A couple of coracles were lying like beetles on the moss below the path and on a moody impulse he turned one over, got it on his shoulders and managed to slap it onto the water beyond the rocks by the edge. There were several paddles in a basket, so he took one and pushed out from the shore into the glare of the moon across the water. The shine was that harsh it would blind a man that didn't squint his eyes."

"Get on with the story. We can do without observations on astronomy and landscape." Mountmellick grudged leaving MacGilla in the pulpit too long.

"Leave him alone, Owen. He's telling it very well in his own way." Loreto was content to allow things to unfold.

"Lookit," complained MacGilla. "If I told the whole story as it happened it would take exactly the same time as the thing itself, give or take a few minutes. It takes longer to say 'The moon's brightness dazzled the eyes and left a silver path across the water' than to perceive it visually. Even then I have to leave out how the trees stood up, some in black silhouette and some rounded by a front light. These are things that two eyes can record in a second. On the other hand, if I say 'He walked along the coarse-sanded path above the lake's edge' I describe an act of fifteen minutes' duration, and I save on it. In practice I tell a lot about some things as they strike the mind and leave out a lot that would overburden the story. A large part of any art is in selection, as the punter remarked, marking the racing page."

"Have it your own way."

"What other way could I have it, barring I was reading it from a book? Anyway, he paddled out onto the water keeping a steady course for the far side with the paddle under his oxter, slipping a bit and turning on his own axis but making good way. Up the lake, on the far side by about half a mile, was a sandbar and a beach, of coarse silver sand, carried by a stream, and it was towards this point that he was making. He pulled in to the far edge where the cliff dropped to a bank, trying to get behind the reflection to see the sand, when he heard a voice. When I say voice, I mean a cry or a human sound. He stopped scooping the water to listen and again he heard it, but this time something more. For the tone of the wordless sound was Liadin's. It's funny how you can recognise a person by a cough or a yawn, or even lying in the next room ye can recognise a person, saving your presence, ma'am, bringing up a lump of morning phlegm.

"He was out of that boat like a bawl from a bull and up to his knackers in freezing mountain water. He had the coracle lifted up on his head in the time it takes to say it, and halfway up a sloping rock with the paddle in his teeth. For some reason he didn't call her name, maybe fearing that she might be out sharing a penance with others, but he listened, his head turned to the rocks, and followed the quiet moans through the clear air.

"Crossing the boulders, some of them as big as a house, he scrambled, climbing and disappearing into deep ravines of darkness. He may have taken a circuitous path, but eventually he got near a sound of swishing and sobbing and sharp cries, so he climbed a sloping granite ramp that stuck up like a tower above the others.

"Beneath him was a clearing the size of a room, with grass and nettles and an ash sapling growing in the nourishing damp. Beyond was a table rock as sloping as his own and by its base, kneeling, her breasts pressed against the lichen, was Liadin. She was as naked as a baby and her skin was as silver as a fish.

"He saw her body shudder and go flabby, but then she was on her feet again, flogging her belly, her thighs, her arms, any part she could get at, with a bunch of nettles as long as a king bull's pizzle. I suppose he must have let a cry out of him, for she turned and looked up, twisting her body in the moonlight so that the flesh stretched and the muscles pulled their weight behind them. Her mouth opened, she stared, then called his name in disbelief and flung herself into a thicket of nettles that would bury a ram and four ewes up to the horns.

"She rolled around in this for ten seconds or more, sobbing and giving quare screams that got strangled in her gullet before they could split the trees. With the cry of a bull seal he jumped, or threw himself, twenty feet into the hollow, flattening a bushel of horse nettles in his fall. Liadin was lying back in the poisonous weeds, like Leda, wondering what the bird was up to, the back of a hand covering her open mouth. Before she could cry, Curither had one arm under her knees and one under her shoulders and had lifted her out of the nettles and laid her on the long cool grass.

"No moonlight lit that grass, which stood a foot high in the hollow of a rock, so he lifted her again and laid her on the slope of granite. The nettle burns on her skin looked like the back of a trout, shining in the moon's cold fire. The only part of her that wasn't mottled in red burns was the part of her that had hair, and the hair on her head had been cut with a knife like a torn skirt. Only these parts and her eyes were free of the nettle burns.

"He said something, but no one would have understood the words, except that there was no metre or scansion to them. Then he left her for a second or two, and tore up fistfuls of broad dock leaves that were crowding the draining end of the hollow. With a ball of these in his fist he rubbed her, like a gilder and his sheets of metal, hard and in circles, missing no part: her feet, her shins, her thighs, belly, breast, neck, jaw, up into her ears and under her hair. Then he turned her over and rubbed fresh leaves into her back parts in the same order, heel to neck. If the moonlight hadn't been so cold she would have shown the colour of a stagnant pond with the green juice that soaked her skin.

"He turned her on her back again and not one sound came out of her, so deep was her silence after the growling and yelping in the nettles. Curither looked down at her for a long second and she threw her arms out like a crucifix, flat on the rough rock.

" 'Liadin a leanbh,' he managed to gasp, and she gave the cry of an otter maybe. A wild cry. But at least it was the cry of a living being. Her face was beginning to swell and along her arms and belly, but Curither was at his breeks, which were laced with ropes of straw, tearing at the knots, and not another word from him in answer. Then she was on her knees, though by now her eyes were swollen to slits and the tears were cooling the burning on her cheeks.

"On her hands and knees like a beast in affliction, she was snapping and snarling with her teeth, like a hound at the shoulder of a boar, and tearing the straw binding from his legs and pulling the woollen breeks away in tears and tatters until he was as naked as she.

"By then her only knowledge of his state must have been by touch, for her eyelids had swollen across her vision. Small matter, for within a second she was half stamped into the rock like a chalice being worked on a bed of soft pitch, and Curither was up through her and out the far end into eternity. She gave a great cry like the plunge of an eagle into darkness, and a cloud cut the bottom off the moon in silence."

"Wow! You certainly pushed that bit to the last word." Loreto was lying back in the pillows, one hand cupping a breast, sweat on her face and her hair hanging over one temple. "That sort of shenaniging can get a girl sorta worked up. Is it all true? How can you know?"

"I know the woman that it happened to. I know the kind of love and the kind of blasphemy that can outlast a thousand years and more. I know that feelings are beyond words and that anything I can say on any point of detail is less than a thousand millionth part of what happened to those two lovers."

"There must be something to be said for a release from vows of chastity," remarked Mountmellick, who looked a bit sweaty about the temples himself.

"Release my left bollock," retorted MacGilla. "That was only the beginning. The agony of love was what followed."

"True, true. What's the use of a tragic love if the fates are not remorseless."

"What happened then?" asked Loreto, as if she doubted if anything could.

"It's the worst part of the story," admitted MacGilla. "Chastity is one thing before it is assuaged, but it's a bloody sight worse after being split up the middle and sucked dry."

"Really!" Loreto laughed edgily and with a slight palpitation.

Mountmellick shook his head. "I cannot fully agree with MacGilla when he says that the worst part of the story is yet to come. We are talking here of human agony, a state or condition that is difficult to analyse. Perhaps science can help, though merely identifying the neurological condition is only a beginning. There is in medicine a tendency to consider a description of the condition as a cure.

"Both Liadin and Curither suffered as much as the human mind can feel. Beyond that point there is only an extremity of physical pain and merciful shock. Deprivation, as the theologians argued, is the greatest endurable pain.

"When Liadin returned from the Ailella to wait for Curither, she became involved with the monkish scholar who later sent her to Saint Cummin. I don't know the scholar's name, but he came to her house, joined the discussions, and what he had to say was exciting. Originally from Cashel, he had returned from France where some of his compatriots had dabbled in neo-Platonism, an attractive system. Furthermore he had crossed Europe in a delegation and knew Milan, Ravenna and above all the Sublime Port. His scholarly excitement was fanatic and his imagination was addled with snippets of Ovid, Horace, Apollonius of Rhodes, Procopius and Heaven knows what other voices from the classical twilight. New verse forms, new attitudes, crowded his head, but the only pathway to understanding was through celibacy. Either you were promiscuous and ignorant or celibate and enlightened. It was a general view at the time.

"Liadin was a good poetess, in the Gaelic tradition, and schooled in native verse forms. Indeed it was a long and arduous training. In order to savour the smell of Ovid, she found herself expected to take a vow of celibacy. I doubt if she ever realised that it was to be permanent: not in her deepest heart. After all, the disciplines of the bardic colleges were as extreme as anything practised in a Christian convent: long hours of meditation in a dark cell, prodigious feats of memorisation and a daily office as strict as that of Loyola, centuries later. She wasn't a young girl, but a mature woman of thirty-two years, eleven of which were spent in poetic training, without rest, under criticism from her teachers and her fellow pupils.

"I don't know how many lovers she had allowed. Three or four? Were her years with the other pupils entirely spotless? Don't forget that one of the tricks of the trade was to roll naked in a flayed bullskin on a pile of brushwood, to trigger off inspiration. Perhaps it was some parody of this exercise that led her to the nettle bed. But it seems that her longing for union with Curither had something of the shape or flavour of the writings of Plotinus. Out of the union of their two bodies and minds would come a child who would also be a poet, a prophet who could so arrange and mould the Gaelic and Brythonic speech as to make each utterance a description of the order of creation: a triple harmony of sound, nous and hymn to existence. This sort of idea was in the air in Celtic Europe at the time, though eventually the pedants from the schools suffocated it with their Talmudic Aristotelianisms.

"So, what the poor woman yearned for was no ordinary tumble in the heather, but to be the mother of a sort of poetic messiah. Now, when this Tipperary man came back from Charlemagne's court, on account it is said of a row about alphabetical scripts, he managed to convert Liadin to the idea that marriage with Christ was the only path to the Truth that contained all poetry and divination: no more than the change in attitude that overtakes many a poet. Alas, no fasting or penetential exercise can wholly absorb the tearing of the bowels or the burning of the breast that betokens physical attraction. Many a night, her belly rumbling on a thin cup of coarse gruel, taken at dawn, Liadin would lie on her couch of slates, her body feverish and open to the Heavenly Bridegroom, but the person that filled her thoughts, crowded her mind and touched every aching secret of her body, was Curither the unbaptised, the pagan poet, glory of Ui Ailella."

"You seem to know an awful lot about her," remarked Loreto.

"You'll start learning pretty quickly yourself," MacGilla assured her. "It is small wonder that creatures like us, rejected and forgotten, love-children of the most imaginative minds of mankind, wouldn't know more of the motives of mythology than scholars that have to stick to linguistics and digging holes in the ground. No offence intended."

"You mean Liadin and Curither are myths?"

"They are in my left bollock, in the strict sense," said MacGilla. "Oh, they existed all right, but their pains and tribulations were taken up in the minds of men and you can still read the poem about them, translated now into several languages."

Loreta half closed her eyes and looked at Mountmellick.

"What happened to them both? Surely it didn't end in the nettle bed?"

"It did not," Mountmellick replied, "though it would have been a great charity if one of the rocks on the mountain had fallen and crushed them both into the same indissoluble pulp. They both died, though Curither lived longer and died far away."

"If they were both people of flesh, how come you and MacGilla want her to join us in our little enterprise? If she died in the Church she should be in Heaven. If she just died in the modern manner, she exists only in the power of an old poem. In neither case could she end up in Limbo."

Mountmellick and MacGilla looked at each other and smiled at the precocious infant logic of their protégé.

"The Liadin we hope to have as a colleague is at this moment a literary particle, in Limbo, awaiting our help in obtaining release."

"You'd better explain the whole story," added MacGilla. Loreto shook her head to his gesture, so he filled a drink for himself and set one before Mountmellick on the bedside table.

"To be brief to a point just short of inaccuracy," began Mountmellick. "George Moore finished *Heloise and Abelard* in 1921. Life was tranquil in Ebury Street, but the sound of guns across the Liffey water penetrated to his quiet corner of London and set him thinking again on Irish topics. He had dabbled in them before, but he could hardly help being stirred by what had happened, and the way Yeats' terrible beauty had been born from common clay. For a discerning novelist, to witness the first mortal convulsion of a vast empire was an exciting experience, by any political standard.

"Lloyd George, Birkenhead and Michael Collins were arguing it out, on the Welshman's terms, and Lady Lavery was holding Collins' hand and saying 'Careful now, Mick. Watch that Cymric centipede.' Moore was only one gossip away from this struggle. He had many Irish visitors. Talk tended along Hibernian lines, rather than on the topography of Parnassus.

"I don't know where he came across the anonymous ninth-century poem about Liadin and Curither. He must have spoken about it a lot, and picked his friends' brains. Not so many years afterwards Austin Clarke, the poet and a man with a particular knowledge of the monastic period, and with an emphatic disinterest in celibacy, had tea with him in Ebury Street. Moore didn't mention a word about it, though by that time the book was half finished.

"Possibly he didn't want Austin Clarke to write a verse play on the subject, or maybe he feared contradiction from a young poet who had a particular and special interest in the period. Moore died in 1933 and his ashes were taken to Mayo, not far from Curither's stamping ground, but the book was never finished. Indeed, within the broad outlines of the story, Moore never decided what happened after the episode by the lake.

"When he died, the characters of Liadin and Curither were too far developed to abort uselessly, so they ended up in Limbo. Over the years, Curither has grown more morose and unwilling to exert himself, but Liadin is quite different. She can't wait her chance to join us. MacGilla, like a good fellow, lay off that bottle of malt and tell Loreto the end of the original story."

" 'Tis hard to tell what is original, as you call it, and what was fashioned to the needs of people, to say nothing of Mr. Moore's notes and jottings. Maybe they are lying around somewhere, too incomplete for a literary executor. Liadin knows a lot about them, of course, and she's thankful to the Muses that he never got it finished, because she died before Curither, as I understand it."

"I think I get you," Loreto remarked, screwing her eyes and grimacing in concentration.

"Seemingly Curither, when he rose up off Liadin, found that she was stiff with the shock of him but stiffer with the shock of the nettles. Her first instinct was to offer up both shocks to God for the souls of the unredeemed poets and heroes of her land. This was the result of her recent training. Her second thought was that since she had sold out to the amiable demons of her upbringing she might as well make the best of it. Indeed she did, but not before Curither had carried her down to the lake and laid her in the cold brown waters and sponged her with a handful of velvety moss that he peeled off a rock. This brought down the swelling a bit but it got both their hearts tingling again, but with more peace and less madness. She stroked his hair and told him that when he leaped down on her she could plainly see the battle light shining above his head, a bit like a halo from Constantinople but more fluorescent, like a vibrating globe. This commonly happened to heroes and gods in battle and it could flatten armies. No poet ever had it, not even Oisín or his son Oscar, and it was quite unlike the love spot on the forehead of Diarmuid MacDuibhne which beguiled poor Gráinne.

" 'Curither,' she crooned, 'you neither wooed me nor ravished me, but you laid me waste with a sword of light, the blind fire of battle.'

"In the heel of the hunt she had them both persuaded that what had happened was no more than a rare but accepted phenomenon that occurred in Celtic chivalry, well attested in the 'Táin Bó Cúailnge,' 'The Battle of Moytirra,' 'The Death of the Children of Tuireann and Emain Allach,' at least in any definitive version of the tales. There was neither blame nor shame to the act. If a Christian warrior of the Gael fell in battle, not even the monks doubted that his flesh would be gashed by the cruel beak of the Morregan, the battle goddess. Did this unavoidable occurrence bar him from Heaven or Purgatory? Not even the unspeakable Synod of Whitby, a Saxon mullarkey of dolorous ecclesiastical consequence, had ever pronounced on the matter. Furthermore a succession of popes of Lombard or Vandal stock had evaded the question and reserved their wrath for Monophysite jackals and similar sybaritic degenerates and hyenas from the Golden Horn."

"Alas for the poor child of innocence." MacGilla shook some vol-au-vent crumbs from a Belfast linen napkin and wiped his creased brow. "Before the day was out, and she so stiff that she could hardly drag her feet behind her, she had let the whole story out to Saint Cummin. It's not the first time that trouble started in a confession box and it won't be the last. To do him justice, he never exactly broke the seal of the sacrament, but what he did do was to get his young men to cover up the jeweled bell in its shrine, hide a collection of expensive imported relics to prevent contamination and pronounce anathema on the pair of them. The two of them, within a year of being respected and revered poets, were now homeless and penniless with barely a rag to cover their shameful flesh.

"Liadin had handed over her fat cattle and fine homestead to the Cashel man from Aix and her pupils were now his flock. Her gold and jewels had been melted down for church ornaments of intricate design and richness. She could never go back.

"Curither had received news some months before of one of the perennial changes in Connaught in which the Domnan people with their strange tongue had been finally absorbed by the Gaelic Christians of Breifne, the Ui Briuins. Although a Gael himself, his return would involve him in prolonged genealogical studies. In any case his house would certainly be ransacked and besides, the belligerent Christianity of the Breifne people, triumphant from their raiding under the cross, would offer little comfort to a blasphemer like Liadin and a cause of blasphemy like himself.

"One of the retired poetesses from Liadin's home crossed the mountains to meet them near the ford at Laragh, having heard news of their disgrace. Though now a nun, and content with her faith, she yielded to old loyalties or Christian charity, maybe. Anyway she brought them a bag of oatmeal and a few small ornaments of Liadin's gold that had not yet been refashioned into croziers or shrines.

"For this the lovers were thankful and they sang a lament together by the tumbling river which caused cock birds to moult and pullets to go broody. Many a virgin egg was hatched that season by virtue of their great sorrow. It has lost its name now, after more than a thousand years, but I hear it may still be going strong after many a change of words.

"Anyway the pair of them set off towards the recent settlement of the Norsemen at the estuary of the Liffey, a few miles from where we're sitting. When the first raiders came from beyond they were worse in many ways than our own lot that used to go marauding in Britain or

Gaul. They came a long way in their ships and set up convalescent centres on islands off the coast until they could gain strength to have a go at the rich pickings. But it wasn't long before they were followed by traders and settlers, not unlike our friends across the water in England a century ago. These were the people, partly Christian, by now, who built the town by the moorings which they called Dublin (the black pool), after the wide stretch of sheltered water. One of the main streets is still called after them, though it has changed a letter of its title from Dane Street to Dame Street. It was a busy place in those days, full of leather merchants, farriers, weavers and the usual export trade that still goes on around the area. Cities are more conservative than people.

"Liadin and Curither made their way there, first of all along the coast and then back inland through the mountains. They stopped at Glencree beside Lough Bray for a while with the women and children of a clan that were putting their cattle to high pasture. These people asked enough questions but were ignorant enough to accept evasive answers. Anyway they weren't so hot on the message of Christ, although they had been baptised many generations earlier. They were Lagin people, though with no memory of their difference and most of their men were of the Luaigni, a sort of Ghurka regiment of British-speaking people with a record of bloody service with the high king at Tara.

"There was a lot of Gaelic in their speech and of course Liadin could speak it anyway. And Christian or not, every bush and ditch was the abode of some godlet or sign so that the place was littered with baskets of unripe berries, balls of barley paste and whatever queer diet satisfied their spirits. They shied away, like humble people, from important gods and that included the Man from Calvary.

"Life went pleasantly for the absconding couple, although it was a bit rough, sleeping in a bower of river stones and living off oats and the odd marrowbone. Strangely, Liadin did not become pregnant, although God knows every stretch of heather on the hills had been a well-flattened marriage couch for them at one time or another. Curither had to cross the flat mountain to Glen na Smol to net birds to keep up his strength, oatmeal being no fodder for a man with a woman's rapacious belly to fill.

"Their art suffered from lack of practice, since their primitive hosts were used to nothing better than a little storytelling and a few work songs to soften the cows for milking. True, Curither, without benefit of a harpist to recite and perform, did compose a few poems which he recited himself, banging the rhythm with a thighbone on a leather bucket. He also composed a satire on cattle raiders, particularly the wild Brigantes from Wexford, who occasionally got as far north as the lakes. This produced a week's eating on a calf which their hosts presented to them. Liadin composed nothing and indeed kept her exalted rank secret from the helots of the Luaigni warriors. Truth to tell, she was a bit of a snob. Though related to them, or their more illustrious ancestors, by language, she had risen to eminence in the Gaelic aristocratic dispensation. Although she had popularised a few poems on pre-Gaelic Laginian themes, these were sentimentalised and were mostly about good Laginians who threw in their lot with the noble Gaels. Usually they were about a Laginian princess, raped by a Gaelic warrior, who forsook her language, claimed descent from some god common to both Lagin and Gael and mothered a brood of red-haired cattle raiders.

"In these particular poems, she was like Tommy Moore, composing sentimental Irish songs for the delectation of the Prince Regent when he was seeking liberal support against his mad ould da above in Kew. All the time near Lough Bray, when she wasn't bouncing Curither in the shielings, she sat by the lonely lake throwing stones in the black water and checking every day to see if she had started menstruating again. This put the fear of God and all the demons of Gaeldom into her.

"Finally, as the Luaigni people were about to take their cattle down to the littoral for slaughter, the pair of them decided to try their luck in Dublin. Neither the Fingal nor the Dubhgal (bright strangers, dark strangers) could be as inhospitable as their romanised countrymen, so there was little to lose.

"Near the crest of the Featherbed Mountain, which hasn't changed much to this day, they looked down on the town five miles below where the river broadened into the bay. Far across the water they could see two ships setting out from the peninsula of Hoffat, which they knew as Ben Edair, a particularly holy place. Smoke drifted up from the river mouth, evidence of Dublin's industry.

"It is true to say that they were well received by Flossie, the king's brother. He could hardly offer them a permanent job. His brother was on a bridal visit to a distant land which Liadin identified as Inis Orc, a Pictish land north of Alba, which is to say Scotland, but as Regent, Flossie was courteous enough, asked questions that could be answered truthfully but tactfully and helped them build a house of heavy timbers, curtained with wattles and firm red clay from the peninsula of Howth.

"Neither Curither nor Liadin had ever put hand to timber before, let alone clay, being of the poetic sept, but it was accounted no shame amongst the Norsemen.

"Olaf, the scald, helped them out of professional courtesy but also out of the kindness that was inherent in these people as soon as their wild blood had run its course and they had found a patch of land to breed children and cure fish. Curither was content enough, learning runic letters for recording useful spells, and finding much to recommend itself in the saga. Indeed he attempted one on the Yule Feast which was equally celebrated as the Norse-Irish Christmas. The general view was that he made a good job of it, particularly the genealogical prologue, but was a bit weak on the narrative and given to elaborate asides on matters of daily observation, such as the colour of fish falling from the net, the notes of a thrush, the snort of a porpoise and such matters. For himself, he could hardly help using a mind trained to lyrical observation and he realised that the meaty weight of the saga took a lot of getting used to.

"To compose without intricate embellishment, balancing ideas and words into an elegant harmony, was a novel idea for which he still felt considerable distrust. Still, he realised soberly that on matters of character and narrative the Gael had much to learn from the Norse, even the most horse-worshiping bastard amongst them.

"Liadin, despite her fine operatic airs, thought it no shame to consult a Norse magician about her gynaecological state. Her heart was like lead at the thought that her breaking of her vow of celibacy had put a curse on her womb, like the breaking of the Gaelic geasa or taboo. A large part of her attraction for Curither was the desire to produce a son of unusual gifts, as I explained, and she had every reason, under the circumstances, to blame the Man on the Cross. It was not as if she could be barren, for she already had two children from her early days of poetic practice, one fostered with a notable File sept in Breffini and the other in no less a place than the seat of the high king at Tara.

"The Norse wise man was less learned than a druid but he had his own divination technique, some of which she recognised. It was the standard practice of drinking mulled ale with a tincture of menstrual blood with pounded haws. But added to this, after poking around her with holy bones in a manner that she found very distasteful, he put her on a diet of broiled fish offal, mostly liver, and a sort of haggis made of seal pâté. She wasn't used to a fish diet and it gave her a bad flux of the bowels, saving your presence, ma'am, but one day, months afterwards when she was squatting in the reed beds near where Trinity College now stands, she found blood running down her leg. Most likely the penetential gruel of Saint Cummin had brought on an anaemia which had been cured by the fish guts.

"Bloody as she was she ran to Flossie's hall and composed a panegyric on the spot. The language was overblown by the pigeon-Gaelic standards of the Norse-Irish, but it was taken as a courteous gesture and people remarked on her good breeding. Intellectuals hadn't queered their own pitch by the ninth century. That wasn't until later.

"Curither at that time was working hard with Olaf and a Norse priest called Torgil on the proper understanding of the saga. He had some hopes of investing the art with what he recognised to be Gaelic advantages of description and detail.

"In Dublin and in the nearby Norse colonies popular belief was pretty degenerate compared with Olaf's vast and complicated cosmogony. There were many good Christians with their own Norse priests, trained in Ireland. Also there was Eógan the missionary evangeliser from Clonmacnoise whose three dialects of Norse would put a skald to shame and whose zeal would allow no concessions to Northern customs despite his wide learning. Eógan was visiting Waterford on the lovers' first arrival, but he was quick to take an interest in them when he returned.

"Otherwise the locals, mostly the women, had a great gradh for Baldur, the beautiful boy. Indeed they were much more concerned with him than with his father Odin, the big chief. Curither realised that harmony and beauty counted a lot in their thoughts as well as the idea of his death, like Christ from a stick of timber. Sife, the wife of the kipper curer, invited Liadin into her home one day when her husband was out with the boats, many of which he owned.

"There were half a dozen women present, gossiping and eating barley cakes and smoked salmon and sipping wooden cups of fine thin ale. Liadin unbent and chatted to them in a friendly way. Indeed she envied them for their numerous children, fine offspring with bright hair and outspoken manner. Then Sife, looking very mysterious, opened a chest and brought out a large bunch of mistletoe that had come from a nearby orchard. No sooner had she hung it from a beam than the women started to pluck the white berries and suck them, without swallowing them, crying 'Baldur's balls, Baldur's beautiful smooth balls. Suck them and see.' Knowing that they were a very domesticated community,

Liadin realised that this must be some sort of magic. And so it was. 'Here, Nerti, you need them most,' cried Sife, handing half a dozen to a young girl, slim but monstrously pregnant, suckling a healthy child at her enlarged and overladen breast. Nerti handed the child to another woman, wiped her vast nipple with grimaces of pain and half laced up her dress. She carefully sucked the mistletoe berries and spat them in the cloth with which she had wiped her dug and then one by one squeezed them between her fingers into a pipkin of ale. As each berry burst and exuded its spermlike pulp the women praised the act, crying 'Gentle juice, God's holy melt. That'll teach him manners. Oh that'll put a touch of decent respect into his hammer and stop him from bashing it like a pickaxe in a ditch.'

" 'Thor never overthrew a monster as bad as her fella,' said another. 'The poor girl hadn't even tightened up after having young Snorro when he was up her again. Merciful Baldur, he might as well have been stuck up an empty herring barrel, but at least a barrel can't feel.'

" 'Well, a good drink of that with his supper and he'll be eatin' outa your hand and lickin' yer lap for more. He'll do the job quiet and gentle, with you lying on your back like a decent Norsegirl and please Baldur, afterwards he'll get up and mull ye some ale and bring it to ye in bed.'

" 'I always pray to Baldur,' said a vast elderly woman. 'He may be a god but he's a gentleman. Not like that carpenter's son that's all the rage up by the River Tolka. If it wasn't for the juice of Baldur's little balls, I'd never have survived that man of mine. I declare to the gods that kipper smoke must have some effect on him. It's neither pleasurable nor decent.'

" 'I thought with a family as big as yours, you'd be used to it, Ulla, from your tonsils downwards.' Sife turned to Liadin. 'But you see, Laginian, why this is a women-only party. These men of ours are out in the fresh air all day. Up where our grandfathers come from the nights are long. That's fine, but the men are a crude lot and that's the truth. It takes a dose of little Baldur's balls to put a little consideration in their cocks, eh girls.'

" 'What about the Christian Danes?' asked Liadin. Very few of the Norsemen could write more than a misspelt runic spell, but quite a high proportion of the Christian Norse could read and write.

" 'Like a winter herring. Yeh lose on the salt what yeh gain on the flesh. What's the use of marrying a man and having a clutch of fine children by him if he's liable to suddenly feel the call of God one day when your figure is a bit gone. Some of them try to force their wives into a convent at the same time. Now, the nuns aren't the worst, but a hard bed in a cold cell is not the life for a woman that's spent twenty years breeding a family under a woven rug with a good warm man. I don't know. Between our lot with their lusts amok and their lot with their celibate ways, I don't know what the world is coming to.'

"Liadin took some berries for Curither, but didn't give them to him. Not that poetic substance is more refined than that of fish curers but their sensibilities are more developed. When he looked at her as she raked the ashes of the fire before going to bed, he saw a grave head and a long neck on which it turned, sloping shoulders, tapering arms. He saw silver breasts and a belly of whale ivory centering on a wedge of hair as comforting as a flowering moss in a rock cranny. He saw her body bending and turning, keeping its balance in a thousand subtle ways, extending an arm, bending a haunch, pulling a breast with a raised arm. She required no gentleness from him and could match his fury at any time, but it was a fury inspired, not an itching hunger of jaded habit like the poor burghesses with their rednecked fish hawkers.

"But in spite of all this, and much had been recorded in a poem, all was not well between them. Not just her passing barrenness but the beginning of the cleavage of the soul. She distrusted his new interest in the saga style of recitation, being a classicist in her own art. A few months earlier he would raise her kirtle as she bent over the quern and stroke her hands, saying:

" 'Better is this arse to me
Firm flesh divided discreetly
Than the champion's portion
In the hall of Conchubhar.
Carved with elegance
On a plate of fine gold.

'Firm fruit, the feast end
With soft melody
Two dishes in one.
Indurable mystery.

'Two dishes in one
Indivisible mystery
Food for my heart
Feast portion
For Aengus and Midir.'

"A few days before, after helping to wash the nets, they had gone together to a small island in the Liffey, floating in clear warm water over sand, to clean themselves. After swimming together, Curither had rubbed down his own skin with a glove of sealskin and thrown her a square of lamb's wool for herself. Fair enough! But scarcely a year before he had taken the torture from her flesh with wads of dock in a battle fury of attention.

"Provocatively, to exert all her power, she stood in the water, ankle-deep, half shaded by a willow tree with patterned shadows, and flaunted her body, drawing attention to each portion, each muscle, each firm and soft mass interrelated. His only remark was that the sea-fish diet had built up her flesh but that she needed more exercise. He picked up a piece of driftwood and threw it towards the north shore. 'Fetch that,' he cried. 'Get some salt into your lungs.'

"She did retrieve it and bound it to another to form a cross which she planted in the sand beside him. He shook his head. 'I've gone too far to start climbing Golgotha barefoot. The more you know of people the less certain the answers. Do you know what Olaf was telling me the other day? It's interesting. . . .' "

Mountmellick stirred in his chair. "I know what was happening. I don't think he was forsaking her: simply readjusting. He started off by using her as his muse. Very good. He couldn't have found a better one in human flesh, but the poetry of his upsurge couldn't last for ever. Verse is discipline, but its decisive moments come in flashes."

"I suppose so." Loreto sighed and snuggled down the bed. Mountmellick offered her some rather warm Chablis, raising her shoulders in the bed and holding the glass to her lips.

"Did he make a breakthrough into a new style?"

MacGilla shook his head and shrugged his shoulders.

"He took up literary politics. I think that would describe it," said Mountmellick. "He was an extremely intelligent man, observant and quick to draw logical conclusions. He knew that the monastery scholars were busily engaged in changing the history of Ireland. At Saint Cummin's establishment a brother called Cairbre had charge of the paschal tables from which various feasts were computed. It had to be done carefully because an omission or an imprecation in the eighty-four-year cycle could throw records out of gear and indeed had already done so. Without some adequate cross-reference it was difficult to tell whether an event took place in year 2 of one cycle or the next, since the cycles themselves were unnumbered or named.

"Gradually over the years the custom had grown up of recording contemporary events in the margin, thus providing a yearbook of historical usefulness. Since every Gaelic event involving people also involved their genealogies, the recorder had to set these down carefully. That's where the dishonesty began.

"Curither knew, as did any qualified poet, that there were several linguistic and cultural groupings in Ireland, as there were in Britain or France. In Europe, the empire founded by Charlemagne was a warlord's collection, like the Congo under Leopold, and in Britain there were Saxons, Welsh, Cornish, Irish and Picts still fighting it out with no certainty of the future. An Irish army had been beaten by the Saxons, a few years earlier, so the Gaelic strategy was to rely on their own white settlers from Dalriada who had colonised part of Scotland and were consolidating a union with the Picts. This area still bears their name: Iar Gael, or Argyle. Those English cartographers were an illiterate lot. A few years earlier Cinead MacAilpin, a Gael, had become king of an extensive Pictish kingdom.

"In Holy Ireland herself, Curither knew of various linguistic groups and kingdoms, speaking at least three different languages. There were the Crinoch in the north who were Picts or Pretanni, the early Celtic inhabitants of the islands. Then there were the Belgic tribes, the Fir Bolg, who had pushed back the Crinoch, and had themselves been overthrown and forced into small Ulster principalities by the marauding red-haired Gaels, fresh from Europe. These fellows established a herrenvolk of cattle barons with their barbaric vigour and soon settled themselves all over the south and in the fat pastures of the royal seat at Tara.

"To complicate all this there were other peoples of a separate Celtic stock and language who had occupied Leinster and Connaught under different tribal names. The Fir Gálion and the Fir Domnan—the Gauls and the Dumnani. These held their own against the Gaels, Scots, Irish, whatever you like to call them, but their culture was slowly absorbed, although there was a lot of give-and-take. Liadin came from Domnan stock, now known as Laginian from the god who gave his name to

Leinster. It was a worse mix-up than Europe today, I can tell you. Poor Saint Patrick must have been a good linguist.

"Now all these people kept their family records carefully since these were their religious records too, and their titles, if you like, to their lands. The red-haired Gaels had no records to speak of, but they had a fair number of gods, more or less in common with the earlier inhabitants. Bit by bit the Gaelic herrenvolk of Tara and the Eoganact of Munster began to spread their tongue and their way of life by various wars and cattle raids. Linguistically they triumphed in the end, though no one will ever know what compromises occurred.

"Berla was the Irish for language, though by now it refers only to English. In Curither's day, Gaelic poets used archaic words to fit their metres. Sometimes this was a lot of jawful for the red-haired paddies and it was known as Iarnbearla, Irish with a lot of Fir Bolg Belgic in it. There was also Berla Fane, Berla na Filid (properly, poets' language) and God knows what else. The English spoke Sacsberla, the Norse Gallberla and Charlemagne's paladins spoke Frangcberla.

"The Gaelic cattle-rustling aristocracy were in bad need of a history to justify themselves as soon as they began to learn civilised ways. They were a branch of the Celts, like all the others before them, so they started borrowing gods. The same thing went on in Greece, hundreds of years before. Don't forget that the Celtic world once spread from Belgrade to Galway and down to Cádiz, with odd pockets of resistance. There were a lot of variations, culturally and linguistically, within it.

"But it suited the early Celtic church to impose a uniform Gaelic structure on the island, and to do this, intelligent monks, learned in Latin and Greek, were prepared to rewrite history. What Curither saw beginning at Saint Cummin's was the beginnings of the *Labor Gabala,* the *Book of the Invasions,* which set out to construct a spurious Gaelic history, starting with the flood and changing every decent Belgic and Amorican tribal deity and executive god into an Irish king. Laginians like Liadin were startled to find their tribal ancestors turned into Gaelic-speaking kings in an improbable and ridiculous line of succession. Of course the Irish had to give as well as take. Laginian Fir Bolgs, Ulidians, Domnan, the lot, were all declared good and true Irishmen, open to the message of redemption.

"Now, among all the Irish, Belgic, Lagin, Gael and Pict, lineage was identity, so what the monks were doing was literary genocide. As a literary man, Curither was outraged and part of the difficulty was that he couldn't get this indignation into Liadin's head."

"Wow," remarked Loreto. "That's a mouthful. You sound very worked up about it."

"Of course I'm worked up. I am, we all are, literary entities. Literary genocide is a matter of concern. Even the South Africans don't go round suppressing Zulu mythology."

"They would if it suited them," said MacGilla, morosely. "Look," he prodded the air. "What you've been saying, with omissions tantamount to untruthfulness, is that Curither's mind had received a series of jolts. There he was, a respected western poet. He gets involved with this accomplished poetess, loses his job, nearly loses her and when he does get her in the end he finds that he has grown up a lot and that she is far behind him in perception. He discovers a Norse culture as complicated as the Irish one. Not that he sought it, but it happened. He couldn't make up his mind whether to spend the next few years studying Norse poetic technique, and then trying himself out in a minor Norse colony, like Man, for instance, or Rathlin Island . . . whether to do that or to go to France, get a grant from Alcuin's successor and spend ten years or so recording what was known to him of the history of Ireland.

"But to do this meant living for a while amongst the Crinoch, the scattered Pictish tribes of the north. He could have gone to Alba— Scotland, that is—but things were still a bit restless after the Gaelic overlordship of Ailpín in the Pictish lands. Here he was, troubled with these possible courses of action, and all Liadin could do was to worry about getting back into bardic harness and keeping his love. He loved her all right in a physical sense and what other sense is there? Without some shadow of that, there can be no other love.

"On Liadin's part, Curither had hooked her on sensual excitement and stimulating company, just when she was having her first doubts about Christian celibacy. It had led to anathema and the hospitality of this stinking Norse trading settlement. What did Curither do? Instead of taking her to a distant port of Gaelic Ireland, some part of the Eoganact domains where the priests were less bigoted and where the high status of poetry would be accorded its proper reward, he kept on about this Norse stuff which was never part of poetic training. It was fancy enough, like all their art. In all conscience she could hardly deny it, but its flavour was alien.

"The tree Yggdrasil contained creation with one root in frozen foggy Niflhel. She knew Niflhel. It was a winter's night in Dublin with frozen mists lying thick across the confluence of rivers and the sottish

leather curers sodden with muddy ale beating their wives and roaring at
the children. Muspellsheim at the other root was no better, an unthinkable land of fire and rancid smoke with its fountain Hvergelmir that
watered the rivers of Mitgard. Mitgard was where men lived. Its waters
flowed from fiery hell. This was rationally and poetically unacceptable.
Many of her poems were about water, rivers, lakes, falls, tumbling and
still. As for Asgard, the abode of the godly Aesir, where was the glory,
the beauty, the eternal blossom of Tir na n-Óg or Magh Mell, the
abode of her own pantheon, which man had visited and enjoyed.
Asgard was a land of prosperous farmers with eternal Yule feasts. True
there were skalds, but unlike Curither, who had delved deeper, she
regarded the Norse poets as no more than household rhymsters. She
was a fine girl with great academic skill and a good public presence but
she was very conservative.

"Apart from all this, her barrenness continued. At first, after Saint
Cummin's, her womb would not flow. Then after the Norse treatment
it flamed fiercely and haphazardly, a worse omen than before. She
could not give up life with Curither for she was drugged by the need of
a man, and the only man was Curither. Her moodiness and spells of
vacant silence which had aided her in her harsh poetic vigils as a student
were becoming more disruptive.

"One November night she left the house to go for a piss around the
back. Feeling moody she walked on past a crowd of noisy children
stacking firewood. The habitual act of the Dublin women of straddling
the legs and rattling into the mud offended her, not in her modesty but
in the social etiquette of her poetic station. She wandered down to the
water's edge across the tufted sea grass and emptied herself pleasantly
sitting across a boat prop, and remained there for a long time staring at
the water and watching the broken clouds passing across the stars. She
didn't think of much but floated in a balmy melancholy broken with
anxieties, fears and doubts. Curither's appearance, after an hour's
searching, caused her neither pain nor relief. She went home with him,
quietly, and spent a long time drawing the fire ashes together into a
neat truncated pyramid.

"Some time after the Yule days had begun to lengthen and soften,
Liadin and Curither went with a party of children and women to gather
shellfish on the far side of Howth facing the pinnacle rocks of Ireland's
Eye, the island where some of the Christian Norse were busy extending
their small monastery. It was a long day in terms of labour, but the fresh
food was welcome and the cockle bake on the sand flats particularly

enjoyable. There were two borrowed horses to carry home the harvest but it was late evening when they had forded the Tolka and taken the ferry home across the swollen pool of the Liffey.

"Women are supposed to have better intuitive feelings, by which it is meant that they can apprehend subtle signals unconsciously and respond with a feeling of unease when warranted. Indeed, the feeling rarely manifests itself if it is not one of unease, or if it does, by no more than a continuation of unmeasured confidence. But Curither had always been the more responsive of the two in this behaviour, and the sight of the dim lights across the water and the distant reflection of the dead sun in the west, towards the Salmon Leap, affected him with an uneasy gloom.

"It was well augered, for they were met in the centre of the town by a citizens' committee returning down the hill from the Thingmote. Vali Agnarson, who passed as king of the settlement, had returned from Inis Orc after failing to negotiate a marriage with a Pictish princess from the mainland. Worse, he had failed in a series of trading negotiations with some Odin-worshiping cousins farther north.

"Stopping at Lambey Island, ten miles north of Dublin, for briefing on civic affairs, he had picked up Eógan the priest, on his way from the Danish port of Waterford. Eógan was delighted at the failure to arrange the marriage. First, because Vali was well married already by Christian and Norse custom, but also because he feared that the inheritance of a Pictish estate in the far north of Britain would affect his influence over the Norse ruler. The Picts and their brothers, the Crinoch of Antrim, were matrilinear, and kingship came through the female line, a revolting and unnatural thought to a Romish god man. Besides it could keep Vali away from Dublin for a year at a time and leave affairs in the hands of Flossie, the king's brother, a farmer and a man whose shrewdness passed for tolerance. Flossie had a kingdom of his own to achieve and to rule as regent prosperously without commitment to Odin or Christ was an elementary prudence.

"Long before noon, when Liadin and Curither were breaking their backs in the cockle beds and watching the children during the tidal surge in the sound, Eógan had addressed the assembled parliament on the Thingmote, where it had gathered to hear Vali make his address. Vali was dejected in failure, whereas Eógan brought news of a proposed trading alliance with Waterford and a potential lenten market in France, of salt fish. To increase his own advantage and to satisfy his own prejudices, he had led an attack on Curither and Liadin, the excommunicated blasphemers, which spread like a xenophobic virus through Christian and pagan heart alike. The lovers were traitors and refugees from the neighbouring and friendly Laginians. The Laginians were deep in Tara politics.

"Poets were the chief officers of darkness and blasphemers bring bad luck. Vali had failed in the Orkneys. In a surge of anger the burghers and more particularly the burghers' wives looked across the water and saw the cause and the cure in the ferry, surrounded by children and young mothers.

"Well, a mob is a queer animal. It has the horns and hooves of a mad bull but no more brain than a gust of wind. Liadin and Curither found themselves faced with a couple of hundred women, with their men in full support, yelling 'Kill the bastards, kill the bastards! Blasphemers! Apostates!' This coming, mind you, from people who were in to Mass one week and slitting a horse's throat to Odin the next. Sife the kipper wife was out in the front screaming 'Kill the bitch! Her with her stuck-up airs. I'll give her stuck up. Stuck up with a boat hook!'

"Cornered on the seashore behind the houses, Curither took the only action open to him, since retreat was impossible with a boatload of children. He hauled Liadin up a ship's gantry of lashed timbers and looked down to face the mob. Liadin was frightened mute for the moment, but Curither opened up on them.

" 'People of Dublin. Ye have betrayed your heritage, and not for the first time.' He picked up a handful of bronze nails from the plank and scattered them below. 'You have hammered rivets in the flesh of Christ and pinned him rigid to the cross. He will hang there till time is forgotten unless one man among you can release him for redemption.' He spoke, or I suppose you would say intoned, in the vocative manner, like the beginning of a bardic delivery. 'Your fathers and foster fathers, brave men, uncorrupted by the foolishness of unhappy women, would have understood me.' He paused and looked down at the growing quiet, and put his left arm around Liadin's shoulders and drew her to him, and continued in Norse. 'They would have known as some of you still know, that a thousand malevolent demons gnaw at the third root of Yggdrasil, the holy tree that supports the world. But more than that they would have recognised here today the gnawing of the serpent Nidhögg, foul embodiment of evil counsel and thoughtless action.' He paused again and watched Olaf the Skald making his way to the side of the crowd and mounting the gantry behind him. The skald spoke in clear and beautiful Norse, straining his declamatory style to Thingmote rhetoric.

" 'Ness men, I invoke the Steed of the Redoubtable and the cruel cold of Niflhel. You must choose your portion. Poetry is the voice of man speaking to God. It is also the voice of God speaking to man. We live in friendly alliance with the people of Lagin and Tara. Are we to endanger our city for the sake of a squabble between righteous priests and proud poets? Who can say which is more important? They both speak the voice of God.

" 'Curither comes from far Ui Ailella on the far ocean which we have tamed. And how many of you have watered your ships and nourished body and soul on the broth and song that was Liadin's unstinted offering to all who passed her bruiden on the Wicklow coast? Remember that the poet is older in the ways of God and gods than some who speak for the Easter Christ, and remember that poetry knows no frontiers of thought and few of language. Curither is as good a skald as I am. Touch him and you live like beetles in the dust, life without meaning. Touch Liadin and never raise your voices again in prayer or song. Write no spells in runic, for the beast Nidhögg will scorch the letters and turn their power.'

"Vali Agnarson chewed his lip, standing amongst his armed men, and looked anxiously at Eógan. Then he seemed to make up his mind and spoke without any counsel. 'This is no place for judgment. In three days the Thing will be convened with all householders from the lands of Danelaw. This must be decided not only by the men of Dublin but by the men of Howth, Finglas, Lambey, Rush, Lusk and Skerries.'

"The prospect of a general parliament in the first days of spring was an exciting one, and a shrewd move by Vali. It turned dangerous hysteria to the anticipation of pleasure. The women would rush to prepare puddings and dumplings and the men would polish their buckles to shine more gallantly on the debating hill. 'May the judgment of the Book condition your thoughts and the spear of Tyr, shaft of justice, transfix your minds.'

"Curither, as his own limbs softened to absorb the shock of escape, felt Liadin's body pressing and softening to his side. She grasped his forearm fiercely and then lost the strength to hold him. He helped her down the scaffolding, half lifting her. Olaf held out his hands, making the Thor sign with his fist, and lifted her to the ground. Holding her by the sides of her hair at arm's length, he pulled her towards him and gave her the Christian kiss on both cheeks. Some of the men in the dispersing crowd cheered and many a woman began to blame her stupid cow of a neighbour for starting the foolishness.

"Late that night in the fine house of Olaf, safe under its carved beams, the decision was taken. Liadin and Curither would travel north to the Crinoch kingdom of Dalriada in a boat bound for the spring fair in Sweden with a consignment of tooled leather. Olaf approved this, since it meant that the Thing would have nothing to debate, but he regretted the loss of Curither and his exciting vision of poetry as the watchdog of a people's faith and the guardian of its heritage.

"I suppose that most literary hopes are stillborn, but there was something salvaged from the Dublin episode to which too little heed is given. Curither's hopes to save Irish genealogy from monkish bowdlerisation and falsification came to nothing. Luckily the tonsured boyos weren't too good at their job and a few clues were left. His scheme to adapt the saga to Irish needs came to sweet—saving your presence, ma'am —bugger all. Before a few centuries had gone by the gap had been filled by Norman claptrap, amour courtois and that sort of Catalan vapourising.

"In place of a flash of white flesh that would inspire a poet to voice his hunger, princes rode on palfreys and the weapons of love became secondhand metaphors: Truth, a commodity hard come by, and difficult to store, is the only weapon of love. It is my belief that the subsequent addiction of the sons of the Gael for their own thumbs and forefingers dates from the introduction of this amour courtois *Peg's Paper* stuff.

"But one thing, as I said, did come out of this Dublin sojourn. Olaf the skald took Curither's fears about monkish bowdlerisation to his deepest heart. Years later in the Orkneys he passed it on, one night in drink, and the idea spread. It was a slow business, much too slow, and it was touch and go. But in the heel of the hunt, over four hundred years later, a party by the name Snorri Sturluson sat down amongst the barking of bull seals and wrote down a manual of verse. It was the first poetic *Edda*. Others followed, but it was a touch and go matter before it was all forgotten."

"At least it was one bright coin salvaged from the ooze of forgetfulness," remarked Mountmellick, sententiously. MacGilla's head remained bowed, but he threw a two-second stare at his master, under heavy eyebrows.

Loreto stretched both legs down the bed, vibrated for a duration in full extension and sat up, gathering pillows behind her back. "Fix me a drink, Mac. Yeah! So what's wrong with Bushmills. I feel a need and something's got to fill it." She accepted a gurgled measure from MacGilla without pressing her preference for ice, in case it brought up an argument about ruined flavour, about which all possible points had already been voiced, and vehemently repeated.

"That's a very interesting story. It's a hell of a sight better than Tristan and Iseult or who's the other pair? Aucassin and Nicolette?"

"Of course it is," said Mountmellick.

"But all these explanations and . . ."

"Peregrinations?"

"Oh the hell with it, what sort of literary corpuscles run in your blood? Everyone knows the form of a short story. Your style couldn't make a grade in East Bradford Tech, Iowa."

"So much the worse for Iowa. The rules of narrative expression are as flexible as an amoeba's foot. You make them to taste as needed and flavour accordingly. This is widely accepted."

"That's more than I can say for you unless you do a lot of editing. What happened to your two poets? Is there any end to the story?"

"There is. Ah yes. I fear there is," Mountmellick replied. "As romantic as anyone could wish. Do you want to hear it?"

"Oh get on, but skip the prehistory stuff."

"You want a picture without a frame. A car without an engine, an argument without a premise."

"Get on with the story before I scream."

"Well, the night before the assembly on the Thingmote, Olaf and Thorgil the priest smuggled Liadin and Curither aboard a trading vessel, partly owned and wholly skippered by Bori Thorgilson, a nephew of the cleric's. 'Smuggle' is perhaps too strong a word in that a couple of hundred people came to see them off, excluding children, and an ale feast had been convened the previous night by Flossie, who hoped to use Curither as a one-man trade mission among the Crinoch, with a view to spreading trade to the overseas Picts of Scotland. Some of the finest battle harnesses outside Danelaw came from one of Flossie's enterprises, a particularly stinking tannery which poisoned more fish than the shore fishers caught.

"Following the southwesterly, keeping near the shore, Bori, who had a small crew, made good speed north, skirting the island of Howth and Lambey and on past the Norselands. The first stop was at Dunleer, to drop off a bale of tannings to the Eldani who wished to invest some of last year's profits from a cattle raid on some black-arsed Gaels, further inland, out of favour with Tara. The Eldani being of the Lagin stock, Liadin was made welcome, since her ecclesiastic enemies lacked jurisdiction there. They begged her to stay and were willing to suffer

Curither. It was tempting, but Curither had sworn to record the history and genealogy of the age-old Crinoch, who had roamed the land when the Laginians, Fir Bolgs and Gaels were scattered across western Europe.

"The next stop, after a perilous journey around Carlingford and Strangford, was Loch Lóg where the town of Belfast now stands. The people thereabouts had thirty skin bags of malt ready for loading and the delay was short. Liadin and Curither stayed near the ship since there was a vigorous church mission in progress held by visiting Eóganact clerics. The Lagan valley Belgae were notorious for their religious backsliding and favoured a cattle goddess whom they had included in the Gaelic pantheon by a deed poll process. Aengus the youth god was supposed to have pleasured her in a watermeadow in the form of a heron.

"This libel enraged even Gaelic Christians, who didn't allow strangers to criticise the gods which they themselves had rejected. Lapsed Catholics often find themselves in the same position.

"Curither wanted to stay, since the people were a branch of the Ulidian Fir Bolgs and worth studying, but Liadin went on strike. She had learned from some sack sewers that the cattle ceremony was particularly unsightly, involving as it did the use of a wooden beak worn by a youth impersonating the god Aengus. As she pointed out, a crusading evangelist dealing with backsliders could put them in a greater peril than in Dublin. Furthermore, Curither would have later opportunities to confer with Ulidian genealogists and poets, since many had penetrated the shrinking kingdoms of the Crinoch.

"The wind turned easterly on the journey up the Antrim coast and the Sea of Moyle was at its stormiest and worst. Liadin was violently and disastrously seasick and moaned between the lockers upbraiding her lover and her bitter wandering fate. Curither saw four swans near a bay at Larne and carried her up to the stern to see them.

"He cried to her, he sang to her the story of the children of Lir, turned swan, to triumph over the wild waters that lay between Antrim and Stranraer. His comforting had no immediate calming effect though it did bring reassurance. Between spasms, Liadin had strength to argue that the swan children were saved by the sound of a Christian bell after five hundred years of pagan suffering. It followed, she argued, that the swans of the loch were an augury that only by returning to celibacy and holiness could she ever return to peace.

"Crouching behind the helmsman's shelter, Curither argued the opposite. The children of Lir, he contended, were celestial beings and not subject to earthly limitations or advantages. The story had been altered, humanised and Christianised until it bore no resemblance to the original. Swan gods as white as the high clouds there had always been, and due reverence and love had always been offered to them. This was inherent in the very appearance of the creatures. To this had been attached the libelous story of a wicked stepmother who turned her husband's children into swans and condemned them to five hundred years living on the lakes and seas of Ireland. This was nonsense, since only Otherworld people could behave like this. Poets were concerned with the description and revelation of truth, and could not possibly accept the malicious hobgoblins of ignorant cowherds.

"Somewhere in the story was the true fact of swan worship and a libelous account of a Crinoch princess who married a Belgic king of Ulster. Since her tradition was that inheritance was through the female line, she naturally took offence at the idea that the children should succeed as their father's issue. She did not turn them into swans, but suggested to them, perhaps forcefully, that they should go to their mother's clan, who held the swans in reverence, and not try to over-turn the natural order of kingship.

"The 'sound of bell from distant shore' that redeemed them was, as MacGilla might say, a piece of monkish mullarkey.

"Finally, on a bright cold day in spring, Liadin and Curither were set ashore near where Ballycastle now sits, on the coast of Antrim facing out towards Rathlin Island. Bori Thorgilson had no wish to delay in the area, or to have any truck with the Crinoch. Perhaps in Scotland things might soon be different, with the new alliance of Irish and Pict, but here the Crinoch were fighting back and had already recovered part of their old lands from the Belgae, some said with the help of Belgic traitors.

"As a mark of respect to various sea gods, Norse, Gaelic and Christian, some fowl were decapitated and a feast was prepared on the seashore and passengers and crew slept in shelters in the lee of the beached ship. Next morning, the two poets stood on the shore and watched the Norse ship making good weather as it slapped and surged towards the Norse settlements in the Scottish Isles.

"Liadin had recovered now and followed Curither as he climbed the high ground to avoid the swamplands up the coast. They saw no houses or encampments during the morning's march, and by afternoon they decided to build a shelter and a fire. After a meal of dried fish and bread they lay in the bright cold sunlight, warmed by the fire and the windbreak that Curither had constructed. Both of them felt a sense of release after the long journey from Dublin and Liadin began a series of apologies for her recriminations during her seasickness. Curither uttered the first draft of a poem that had been on his mind about the altered significance of a homestead on a hill, seen by a seafarer passing, a being from a different world, offered a glimpse of heaven. And yet, as everyone knew, the homestead, secure in its green pastures, was not heaven. How then can visions of heaven be trusted?

"Liadin dissected and amended some of his lines, and they both sank into affectionate love play, gently stroking, combing each other's hair and licking salt from each other's skin. For the first time since before they left Dublin, they copulated freely and happily, rolling in the warm embers and back onto the cool grass. Then they lay, still joined in blissful release, staring at the clouds above a far hill, when Liadin gave a cry and went crawling for her cloak. Curither thought she had been stung by an early wasp and caught her ankle as she scrambled, but she pointed to a fold of green, edged by hazel bushes, which grew along a stream. It took him some time to catch the movement, but then he discerned a file of people approaching them, scrambling uphill and cresting the ridge.

"There were six men, two young women and an old lady, apparently of some consequence. Hastily drawing on breeks and shouldering his cloak, Curither advanced towards them and addressed them formally in verse:

> " 'Blessings on this land
> Men, women and supple children
> Fruitful its pastures
> And our sanctuary secure.
>
> A blackbird rejoiced at our landing
> Trees sweetened to bright green
> Boiling sea and cruel wind
> Were silent in its peace.'

"He then offered a diplomatic genealogy tracing his ancestry through the filidhe of Brian and Fiachra and the line of Eochu Magmedon, but carefully stressing his personal allegiance to the Ailella and the tribes of sen Connachta whose domains diminished under Gaelic penetration. Liadin's genealogy, being nearly pure Laginian, he gave accurately, though stressing certain ancestors more than others. It was four hundred years since the Amorican Laginians had showered spears at the

Crinoch, and poetry can easily sacrifice a small truth in favour of the greater truth of expedience.

"This peaceful utterance was accepted in silence by the Crinoch people, who rolled their eyes and made signs with their hands of a prophylactic character. Liadin was terrified of their tattooing, which consisted as far as she could see of overlapping circles across their foreheads. Their hair was elaborately dressed in coloured clays, blue and red, tasteful but alarming, and their cloaks were of soft tanned leather, painted in geometric designs, haphazardly. But they were not, apparently, absolute savages, since one of the young women had taken off her cloak and was dressed beneath in well-woven breeks held by leather straps. Her breasts were large and bare and had circles painted around the nipples.

"It was the girl who spoke, and her flood of speech worried Curither and made him despair of learning the language.

"But the intruders were friendly. There seemed no doubt about that. The old lady presented Liadin with a piece of cheese from a wrapping and then offered the rest to Curither. By signs and gestures they succeeded in persuading the poets to accompany them, carrying their gear and touching and stroking them playfully, like children. Together they took a cattle path over the hill and along a series of ridges, avoiding wet ground and thickets. There was as yet no sign of habitation, and Curither expected them to camp for the night, when suddenly, as they rounded a dense isolated wood, there appeared below them a scattering of lights, and the sea, beyond.

"The Crinoch stronghold was a circular stone structure, twenty feet high, elaborately constructed and sheltering several pavilions of wood, stone and leather built against the inside of the wall. They seemed weatherproof and commodious, but quite unlike the halls or bruidins of Gael, the Lagin or the Fir Bolg. Several fires burned in stone hearths, in the open enclosure, protected by dry stone walls that formed small courts.

"People came running out to meet them, chattering loudly, and Curither found himself facing a king or chief who came towards him with a woman at his side. Putting his arm across Liadin's shoulder, Curither issued his formal address a second time, being careful to remember the lineages accurately. It seemed to be acceptable. There was a short conference amongst the royal retinue and a sandy-haired man in a skirt and harness stepped up and spoke in bad Gaelic with many recognisably Belgic words and comical grammar. He bade them welcome in Liadin's honour. Her reputation was known. Curither was made welcome as her prince and druid.

"Carefully but truthfully Curither explained through his interpreter the reason for his presence with Liadin, stressing his role as that of file and companion. Since the Crinoch were still matrilinear, despite the intermarrying with the Fir Bolgs and Gaels, it seemed more prudent. That men were highly considered was obvious. There was no sign of petticoat government. Nevertheless he noticed that Bruide, the king, took the bowl of milk from the hands of his consort Bidba before offering it to the visitors. Gaelic queens and goddesses for that matter had a great deal of power in their own right, but ultimately the king was the war leader and both power and the giving of favours were in his keeping.

"There was no evidence as yet that Bidba, a tall flat-chested woman, wielded power, but there were many indications during the ceremonial welcome that, for ceremonial purposes at least, power derived from her.

"Both Liadin and Curither were extremely tired and hoped to be offered a cubicle for sleep, or whatever the Crinoch equivalent might be. When they were taken, by Bruide and Cinead, the interpreter, into the largest pavilion under the walls, they saw no sign of any partitions or stalls, or anything resembling the architecture of the Bolg or Gael. Along the wall side there was a continuous bed of heather, boxed behind a plank container, and covered in deer skins, some of them stiff and badly cured. There were about fifty people of both sexes, some naked, and others wearing kirtles or trews. All the women, until past childbearing age, had patterns tattooed on their foreheads and circles or chevrons painted on their breasts. Senua, one of the young women who had surprised them resting in the fire ash after lovemaking, ran to greet them, followed by an old lady who had been repainting the girls' breasts and back, from a bowl of fatty clays. Nursing mothers, often very young, and matrons of all descriptions, however naked they might be, seemed careful to keep in place two little banners of yarn or decorated leather covering their front and back apertures. Liadin noticed that a woman with a round patch carefully shaved from her skull was extremely apologetic when she exposed herself inadvertently when scrambling to pick up a crawling child.

"This showed some sense of decorum, which gave Curither a little relief. As a file, he was also a professional diplomat and under the obligation to observe and respect other people's customs.

"Both he and Liadin expected to be undressed by the women and washed with dippers of water from a warm cauldron. This was usual after travel, hunting or battle, and all the nations of Ireland practised it in one way or another. Not, apparently, the Crinoch.

"A small elderly man, the only naked male in the entire assembly, had been smeared in fat and coated in powdered chalk and small feathers. He pranced around Bruide and Cinead, shaking a rattle, chanting a song and making obscene gestures with his appendages which were so decorated with a corona of coloured feathers as to be invisible.

"He wriggled in front of Curither and made a miming gesture in front of Liadin that would have caused a ten-generation blood feud elsewhere, but the only reaction of the Cruithne was to smile politely and clap their palms. Liadin rose to her stretched height and was about to put the full power of her poetic abuse on him and all that favoured him, but Curither muttered, 'Still your mouth, woman; our only weapons are our words. Use them carefully.' It was wise advice, for Cinead explained to them later that the man was a druid. He plainly wasn't but that was the only word available to express the idea.

"The Crinoch had no poets, file or any such rank. Nor had they druids or lawgivers. Matters of a religious kind, relating to birth, marriage, death, harvest or hunt were regulated by societies, practising secret rites with some public ceremonies. The function of the whitened clown was to draw all luck from each person present, protected by his own covering of chalk. The chalk was later scraped from his body and buried, and if necessary someone was sent underground with it to ensure its safety in the dark dumb land which they feared.

"After a meal of barley and venison, taken al fresco by the entire company, without any apportioning of pieces in order of importance, there was entertainment, partly out of courtesy to the visitors. The social process was very strange to Liadin and Curither. Everyone, even the older children, ate from two cauldrons. This caused a little squabbling but there was no danger as elsewhere of a blood fight between two men who both considered themselves entitled to a shoulder portion or any other portion befitting their station. There was no adjournment afterwards around the centre hearth to hear the bard singing the poets' compositions or to listen for flattering genealogical niceties to give one man pride and another pique. Instead, the Crinoch sang songs. Anyone with the skill and voice seemed acceptable, and both Liadin and Curither had to admit that for uneducated people they did it well, or some did.

"Cinead, who had spent many years hostage at Emain Macha, the old Belgic capital, translated some of them. They were love songs. One, which combined a tender melancholy with a fiddle-de-dee chorus, was about a girl who loved two boys. One was dark and one was red-haired, both had straight bodies and bold eyes. But only one could quicken her belly with a girl with small ears and white teeth, and he was the shyer of the two, and of the wrong clan.

"There were hunting songs, sung by the men, and work songs sung by the women, some of which were onomatopoeic in structure. A weaving song imitated the rattle of the loom weights and Curither was very impressed by a hunting song, sung by three young men, the words of which were unintelligible, but which caught the feeling of a hunt: the long search, the sighting, the chase, the cornering and the howling of the hounds. Finally there was the kill and the grunts of the spearsman and the death of the boar. One of the men seemed to know boar language, so excellent was his speech mime. Then there was the procession home, with rattle music and triumphal horns. These Crinoch might lack the aristocratic pomp of the Gaelic clans, or their sophistication, but they were not without art and grace to suit their own secret needs.

"Liadin and Curither were so weary that their ears were singing. As yet, no one had apportioned them a sleeping space, but before collapsing into rest, Curither drew Cinead aside to ask where they could both relieve themselves before the night. To his embarrassment, Cinead transmitted the request to Bidba, who stood up with her consort and made for the curtained door, beckoning the strangers to follow.

"A couple of dozen Crinoch of both sex led and helped the visitors down to a tongue of sand washed by the sea where they all proceeded to relieve themselves. Many of them wore long worsted cloaks with embroidered chevrons and similar patterns, and half sank into the darkness, like small conical tents or poetic contemplation booths. The process astonished the two poets. In the Gaelic and Laginian courts and bruidins, relief was allowed as nearly as custom or convenience allowed, a token aversion of the eyes being the only privacy. Curither suspected that, clearly as the custom might be, its purpose was magical or religious. Bidba had used the occasion to purge the company of harmful goblins, humours, spites and pookas in token of amicability. Whatever the reason, Curither reflected that the native lords as well as the Saxons, Franks and Romans could learn a lot from these strange people from Antrim and Strathclyde.

"Back in the royal pavilion, Curither looked for Liadin to find or be granted a place to sleep. He caught her eye, but she frowned a warning and he watched her being whisked off by more women, mainly chattering and curious young girls. They all lay down together at one end of the vast heather bed, covering themselves with their cloaks, laughing, giggling and whispering to each other. Liadin, queen of the feast, lay unapproachable in the middle of them.

"Bruide and Bidba slept near each other, but separated by several children and youths of both sexes, and Curither was left to lie down with Cinead and a group of members of the official classes, a soothsayer, a smith and a boatbuilder. He lay there on the crackling heather wondering how the generations of Crinoch continued, considering the sexual segregation of their sleeping habits. They were a shrinking nation, victims of all the invaders of Ireland and a prey to slave-raiders, Gaelic and Belgic traders and husband-seekers, to say nothing of the Romish clergy who beheld them in horror, despite the fact that Patrick had once lived amongst them and loved them.

"Next morning there was a hunt which Curither attended. To his surprise, several girls came along, including Senua, who was a skilled net weaver and a consummate caster. Two badgers, a resting seal and a host of birds fell to her throwing, and also a fox, which she presented to him. The men raised a stag and led it with their dogs into an angle of net which she and her companions had erected between some trees. In the kill, the hunters drove their weapons by hand, rather than by throwing, but Curither observed that the weapon heads were mostly of Belgic design, except for a few native ones with neat leather binding to hold the small narrow blades. There seemed to be no distinction between hunting spears and war spears, and Curither noticed that several shafts carried prophylactic ornaments.

"The hunt was a reasonable success, and the men carried back the spoils, while the girls walked behind, singing songs, apparently of praise, thanksgiving and apology to the animals. Curither had often heard men apologise to a tree, before hewing, but this was an odd custom which he considered picturesque. By this time his feelings to the Crinoch were paternalistic and sentimental. They seemed to be a simple people, whose old manner of life was slowly giving way to pressures stronger than their countless centuries of conservatism.

"As a fully ordained poet, Curither was aware that it was a secondary function of all art to conserve as well as to innovate. Every glen and every plain has its beauty and the record of these attributes or the lament for their destruction is a proper function of poetic skill. Equally, the new delight in learning or the fascinating propositions of the Greek and Roman druids seemed worthy of praise, although they might, in their spread, lay vacant every feasting hall and fortress in the five portions of Ireland and leave the grandeur to shy foxes and desolation.

"The Crinoch people were being bested not so much by battles as by new movements in the thoughts and lives of men. Once the Fir Bolg of Ulaid sang the greatest songs, and Cuchulain in his battle madness fought singlehanded against the armies of the men of Ireland. Now the chariots of Conchubar were remembered only in song and story and no one hurled spears of light from the leaping harness poles.

"When Bruide and Bidba traveled to their neighbours' forts they still rode in an old Ulster chariot, shining with thin gold and painted wicker and drawn by four ponies. It was considered an historical relic. No one would have dreamed of fighting from it. Indeed, no one knew how. The Crinoch hadn't invented it or even built it. It was a tribute to their old Sky Wheel, which they had adopted after some disremembered battle against the Fir Bolgs of Emain Macha, centuries before: a forgotten acknowledgement of the power of the foreign Ulster men, with their vast feasts, strange language and omnipotent battle goddess.

"No one fought from chariots now. Even when Patrick faced King Leoire in the Tech Midchuarta, the vast palace at Tara, there were no chariots among the fighting men and no one would have been skilled enough to drive one.

"It was this process of change that Curither wanted to understand and record: without a record there could be no understanding. It seemed a more important phenomenon to him than the mystery of syntax or the mystery of the Trinity. These were only ways of describing Providence or trimming God to fit a metaphor, but the diverse land in which he lived, and the outer world of which he knew were subject first and foremost to change and alteration. The warriors of the Gael, the courts of the Franks and the first fury of the Norsemen were only symptoms: this upheaval was the distant stirring of an all-father, a movement in the stars that no one had noticed. If he could have explained his feelings to an intelligent Crinoch, he would have been told to look for an all-mother, not an all-father, since it is a stirring womb that thrusts forth both the novel and the expected. He was aware of this odd attitude of theirs, but felt that it hardly mattered whether the Being was generously hung or deeply cleft. If men and women were formed in His image, as the Christians reasonably suggested, its delineation must needs be either sexually ambiguous or all-embracing. Any competent theologian could handle either proposition.

"Of course Curither wasn't anything remotely resembling an anthropologist. He had no method of enquiry, and saw most things in terms of his day, but just as his body fed on Liadin, his mind fed on questions which required acceptable answers. A few centuries later, logic was bent to serve the needs of the Church and intelligent men spent lifetimes setting out the Christian mysteries in terms of Greek logic. With Curither, poised between two cultures, it was simpler. The old Celtic world, whether Crinoch, Belgic or anything else, had sufficient gods and goddesses, but the plain people stuck to forces that threatened and forces that benefited. Some might see destruction by lightning as the power of the magic spear, the gai bolga, or the burning eye of Balor on a summer pasture, but most kept to smaller gods that hid behind standing stones or in the roots of thorn trees. The Crinoch were given to this sort of thing as were the ordinary people everywhere, and Curither wondered how much the various invaders, over hundreds of years, had penetrated into the matrix of the old ways that had gone unmodified for thousands of years. There was some suggestion that they had only overlaid them with top dressings of different colours.

"For several weeks Liadin and he lived diligently with the Crinoch. Life was orderly and rude, but sufficiently full of new things to be interesting. Liadin seemed to expand in her female half of the society. Her fame as a poetess from Gaelic lands seemed to have entitled her to high standing in the archaic society of their hosts. Bidba firmly commandeered her for the milking, the complicated rituals that went with cheese-making and in the hand-feeding and stroking of pregnant cows which featured largely in her duties. She and Bidba would spend hours subduing the fierce little black beasts into docility, which was considered very important. Herding was a form of husbandry foreign to the Crinoch, and only adopted by them from the neighbouring Belgae within historical memory, but they had extended their agricultural practices to the animals, and offered vegetable sacrifices to their cows, before and during pregnancy. Bulls were esteemed less, although among the Belgae and the Gaels they were the royalty of animal wealth and admired and coveted. The Crinoch however revered the little brown cow and used it as a term of endearment.

"Curither, with the doubtful help of Cinead, tried to get some idea of the Crinoch speech. Since he was poetically trained to remember, he amassed dozens of words in a few days, and isolated verbs from nouns. Many of these words were half familiar, through Gaelic, but he thought nothing of that since he had observed the same thing in the Latin tongue that he had begun to study at Saint Cummin's. Their grammar was very simple, though full of irregularities that made him despair. He was very doubtful indeed of their tongue as a medium for poetry. They had no poets; need any more be said. Nonetheless, their songs were not without some skill and poignancy. There was plenty of evidence of normal sexual awareness amongst the children. Little girls played with little boys' bods and boys teased girls for the absence of the same. But this was normal child play anywhere. Life in Ireland, Alba, Saxonland or Frankland was pretty communal. People crowded into hovels or halls wherever they lived, but the Crinoch seemed to lack a sense of privacy, over and beyond ordinary living. They were a dying nation anyway. . . ."

"I don't know anything about them," complained Loreto. "Are they necessary for the story?"

"All Irish matters, all considerations of the western Celts, are suffused with genealogical patterns," Mountmellick explained. "To this day, if two Irishmen or Welshmen meet anywhere from home, they sniff around until names and birthplaces supply some measure of identification."

"It all reads like something out of Tolkien." Loreto had passed the point of further interest.

"Listen to me briefly," Mountmellick begged. "Western, and for that matter northern eastern Europe was being formed after Rome's political collapse and Rome's religious triumph. The Picts or the Crinoch as we called them had allied themselves with the Scots or Ulster Belgae from the north of Ireland and were trying to hold Dumbarton in Scotland against the advancing Saxons. In Ireland the Crinoch had been driven into a small principality in the north of Antrim, around the Giant's Causeway, by the conquering Gaels who had squeezed the Belgic Ulstermen into a small kingdom on the west of Lough Neagh called Airgealla. This was the end of the heroic dynasties of Emain Macha, near Armagh, whose whitewashed citadel had been razed by Niall of the Nine Hostages and his pitiless three sons, the Collas. The Church was entirely on the side of the Gaels and it would be true to say that every man or woman of the Crinoch or the Ulster Belgae who suffered baptism, either at spearpoint or by adopting a tribal saint to operate a local holy well, became Gaelic in speech and

behaviour within a generation. Only a few pockets of the old tribes in
the high mountains or on distant islands and peninsulas remained.
Some say that the Gaels of Ireland and Argyle came originally from the
Mont Blanc area."

"Are we going to sit up all night?" enquired Loreto without, as far as
could be judged, sarcasm.

"Yes! There's a lot to be done. Sleep is for frail cellular beings. We
mustn't emulate them. Let the pulse beat of words continue."

"Oh."

"About fifty miles to the south of Dalriada was the Crinoch principality of the Echoch. They were more desperately squeezed than the
Dalriadan Crinoch because they were surrounded by Gaels, Bolgs and
Lagins, apart from warrior septs, originally Lagin but who had sold
their swords to the Gaelic high kings at Tara. I tell you there was a
pretty Balkanised situation in one small corner of a small island.

"The Ui Echoch who were all first cousins of the Dalriadic Crinoch
sent word that the rump kingdom of the Bolgi was about to raid
Dalriada for cattle and women, and whatever else was available for
easy collection. Needless to say, the Airgealla overlords did nothing to
inhibit this action, knowing that it was the easiest way to deal with these
pockets of resistance. Whatever happened, the Gaels would mop up
the remnants and penetrate the victors by intermarriage. Indeed, the
palliasse of the marriage bed was one of the most effective landscapes
for conquest. Like the surface of the land, the less bumpy it was, the
more effective the victory, with both sides satisfied.

"News of the raid, expected in midsummer, set the Crinoch elders
and advisers into a frenzy of organisation. Half-Gaelic septs on the
perimeter of their domains were approached for help and there was
a plan to send a poet to the Airgealla courts to collect whatever
mercenaries were available. The Crinoch had a dwindling stock of
gold and a vast surplus of girls to pay for military service.

"Curither was approached by Bruide to visit the Airgealla court and
perform a poem that would set greedy Gaelic hearts stirring, but he
pretended not to understand the request, so there the matter lay for a
few days. No such request was made to Liadin, presumably because the
Crinoch wanted a prophetess of non-Crinoch origin to check on their
own magical prognostications, and women were more highly considered in this sort of judgment than men.

"After a hectic day of spear-sharpening and smelting cauldrons
into spear moulds, there was a big feast held in the main courtyard.

Everyone was there, except those who were fishing or visiting periph-
eral allies. Two vast cauldrons bubbled with barley and seal meat, to be
followed by a bird-bake of dozens of thrushes, blackbirds, curlews,
geese, rock pigeons and any edible delicacy permitted by season or
taboo. A live hare, at all times inedible for reasons that no one would
question, crouched in a wicker cage, round-eyed, sniffling at the bars.
The ale was half solid with pounded grain and flavoured with a dozen
tasteful leaves and saps to give it pungency.

"Curither recited a poem of considerable length, to his own accompaniment on a harp, found and repaired by his increasingly nimble
hands. Liadin, accompanied by Curither on the harp, invoked the
growing sun and the Virgin Mary in a diplomatic hymn that was translated, verse by verse, to the assembly by Cinead, though Curither had
grave doubts as to the translation and the interpretation of the allegories
by the Crinoch. The stanza where Mary praises the sweet radiance of
the sun's long arms on the pastures won wild applause from people who
regarded virginity as a brief passing state of magical potency and the
sun as a source of male potency to be welcomed on proper and
prescribed occasions. Holy fools leaped around, troy dancers wove
about the compound, and the hare was released, carrying in its bony
frame a long list of minor tribulations such as boils, toothache, barrenness and depressive melancholia. This useful purging left everyone in
an exhilarated state.

"Neither Liadin nor Curither could follow the conventional phases
of the feast. No one sat in a position granted to him, no one contested a
place. No man divided the meat, for one cauldron contained porridge
and one contained seal meat in morsels. There was no fighting and no
struggle for precedence or glory.

"Lastly, there was no bard to sing appropriately composed poems.
This upside-down social system was becoming known by now to Liadin
and Curither, but they still felt a void when the smoke receded to a
glow and ale softened the tongue.

"There was some singing and the company sat on the long bed
applauding and calling for other songs. Then three old women brought
a basket of eggs to Bidba, who turned them sunwise and addressed the
people. 'Who is for an egg? What fruit is ripe tonight?'

"Liadin was about to ask for one to suck when a young woman
nursing a baby, setting the child across her hip, advanced laughingly to
the basket and took one, saying 'I declare to all here that I still have
need of it.' Curither could just catch her utterance, but was nonplussed

by the roar of laughter that followed. 'Have I need of it?' the girl cried again. 'Ask Bidba. Bidba will judge.'

" 'The need is in your heart, maybe, or in your body. Take it if it is in both together.'

"The girl set the baby down and removing her apron put the egg between her thighs, against her crotch. 'Do I need the egg?' she called. Everyone laughed and an unmarried girl in breeks ran up to her and said, 'If any shell is to be broken, it should be mine.'

" 'You have spoken rightly,' replied the young matron, who then handed the egg to the girl. 'Whose season matched this egg?' cried the matron again. 'You can all see that it cannot be me. Mine is well hatched.'

"Half a dozen girls, some brash, some shy, came forward, or were thrust. 'Take an egg each,' cried the young woman. 'May they hatch soon.' General laughter followed this remark and some old hags became hysterical and had to be quietened and given dippers of milk.

"Both Liadin and Curither felt foolish. He was able to understand most of what was being said and she could get at least the gist of the words, but they bore no relationship to Gaelic or Lagin humour which was based on exaggeration or mock boasting. Nevertheless they both laughed politely and uncertainly, looking around for some clue. It didn't come quickly. The young matron, who seemed to have a planned part in the ceremony, handed each girl an egg. As they took them in their hands the laughter was renewed. Someone began to sing:

" 'Who am I that is
Rounded but not globular
Gently pointed and smooth
(I am) broken
So a chicken
May crow to the sun.'

"The girls, seven in all, removed their nether garments, woollen breeks, aprons, kilts, to catcalls and whistles. An old man jumped up and took a cock stance on a log and crowed loudly. There was a brief silence of attention when the girls, each one in her own way and according to her temperament, placed the egg under her crotch and held it delicately between the fat of her thighs, one grinning, another pale with anxiety. They stood, in an outer arc beyond the fire, apparently motionless, until one began to giggle, which caught another by contagion. Two egg whites and golden yolks rolled down their legs and pieces of shell dropped to the earth. Another dropped her egg so that it broke on the ground, but she was immediately given another. Eventually, all the eggs were broken, but only one was neatly divided into two halves. People leaned forward to touch the lucky one.

" 'Calda has revolved,' announced Bidba. There was another silence. Bruide went out of the building, followed by half a dozen men. Curither thought that he had understood the words and he asked a man by his side. 'Revolved?'

" 'Yes, the praises be, and Mary guard her likewise: with the cracking of the eggs. She chose the moment well.'

"Liadin drew near her man and pointed to an occurrence beyond the central fire, in the darkness. Several people, including the egg girls, who by now had donned the all-purpose long cloaks or ponchos, were lifting an old lady and wrapping her in a blanket. They carried her to a stool and heaped up heather around it, strewing skins and blankets over it. The old lady was left seated, resting back on the heather, watching the firelight which shone on her face. A girl left a wooden dish of broken eggs by her side but they remained untouched.

"There was a castanet rattle from outside and everyone turned to look. A creature jumped in followed by several others. Their appearance was horrifying. Chalk white from crown to toe and covered with herringbone zigzags and spirals, they were far removed from human appearance. Liadin crossed herself and thought of the quiet convocation house at the nunnery and the safety within sound of the holy bell. It took her several minutes to recognise the leader of the ghosts as Bruide.

"The dance wove around the building, through the embers of the fire and out again into the night. A woman who had apparently been waiting outside for her cue came in, bearing a large flat dish of earthenware, a rare thing amongst the Crinoch, who used wood or baskets more commonly.

"She set it down before Bidba, who stood up, crossed herself, took a bag from a nearby woman and held it out. Dozens of hands reached towards her, and she distributed what seemed to be grains of rye. Someone gave three to Liadin, who, following the others, poked a finger in the earth-filled platter before Bidba, and planted a seed in the hole.

"The men took no part in this, and Curither watched with curiosity. It was apparently a piece of magic, a ritual, or a folk custom. Several people made Christian signs. No one knew for certain the religion of the shy Crinoch, although there had never been any trouble about converting them to Christianity. Indeed they were particularly eager. Nevertheless it was a known fact that they never endowed monasteries, took advice from bishops or adopted a way of life that would allow the development of a settled clergy.

"The men of Rome had relatively little difficulty usurping the position of the druids in the Gaelic clan leadership. There wasn't all that much change, and it was generally agreed that they were quite good at prophecy. Furthermore they were less of a closed shop and cheerfully taught the magic art of writing to anyone willing to shave the front of his head and give up women. Otherwise they lived in colleges, as druids had always done, and advised on matters of state.

"With the Crinoch it was different. How could the clerical men, trained to act in a certain way in a society, fulfil their purpose, when that society had an alien form, with few resemblances to their own? The Crinoch had no druids to replace and relied, as far as anyone knew, on amateur magicians, like any group of mountain herdsmen. There were few Crinoch anchorites. The most that Columcille was able to manage in Iona among the Scottish Crinoch was to approve a few settlements of anchorites who lived on shellfish and birds' eggs, said their prayers, learnt no Latin and harmed nobody. Their existence in an area, however, vastly increased the bounty of the harvest, led to victory in cattle raids and was particularly efficacious in preventing fishing lines from snagging.

"The saint was pleased enough and knew that in a generation or two a good abbot could take control and set up a sound Irish organisation. Like many other Celts of sanctity, he was a sound organisational man.

"Curither was turning these thoughts over in his mind when he spun around to the alarm of a furious rhythm of clatter bones and cauldrons gonging. There was a wild yell from the company more alien, more terrifying than an Ulster war cry, and the flickering darkness of the fire blazed into white light when someone threw a bunch of dry straw on it. The wicker supporting the sod roof started to singe, but luckily held.

"Everyone was tearing off clothes, though in many cases, in view of the Crinoch habits, this didn't take long. He had, since arriving at their fort, found them a gentle people, kinder in their ignorance and their strange tongue than many a king and a king's retinue in the halls of Tara, where golden words of rhetoric and gateposts of beaten gold distracted from treachery and greed. He began to see them differently.

"Women, screaming, with wild starting eyeballs, were throwing themselves at men, fighting and clawing with each other. The men offered no resistance or made no choice, as far as he could see, but his objectivity was interrupted by young Senua whose thighs were still covered in egg white and black with fire ashes. She leaped on him from a pile of sacks, clawing at his clothes and his first thoughts were for them. He still wore Norse drawers of fine Frankish linen, a gift from Olaf, and a waistcoat of sheepskin under a long tunic, the last of which was a parody of his old poetic livery. Senua was a plump girl and strong. Furthermore she had all the strength of a person possessed by a demon, which he could only counter with alarmed sobriety. He was overlaid by anxieties of an inhibiting nature: he was worried first of all for Liadin, and concerned about sexual initiative. For years he had been used to putting an eye of lazy greed on a girl and confidently expecting her concurrence. Usually it worked. Most people expect life to fulfil itself to the threshold of their status, and reasonably. But to be clawed by a nubile child, and to worry about the state of a lover, a conflicting amalgam of obligations, bewildered him. If someone, probably another rapacious girl, hadn't slit his Norse linen drawers down the seat, he might have extricated himself from the urgency of the dilemma. With his trews in shreds from betrayal and his resistance betrayed by a hundred tooth marks around his shoulders, what could he do but react as he did. People around were screaming. Distantly he could apprehend conjunctions of quivering flesh, so close to his eyes as to be beyond focus. Senua was on top of him, underneath him, pivoting on his fulcrum, demanding, taking, growling like a starving wolf. There was no way of describing her particular role.

"He staggered to his feet and stepped over arses and tits, sacks and baskets, fowl and animals, searching for Liadin. He found her, naked as mattered a damn, lying half buried in the mud ruts of the entrance, her head in a heap of pig shite and her hair plastered and besmirched in pools of muddy water.

"As he had once done before, to lustrate her agony by the lake, he lifted her and carried her weight to the seashore. She was heavy, and the distance five hundred yards, but he managed to roll her in a shallow rock pool and rub her flesh with a cloak which was lying on an upturned fishing boat of wicker and bullhides.

"It took a long time for him to find a response, though her heart was beating. He lay on top of her and tried to warm her. Her eyes unglazed to catch his glance briefly, and then closed to exclude him from her experience.

"It was cold by the seashore. The stone fort was dark above him, concealing the hearth fires within it, and the land on either side was wild and uninhabited pasture and waste. The sea was flat and empty, offering no answer to his hopes of flight. Since he had no choice, he wrapped Liadin in the stinking poncho, stiff with fish scales, and carried her towards the shelter of the fort. Whatever had happened was not directed particularly against himself or his woman. That was some consolation. At any rate it solved the mystery of the sexual segregation of the Crinoch during their sleeping hours, and the wild manner of their domestic alliances when they were finally permitted could perhaps be excused by the pressure of stored passions. He knew, however, that there was more to it than that. The girls and the older women knew that they were taking more than a man, or a few men. They were taking into their bodies the whole future of their race, the crops, the cattle, the fish harvest, and the seed of humanity. Bellies had been filled, not just with the seed of men but with seeds of beneficent nature.

"Poets sometimes made statements of a metaphysical kind, to this effect, but the Crinoch took it literally. To them it was as significant and as transcendental as the Christian Mass. Those women lying exhausted in the queen's pavilion had opened their bodies to the seed of the barley, the rye, the seed of black bulls, the melt of salmon, the honey of bees and the sweet nuts of the bushes. The harvest fields, the calving paddock and the fish shoals were one and the same thing as the bellies of their girls. As for the men, he couldn't be sure. He himself was black and blue, torn and scratched and aching in the joints. The men of the Crinoch must take no more pleasure from love than a sunbeam enjoys the quickening of a furrowed field. It was hard to tell. Perhaps each man was the long hand of Lugh the god.

"He set Liadin down beside an outdoor hearth ring of warm stones in the enclosure of the fort and covered her carefully, chafing her frozen feet and hands. The noise from the queen's house had diminished, so he called up his courage and went inside, through the watery ruts at the main entrance. Although there was some light from the fire, it seemed darker than outside, but he could still identify shapes and shadows in urgent entanglement. Some were worn out. Women lay sprawled, face downwards in the ashes or sleeping pillowed on the bellies of their men. Two men, near the entrance, appeared to be dead and a young girl was sitting on a sack, crooning and combing the hair of a youth who sat at her feet, staring into her eyes. She kissed his ear and he kissed her knee. A tall flat-chested woman with the shadow of age upon her sat staring into the firelight, pensively and quite tenderly stroking the shoulders and spine of a big hairy man who lay motionless. There was nothing impersonal about these two examples of behaviour and Curither realised that he was witnessing ordinary human tenderness. This surprised him, after the savagery that he had seen and suffered, but it also reassured him. The older woman stood up from stroking her man and he saw it was Bidba. Tall and gaunt as she was, naked, her paint rubbed and dirtied, she had a certain majesty of bearing. 'Warm yourself,' she said. 'Seven fine men have been granted to me. I had hoped for you, but my womb tightened at a holy number. Where is gracious Liadin?'

"Curither could hardly voice a reply. Bidba was apologising for not having raped him. She had asked sweetly for his woman. He mumbled, 'Outside by a hearth circle. She is unconscious. . . .'

"Bidba wrapped a blanket across her bony frame and said with some excitement, 'The rays of light have blinded her. She is fortunate. We must share her luck.' She raised the couple with the hair comb and kicked another couple into awareness. It was disastrously evident that they were not quite ready for interruption. 'Find Liadin of the Lagin and bring her to our hearth.' Curither made to accompany them but she held him back and bade him sit by the fire.

" 'For more years than can be measured between the high stones and changing stars, the gods have fought amongst themselves, and Mary and her son have not shirked this conflict. And where the Powers go, men follow. But in dynastic battles many die and many are injured. Liadin has been wounded by a spearman and she is hurt. But she has seen armies join in splendid conflict, and winter change to spring. She has lifted her heart to the wild growling of the hunting horns: and she has opened the earth to the sweetness by which all the gods are known.'

"Liadin was carried in and laid on the heather settle nearest the fire. Bidba unrolled the stinking cloak and rubbed her body with sour curds, slowly, firmly, examining the Lagin woman's belly, breasts, nipples and face, gravely and expertly. With a low moan Liadin opened her eyes and Curither leaned forward to grasp her hand.

"Bidba stood up and smiled down at her. 'The shining wheel has blinded you. But now you will see better. Your blood is warmed. Stay with her.' She turned to Curither. 'Your place is by her.'

"He slept, or thought he slept, by Liadin, wrapped in the square coloured ponchos of the Crinoch people. At one point, when dawnlight brightened the gaps at the gable end, he thought he had made love to her. It was difficult to be sure. Maybe it was no more than the heat exchanged between their battered bodies.

"Next morning the sun shone warmly and the trees were noisy with birds. People seemed bright and purposeful, setting out early to the fields or to the birdnets, without allusion to the dark night. There were signs, however. As the women turned the sods and buried the seeds beneath, they sang in chorus. The music floated down the hill and hurried the men at the fishing nets so that they cast and drew with greater skill and more impatience than was their slow ageless custom. In pairs, whispering, they climbed the hill to where the women worked, not daring to help, for fear of ill luck, but making jokes, false insults to avert the evil eye and waiting for the field-workers to finish. Their insults seemed carefully conventional to Curither, who was watching them with interest, sitting with Liadin on a sunny bank. If they had been offered to a Gaelic woman it would have started ten generations of blood feud. A fine lump of a rosy-cheeked girl with bouncing breasts quivering as she dug and turned the earth would be hailed as 'empty bags,' two bladders drying on a wall, dry slit, periwinkle hole and similar enormities. The women in turn would boast fondly of men elsewhere who were hung like leaping salmon and not like certain miserable creatures, unskilled in hunting or craft whose kirtles concealed dried shrimps, fit only for the famine pot of midwinter.

"The cheerfulness of these traded abuses, and the giggles and gestures that accompanied them, convinced Curither that their purpose was to delude or misinform malicious spites who might prevent a belly from swelling, a breast from filling or a baby from being harvested safely. He began to compose a satirical poem on Liadin's imaginary deformities, her breasts, her hair, her stance and her metrical judgment. She didn't like it, and pushed him down the bank to the loud laughter of the Crinoch peasants.

"The euphoria following the night that the earth was opened, as they called it, lasted for no more than a week. Curither never learned what had happened to Liadin. Bruide and his ghost clan were involved, and he dared not ask further. But returning to the fort, leaving the fishermen and the land girls rolling shamelessly in the mud, surrounded by a hand-clapping circle of wellwishers, his feeling for the settled things of life received a second rupture.

"Calda, the old woman, lay on a pile of furze and faggots, in a fissure between two rocks above the sea. She was dead, and it struck Curither that she had died at the time of the egg-breaking. This ritual puzzled him, when he remembered it through the distance of that long night. When he asked Bidba she rose from the bowl of curds which she was squeezing and answered, 'Every girl must break a golden egg before she takes the strength of womanhood.' He couldn't grasp it, and it was Liadin who suggested that it somehow represented defloration. In more scattered Crinoch tribes, now shrunk to forgotten settlements on distant mountains, the tribal prophet, who is the queen's first husband, did the job with a hazelnut shell on the tip of a finger, while the women held the girls down. The egg was an improvement, Curither reflected. It was interesting how crude magic changed slowly to sacrament. The same had happened to poetry. Buried deep in the elaborate structure of verse were the shadowy patterns of gods that had lost their power or had sold out to usurpers with broader spears. The Christian prayers were not exempt from this, which was why, perhaps, people found them so acceptable.

"Curither went with Liadin and a party of children to gather kindling. The winter's demand had exhausted dry sticks nearby and they had to go beyond the wood to a sally thicket by a stream. Its branches had been slain by a heather fire the previous summer and the charred canes made excellent kindling though rather sooty to handle. Not that the children minded. A covering of carbon was a more agreeable garment than the incrustation of tears and snots and shite that built up during the winter months. A few hours cockle picking would reduce them to their original pink.

"On the way back, passing the ghat of the old lady, Curither paused to look at her face, which lay now, released from the ravages of half-savage age. It was the face of Bidba, and the face of a dozen people whom he could clearly recognise through the high-furrowed forehead and the long nose pointing towards a jutting rounded chin. She must have been the grandmother of the sept, or whatever divisions the Crinoch had. Crouched by her side, naked and bound with straw ropes, his skin star-tlingly chalked and painted, was one of Bruide's ghost men. A leather strip was buried in his neck and his strangled eyes stared wildly down his shins, his chin pressed onto his knees. Calda would not go unattended to the glass castle or the holy cave or whatever dismal abode the Crinoch favoured. They had a fear of caves and burrows, so he reckoned it was a gloomy kingdom, of dark and cold. Nobody ever spoke of it.

"It was a disquieting discovery. Up to a few generations earlier, the Lagin and the Fir Bolgs were prone to strangle a stranger in times of stress. Even the Gaels approved of this. Gods were very parochial entities. There were a thousand Aenguses, a thousand Lugaids and a hundred thousand Brigids, each to his plain or her valley. It took the sophistication of a druid, a poet or even a Christian monk to draw them together into one, and that was no more than a scholar's conceit. A nut copse, a lime kiln or a salmon trap were all the better, in times of scarcity, for the gurgle of a stranger's strangled groan, providing the time and occasion were propitious. If the Fir Bolg, those ale-sodden, half-Christian detribalised hoodlums, with their slaughter spears, captured a couple of dozen cattle or girls in a raid on Dalriada, either he or Liadin could end up like this white ghost. How could these simple earth-scratchers understand the inviolability of apostate poets?

"He made up his mind to leave. There was nothing to learn here. The Crinoch had no fathers and no genealogies. Their religion was the deepest and most buried kernel of other religions, a dim shapeless mother who had to be served and nurtured, and her lover, a temporary being, with his brave golden spear, who sailed across the skies each year and helped the mother in her talk of producing life.

"It was Liadin who suggested a way out. Curither should accept the suggestion to go to the Airgealla court to raise mercenaries and, if possible, arrange an alliance. The matter was discussed with Bidba, with Bruide and finally with the assembly of councillors. Agents arrived from other Crinoch strongholds and the discussion went on, day and night, for a week. Every emissary demanded a new hearing before the assembly.

"In the end it was decided. Curither would travel with Liadin to the Airgealla lords. The Crinoch spoke of them as one kingdom with one ruler and Curither had the greatest difficulty explaining to them that they were a confederation of principalities who had won a large part of Ulster from the Fir Bolgs and the Crinoch. There was no central Airgealla court but several. The Airgealla were the Gaelic ruling class of the now fragmented Belgic kingdom which they had conquered before the coming of Saint Patrick.

"Their foundation had been encouraged by Niall of the Nine Hostages, four hundred years earlier, as part of his attempt to rebuild the high kingship at Tara, which had sunk very low under its previous Laginian dynasty. Each state supplied a hostage to Niall, nine in number, and so it continued after the coming of Patrick. By now, however, they paid cattle tribute to the Eógonact of Munster, a more southerly branch of the Gaels, and the halls of Tara had more sheet gold on its carved pillars than it had power or respect.

"The Crinoch, living in the earth shade of forgotten centuries, knew little of these matters of world politics, but Curither felt reasonably certain that he could act as ambassador and compose flattering genealogies in the Christian manner. This involved jumbling together every venerable name, superhuman or human, from all the peoples of Ireland, gaelicising their forms and stringing them out into an impressive list. He had memorised a useful collection of Biblical names from Saint Cummin's foundation and had no doubt that he could include a stepson of David and Bathsheba or a warrior lineage from the Book of Maccabees. The clergy might be suspicious, but if their kinsmen were flattered they would happily approve. At the same time Curither knew as well as any certified poet that the Airgealla were no more than a ruling elite. Most of their men were of Fir Bolg stock. After several hundred years it could do no harm to extol the praises and compose lavish descriptions of the old Fir Bolg capital of Emain Macha, citadel of glory. A yearning for old glories lay deep in the hearts of all Ulster men, whatever the changes of history or power.

"He felt confident of getting a hearing. The rest was in the hands of various fates, the only deities for which he felt any deep faith. There was the complication that he was expected to take Senua with him. Although she appeared to him no better than any other healthy young girl in the Crinoch territory, he soon learned that she counted as a princess, being the daughter of Bidba's sister and the granddaughter of Bidba's mother, whose ghost, consulted oracularly, was one of the principal deities of the tribe. In twenty or thirty years' time, Bidba herself would be a consultative ghost.

"Senua was being sent as a manufacturer's sample. Crinoch kingship was achieved through marrying a Crinoch princess. In turn his successor would rise to power by marrying one of the daughters or, under certain circumstances, a niece. By putting Senua on show around the Airgealla petty courts, Bidba and Bruide could reasonably hope for a vigorous young warlord as a son-in-law, who could organise them in battle and involve them in clan ties and alliances with other Gaelic petty kingdoms. Neither the politically impotent high king of Tara nor the Eóganact overlords from Munster and the midlands would interfere, they surmised. It was a good plan, but it had to be put into practice immediately. The Fir Bolg raid was expected in late June or July, and the enemy was only three days' march away, beyond the shores of Lough Neagh. Equally, the nearest of the Aegealla courts were hardly much farther. The difficulty was likely to be in getting these contentious princelings to stop their tedious quarrels, their endless boar hunts, long enough to send out a call for men and to submit to any sort of leadership or common strategy.

"Curither thought of Flossie in Dublin, a useful levelheaded man, but could think of no way of introducing him into the scheme. He would need a war party of his own, from Man, perhaps, or one of the Scottish settlements, and this would be a risky business. Only trade and marriage, with a dash of holy water, could induce any loyalty or reliability into these northerners. On formal invitation they would happily sack the bruiden of Connor, king of the Fir Bolgs, but if they met anything else on the way, including their employer's women or bullion, they would settle for that, and call it a day."

10

"Now listen to me," said Loreto. "This is all very interesting. But it seems to me . . ."

"She's dead right, captain," added MacGilla. "Well . . . What I want to say is this. You set out to tell the story of a couple of lovers in the ninth century, ah dee. Fair enough. I helped you out myself when ye got winded. It's a story about two people caught up in a fashion: for that's all celibacy was, a fashion that got involved in European religion at a formative time, and got written into the rules."

"Yeah. And I don't see why you have to give us the decline and fall of the Celtic Empire in dynastic detail. Why not like Heloise and Abelard or Tristan and Iseult?"

"My dear woman." Mountmellick raised a pontifical index finger. "I cannot allow this couple to divorce from the social and political ambience. If their lives had mingled during, say, the sacking of Magdeburg, this event would alter the texture of the story."

"Be Jasus," remarked MacGilla. "We have a critic amongst us. Ora pro nobis."

"Furthermore," pursued Mountmellick, raising his voice, "their most intimate moments would be conditioned by other events. The Defenestration of Prague, the Holy League, the Treaty of Lübeck, Gustavus Adolphus, Wallenstein, the rise of baroque, the States General, the Peace of Westphalia and Mother Courage. Perhaps I stretch my point a little, but . . ."

MacGilla sighed and hunched himself over his glass, gripped in both hands.

"No. No. I must make this clear." Mountmellick was virtuously defensive. "What's the use of trying to put some flesh on the poem of Liadin and Curither if people think that she was some sort of Enid Starkie who joined the Carmelites or that he was a Penguin Poet who became a Jesuit? As for the fair Iseult, if people don't know that she was a decent Laginian girl from Dublin, imported by the Irish monks of Padstow to sap the cockiness out of an ageing king, and make him more amenable, they know nothing about the story."

"What about Wagner?" Loreto got a few words through.

"Exactly. You have answered yourself."

"How," enquired MacGilla, slowly, "do you know that the Irish clerics wanted to control King Mark? They were doing all right. There wasn't a Saxon within a month's march. It could have been the other way round, you know. A soft warm girl was considered a cure for more than the colic in those days. 'Suffer little children.' What about David and Abishag? Even if all he could do was to pee in her bath, it would have given him a new interest in life."

"You mean . . . the monks wanted to rejuvenate King Mark?" Loreto raised an eyebrow.

"It's an equally good argument. Saint Patroc knew more than his matins. The ould fella's death could have been followed by a civil war. You know what Celtic succession was like. It's my belief that Tristan was in the pay of the Welsh, or even the North Britons. Tristan . . . Drustan, Dróstan. It was a common name up north."

"What are you trying to say?"

"I mean that the historical ambience flatters the mind, but that it's like a lump of clay. Ye can shape it in any direction. Yerra, what's a story but a way of passing a few hours."

"If that's the way you see it . . ." Loreto tilted a pharisaic nose.

"There's more comes up in spa water than haitch two oh. The water brings up whatever it finds. And whatever lies in the mind of the writer comes out stuck to the words, whether he likes it or not."

"What are you arguing about?" interjected Mountmellick. "Are you trying to say that my account of Liadin and Curither was wrong?"

"Not particularly. I'm only drawing attention to the fact that it doesn't sound like George Moore."

"I don't know if you are aware," pronounced Mountmellick, "that George Moore had a lengthy correspondence with various historians, philologists and Celtic scholars on this subject. He had originally intended to write a play based on the life of Duns Scotus. Patiently, week by week, he fed muffins and Earl Grey tea to a succession of eminent advisers. The sexier bits he culled, with permission, from some anecdotes by Frank Harris."

"Frank Harris? How did he get into it?" Loreto was incredulous.

"Pooh! Who better? And he liked talking, which made it easier for Moore." He stood up. "And now I think the time has come to welcome our future colleague. You realise," he turned to Loreto, "that I had a deeper purpose than lay on the surface in continuing this story so long. It is the only method known to me to give strength and body to the ghost of Liadin, in Limbo. By now, the fellow up there," he gestured towards the unseen scribe, "by now he will be loosed in his resistance to her appearance. For her it will be a quick jump from stultifying inertia into the busy world of fiction."

MacGilla got up and started to collect empty stout bottles and stack them in a laundry basket. "You, miss," he addressed Loreto, "had better get ready. It's been a long session and we're all a bit tired, but there's a bit more to come."

"I didn't understand. How could I guess that all this was some sort of a calling-up ceremony. What should I do?"

"Take off that teddy bear dressing gown and try to look like a welcoming hostess. Something dignified, but without denying either your sex or your personality."

"I'm not sure what I have. I need to look."

"Get something new, my dear. It's on expenses," Mountmellick advised avuncularly. "It's the fellow up there, writing, that has to pay."

"What does he pay with? I thought he was broke."

"He has to pay in the ultimate coin," said Mountmellick. "He has to buy it with the electrical impulses in his questionable brain. He has to pay for it with charity towards a literary creation. Most importantly, we call the tune, and he has to do the paying. What sort of dress do you want?"

"I'm not sure. Something original but appropriate."

"Very well. Take off your dressing gown slowly and see how quick
he is off the ball."

"But I'm wearing these ridiculous polka-dot pyjamas. You told me
to."

"Ah yes. Our little joke. Well, it paid off. We don't need them
anymore. I must change. But you do as I told you. MacGilla, is everything arranged for the supper?"

"It's probably desiccated by now, but I'll see to it myself. It'll only
take me a minute to change. I have the pants on already." MacGilla
indicated a pair of Rommel stiff riding breeches in navy blue, piped in
red, the previous impact of which had been negated by an enveloping
bainín sweater, reaching towards his knees.

The three parties departed to their various preparations. MacGilla
shed his woolly sack and uncharacteristically preened himself into a
uniform jacket with military suggestions, but equally suitable for
driving a car with CD plates. Mountmellick went to his room and
occupied himself sliding coat hangers up and down the rod in a cupboard and selecting a suitable suit. He fixed a Chekhovian pince-nez by
its chain to the lapel hole and slid the device into the breast pocket.

Loreto stood where she was, beside the bed, and looked up beyond
the leaves of the manuscript, doubtfully. Then she shrugged and took
off her dressing gown.

She was dressed in a single loose smock reaching halfway down her
thighs. Its fabric consisted not of woven fibres but of an interlock-
ing chain of small medallions in gilt and silver enriched with Irish
Romanesque enamel work and gilt bronze decorations. Its mobile
reflections twinkled on the floor and on surrounding objects and
her sallow smooth skin revealed itself decorously enough, by beach
standards, but startlingly by salon custom.

Satisfied by its unique impact, and giving no thought to the inventive
generosity of the donor scribe, she set a table lamp on the floor behind
her and surveyed herself in a long mirror glass, to judge the general
effect and to check for transparency. Her body showed through as
though she were covered by no more than a spray of water. So much
for male designers. How could one expect them to think of an under-
slip or a body stocking?

In the dining room attached to the suite, a sleepy night porter and his
wife were laying a table with the requisites for a simple but appetising
supper. On display, suitably chafed or chilled, lay an haricot of mutton.
Baked barbels, a quince pie on ice and a jar of Drogheda usquebaugh

smelling strongly of coriander, liquorice, cloves, mace, fennel and appetisingly tinted with the finest English saffron. There was wine from the Royal Pope and Spanish ale to give them hope. Also Polish vodka. An oatmeal flummery, well sugared and fortified, lay in a side dish, previously prepared by MacGilla and laced with vodka to expedite its purpose of instant nourishment.

Mountmellick came into the room and was joined by Loreto. They stood together by a renovated settlebed which served as a cupboard. The laden table lay in a greensward of lime green carpet from door to windows.

"I think I hear something." He cocked his ear towards the staircase beyond the door.

Sounds of confused movement rose from below. A voice was raised outside, so that it rang around the converted stableyard. There was a female cacophony and tones of protest, without discernible words.

Loreto was extremely curious about Liadin, their expected guest. Somewhere, behind or below her faith in the Mountmellick literary cosmogony, there was a tiny irreducible doubt which all the printing ink in the world could not dissolve. It was hard to believe that the unfinished love story of Liadin and Curither, full of footnotes and explanations, could have drawn the shade of George Moore's Liadin from the icy confinements of Limbo. Many a nonconformist zealot, awaiting the Last Day to begin at twelve midnight, shivering in a duffel coat on the top of Primrose Hill, must have had such a doubt, watching the city lights of London reddening the night clouds. If the doubt had weight, it meant that Mountmellick was either a fake or a lunatic. Of MacGilla, she was uncertain. Sometimes he agreed with every suggestion, sycophantically. At other times he could express his own contrary views most emphatically indeed. At the same time he was responsible for formulating her own literary lineage which her parents had concealed from her.

Standing in the hotel room she waited alone, to make a final judgment on the tenets of her new faith. No act or word on the part of her two companions could influence her impressions of an alleged literary entity straight out of the top drawer of Hell.

11

MacGilla came up the short staircase first and opened the room door more fully. He grimaced fleetingly at Mountmellick, and ushered two people into the room.

"Here she is at long last," he announced, "and she's brought a friend."

A woman in a long yellow cloak with dark gold hair held by a gold circlet stood behind a woman of more conventional stature, dressed in a long grey linen garment, held below the bust and falling in heavy folds. The woman in the yellow cloak was well over seven feet tall, nearer eight.

Loreto's stomach shot up her esophagus and pressed desperately at her tonsils. Mountmellick froze in thought and deed before the loud beating of his heart awakened him to acts of courage, courtesy and hospitality.

"Welcome, ladies. A thousand welcomes. We have been waiting for you all night. I am delighted that you were able to bring a friend, Liadin."

The woman in grey, of medium height and agreeable aspect, smiled and came forward towards Mountmellick.

"I am well pleased to greet the light and all who live in it. Many an empty decade have I spent in darkness. But stay, that I may present to you my dearest friend. She hath lighted the shade with her fierce hopes and hath proved steadfast in loyalty." She turned to the startling female entity behind her and bowed. "Eevell of Craglee, Queen of the Munster Hosts of Fairy, may I present unto thee thy servant, Owen Mountmellick, a poor scholar and gallant captain, and his sweet leman, Loreto, a maid from Hy Brasil who hath favoured thy shores, and seeketh sanctuary."

The extraordinary creature raised her head and shook her heavy cascade of hair, revealing a face like the Statue of Liberty, firm of brow, clean of nose, with a round determined chin. Her cheekbones were high but well covered with firmly sculpted flesh which gave her face a chiselled dignity. Putting one hand to the brooch of her cloak, she unfastened it and allowed it to drop into the servile arms of MacGilla. She was clad in a long, tightly tailored dress of green velour, high waisted and tightly bodiced to emphasise her strong Roman breasts and her firmly caged and muscled torso. A two-inch border of Celtic interlace, embroidered in lustrous floss, weighted the hem of her garment, and brushed on her slippered feet, bright in Spanish leather. She raised her right arm and orated like a contralto in a Gilbert and Sullivan opera.

> "It gladdens the heart with dolours pressed
> To rise from Hell and pass the test
> For any creature with claims on life
> Who faces battle and fears not strife
> I am no patronising queen
> With a lofty nod for a base sliveen
> But a battleleader of many fights
> For petticoat justice and women's rights."

"God's sacred dentures," muttered Loreto, licking her dry lips and struggling to secrete enough saliva to irrigate her tongue. Mountmellick, his alarm concealed behind a splendid savoir faire, or possibly even courage, said respectfully:

"If you will come to the table, ma'am, and refresh yourself after your incarnation, it will be our honour, later, to listen to your adventures and tribulations."

"Exactly, ma'am," interposed MacGilla from the doorway. "You are amongst loyal friends who will give you every help in regaining your heritage." At the same time, half hidden by Liadin, he attempted to ticktack Mountmellick to indicate that he hadn't the slightest idea who Eevell might be. "This way, excellency, over here, your reverence," he cried, drawing her away from the totally inadequate Hiberno-Finnish dining chairs and urging her towards a daybed. "And Madame Liadin, perhaps you would care to sit by her. It's only a light refreshment, because I thought that, being newly encorpified, your guts would need to get used to digestion."

"A light repast would refresh my soul," replied Liadin, who was eyeing Loreto's see-through chain dress with curiosity. "Methinks the body is a burthen, but truly it must needs be nourished, for it is the receptacle of the soul. Later we will give tidings of our delivery and our journey thither." She followed Eevell to the daybed and curled her legs on a small cushioned stool at its foot.

MacGilla stood nearby, respectfully, and enquired, "Which dishes do ye fancy? Ye had better be tactful to the bellies. What about some of this." He indicated the richly laced flummery.

"It seemeth a fair dish," observed Liadin. Eevell replied,

> "When eating and drinking are served as one
> With the solids bland and the liquor strong
> The soul and the belly are granted their share
> And each is nourished on suitable fare."

She started slurping down the fiery porridge noisily while Liadin began picking at two baked barbels. Having filled the dishes and passed them to MacGilla for serving, Loreto caught Mountmellick's eye and semaphored for an urgent rendezvous outside the room. The subsequent silent slurping and mastication gave them both a chance to retire, unnoticed, to Mountmellick's bedroom. Loreto was at him like a flash.

"Jeesus! What have you got us into now? Those two are nuts. I thought the big one was dangerous until I heard her talk in verse. She's lethal. As for Liadin, she may be all right, but she talks like a children's film of Robin Hood. We couldn't produce them in public without being arrested."

"I don't know a thing about Queen Eevell," protested Mountmellick. "We'll have to do a bit of research. As for Liadin, I think I can explain. I'm not so worried about her. She'll learn quickly."

"She'd certainly need to, gadzooks," said Loreto sarcastically.

"You've got to remember that when George Moore forsook the realism that he had imbibed in France, he made a bit of a hash of his dialogue writing." Mountmellick was defensively apologetic. "Esther Waters spoke like any girl of her time and station. So did the Mummer's wife. But did you ever read *The Last of the Essenes,* about Jesus living in retirement as a shepherd after escaping off the cross? All the characters spoke like Liadin. And the person we have inside there isn't the Liadin of the ninth-century poem, or even the Liadin that I tried to reconstruct for you, but someone thought up by George Moore in Ebury Street, London, SW1. But don't worry. I was nearly as bad as her at first. Luckily I didn't have to barge into the middle of a story. I had time to flex my tongue. But that other monster is as tall as a giraffe. Oh come on, we'd better ask."

"Ask who?"

"*Him,* of course. We didn't ask her into our life. Liadin, yes, but the giantess, no."

"Who is *him?*"

"The bloody idiot that keeps us alive. The creature upstairs recording our actions. I know! It's his revenge for the trick seduction scene
that we fooled him with."

"But I thought he had to faithfully record whatever we told him.
Are you trying to tell me that he is able to have creative ideas of his
own? I don't like the thought."

"Of course not. Look, my dear girl . . . He must have sensed the
moment of Liadin's escape from Limbo and given an opening in his
own mind to anybody with her. He must have guessed it would foul
up our careful planning. Anyway we are lumbered with her. I've
nothing against women's rights. Good luck to her. But maybe we
can direct some of her undoubted energy into furthering our aims
for total independence from human assistance."

"Yeah. But I wish we knew who she really is. I'm afraid to ask
her."

"As I suggested, we can try a direct appeal. Are they still eating
inside?"

Loreto tiptoed to the door and peered down the corridor into the
salon. Both visitors were tearing through the quince pie. MacGilla
was in fervent attendance and the record player sawed, moaned and
percussed to the sound of rebecs, knackers, crumhorns, portative
organs and other sensual stimuli. Liadin appeared bemused.

Loreto returned to Mountmellick and whispered, "I guess they
haven't missed us. It's OK for a few minutes."

They crept past the open door of the salon, observed by MacGilla
alone, and went down to the courtyard. On the far side was an archway looking onto a walled garden. Against the sky a fig tree exhibited
its glossy polyvinyl leaves and a yew bisected the moon's nimbus.
Mountmellick stood framed in the archway and raised both arms,
like Moses on the Mount. His supplication was unsuited to wild
rhetoric so he spoke in the firm tones of an urgent but courteous
enquiry.

"May I enquire," he boomed into the night sky, "the genealogy
of our unexpected guest? I think we ought to come to an understanding. If we both play straight in future it could make both our
lives easier. The tranquillity of our lives is at stake, and the harmony
of your writing. Please indicate your answer in the usual way. By a
footnote."

They both stood in silence in the courtyard, waiting for something
to happen. Loreto did not know what to expect. What she finally

saw was so familiar as to take her several seconds to adjust to its unexpected context.

Across the dark shape of the arch, against the stones of the walled garden, appeared words, like a subtitle in a foreign film. They tapped their way through the following announcement:

1. Brian Merriman, despite his name, was a Gaelic-speaking poet of intellectual and classical tastes. Born in the middle of the eighteenth century, he lived in the remote village of Feakle, Co. Clare, at a time of rebellion, repression, Union and decay. Educated under some draughty hedge, he became obsessed with enlightened protest in the shape of Swift, Goldsmith and Rousseau. Adopting a classical style, previously unexploited by Gaelic poets, he wrote a savage but tender bacchanalia in five hundred couplets on the subject of marriage, its failings, change of social function and lack of intended purpose.

The language was lively and beautiful and its vitality can be judged even through the limitations of translation.

Down with marriage! 'Tis out of date.
It exhausts the stock and cripples the state.
The priest has failed with whip and blinker
Now give a chance to Tom the Tinker
And mix and mash in nature's can
The tinker and the gentleman.
Let lovers in every lane extended
Follow their will as God intended
And in their pleasure bring to birth
The morning glory of the earth.

Need I go on? That was translated by Frank O'Connor. Arland Ussher also produced a version, extolled by discerning scholars. This is a very long footnote.

Mountmellick clicked in irritation and turned to Loreto, who shrugged and said, "That's fine, but where does it get us? What about Eevell?"

"I'll try again."

He resumed his imprecation by the arch and begged further information. There was a long pause before the ghostly subtitling appeared against the blue-black wall, line by line in staccato bursts.

2. Footnotes can be overdone. Some people skip them. The poem, although classical, follows the familiar Irish aisling or vision form. The poet, in a dream, is summoned by a fearful twenty-foot female bailiff, to attend a court held by Eevell of Craglee, Queen of the Munster fairies. The unmarried and unhappily married women of Ireland are to plead their marital problems and all bachelors are subpoenaed to attend the judgment on Moinmoy Hill.

Since the courts of the English are useless in such important deliberations, the desperate women appeal to Eevell the fairy queen to sit in judgment. Being an Irish fairy she is larger than human size.

"Now we're getting somewhere," said Mountmellick. "Continue, please," he bawled at the night sky.

The footnote subtitles continued petulantly with errors of punctuation, grammar and spelling.

3. In the sombre court, a girl describes her difficulties in getting a suitable well-thewed shapely man to match her own charms, which she lists. A wizened old man jumps up to describe with indignation his marriage to a lusty wench, flattened by every bog-worker in the parish and pregnant on the wedding night. Then the girl describes the feelings of a young wife married to an old man, the fretful nights of unfulfilment and the waste. She advances useful theories on clerical celibacy in the Catholic Church, in rather rumbustious language.

Finally, in judgment, Queen Eevell orders that twenty-six selfish bachelors are to be arrested by the guard, stripped, and tied to the gate while the angry plaintiffs decide the extent of the punishment.

Mountmellick, still dissatisfied, and anxious about the neglected guests, spoke less respectfully.

"Is that all? What we need to know is which Queen Eevell have we got, Frank O'Connor's or Arland Ussher's? It's important. Does she *have* to speak in couplets?"

The footnote recommenced, white and luminescent in the darkness:

4. This is more of a monograph than a series of footnotes. It is the ruination of any modest attempt at style. Your Eevell is from a translation by Brendan Behan. It's not the couplets you have to worry about, but worse.

Mountmellick looked shaken and Loreto, in a moment of comradely solidarity, gripped his hand.

"God pity us," he croaked. "What have you done?"

The lettering began again.

5. Nothing that a resourceful collection of UDI literary characters can't handle. Ha. Ha.

Brendan, on entering the Borstal institution, filled in POET under the line on the document indicating his trade, and demanded a copy in the original Irish of Merriman's poem as necessary tools. With bombs falling, and Albion beleaguered, the dauntless Home Office officials obtained him a copy, in Glasgow, I believe.

On returning to Ireland he lent his somewhat rumbustious translation to a servant of the Muse, who shall be nameless, who lost it, visiting Brendan while he was painting gutters on the scaffolding of a Georgian house. The visitor suffered from vertigo, as did Brendan. There was drink taken, including the foreman. Large remnants of the poem remained in Brendan Behan's head and were uttered occasionally, to separate the grain from the chaff on tedious social occasions. This is positively the last footnote. What you lot need is a good appendix: or an epilogue. Full stop.

Mountmellick clamped his teeth. "What that biped needs is an epitaph. I'd be delighted to oblige. But not yet. The humblest creature serves a purpose. Well now, Loreto, dear child. We must exercise the greatest tact and diplomacy. Survival, I fear, is at stake."

"I'm not sure what she can do. Is she really a queen?"

"We'd better go inside. Her royalty is unquestionable. As head of the Munster sidhe, she must belong to one of the oldest royal lines in Europe. No question. The trouble is this: in Merriman's *Cuairt an Mbean oidce* she was fearsome enough. He made her into an avenging sword of women's rights and privileges. But as translated by Mr. Brendan Beham in a Borstal institution she must have taken on some, at least, of his splendours and disabilities. God knows what unpredictable behaviour or wild carousings lie ahead."

"What about Liadin? She seems a reasonable woman." Loreto passed through the door ahead of Mountmellick. "Apart from the fact that she speaks like the Sheriff of Nottingham on the telly."

"She may be a restraining influence."

The room was empty. A platter of flummery lay inverted on the carpet. There were signs of drink having been taken and of departure. Liadin's strange clothes, which had a neo-mediaeval Eric Gill cut, were scattered on chairs. A pair of cambric drawers, with broken tapes and frilled lace, lay, dropped by the space heater. George Moore evidently dressed his heroines to his own taste, formed in Impressionist Paris.

Mountmellick, a terrible thought in his mind, searched in all the rooms for garments dropped by Eevell. The thought of a naked giantess loose in the countryside, declaiming in heroic couplets, was alarming. There was no sign of them. She was apparently still clad in the early Abbey Theatre props in which B. Behan had vested her.

"MacGilla must have gone with them under some duress," Mountmellick mused.

"He can't have had time to write a note. Perhaps he thought it safer to stick by them. I'm sure it was that awful Queen of the Fairies. We will have to find them somehow." Loreto was worried.

The pair of them were some time waiting for a taxi, summoned from the nearby airport.

"Wherill it be, sir?"

"We are looking for two friends of mine who may have gone on a tour of the city. It is possible they might stop somewhere for a drink."

"If that's how it is, they must be at the cattle markets. There's nowhere else open. How did they go?"

"I saw a taxi list open on the table."

"Well, the markets will be open by now. Will I take ye there?"

"Oh please. I'm worried in case they come to harm."

"Oh the markets is as safe as the altar steps, barrin' the whiskey, that is. Tell me, did your gentlemen have much taken?"

"I think so."

"Oh well, that's the exact place. Even the cattle jobbers don't start there sober. A few of the clerks, maybe."

"They weren't men, I'm afraid. Two ladies. Foreign ladies, um! One of them is eight feet tall. Should be easy to locate."

"Christ Almighty! Oh well, she'll make a match for some red-eared Roscommon drover. Anyway I'll do what I can."

The wheels of the taxi drummed with tension on the empty roads towards the city, through villages grotesquely swollen with the elephantiasis of corporation building development. Driving into the coming dawn they turned smartly west under the spreading rococo of the Five Lamps and were carried towards a darker sky.

"Saville Place . . . Russell Place . . . This is near Behan's birthplace. It's ominous. He often ended up in the cattle markets. Mountjoy prison is up there to the right. I hope to God we're in time to stop any misunderstanding."

Down the back streets of the 'Boro they sped, the coachwork sounding the throb of cobbled relics and patches, past forlorn monuments to the balls of Henry Tudor, ecclesiastical relics of an Anglican empire. The taxi made a smooth landing between abandoned cattle trucks, some empty, some weighted with patient beasts, cloven, melancholic and soft-nosed. The Coleridge towers of Grangegorman Mental Hospital stood witness to the steaming flesh for sale, on the hoof. Sodium lights thinned unpleasantly over a thousand iron pens, as the lightening sky pushed the cosy darkness westward, towards Mullingar, Athlone, Ballinasloe, Galway, Boston and Rhode Island.

There were signs of alarm and recent tumult, outside the pub. Liadin, in polka-dot winceyette pyjamas, was integrating herself into the late twentieth century. Seated on the bonnet of a large Buick, she seemed to be accepting a glass of colourless liquid from a Clare cattle jobber, a glyptic Eóganact creature, monumentally designed, with red hair matted to a golden felt on his head and bursting in glowing sprouts from his hands and knuckles. There was no immediate way of knowing whether the glass held sal volatile, Catalan, Lucan Spa or fiery Geneva.

Mountmellick directed Loreto to join Liadin to smooth the certain confusions and distract from the unseasonal winter nightwear. Presumably Liadin had chosen this schoolmarm garment, abandoned by Loreto, on the supposition that it represented the most advanced example of contemporary fashion. Then he opened the pub door and pushed his way through the hulking affluence of crowded cattle barons, towards the bar.

Flanked by the brass pumps, like altar vessels, stood Eevell, her head as high as the highest rare liqueur on a top shelf, drunk only in Christmas lunacy. Both her arms were outstretched and her gorgon gaze had cleared a space among the pastoral people driven from their drinking and bargaining to face her onslaught.

She seized an ivory froth knife as a sceptre or gavel and banged on the red mahogany. Rows of whiskey glasses, full, virgin, unviolated, from a recent and astronomical round of drinks, vibrated to her blows and the golden maltfire left parabolas of fusil oil on the glass as it shivered its fifteen-year-old surface molecules.

The pastoral men, victors of a thousand bargains, sealed with spits or massive paws, stared at her sullenly. It was apparent that many words had been spoken before the Queen of the Munster Sidhe had cowed them to sullen silence and hostility.

Her voice penetrated every corner, ingle, private snug, the Gents urinal, the cellared labyrinth below and the core of rosewood on the gleaming bar pediment.

"Stinking offal from stony shielings
Ditch-got drovers devoid of feelings
'Tis plain what you'd choose, if forced to vote.
Not a woman's charms, but a five-pound note
Not the wisdom of Pallas, the belly of Helen
But a greasy wad from the paw of a felon."

"Hew does that one think she is? Grawnye-fuckin-ail or sumptin'?" A thin city whine spoke for all, including the cowed kulaks from the outlands. "Granuaile the pirate queen," said another city voice, iconoclastic, sceptical, free of rural superstitions. "Or Caitlin ni Houlihaun?"

"Kathleen Mavourneen mebbe," said the first voice, its nasal drone stretching the syllables. "And Janey there's a fine red dawn breaking in this place, today."

Her Majesty stepped forwards, parting the packed audience. The tallest man, high as a Guinness's dray horse, wasn't up to within an inch of the bronze tips of her tits. She seized one undersized slum-starved tenement jackeen by the crotch, shook fiercely, hurled his hulk into the corner and threw his balls into the cork bin; or that is how it seemed. The edges between illusion and reality were extremely blurred. She then repeated the process with his fellow citizen, but as she shook him high in the air, like a dog with a rat, she boomed:

"You tomcat's melt from the tenement kips
This'll put paid to your jibes and quips
Your wife won't miss what you're going to lack
When I palm your deuce of Jacks from your pack."

There was a silence of desolation. A hundred red necks grew redder as the blood ran colder and by efficient heat exchange raised the temperature of the long bar. The barman, or owner, who had the mixed innocence and guile of a Mayo man across his grey eyes, moved bravely from the curved retreat at the end of the counter, and approached the outraged Majesty, impelled either by courage or folly, insofar as these can be distinguished.

"Now ma'am. Fair's fair. Ye can't expect every man jack of these decent gentlemen to take three wives each." Eevell looked down at him in terrible silence, but yielding to a herald's inviolability. "As well," he continued, politely, "as maintaining them in a decent state of living. Never mind the providing of young fellas to keep them happy and outa mischief. It's askin' too much. A man 'id be better off in a monastery, doin' his comfortable daily office, with bare feet on the frozen flags. Ye have a point, mebbe, in the way women is treated. Sometimes it's shockin'. But your propositions, saving your pardon, is stretchin' human credulity a bit far."

"Too true for you Mick, boy." A voice raised itself from the back of the beleaguered crowd of pastoral types. "My money on that." The courage of the plain people of Ireland, never wanting in times of terrible toil and crisis, was reasserting itself.

Another voice, thin and melodious, gaining in certainty, arose from the uncomfortable silence.

> "But hark, some voice like thunder spake
> The West's awake, the West's awake.
> Sing ho, hurray! let England quake
> We'll watch till death, for Erin's sake."

At this moment, for every man has his moment and the wise man is the one to recognise it, MacGilla separated himself from the back of the crowd of cattle jobbers. Clad in livery of his choice, like Baron von Richthofen or Atatürk at the walls of Baku, he trod firmly the hearth before the stove and took up the stirring song.

> "To triumph dashed each Connaught clan
> And fleet as deer the Normans ran
> Through Corlieu's pass and Ardrahan—"

He faced the cattle men, arms outstretched, and cried, "Come on there, Connaught men. Speak yer bit aloud before yer wives have yer stones for pickles. Tunefully!

> "And later times saw deeds as brave
> And glory guards Clanrickard's grave
> Sing ho! they died, their land to save
> At Aughrim's slopes and Shannon's wave."

A sufficiency of the stricken kulaks bawled in response to give the illusion of victory. Mountmellick seized the instant of initiative, pince-nez in place, exuding a feudal certainty, which, however lacking in warrant, was at least more positive than the uncertainty that followed when the song's euphoria had ended.

He strutted forwards. "Gentlemen! Gentlemen! A little cooperation please." His cosmopolitan suavity gained him some startled ears, with provisional respect. "Don't forget that we have some very important guests with us, from time to time—" he caught Eevell's imperious but so far uncomprehending eye—"in our little castle yonder." He nodded his head backwards and a little sideways towards the high walls of Grangegorman Mental Hospital.

"What is she, docther? They don't breed her sort even on the Curragh." Mountmellick smiled conspiratorially at the questioner, out of Eevell's direct gaze. "If that's what comes outa the National Stud, they oughta hand it back to the Aga Khan."

"I think we can sort this out: with a little help from the proper authorities." His heart belied the brave words at the prospect of several squad cars of the Civil Guards handling her Immortal Majesty. If only they have the wit to send policewomen, he prayed. Then followed a counter-prayer. Eevell would certainly take command of any female force.

As if to emphasise this second fear, Eevell extended a vast hand of Renaissance marble and knocked the necks off two random bottles from the top shelf of alcoholic capriccios. An enormous imitation brandy bubble, occasionally used for flowers when the licence was in jeopardy before the Sessions, was splendidly filled with a bottle of kümmel and a stone jar of Bols. She savoured the mixture, and finding it short of the standards of nectar or hydromel added a venerable bottle of sake, used for ornament only.

Mountmellick's potential control of the situation waned, and the cattle jobbers developed a new confusion and uncertainty.

Eevell drained the one and a half litres of potion in a convulsion of rapid gulps and threw down the vessel slavonically.

> "I stand by my duty, a verdict is needed
> I warrant its lesson will long be heeded.
> May every noggin that wets your pipes
> Corrode your bladders and rot your tripes.
> May sweetbreads, kidneys, liver and bile—"

There seemed no stopping her. The chance to castigate the assembled flower of the wealthy peasantry was too much. Her couplets faltered more frequently and lapsed into discontinuous volleys of Behanistic abuse.

"Bog Indians! Get back to yer bald mountains and scratch amongst the rocks! Put a loop in yer rosary beads and dock a bull! Shut up there, Dundalk, before I have you crucified on a Ferguson combine! If Jesus Christ came down here amongst yiz a second time, he'd get back onto his comfortable bloody cross."

Fights are very rare in Irish pubs, except amongst tinkers at horse fairs, when settled people withdraw until the travelers have departed or been arrested. Tavern brawling in general is the preoccupation of a migrant bachelor class living a detribalised life in cities or around isolated sources of mass employment. There was no fight in this pub in the cattle markets. Let no one suppose so. Peace was breached, and excessively, but only in the confrontation between the massive queen and the cattle jobbers. Two native Dublin yard sweepers, uncouth, irreverent and sceptical, had been injured, it is true, but only as a warning to the cattle jobbers to listen respectfully to the gospel of the Fairy Queen.

Both Mountmellick and MacGilla were attempting, in brief judgments, to assess their gains and losses in extricating their bookborn brood from the market pub, when an unusual sequence of events occurred.

Two squad cars of Civic Guards, splendid men, of hostile intent, without favour, drew up outside, double-parking by the cattle trucks. They had hardly emerged, opened the car doors and made audible the nasal inflections of their two-way radios when a large two-tiered truck, suitable for the conveyance of calves or sheep, drew up behind them. The cab door opened and a tall red-haired young man jumped down and approached the Guard with sergeant's stripes.

Commencing politely, with imprecations and in the vocative case, he addressed the policemen in Irish.

"My blessings on you, O Sergeant. Great would be my pleasure that you should bear (suffer, endure) the burden (weight on mind, Manga mor) that does be on me at this particular time."

The Sergeant pondered on the grammar, syntax and general bearing of the young man, and enquired in English:

"What's your trouble?"

The reply was lengthy and, as was latterly apparent, accurate as far as it went. There were, alas, linguistic problems, since the Sergeant's knowledge of Gaelic was limited to specialised civil service clichés, and in any case the young man's reply was unusual in content.

Guard MacAoda, wearer of the Gold Faíne, handball champion runner up, Department of Justice golfing tournament final heats runner up and impeccable speaker of Castilian Gaelic, took control, by advice and suggestion.

Inside the pub there was silence. No blood oozed under the door, but neither did anyone emerge to claim sanctuary under the Civic banner.

After Guard MacAoda had listened to the lorry driver, and subjected him to various necessary questions, such as name, age, insurance number, blood group and by inference political allegiance, he turned to the Sergeant, who stood at the head of his waiting men, including the drivers.

"He says he has a lorry load of refugees."

"Yerra man, we have to answer a complaint about a breach of the peace in the pub forninst you. It's my belief that he's trying to obstruct. What refugees? From where?"

Guard MacAoda stroked his nose and rasped his chin with splayed fingers. "Aughrim, Sergeant. The Battle of Aughrim."

"If I didn't know your sister to be a decent woman I'd have you disciplined. Quit arsing around. Come on lads."

He urged his troop towards the pub door, turning back to call to Guard MacAoda. "Hold that fella there, I want him later for questioning."

Marching to the door, he slowed to an amble, tried to peer, unsuccessfully, over the cut-glass brilliances of the window, and nodded to two of his men to enter first, which they did. When they failed to report back within five minutes, a further two were despatched up an alleyway to effect a rear entry past the stinking urinal. After a further lapse, they too failed to reappear or otherwise report or request reinforcements.

The Sergeant deputed that a request for assistance be made by radio, and considered the grave situation. Word had originally come to the patrol car that a woman was causing trouble in a pub at the cattle markets. But despite the many improbabilities of his rich experience, he had yet to meet the woman who could best four trained peacekeepers *in silence*. There were a few, well known to many in the metropolitan area, who could hold their own for a few minutes at least, but extremely noisily. There were mature matrons from the neighbourhoods of Stoneybatter or Black Pitts who could have charged the Russian guns at Balaclava, but they lacked staying power. Within minutes, such sounds could be heard as far as the next parliamentary constituency.

The Sergeant beckoned Guard MacAoda to relinquish custody of the red-haired lorry driver and join his four colleagues. Five in all, in blue and silver, the pick of the land, they effected a frontal entry to the silent pub by the strategy of applying a small manual force to the door-spring in the usual manner.

Within, they encountered their colleagues unharmed, standing amongst the cattle men. There was no sign of violence, since the yard sweepers were huddled and shamed behind the bar, almost forgotten. Mountmellick, in desperation, flanked by the impressively caparisoned MacGilla, was trying to regain his lost mastery of the situation and get Eevell away to safety; an effort which she in her arrogance or innocence did little to assist. The entry of the last five guards seemed to Mountmellick the final blow to the vanquished. In the back of his mind he remembered Liadin, but could only pray for her safety, outside. The Irish like the Poles had streaks of metaphysical fat running through their empirical tissue, but the thought of having to explain Liadin and Eevell, to say nothing of himself and MacGilla, to a District Court did not heighten his joys or increase his confidence.

In the few seconds as the newly arrived guards stared in amazement at the eight-foot queen holding the beef burghers in restive equilibrium, Mountmellick, with sickening recall, remembered Loreto whom he had left outside to cope with Liadin.

Eevell, though undoubtedly in royal and indeed supernatural control of her usual self, had long passed the stage of rhyming couplets and had descended to Behanistic abuse.

"Ye bog-begotten gets," she roared at the guards. "May ye be the fathers of labour exchange clerks."

The Sergeant, confronted with her extraordinary appearance, found it difficult to put her in a category. Quite apart from her size, her dress looked like an early production of a Yeats verse play, run up by Miss Horniman and Lady Gregory on a Singer belt drive, out of curtain lining. Such eccentricity could have literary and/or political connections. She appeared to him like the kind of woman who could ruin his pension prospects and cause endless embarrassment by going on hunger strike. Driven by the need for action, he approached her, across the neutral zone of vacant floor space.

"Now ma'am," he pronounced cautiously. "What's the trouble?"

Mountmellick adjusted his pince-nez and with the bravura of a Minoan dancer took the bull by the horns.

"Ah Sergeant, I'm glad someone in authority has arrived." Deep sigh. "You've no idea how relieved I am." Taking the cue, MacGilla moved towards him with the deferential authority of a trained lackey.

"I think we have it under control, Herr Mellickberg. Do you suggest a sedative?"

Mountmellick looked startled for a moment before nodding. "Quite so. Quite so."

The Sergeant remained without action while the cowed pastoral men stared in unprotesting silence at the rest of the assembly. MacGilla approached Eevell at the bar and produced a large pill from a fob pocket in his uniform jacket. Pouring some water from a jug into a glass, he offered it to her with the pill. "Your hydromel, Your Majesty. There's eating and drinking in it." Eevell accepted the offering and pulverised the tablet with her splendid mandibles. The water she scorned, after carefully smelling it.

The Sergeant drew near to Mountmellick and spoke courteously. "I'd better have a few words with you, sir." Mountmellick experienced again the frustrating agony of having to explain the unbelievable.

"Yes, of course, Sergeant."

There was the beginning of a relaxation amongst the cattle jobbers and civic guards. Eevell, with more wit than she had previously exhibited, stooped to a hidden corner and raised the two yard sweepers and set them on the bar counter. She muttered something to them and they laughed.

"True for you, ma'am. It could happen to a bishop."

She handed each one a large whiskey from those still standing on the counter since having been abandoned by the cattle men when they were still counting their crumpled wads of money before the fairy invasion. Watching the Sergeant, searching for the best wording, diplomatic but authoritative, Mountmellick began to see the pink dawn of hope reflecting in the eastern sky. His mind was distracted by a rising sound from outside, a tumult of voices, the bass predominating, but broken by random sounds in the treble. The Sergeant heard it too and the civic guards turned their heads professionally towards the windows. Half a concrete block shattered the glass, stilling for ever the engraved and gilded announcement "Dublin Whiskey Distillery. Finest Wines, Stouts, Ales."

The double doors were pushed open and filled by a wedge of unkempt tinkers or some such second-class citizens. Beyond them, more could be seen, carrying cudgels, staves, pikes and hackbuts. The confrontation was brief before the rearguard injected the vanguard into the licensed premises. Mysterious cries filled the air. "Rí Seamus Abu! Vive Saint Ruth! Vive la France! Vive le Roi!"

Both the Sergeant and Mountmellick, pressed against the paneled partition of a snug, tried to change gear in their minds to comprehend the possibility of bilingual tinkers; bilingual, that is, in English and another European tongue other than Irish or Sheltie. MacGilla threw down a bundle of notes beside the till, vaulted over the bar and began to draw glasses of ale and stout indiscriminately. As he set them on the counter, they were passed on to the invading tinker mob with surprising decorum and social ease.

Mountmellick, still with the Sergeant, dumbly grateful for the procrastination of the questioning, was surprised and delighted to see Loreto and Liadin pulled through the crowd of strange invaders. Liadin had hold of a particular man by his frieze cloak and urged him towards the bar.

"Speak, as thou didst to me, that their hearts may be melted." Apparently she was slow to shake off the language taught to her by George Moore in Ebury Street. Indeed she still spoke with an Ebury Street accent, with a mouthful of muffin in every broad vowel.

The man, aged about thirty with warm fair hair and high cheek-bones, climbed on the bar and held out both hands. His flesh was pulled tightly on his bones and his eyes had the hard protuberance of shock and exhaustion. His open cloak showed a jacket, belt and breeches, with torn woollen stockings to his knees. He had only one shoe, like a mocassin, and he spoke in Irish, quietly, softly, audibly.

"The passion is broken at me, and me to be here and you at your drinking.

"This morning past, the hanging they gave to my woman, in the tree that is by the well. Not any word did I speak for King James, nor the Dutch, nor the English, nor the French, nor for any man, native nor Sassenach; nor she neither, before the last words were choked.

"Four others they put death on with the rope that was on Jack Connor's ass. And the girls they cut with swordplay when the sport was finished. I got my escape when I was hit with a black swoon. May God be praised, but sparingly for the terrible times that do be in it. That is all I will say."

There was a silence as the pathos lingered briefly. Then a man shouted, "We were bet at the Boyne, but we held the bridge at Athlone. Yesterday was a bad day, but we'll carve the bastards at Limerick." He shook the honed complexity of his pikehead, fixed to three feet of shattered ash pole.

"A very offensive weapon," the Sergeant observed to Mount-mellick, nervously.

"I don't give a hog's tit for King James, nor for Dutch Billy neither.

I fought under Mountcashel but not many got away from Wolsely at Newtown Butler. Is there any man here will travel on with me, to Kilkenny?"

A few took him up, ragged men in nondescript dress and stiff baldricks.

"Right then. Follow me up to Carlow." There was a laugh.

Loreto and Liadin handed out drinks at the bar, unmolested. The Sergeant and his men seemed devoid of any initiative. A bony-faced man wearing what appeared to be a sack over his head threw down a pint of stout so that the glass shattered. As he stopped near the light from the window it was plain that he was wearing a long and rather unkempt periwig.

"Sals paysans! Vous m'avez contaminé. Sa Majesté doit être folle pour venu à votre secours. Qu'on dise la messe et qu'on sonne le glas pour courageux Maréchal."

Liadin and Loreto went on dishing out drink. The French captain got a half pint of Hennessy's brandy and the Dutchman was given a bottle of Bols Hollands gin. There was a row going on between two Frenchmen, one Huguenot and one Catholic, enemies, it appeared, and around all this there was a furious heaving of flesh and a burning of words as the Irish, civilians and military, tried to sort out a thousand unsolvable problems. The Civic Guards were fraternising with the invaders.

"I never seen the like," complained the Sergeant to Mountmellick. "They're not tinkers, or any kind of traveling folk. Who in the name of Jaysus are they? There should be help along soon."

Mountmellick couldn't say for certain who they were, beyond feeling in his bones that they had escaped from the hell of some unpublished literary effort, like himself and MacGilla. But never before had there been such an outbreak, and never before, except in the difficult case of Liadin and Eevell, had anyone manifested in the flesh without first adjusting to mid-twentieth-century speech and custom, by absorbing the flotsam in the mind of the literary host first. Then he realised, and it gave him no reassurance or pleasure, that something had gone wrong. The huge gaolbreak, unforeseen, and connected somehow with Liadin's escape, was too much for any literary host to cope with. The characters were coming in raw and unfinished, without protective conditioning, and no effort was being made by that scruffy dim-witted writer to adapt them or give them the smallest veneer of conformity.

"Who the hell are they?" he yelled out of the hole in the broken window. "Have you gone mad? This is a terrible mess."

"You're right at that," remarked the Sergeant. "Can you see if our squad cars are on the way?"

"Hey you!" Mountmellick bawled at the sky. "We need a footnote, any kind of bloody note. An appendix," he appealed.

After a short pause, letters stuttered across the scene in staccato bursts, revealing words.

Can't help it. You started it. They have escaped from the Battle of Aughrim, near Ballinasloe, Co. Galway. July 12, 1691. Don't blame them, civilians and soldiers alike, they have been under a great strain.

"What's that queer writing?" asked the Sergeant. "Is it a kind of advertising?"

Marshal St. Ruth arrived from King Louis with stores, arms and some officers. He gathered the defeated forces from the battles of the Boyne and Athlone, 15,000 in all, and made a stand on the hill of Aughrim, west of the Shannon. Unfortunately his head was blown off and General Ginkle, William's man, a decent Hollander, carried the day. The Franco-Irish forces retreated to Limerick. King William's army consisted of Dutch and Huguenot French as well as some English. There was a lot of confusion—

The Sergeant stared at the lettering flickering down the scene, pushed his cap back and scratched his head. "Is this some sorta television news service? I never seen the like. Are they Orangemen?" he enquired.

"I suppose some of them are," said Mountmellick, "literally."

"Then this must be some sorta unlawful assembly. Some of them is armed with shockin' devices."

"They are not all Orangemen," Mountmellick theorised. "Mostly they seem to be from the other side."

"Well, Black Tories or Green Tories, this has gone beyant the beyants. Let them keep their civil disobedience to them that can suffer it easiest. We should have double Partition in this country, with barbed wire and landmines to stop them contaminating decent citizens of the Republic."

"Who the hell created this lot?" Mountmellick complained loudly. The place was awash with drunken soldiery and peasantry. Three men were priming a flintlock, assisted by a Civic Guard who had donated

fragments of his cigarette lighter. Eevell was beaming down at the
riotous assembly and Loreto tipped him an optimistic wink.

"I have a few clues," announced MacGilla, dragging a septic-
looking battle brand behind him.

"Well?"

"Well, Mister Mountmellick, they're recent. Very recent. Not
properly formed. No depth of character yet. None of them is capable
of adaptation, you might say. I think they're out of a first draft, not a
finished work. Furthermore," and he raised the rusty weapon and
leaned on it impressively, "I don't believe they're out of a novel at all."

"Good God." Mountmellick was aghast. "Not a film script?"

"No, not that. Worse in a way. More emotive. More intense."

"Well?"

"I think they are from a pome. From one of the first drafts of
Richard Murphy's *Battle of Aughrim,* published in 1968."[1]

"Remind me to see someone about this." Mountmellick was
indignant. "I am not without some influence. Heads will roll."

"They will if you stay here. Come on, now's our chance. There's
going to be a most peculiar battle when the Sergeant's reinforcements
arrive. Matchlocks and batons."

Taking the excellent advice, Mountmellick turned back to the
bemused but unharmed Sergeant. "Sergeant, I think it would be better
if I took the ladies outside. Perhaps the clerks' office by the weigh-
bridge. There's going to be trouble here."

"Oh yes, you do that, sir." The Sergeant had dropped his earlier
plans to capture Eevell with tranquillising darts from the nearby
Zoological Gardens, in the face of civil disorder by armed persons.
Two Irish levees, assisted by a Huguenot and the Civic Guard, had
primed a fearsome gun and were busy ramming half a pound of
gunpowder up the yawning muzzle. Eevell was haranguing a small
group of soldiery in what could be fairly and honestly described as
gutter Gaelic. Soldiers on campaign are a desperate lot at any time, but
for one reason or another they seemed to find Eevell's dissertations
diverting, and the tone of their laughter suggested that the subject was
bawdy.

---

1. MacGilla's guess was a near miss. The characters came from a series of translations of part of Richard Murphy's dramatic and epic poem, commissioned by
the BBC from different translators for the Overseas Service. The translations
were extremely free and varied from the original considerably, particularly the
Somali version.

Loreto and Liadin had not been molested or outraged in any way, or not at any rate in a language they could understand. When MacGilla beckoned them to leave, they allowed themselves to be ushered through the refugee throng without apparent fear. Mountmellick coped with Eevell more easily than he expected. She was reciting an aisling or vision poem to the muse of Ireland.

"Seven times in a night have I pleasured you
At a cost of four strong castles and a princedom
By the silver Boyne you slaughtered my strength
In the whispering sallies you tore my entrails
Naked and wounded my stiffness arose.
Hard and terrible with a madness and longing
O Trollop, my cruel Queen, my only love."

"Better a succubus from hell than Jamie Stuart," remarked an Anglo-Irish captain, festooned in bandages. "They do say that William of Orange fancies choirboys. I hope the pope sends him a few, done up in ribbons."

"Your companions are awaiting you, Eevell of Munster," interposed Mountmellick hopefully.

"Tell them to get screwed. I'm all right Jack."

"But the Council cannot sit without you," he protested.

"You expect me to leave with all those rozzers only half corrupted? I'm not stirring a foot until you can bottle the scent of decay offa them."

"You don't want to demean yourself with a crowd of windy metaphors like this lot. There are empires to be won, decisions to be taken. We can't go without you." Mountmellick was firm, courteously authoritative.

"You Anglo-fuckpig. Who are you supposed to be, Arthur Griffith or Anton Chekhov?"

Mountmellick adjusted his pince-nez.

"The drink is running out. Anyway the other pubs are open. MacGilla knows a particular place."

"That arse-licking publisher's nark. All right then. Have you rung for a taxi?"

"I understand there's a vehicle waiting."

"I'll be seein' you boys." Eevell addressed her listeners. "Keep the oul' hammers hangin'. If the heads work loose, soak them in cold tea."

Outside, drawn up at the door was the cattle truck that had brought the refugees from the Battle of Aughrim. The young driver, his hair

aglow in the white light of day, had helped Liadin and Loreto aboard
and was standing with MacGilla. A drummer boy stood by, beating a
slow tattoo. Up the street, at a barricade, hung the white banner of the
Stuarts and the golden silk of the House of Orange. A small crowd was
loading a culverin.

"This lad says he knows a way out into the back of the 'Boro, up a
laneway," announced MacGilla. "We're surrounded by police, but
they are well down past St. Michan's and the Bridewell."

"Anything you say. There's going to be trouble here." Mountmellick and Eevell were helped aboard.

They negotiated a few laneways, two inches wider than their rattling
vehicle, through a gate in a large yard used for curing rabbitskins, and
out through another gate. Through an archway of a forgotten century
they rattled past a concrete and wattle sweatshop full of young girls
machining polychrome heaps of nylon knickers and slips. They drove
through the surround of a deserted Protestant church and out by the
vicarage gate.

Eventually they were out in the main thoroughfares, trodden by
Swift, Congreve, Goldsmith, Sheridan and their creditors and debtors.
Rattling through Stoneybatter Eevell banged her head against the roof.
"Name o' Jaysus. What manner or shape of vehicle is this? A confession
box on wheels! Hey there son! Aisy on a bit or I'll have your sweet-
breads on toast."

They sailed up Aughrim Street, ominously named, without obstruc-
tion, and were soon trundling and creaking westwards through the
Phoenix Park.

"Meseemeth 'tis a fair parkland," Liadin offered conversationally.
"Broad and noble. See, the noble stags rear in rut."

"You'll get a rut up your arse with a king-sized antler if you can't
talk like an ordinary Christian," observed Eevell tetchily.

They rolled more smoothly through the green parkland, past the
Presidential Palace and embassies hidden by trees. Green woods and
geometric plantations turned their path southwards, until they circum-
navigated a deeply wooded hairpin bend where Mountmellick tapped
on the glass panel of the cab. The lorry stopped, the rattling ceased and
the birds sang loudly. They were beside a small lake in a hollow, wood-
fringed. Above them was a steep hill covered in furze, crisscrossed with
narrow paths and tunnels through the herbage.

"Ah. The Furry Glen. It's the sexual academy of the Augustan City,"
remarked MacGilla. "It's quite a while since I lay for my finals here."

"Now listen." Mountmellick raised a finger. "We are as much refugees as that lot of war heroes up at the cattle markets. We must stop here for a while, until MacGilla can get to the hotel and collect our stuff. We've got to get out of this country."

"Where to?" Loreto was anxious.

"We have a choice of various capitals, but London is the most convenient for the moment, if we can set up as publishers. Let's talk about it later. Our friend here," he nodded at the red-haired lorry driver, "has to leave MacGilla to a taxi rank. Then he will rejoin us."

"I would fain dally an hour with him on the green hillside yonder," remarked Liadin, appraising the young Connaught man's appearance.

"And I would fain ye'd stop talkin' like a Protestant Bible and speak like a Christian," said Eevell. "Yer a dirty pack of liars. You told me you were going to a boozer."

"Later, later. Soon we'll be safe and away by aeroplane."

MacGilla departed to collect the possessions from Malahide and to importune the host writer for money to meet the new emergency. "Tell him we need a lot, but I hope it will be the last. If we get safely set up on our own we can be completely independent. No! Better not put it like that," added Mountmellick. "Say we don't want to be too much of a burden on him. We've got to treat him diplomatically. I think he's a bit lost with all this carry on."

"I think he has only himself to blame," remarked Loreto indignantly. "If only he would confine himself to taking shorthand notes of the proceedings, instead of getting worried because we don't have any literary coherence, his life would be smoother."

"Methinks we might think more gently of him," Liadin suggested. "Every soul seeketh some pride, some small estate. E'en a scribe hath rights and privileges."

"Never mind that now." Mountmellick called the déjeuner sur l'herbe to order. "We have things to discuss. I'm afraid that we are in a bit of a mess."

"If you're worried about that lot of Jacobite bowsies above at the market pub," observed Eevell, "ye can forget them. I know their sort. I lay ye ten to wan." Here she peeled off ten filthy Irish currency notes, obviously of cattle jobber origin, and laid them on the sward. "Ten to wan they'll evaporate be tomorrow."

"Evaporate." Mountmellick was incredulous. "At this very moment they are attacking two squadrons of the Civic Guards with matchlock guns. And I noticed two prison vans from the Bridewell with their tyres slashed with halberds."

"Look here you." Eevell spoke with intellectual arrogance and a certain menace. "I didn't come up on the last train from the bogs. Cover my money. I'm telling you that by now the television people, Tellyfish, BBC, Rediffusion Français, and all the papers are busy covering a Paisleyite invasion from Ulster. What's the difference between frightened ghosts from a poem about the seventeenth century and a row between people who still live in the seventeenth century? I tell you we're as safe as houses fully insured."

"Yet I feel we should take refuge with the gentle Saxons. Mount-mellick may yet be right." Liadin had begun to modify her appalling pseudo-archaic style.

"Oh Liadin! I meant to ask you." Loreto spread herself odalisque-wise on the grass. "How did your affair with Curither end?"

"Evil befell us at the hostelry of Saint Ferdomnoch in Armagh."

"What took you there, daughter?" Eevell enquired. "The place was alive with bishops and cardinals. Still is."

"Seeking judgment between contentious princelings. Above all, amongst the Scotic nations, its decisions had God's authority."

"Yeah, I see that, but what was the trouble?" Loreto wanted no generalisations.

"Better to be smitten by a crozier than to die with a burning sword in the throat. It was that hot-holed polecat Senua that caused our miseries."

"Every royal palliasse in Ulster was pressed to her imprint. She bore the weight of Curither when three deacons and a lawyer came to take depositions."

"What happened?"

"I was much overwrought, and near to death, when the good Saint Cummin bore me to his bowered cell by the lake and tended my ills."

"What happened to Curither?"

" 'Tis said he journeyed to Argyle and to the hospitable halls of the Saxons. From there with him to Frankland and the arbours of Laon where he found a second mistress fashioned from the fancies of John the Irishman."

"Come again." Loreto was out of her depth.

"She means Scotus Erigena, the philosopher, I think. The man who had to be protected by Charles the Bald for fomenting neo-Platonist heresies."

"You mean John the Scot got him a woman?"

"Not so," replied Liadin. "For to do him some justice, he often said that only a substance more rarefied than my flesh could assuage his yearning."

"His mistress was Sophia, the harmonious concord of the universe."

"Oh, I get you. He gave up women to concentrate on philosophy. Well, at least he didn't leave you for another woman."

Liadin gave a grating sympathetic snigger. "The stink of that Crinoch bitch clung to him until the last bell tolled o'er his flattened clay," she snarled, betraying for the first time the less gentle side of her character. "For many long days and measureless seasons I mourned him on the rock where he first took me. When all was past and done, by command of Saint Cummin, that rock was made to seal my tomb, unconsecrated but remembered and adorned with verse."

"Well, by Jaysus," remarked Eevell. "That verse had very persistent qualities. You are the first person I've known to describe her own funeral."

"Know ye not, as Curither believed, that the soul hath diverse parts. What John the Scot and his master, Plotinus, did not reck was of its most dramatic particle, which lieth waiting for nourishment in the imaginations of later generations of men. All gathered here are germinated from such soul-seed."

"We're all acutely aware of that," replied Eevell. "In my case it's even more complicated. First there was Merriman's Eevell in the original poem, then there was Arland Ussher's Eevell in the first trans-lation, and then there was Frank O'Connor's Eevell in his translation and now there's me. Be Jaysus, I'll tell you, we'd make a fine oul' trinity if we got together."

"Nature is ever bountiful," remarked Mountmellick, "but of course this cannot happen on earth. Your three previous cousins are living the life of Riley on Parnassus, or Slieve Luacre or wherever Gaelic poetic concepts go when they are published. It is because you have escaped, like all of us, from the hell of the unpublished that you are now able to sit here with me. It may seem a terrestrial paradise to you, but the emphasis is on terrestrial. It's full of snares and delusions. You've just escaped from one. By the way, Liadin, what happened to Curither, I mean your Curither?"

"We met but little in Hell, but I had known that he escaped and flourished mightily in a fictionalised biography of Danilo Dolci and wrought much good amongst the Frankish Saracens of Sicily."

"Here comes our friend with his lorry," Mountmellick announced. "It's about time you ladies changed clothes. I don't think that enameled see-through is suitable for travel, Loreto. And I hope there is something amongst your stuff for Liadin. I'm not sure what to do about Your Majesty. No matter what you wore you would look . . . distinctive."

The driver nodded. "Mr. MacGilla did say that I was to leave ye by the airport. 'Twill be a bumpy oul' journey but the ladies, God willing, can travel in the cab with me. I'm not sure about you, ma'am," he added, eyeing Eevell, whose head was hidden in the branches of a larch tree.

"That's all right, son." The queen was gracious to any young man with positive sexual attributes. "But don't forget to stop at a boozer. Me tonsils are desiccated with constant evaporation."

"There's a special offering from Mr. MacGilla in the back, for you. Half a dozen stout and a quarter bottle of Jameson. He says that'll be enough to get you through the journey."

"The dirty gate-lodge quiff-toucher. Still and all, maybe he meant well, in his innocence."

They mounted the vehicle to their several places and sinuously descended from the Furry Glen towards Chapelizod before turning north across the park towards Collinstown airport near the monastic settlement of Swords. Passing the Civic Guards training depot, a fine spread of British Colonial architecture, Eevell delivered a brief incisive speech in rough demotic Gaelic addressed to the trainee policemen. She had the wit to call down a cloud of invisibility on the lorry, which impressed Mountmellick and Loreto with its strategic potential. With the first faint hopes of tranquillity, they sped, lurching and invisible, out of the park and north towards Cabra. Civic Guards ran out from doors, carrying carbines, batons and paperweights. One man appeared in the quadrangle pulling up his trousers and shaking a vast red fist. Questions were later asked in the Daíl, but were ruled out by the Speaker to Opposition catcalls. Eevell's message appeared to have had the nature of vulgar abuse, but playing skilfully on each man's private weakness and shame.

Invisibility landed them in some dangerous situations with regard to traffic until Loreto reminded her to visibly revert. This was not as easy as it seemed, since the queen maintained that it came and went like hiccups. Somewhere near Glasnevin Cemetery they reentered visibility to the driver's relief, since the highway was strewn with fragments of funeral cortege and isolated cabs, starting to follow wrong hearses. Eevell had to be distracted by the inadequate quarter bottle of whiskey from paying a visit to the grave of Brendan Behan, her maker. It wasn't an easy passage.

Loreto made the expected remarks about the phallic nature of Round Towers, which irritated Eevell.

"Listen, allaniv, you climbed up a few phalluses in yer day, when ye didn't have a big Norwegian with a battle-axe tryin' to carve lumps outa yer arse. Anyway they were bell towers, mostly. If they *are* phallic, it's a pity every man doesn't hang a warning bell on the end of his cock. That's not a bad idea. . . ." She fell to musing. Loreto stared out at the cypress tress and drilled ranks of tombstones and announced peevishly that if that was the setting for one of the adventures of Ulysses, then Joyce must have been slipping.

Eventually they neared the airport and coasted down the main Belfast road looking for MacGilla. They found him near a parked hackney scanning the traffic. After paying off the decent man of the lorry, MacGilla detained him to use his vehicle as a changing room. Loreto fished out suitable garments for Liadin and herself, while Eevell stripped herself naked and waited, standing on a folded tarpaulin, expectantly. Liadin was able to follow the lunatic logic of a pair of tights, a slip, a dress and a coat but was unable to fit her feet into any available shoes.

Both of them stared, nonplussed, at Eevell who complained loudly of the cold. Goose pimples the size of lentils erupted over sensitive areas of her skin. MacGilla and Mountmellick came in to advise and left hurriedly.

"Nevertheless, I am sure she would make some man a fine wife," Mountmellick ended his comment charitably.

"She would, providing he was a Zulu folk deity," observed MacGilla.

Eevell's body was quite human, devoid of wings, gills, vestigial webbing in the toes or even scales. In bronze, lining an Olympic stadium, she might pass unnoticed. But in pink marble flesh the totality of her eight feet, long golden hair, high regal breasts, muscled belly and pillowed limbs was startling. Liadin noticed for the first time that the royal nipples were virginal. In the end they had to dress her again in her Celtic embroidered gown. With a cloak heavy with woven interlaced Celtic serpents, she looked less like a carnival decoration.

The driver of the lorry departed in a friendly manner for Ballinasloe, promising to keep a lookout for any refugees from the cattle markets, making their way back to the battlefields of Aughrim. Hopefully, he suggested dropping them off at Lynch's library in Galway, the only place he could think of that was both antique and literary. Mountmellick told him to do just that and Eevell protested that they would

mostly be disembodied metrical stresses by now, or disorientated metaphors, "not having," and she punched her huge breasts, "any literary
persistence or staying power."

Fortunately, by mutual agreement, passports are no longer necessary
between the realms of Ireland and Britain. Not that they would have
been unobtainable: Mountmellick had long been aware that many civil
servants in the Department of Foreign Affairs lived double lives as
writers, poets and critics, and were open to literary corruption or at least
persuasion. But no document could guarantee the admission without
let or hindrance to Eevell, in any human society. She caused a stampede
in the airport buildings, in particular when she recovered her dignity
enough to harangue the resident journalists in hexameters, after
demanding to see their NUJ cards.

To Mountmellick, the jumble of events in the departure buildings
was a nightmarish confusion. MacGilla, the paymaster, was unable to
book seats on the next flight since an indivisible block of five was
needed. Long before he had returned from the booking desk Eevell
had smelt out the bar and had made a royal entry, followed by the
others in a condition of apprehension. She searched the faces of the
white-coated barmen from her bird's-eye view and picked on a small
rat-faced youth with lank black hair.

"How are ye fixed, O Declan," she addressed him in Irish.

Startled at his first sight of an immortal and at being summoned in his
own name, he made the sign of the cross. Eevell glared at his act of defence. "I don't give a tinker's chancre about the extent of yer piety as long
as ye keep the holy wather out of the whiskey. What'll it be, comrades?"

Mountmellick ordered a twenty-year Lockes of Kilbeggan and one
for the absent MacGilla. Loreto requested a Scotch on ice, at which
Mountmellick, concerned for her education, suggested that she try a
superior malt. Eevell turned on him in wrath. "Don't you say a word
against blended Scotch whisky. It's the world's finest soft drink. Far
ahead of Coca-Cola. If yer stomach's tender and ye want to lay off the
booze for a while, Scotch is yer only man. And you, pet?"

"A firkin of ale or a stoup of wine as it pleaseth you."

"Talk like an effing Christian. OK. Declan, a double schooner of
San Patricio for the lady and a treble anis for me."

The drinks came up and Eevell pushed through gaping travelers and
their relations to stare at the tarmac beyond the windows. A plane took
off for Rome, lifting its vast belly desperately from the runway as it
beat gravity on points only, and circled above the distant mountains.

"Christ! I may be immortal, but I'm not risking me litherary future in a device like that. I'd as lief put to sea in a prefabricated bungalow."

Mountmellick was soothing, reassuring. MacGilla, arriving and seizing his drink, supported him. Eevell put her arms around Liadin and comforted her. "Don't mind them, allaniv. You and me'll turn into swans and follow them on our own. I'm not agin progress, mind ye, but sometimes the ould ways are the best."

The possibility, even probability of this act turned Mountmellick's blood cold. A passing American senator ordered a repeat of the round of drinks and spoke jokingly but politely to Eevell. "I'd sure like to see you doing that, ma'am. I certainly would."

Eevell glared at him. "If you were as flahool with your money for social welfare as ye are over that bar, life'id be the better for all concerned. Still, I never begrudge a generous elbow, but," and she grabbed his lapel, pulling him up from the floor, "if I weren't amongst friends I'd turn ye into a councillor on the Dublin Corporation. It's about yer level."

Mountmellick was very alarmed. Absolute discretion was needed for their future prosperity and there was little of that diplomatic virtue available.

MacGilla, as usual, solved the problem. He it was who muttered words to the grey-haired foreman barman and directed the concoction of oily liqueurs which he offered to Eevell. Before handing it to her he dropped a lump of dry ice into the glass. It foamed, smoked and bubbled and the queen regarded it favourably.

"They must have distilled this in the lavatory cisterns," she remarked, tossing it back. Within a few moments she was hiccuping like a quasar in convulsions, and between each spasm she lost her visibility. Only a few people saw this and they foreswore the drink. A stripper returning from the family cottage in Clonakilty vowed to make a general confession at the earliest opportunity and to institute enquiries about a religious vocation.

Eventually Eevell was asleep, uncontrollably invisible. Mountmellick and MacGilla erected and occupied an effective barrier of chairs around her and many awkward situations were avoided. Luckily the changeover in clientele at the bar was regulated by air traffic and was briskly fluid. The others, not daring to go to the restaurant, chewed sandwiches and waited.

Early editions of the Dublin evening papers were black with headlines about a three-cornered battle between Sinn Fein marchers, invading Paisleyites and the police. Television teams disembarked and famous faces were greeted uncertainly by people who dimly remembered their shadowy images and tried to remember the pub, racecourse or social occasion where they might first have been encountered.

When Eevell awoke, after an hour's invisible sleep, she was sufficiently wraithlike to be taken to the departure gate without starting a stampede. People stared. A coven of nuns sought in their reticules for fortifying rosary beads, but nothing really serious occurred. "I hope you've forgotten this nonsense about turning into a swan," said Loreto, undiplomatically.

"I'd chew the tits off you only I'm a vegetarian," grunted Eevell. "I couldn't turn into a fucking sea gull, the way I am now, barrin' I had a sewage outflow to tempt me. Jaysus, what did that yellow-fanged ostler put in my drink?"

"Come on now. Up the steps, ladies. Eevell, perhaps you had better go through the door on your hands and knees. The stewardess will understand."

At that moment two figures appeared, struggling with the boarding-ticket girl at the exit part of the building. Thrusting her aside, they ran towards the bottom of the boarding steps leading to the *Saint Molaise* flagship of the Aer Lingus fleet, where the literary entities were handing necessary documents to a pretty girl with attractive bones. They were revealed as a young man wearing a beaver forage cap and a girl dressed in the walking-out uniform of a trainee nurse, complete with black cape and a diminutive Polly Flinders cap. Her youthful and generous breasts bounced in the trivial confinement of a linen dress. Both of them were holding hands, the young man with long Ivy League legs pulling the girl behind him. Their arrival was breathless.

"I say! Mr. Mountmellick sir!" Mountmellick sought to keep his heart four-square in his rib cage.

"Well?"

"May I, sir, in a manner of speaking, intrude on your privacy. A word alone is called for and must be granted."

Mountmellick detached himself two yards from the group at the bottom of the steps. "You had better be quick. This is an outrage."

"Take us with you."

"What? Why?"

"We want to, and I use a common cliché to express it, better ourselves."

"Are you trying to have me on, young man?"

"Oh no, sir.

> "Airports are vast
> And lonely.
> They look alike
> But their runways
> Are the portals
> of discovery.

Not to mention escape, sir. This is Cynthia, sir. Her father is well considered and is the Chief Veterinary Officer for the Leix-Offaly regional stud."

Mountmellick was beyond words and looked frantically for MacGilla.

"You see, sir, we share a lot in common. Origins. For many years, growing no younger, exiled near Kilcool. A damp place you will admit, when there are clouds on the mountains. And the pounding of the surf. Erosion. Deal with us charitably."

MacGilla dared to leave Eevell in the care of Loreto, to surmount the boarding steps. "Now then," sharply, "what's all this about?"

The girl spoke. "He's only trying to tell this gentleman that we are the same as you. Out of an unfinished novel by Mr. Donleavy. We want to come with you."

"That's it, sir. Mike Donleavy left us in a barn near his cottage in Kilcool. It's been years. And Cynthia. It's not fair. She has a terrible sense of sin. And that's what we've been living in. There's nothing else around. Only sin. A desolate place."

"Are you two created by Mr. J. P. Donleavy?" enquired MacGilla stiffly.

"Yes sir. He left us in a state of impending sin. For years. Forgotten. And Cynthia has such big soft breasts, sir. When I bury myself between them I get impure thoughts. How can I help it?"

"Ah, men are always impatient," Cynthia observed fondly, sadly. "Can't even wait until the end of the chapter."

"Will you both please curb your animal proclivities of pleasurings. What you ask is impossible, just now."

"But sir. Cynthia! Show him your tits. We've got to make the fellow understand. God's teeth!"

"Cover that up, miss," said MacGilla, sharply. "Put it back beside the other one. I'll allow it's a beauty. High lactation potential. But there's a time and a place. Please now." He paused and appeared to cogitate and give a reasonable, charitable reply. "Look here. At the moment we're tied up. But we are launching an enterprise. There could be a place in it for two forward-looking entities. We'll get in touch, very shortly. You can see we have immediate problems." He nodded towards the place where Eevell's entrance perforce on all fours had caused the hostess to scream. "What's your name?"

"Bartholomew MacAboo, graduate of Trinity College, Dublin University."

"And you, miss?"

"Cynthia Philomena Fitzgroyne. St. Fatima's Hospice for the Hopeless, Kil of the Grange, Co. Dublin. It's on the 24 bus route."

MacGilla scribbled in a notebook. "And you are now temporarily resident for more than twenty years in the junk barn beside Mr. Donleavy's cottage, Kilcool, Co. Wicklow? Why were you not sent to Limbo?"

"Please sir. I can explain that. After all, Limbo is the first-class section of Hell. It is permissible to enter in a state of error, but not of outright sin. We couldn't get to confession. Both of us, sir, have a terrible sense of guilt. Enough to destroy the entire Federation of Pan Daemonium."

"I see." MacGilla breathed heavily, tore off the page and handed it to Mountmellick, who put it in his wallet. Mountmellick coughed.

"I endorse my colleague's promise. Soon you will be hearing from us. Do you know anything about publishing? Ah well. However!" He raised a cautionary finger. "Earthbound you may be, and not properly incarnated and freely mobile, but I have a feeling that Mr. Donleavy may not have forgotten you. He has a sharp memory and a black plastic notebook of memoranda. At any moment you may be called upon to give your services. I think you'd like that, wouldn't you?" He smiled faunishly, sexily. "Of course, you might have to change your names. He often insists on that. I'll see what I can do. Drop a note to the Mullingar house and see if he'll clear them. After all, he has the copyright."

"I'll do that, sir." MacGilla stiffened in token of eager obedience.

"Well. It was so refreshing to meet you both. Young love is charming. Slán leat. We hope to meet soon."

Mountmellick bowed with Bourbon courtesy and ascended the steps, followed by MacGilla. At the top he turned, removed his pince-nez and waved gently, with infinite and tender understanding.

MacAboo looked disconcerted and then perked up. He threw an arm around Cynthia's shoulders and turned with her towards the terminal buildings. As they walked across the endless concrete tundra, his hand slipped from her scapula, beneath her nurse's cape, and began to stroke and squeeze the cheeks of her arse, fondly.

> "Soft breasts
> Smooth haunches
> Moving slowly
> Past endless concrete
> And glass."

At this more purposeful point in an otherwise haphazard drift of events, the host scribe took to his bed with fluxes, agues and the yellow staggers, a stress syndrome.

The Fates, in whom he believed, are capricious deities, benevolent aunties to some, but wicked stepmothers to others. They confound all liberal illusions of eschatology. The scribe belonged to the less favoured class of catechist, but for once his demiurges granted him a small mercy, and comforted his anxieties. Between fevers he was allowed brief and very discontinuous glimpses of his parasites, but below the threshold of coherent narrative.

Between aspirins, the group of errant and perverse entities revealed themselves briefly. There was an altercation in the toilet, on the plane, in which Liadin complained about the unsuitability of the fittings for either footwashing or baptism. Being shoeless, she suffered from anti-skid gravel between her toes.

An aspirin later revealed Eevell lecturing the Immigration officials on the prose style of Rabindranath Tagore. She had, she protested, two husbands in Wolverhampton and three uncles and a sister at Luton, all gainfully employed. She name-dropped several junior ministers, and demanded references from her old and valued colleague, Wayland Smith.

There seems to have been an episode involving the ladies alone in a hairdressers on the Finchley Road. Mountmellick and MacGilla, it is to be assumed, were desperately seeking communal accommodation at any price. A Persian hairdresser, young, attractive and well-inten-tioned, came upon Eevell, sitting down, shrouded in a cover, and being unable to gauge her proportions, went to work on her thick Munster tresses. The process added eighteen inches to her height. In faultless Iranian interspersed with coarse Sufi images, the queen called down the malevolence of yazatas, daevas, drujs pairikas, yatus and other goblins on the girl's trembling head. Her coiffure entangled in a perspex chandelier, Eevell declared her to be the result of an unnatural union between Abu Bekr and Othmon, arch-heretics, with Omar acting as pander.

Scenes like these, without beginning or final outcome, absurd and embarrassing, interrupted the fevers of the wretched scribe to the extent that he was unable to judge between his literary rapport and his disordered fancies. No absolute reliance can be placed on such feverishly garnered archives.

A couple of days later, the scribe, now recovered from fever, but still reduced by secondary infection, visited the Burgundian, ostensibly for a drink but really to see if the world still spun on its customarily enclosed axis. Bibi was drinking Harp lager, wrapped in his own adequate suffering, a rheumatoid affliction of the shoulders. Dédé nimbly evaded bores, her mind on bills, wines and responsibilities.

This reassuring familiarity was shattered by a glimpse of two figures at a corner table, drinking whiskey, deep in communion. Without a shadow of doubt they were Mountmellick and MacGilla, both dressed rather informally in bishop-sleeved silk shirts and fringed suede trousers.

Retreating behind Bibi, tallest and bravest of the Belgae, the scribe kept watch, concealed from the eyes of the literary entities. Ten minutes later Liadin entered, wearing a faultlessly tailored boiler suit. Mountmellick fussed over her chair and went to get her a drink. At the bar, as he went on fussing characteristically about the whiskey, he searched in his pockets and then strolled horribly towards the cigarette machine. Fumbling in his pockets, he turned to the scribe and said, "Excuse me, have you got two fifty-pence pieces for a pound?"

In petrified fear the exchange was made, without words, for on the scribe's part none were possible. "Thanks very much." Mountmellick inserted and extracted.

He rejoined Liadin and MacGilla and said, loud enough to be heard, "Where is she now?" It could only refer to Eevell. The reply was inaudible, and they went on talking with nods, statements, replies and interjections.

It was then that the scribe realised that they had not recognised him. Apparently their sense of the percept was not visual but an amalgamation of recognisable foibles and patterns of personality. It followed that as long as he could remain remote and unrevealed to them, he could watch their public acts with perfect safety. Nevertheless, it was something of a shock to discover that they were now neighbours, breathing the same air and sharing part of his environment.

On leaving, Mountmellick and MacGilla paused by the chimney-piece to make some comment to each other on a large bronzed relief of Socrates corrupting the youth of Athens, pinned to the fabric of a supporting wall. Liadin stood, briefly irresolute, by the door, and with Hibernic-Castilian gallantry the scribe held the door open for her to pass out, remarking that the weather was a trifle humid. The rain was bouncing off the pavement, inducing Liadin to refuse his gesture with easy grace and a flashing smile.

12

Towards the bottom of Frognal Hill in the district of Hampstead is a large Gothic mansion, detached from its neo-Palladian peers. Above its transitional porch rises a high stained-glass window depicting Roger succouring a chastely clad Angelica, which rises up the façade to below the eaves, allowing dapplings of amber and ruby light to illuminate the fretted staircase. It has a semi-basement, recessed in the hill by a shallow ramp of daisy-speckled grass, and cavernous and labyrinthine in extent and shape. The back of the house overlooks a garden on two shallow levels, suitably planted with flowering shrubs and trees. The windows of the solarium return of the apartments give onto the garden.

From this architectural relic of old decency Mountmellick, MacGilla, Loreto and Liadin began to put into effect their plan for complete independence.

Having wound up his connection with documentary films, Mountmellick obtained, in a dingy pothouse near Swiss Cottage, forged National Health cards for Loreto and placed her in a secretarial position in a well-known literary agent's. From this vantage point she made comprehensive lists of publishers, their personnel, moods, tastes, acumen, Achilles heels and fiscal conditions.

From these Liadin, who had a Romanesque aptitude for unraveling interlaced facts, isolated the most likely enterprises for a takeover. It was a modest and nearly bankrupt undertaking called the Eros Press, with offices in Frith Street, Soho. MacGilla was the first penetration, as packer and storesman, a function which he increased in scope and importance within a few weeks by subtle backroom politics.

The publications were tenth-rate imitations of the Traveller's Companion editions of the old Olympia Press, paperbacks, but with lurid and misleading covers to tempt semiliterate proles into the pleasures of reading. None of the books was remotely pornographic or even erotic. The writing was the shabbiest hackwork, done by stray journalists and members of the literary demimonde, for five hundred pounds a manuscript, outright. It was said by the author of *The Strange Case of Polly Proctor* and *Manao, City of Tropical Vice* that the greatest difficulty was to write sufficiently badly or drably. No metaphors were allowed, by editorial decree, unless they were well-tried and tested clichés with a Ministry of Transport roadworthy certificate.

In their three-colour paper covers and coarse thick woodpulp paper, these books were read by nightwatchmen, Irish navvies living in bachelor communes in Camden Town, army recruits and the occasional Pakistani machine-tool operator, attracted by naked houris on the cover and nonplussed by a rehash of the trial of Oscar Slater within. Like padded brassières, the publications were falsies, less titillating than an evening at the Bunny Club.

When Mountmellick moved in as majordomo the authors' list continued to keep to the lower end of the market: strip cartoon paperbacks of the *Heptameron* of Marguerite of Navarre and the diaries of Casanova. A slightly more imaginative venture was an edition of the Song of Songs from the Bible heavily illustrated in line drawings and printed on tissue paper. These sold excellently in the Far East, mostly for burning at funerals, thus guaranteeing the departed grandfathers a vigorous afterlife. A companion facsimile of a Japanese pillow book was less successful although Mountmellick reserved the idea for a second edition in video-cassette form as part of a projected series on the history of art.

Part of the reason for this level of publishing, the scribe realised, was that it was cheap, irresponsible and served largely to generate experiences, but some of these innovations in publishing led to endless arguments with the British Board of Trade about taxation categories, which were never satisfactorily solved. In desperation, Mountmellick thought of letting Eevell loose in the corridors of Administration, but forbore because of the uncertain outcome.

She was a considerable problem, far greater than those posed by novelty publishing on a modest level. In business, Loreto and

Mountmellick were never lacking in a bold enterprise. The coarse grain of their sensitivities made it possible to undertake ventures which would fill others with shame. Their low-pressure dignities could absorb the impact of the brashest gimmick, but every evening, when they gathered up their paperwork to carry it home to Frognal, Eevell was there to damp their elan and diminish their industry. When she wasn't there, it was worse. The situation was impossible.

She had a gregarious nature, drawing energy from others and condensing it to a white heat through her own personality. Left alone in a house, she would browse through books, newspapers, tenancy agreements, the small print on guarantee forms or copies of the *Watch Tower* left by an elderly lady in Jehovah's Witnesses.

She could spend a contented day absorbing anything, from the horrors of a novel by Céline to Live Letters in the *Daily Mirror,* and apparently derive an equal edification from both. But as the hours passed, the need to charge her batteries on other people's energy drove her out to seek a likely source. This was a violation of the house rules, laid down by Mountmellick as soon as the literary coven had been set up in the Frognal maisonette.

The strategy whereby these literary dropouts sought to cushion their precarious environment and achieve a measure of security depended on controlling a publishing house. In their case, something more than ordinary business discretion was needed. Being of literary origins themselves, they were without artistic pretension. The kinds of books that had brought a new life to the shaky typewriters and haircord carpeting of the Eros Press were as effective as any others: probably better. Prosperity allowed them to commission a few biographies and novels from obscure writers, merest hacks and easily controlled. These writings (there was a book on Celtic Romanesque indoor domestic fitments, in the form of an interview with Liadin) could provide the entities with enough energy to last several years. MacGilla with great ingeniousness had himself written into a saucy manual on the imprisonment and torturing of nuns under the Inquisition. Practically under his dictation, the writer was forced to include a chapter on Sorley McGill, Master of Novices at the Irish College of Salamanca. This monster, who naturally enough reflected enough of the substance of MacGilla's personality to pass muster, practised outrages on unfortunate nuns guilty of minor breaches of discipline, such as feeding a canary before the Angelus or refusing the amorous advances of the Mother Superior.

MacGilla was at all times a rough diamond, as they say, but not without certain virtues and a craggy but effective morality. He would allow no harm to come to the girls, physically or, as far as he could help, psychologically. Realising that the human soul is pretty durable, he contented himself with visual orgies behind sealed cloisters. Seated on a bishop's throne, he would survey benignly processions of naked girls singing offices and penetential prayers with rosary beads draped round their hips and loins. He found this elevating, and rewarded the sweetest voices or the most demure countenances with sweetmeats. Afterwards, he always found them good homes, preferably in the Indies. When the completed manuscript was submitted to Mountmellick, this chapter was removed before publication, leaving MacGilla with a harmless non-habit-forming fix of literary energy, and a reasonably profitable book in hand, less a few pages which no one would notice.

This device was so effective that Mountmellick included Eevell in a scruffy coffee-table volume on *Erotic Aspects of Norse-Celtic Mythology and Folk Tales.* Eevell appeared in this in an unreadable footnote on the social and marital customs of troll queens and seal women. To make doubly sure that the daring act of publication did not consign her to Parnassus, the footnote was printed in very indifferent and recondite runic. A passable portrait of her appeared in a three-colour plate of thirteenth-century walrus-ivory chess pieces, but sufficiently idealised to be of no danger.

Not that all of them, Mountmellick, MacGilla, Loreto and even Liadin, had not at some time or other dreamed of disposing of Eevell by having her published. After all, it was humane. Her soul, transported to Parnassus, would live in bliss. Even the smallest ledge on its golden crags was ineffably delightful, but tribal loyalty is too strong amongst the Irish and never more so than between citizens of different opinions facing an alien adversary.

Eevell's appearances in the streets of Hampstead were disturbingly memorable. Generally she carried herself well, in pubs or restaurants, but her extraordinary appearance transformed her smallest idiosyncrasies into major assaults on the social system. She had, it must be confessed, certain prejudices, unpopular in cosmopolitan urban society. Unlike her creator, she could be viciously abusive to male homosexuals. A request, near the closing hour, to an overworked but fastidious barman in the form of "Hey there, get's a coupla scoops of gargle, hot cock" caused a lot of resentment, even amongst heterosexual neutrals of both sexes.

Typical of her minor eruptions which nonetheless drew more than its share of public attention on the high hills of Hampstead was to bawl at elderly owners of large dogs, occupying floor space in saloon bars, "Hey misther! You keep yer dirty hands offa my granny. I won't warn you again." An injunction that was quite impossible to answer.

Eevell rarely mentioned women's rights in the latter days and her real attitude became more apparent. It had little to do with rights in a civic sense but a great deal to do with privilege. She saw it as her duty to further their happiness at the expense of the male or even the neuter, much as a trades union official acts for his members.

She was not against men, but as an Ottoman pasha might be indifferent to female underprivilege and could yet hold certain women in high sensual and intellectual esteem, so she was with the male of the species. She certainly enjoyed their company.

What she really enjoyed was to see young people enjoying their sexual differences to the fullest, and not frittering their fleeting youth because of the mores of a male-dominated society of greater age and selfish sobriety.

She was a notorious maternalistic pander and often gave the spare key to the flat to unmarried couples that she found in the passages and roads of Hampstead Village or Kentish Town. What they thought of her it is hard to guess, as she unbent from her altitude and sent them off to stud with a pat on the head and a Rabelaisian benediction. She may have seemed a monster and yet, somehow, her immortal qualities, together with her characteristics inherited from B. Behan, minimised suspicion or fear, though it may have left a feeling of awe.

Mountmellick was enraged, though at pains to reveal it diplomatically, when he found Eevell hunched over an electric fire at five in the morning, crooning musical praises of her husband, Lugoid MacCon, or MacEógan. Whether they were two people or one, no one knew for certain. Above this melancholy panegyric could be heard the beat of pop music, coming from Eevell's room overlooking the garden. When he entered it, in purposeful enquiry, there was one couple sitting in an armchair, dazed, drunk or entranced, another couple facing each other twitching fingertips to the beat, and a third couple, undressed but modestly sheeted in the bed. On an irritated impulse he snapped off the record player and pulled the sheet from the bed. The others watched him in Incan detachment, silently. The boy sat up and put his feet on the floor, while the girl grabbed a pillow, hugging it to her front for startled concealment.

"Disgraceful," Mountmellick was shouting. "I'm broad-minded but . . ."

Eevell lifted him from the floor with her two outstretched arms. "And is it any different from the way it has always been? In a barn, after a pattern or fair, or on the dry side of a ditch when the hay is out. Would ye rather have them fumbling in a cold bed while the wedding guests puked up the whiskey below in the kitchen, arguin' about the dowry or the mean thoughts that can be got from ten acres of sour land? What I'm telling you is that young people have always behaved like this, whenever they got a chance. Maybe they lack judgment but, by Jaysus, they don't lack style."

She set Mountmellick down, and turned to Liadin and Loreto, who had entered the room. "There's more to living than the joy of giving life to others, and in the eternity of our nation this sort of thing was well thought of. If any of you had ever wandered in Magh Mel, the Plain of Sweetness, you'd be surprised how the nobility of the Sidhe comport themselves. Maybe they are immortal, maybe their flesh glows like the fingers of Lugh, but how do you know how these kids see it? Not the same as you, that's a certain thing. For a couple of years when they are young they can exist without a sense of time, and what else is immortality, answer me that? I'd like to see it on a summer's night, with a young couple stretched out on every well-mown lawn in this city."

Mountmellick, knowing by now that Eevell's fury was of a transcendental and rhetorical nature, rather than malevolently aggressive, dared to counter her argument.

"We are adapting to the society of men and women, and we must never forget it. Their foibles and conventions may seem illogical. In some ways, things are getting easier now, and we should not forget that writers are in the van of the struggle. Nevertheless, this is no time for us to form the spearhead of the phalanx. We must act privately and with cunning and never forget that we are aliens, a fifth column of Muse-begotten souls, penetrating and assimilating the habitations of our creators. To you, Queen Eevell, discretion is a dirty word, a bourgeois camouflage, but I want you all to understand that it is our secret and most potent weapon. Until the day of our final public triumph, when man's noblest thoughts are compatible with his basest actions, we must subordinate our most passionate beliefs to the cause of our kind."

He looked around at the assembled entities, scorning in his rush of blood the startled and hypnotised students and au pairs, and concluded, "Certain conventions may seem irritating to some of us, but let us never forget that all art is conventional. Convention is the matrix of artifice and skill. We may stretch and remould this structure, as indeed we do, and to sublime effect, but it still remains conventional. The word 'convention' is a semantic trap which can, and is likely to, ensnare us. We must step over it lightly using our cunning learned in the pit of Limbo, if we are to attain full human dignity and untrammeled freedom."

Mountmellick's rolling rhetoric ebbed to a short silence, until MacGilla said, "That's a fine speech, Mr. Mountmellick. I haven't heard the like since the Parnell split."

Liadin walked across to Eevell, who stood, pondering. "He means we mustn't be found out and that these boys and girls increase the risk. That's all it is, and there's a great deal of sense in it."

Eevell pouted her lower lip and then announced, "He doesn't have to give a speech like Joseph Chamberlain after the Jamieson Raid. OK. Na h abair aon focal eile. I'm not the head of the oldest royal line in Europe for nothing. Get these kids home in a taxi, but not until they are ready. If I abuse the laws of hospitality that I am supposed to administer myself, I'll end up as much a hypocrite as I still think he is, for all he says. Here, daughter, you with the goose pimples on your arse." The girl from the bed made a brave show of trying to hold the pillow nonchalantly. Eevell laid her hands on the girl's shoulder. "Here's something that'll put Jersey cream in your tits."

The girl stared at her without comprehension until her companions hissed with indrawn breath. Even then she did not comprehend the change that Eevell had wrought in her. Rather did her attitude or bearing alter so that her eyes seemed deeper in her countenance and perceived the world with the detachment of wisdom. It was not that her skin became luminescent, as Liadin first imagined, but that its texture refined itself to catch and offer to the viewer as much light and colour as the room offered, without loss or blemish. She shook her hair, which seemed heavier and more lustrous, and started to walk, with graceful carriage, out of the room, towards the street door. All trace of gaucherie had disappeared, and she might have been a woman nursing a child or a steeplejack on a lofty girder conferring grace to a commonplace act.

"You mustn't go outside like that." Liadin blocked the girl's path, anxious but with a tenderness that the girl's innocence compelled. The boy rushed across the threshold of the room and jumped on an ottoman.

"No. She's right." The boy spoke as if he had seen a revelation. "I mean, like, well! you've never looked like this before. But you'd better cover yourself up before you blind someone." In an inarticulate way he echoed the feelings of the entities and his apprentice adult companions about the change in the substance of the girl.

She stared at strangers, casually, seriously. "You mean me. Oh! My clothes. Very well. Bring them to me."

She pulled a dress over her head and shook her hair in heavy convolutions.

"I can't stay. I still exist in time, I realize. It's a wasteful dimension. I've got to plan how to use it."

She opened the street door and walked barefoot down the front garden, past the monkey puzzle tree. Loreto ran to the door to watch her, anxiously, but made no move to stop her. The others stared silently.

"She'll be OK," remarked Eevell, aware for the first time of the others' unquiet. "I've done this before. Usually it doesn't last long. A friend of mine brushed her nimbus on Willie Yeats in the tram, coming up the tunnel at Holborn, and he nearly climbed up the front of the Imperial Hotel. But he got over it. He grew old and godly and wise and wore a senator's toga over his Mason's apron."

"What did you do to her? I didn't notice a thing." Perhaps Loreto felt an envy of the girl's refinement of substance.

"I gave her the grace and indifference of two thousand years. I wish I had it myself, whenever I needed it. It can't be done to order. For the first time in my life I'm going to ask someone to make a cup of tea. I have the need of it."

13

Mountmellick convened a meeting of the coven in the front room in Frognal to consider short-term plans. Decisions were in need of making and a discreet augmentation of the board was now, for the first time, a possibility. Everyone was present, including Eevell, who had been keeping to her room recently, in voluntary house arrest, making her way diligently through Gibbon's *Decline and Fall.* Her only domestic contact was Liadin, who prepared food when necessary and answered, inadequately, her queries on early heresies. She had to be solemnly assured that there was no Donatist church in London and dissuaded from visiting the offices of the *Daily Mirror* to draw the attention of the editor to the dangerous Manichean inferences in a comic strip. "If that one put one foot in Fleet Street," as MacGilla pointed out, "every paper would have her hanging out of the headlines, even the *Bee-keepers' Gazette.*"

MacGilla laid out chairs with more formality than was necessary and arranged agreeable refreshments. Loreto had a lengthy report on past success and present quandaries and Liadin held her day diary nervously on her lap, ready to answer or ask, according to the play of events. Eevell was in the bath, sitting in its enameled confines with her head and back soaring up in the air, her toes against the taps and her knees crushed against her Olympic breasts. With loud bawls and rough coaxings she sometimes managed to persuade MacGilla or Loreto into playing a hand shower on her monumental person. Finally she stood up and allowed Liadin to massage her flanks with a couple of nylon pot scourers. "Oh that's gorgeous. Lovely. Do that bit again. Behind me knees. Up me back. Oh yes, just there, below my shoulder. Ach, you're a grand girl. If you die before me I'll have ye stuffed and put on show, and your blood sent for bottlin'.'"

Mountmellick waited, with considerable patience, until this charade was finished, and Eevell had joined the company, wrapped in a vast bunting drape which revealed itself as the blue flag with the gold harp of Grattan's Parliament.[1] Nobody knew where she had acquired it, but she often wore it, being short of clothes. "Whenever I feel too benevolent I take a look at it, to restore my sense of outrage and despair."

The master, urbane, smoothly controlled, looked at his fellow entities and noted their glowing flesh and incipient crow's-feet around the eyes. Without a doubt they had adapted and flourished in the turbulent world of the bed-begotten. Except for Eevell, any of them could have passed unnoticed, even in select and discriminating company.

---

1. Grattan's Parliament was the white settlers' legislature in Ireland towards the end of the eighteenth century. Its limited powers represented the interests of the large landlords, but its flag, a gold harp on a blue ground, is still regarded sentimentally, for some grotesque reason.

Loreto was very much the careerwoman, feminine, good about the house, but effectively devoted to the tedium and problems of business administration. Liadin now spoke with a quiet deep Anglo-Irish accent with the faintest touch of a Gallic emphasis on certain syllables in certain words, which she had inherited from George Moore. MacGilla had put on weight, but was too conditioned to being a tower of picaresque servile strength and reliability to be able to change if he wanted to.

Eevell, of course, was a problem. Even she herself realised that. Nevertheless she had made some effort to live without noisy entanglements since the episode with the teenagers. The girl Sue, whom she had casually rarefied, had gone on to become a nationally and even internationally known model whose draped body was to be seen in every second newspaper, on any particular day. Presumably she had kept her friends quiet, for there had been no comeback from the transformation. Probably, as Eevell suggested, she had reverted now, but was able to keep going on her own self-engendered elan. A good hard shake will often keep a broken alarm clock tocking noisily for years of good service.

Mountmellick cleared his throat, stood up and suddenly decided that a Masonic dinner-type of delivery was out of character. Instead he took a memo pad and a pen and laid them by the chimneypiece. Then he removed his jacket and lay down on the rug, supporting himself uncomfortably on one hand. It was awkward but had, he hoped, the advantage of appearing informal: Brian Epstein talking to a Beatle or Diaghilev fixing important strategy with Bakst or Nijinsky. But his opening statement, contrapuntally, gave the impression of forthrightness.

"Things have gone quite well with us in our little venture, but I feel it is time for us to move up to the carriage trade."

"What the hell is that?" Loreto's question was less explosive than its wording suggested.

"I mean that I've had enough . . . we've all had enough, of the Eros Press. All right, all right. I know it is flourishing. Its titular owners are doing better out of it than they are on their strip cellars and gaming clubs, percent-wise, anyhow. We have transformed it managerially, and nobody wants to change that. Loreto and myself have seats on the Board, and we can retain those and use them in an advisory capacity. MacGilla, I am sure, will see that nothing goes on behind our backs. But I see a more exciting time ahead for us. All of us, I am sure, practise our religious duties punctiliously. That is to say, we all read and discuss the weekly book reviews every Sunday afternoon.

"It was Loreto here," he patted her foot on the rug before him, "who pointed out that religion pays dividends. An excellent American maxim, for it has given me, us, that is, a perfect opening in prestige publishing. Money is available. MacGilla has a promise that the assets of several gaming clubs, threatened with closure, are at our imminent disposal."

Obviously the inner cabinet had been at work. Liadin wriggled the pelvis, rib cage and shoulders of her smooth person so as to sit higher in her deep chair. She made an effort to cover her thighs more modestly, a characteristic of some women with a deeply sensual nature, and failing to succeed bent her limbs sideways in elegant discretion. "Could you get to the point, Owen." There was no offence in her tone.

Mountmellick frowned and quickly covered it with his blandest mask. Then the excitement of his idea brought a strain of sincerity into his tone. "You may recall the publication by Faber of *Giacomo Joyce* by James Joyce some years ago. Oh, I know that it was around for some time before, undergoing deep analysis and carbon dating. That's not the point. We," and he looked around him, "are in a position to gain access to any unpublished or unfinished works, by anyone of conse-quence, or for that matter, inconsequence."

"We all know," remarked Eevell, "that you could get a bent finger into a red-hot chastity belt, providing there was money inside and not what ought to be. How do we lay our hands on this verbal loot?"

Mountmellick stood up, tilted his torso sideways and inclined his head. "By carefully selecting literary characters who are still imprisoned in the literary confines of Limbo. There must be hundreds of high quality entities who have escaped the literary archaeologists. Now, we have no desire to bring them to the earthly sphere. I hold no brief, I hope, for prejudice of any kind, but I wouldn't care to cross swords with official-dom about our identities. A small select coven of a few dozen in every sizeable country is just about the safety level. I may seem absurd to you, and extremely unjust, but literary creations have no rights, apart from those incidental to the laws governing plagiarism and libel. These are, of course, framed to protect not us, but those who engender us. No! What I propose, and I hope you will all agree with me, is to rescue from the freezing Hell of the unpublished such characters as are willing, unlike us, to suffer publication and apotheosis and would be happy to exchange the ice of Limbo for the tedious zephyrs of Parnassus. In exchange for this service," Mountmellick drew his feet together and extended an indexed hand, "in exchange for this, they would offer us a complete tape recording of their womb of narrative, and renounce any further claims on it.

"We would look after them in comfort, perhaps even luxury, until the act of publication and critical acceptance allows them to ascend to the realms of the Muse triumphant. There are a few hazards and a few difficulties to be ironed out, but I think the scheme is well within our capacities."

"We could have a right oul Finnegan's Wake be way of an Apotheosis Party," remarked Eevell, who stood up, opened her arms, displaying her godly splendour, and wrapped herself anew in the flag of the Landlords' Republic tightly, like an Incan mummy.

"It would, of course, be an important social occasion," admitted Mountmellick.

"I fancy the idea," continued Eevell, "of some character from Italo Svevo, or maybe from one of our own lost masterpieces, like the *Labor bod Breac*, the *Book of the Spotted Cock*, floating up from the garden beyond, standing on a bank of little clouds festooned with pink-arsed cherubs: like a Murillo painting. By Jaysus, that'd give the Hampstead Festival Committee a wad to chew on."

"And a bull's-eye to suck the stripes off," added MacGilla. "But I'm sure all this can be arranged, providing it doesn't threaten our security. But first things first. Who's in favour?" No one dissented. "Now," continued Mountmellick, "we have to consider what extra help we may need for our expansion. None of us is, I am sure, snobbish." He looked around with a self-conscious liberal leer. "Nevertheless I feel that we must have characters of impeccable literary origin: for reasons of prestige. MacGilla was deputed to check on the amorously thwarted young couple who importuned us in Collinstown airport. Perhaps he can tell us what he has discovered."

"Give over the oul chat. You can save it for your royal memoirs. What went on with Donleavy?" MacGilla had a lackey's licence for familiarity with Eevell.

"Well, you lot kept me locked up in this bloody burgh of Saxons, but I managed to reach him by phone, although I don't fancy the same instrument very much. Still and all, Brendan Behan knew him pretty well. They once had a fight in Fleet Street over a ten-dollar bill. There was a fella called MacNamara trying to hold the stakes. It was the same Brendan who helped him to get a first publisher for *The Ginger Man*, in the Travellers' Companion edition which paid for the Olympia Press, in Paris. Other books in the series had gorgeous titles: *Roman Orgy, The*

Chariot of Flesh, White Thighs, The Secret Life of Robinson Crusoe. The latter was about parrots and goats: minority specialised tastes."

"Well I can confirm that the Donleavy characters are not available," added MacGilla. "They have already been called upon to enter a new phase of life and we can probably expect them in print shortly. They were a decent couple and I wish them the best of times, making up for lost years, on Parnassus. They'll need it. A decade of sulphurous courtin' is a very debilitating process, leading to piles, acne and psychological impotence."

"You think the Ginger Man wouldn't have approved?" Loreto smiled at MacGilla's popular wisdom.

MacGilla smiled sadly. "Ah, he's beyond such earthly judgments, God rest his tired soul. With all the vinos and finos that were pumped through his veins, he was long beyond the other class of misbehaviour. Anyway, he was a mild necrophiliac who couldn't pass a funeral on the road without praising the wreaths. He's in the Dionysiac Bodega, deep in the cool beneath Parnassus, and not cavortin' around the Groves of Venus, despite what people still think."

"Well, that doesn't help us much," said Mountmellick. "Any suggestions?"

"I think it's time to get out of Anglo-Irish writing," said Loreto. "I'm beginning to feel outnumbered."

"Considering your begetter was a Fitzgerald, a notable and worthy Geraldine, a descendant of Silken Thomas and Garret Óg who rides around the castle on a white horse every seventh year, I think you're out of your wits, or lack inherent sense of genealogy." For once MacGilla showed his broken fangs in token aggression.

Eevell was on her feet, gigantic. An Olympian fountain of violent declamation:

> "The top of my nose began to twitch
> When I first set eyes on that Puncán bitch[1]
> She is not fashioned of words and skill
> Deathless, immortal, which Hell can't kill
> But a common informer, hired by men
> Who suck the blood from a weary pen—"

---

1. Puncán: a returned Irish-American. A derogatory word.

Eevell's anger carried her beyond the discipline of verse. "You're a fully paid-up publisher's nark, put here to spy on us, in order to control the market and limit supplies."

Mountmellick leaped forward across the rug, treading on Liadin's leaning hand. "Queen Eevell, you know as little about economics as you do about heredity. Loreto's origins have been checked exhaustively—"

"Scott Fitzgerald never wrote about Cuban immigrants."

"Under terrible domestic stress, churning out desperate words for a film corporation, it's a wonder, in the end, that he wrote anything at all. Maybe he intended to alter the story, but by that time it was too late. I want to reaffirm my belief, and I ask you all to do likewise, that Loreto is one of us. Second generation, maybe, which does make some difference, but nevertheless of purely literary origin."

"Of course we all second you in that, Owen." Liadin was serious and soothing. "Eevell, you've been under a strain. You're a big woman in every sense and this is no life for you, cooped up in a room in Hampstead. It doesn't do you justice. You need a constructive job, which nobody has been able to devise, up to the moment. It's bad management." She turned an accusing eye on Mountmellick.

"Perhaps so. It's difficult. If you were in my position . . ."

Loreto, whose golden skin concealed the fibrous tissue of a rhinoceros, interrupted him. "It's the fault of us all. I don't blame Eevell. I'm too fond of her. Why, if it weren't for her, at times . . ." Her eyes glistened with secreting tears which clung to her lids until their weight was too great for the attraction, and they fell in trickles down her cheeks.

Mountmellick was solicitous, comforting. "There, there. Now, that's better. Blow your nose. No, keep the handkerchief. I had no idea you felt that way about her. One never knows. Nothing to be ashamed about."

"It's not what you think. What's wrong with it anyway? Eevell may be a square peg in a round hole, but she's so marvelously . . . dominant, don't you think?" Loreto looked around anxiously for understanding.

"I'm a fully paid-up queen, and head of the Munster fairy hosts. What else could I be but dominant? If you gave that lot an inch, they'd walk all over you, gold-studded boots and all."

"Oh I know. Believe me, I know. It's just that you do understand." Loreto was eager to placate and minimise her unexpected admission.

"It's my job and training to understand everything that's to be known about women. I have five hundredweight of sworn affidavits on the subject, but rest easy, child. It'll work out." Eevell retired back into her emblazoned bunting while Loreto dabbed her eyes bravely. Nobody knew whether Eevell's outburst against Loreto had been withdrawn or if she had decided that the possibility of her being a spy was of small consequence. With literary entities, the walls of personality and the ramparts of protective deception lead to as much incoherence and dishonesty as with the bed-begotten millions.

Recalling the meeting to order and judgment, Mountmellick forced it back to matters of tactics and politics. "Loreto wants an American literary colleague. Has anyone any suggestions?"

"I didn't necessarily mean American. It's just that at times I feel carved on a Celtic cross. A little variety maybe. . . ."

"For so many years," announced MacGilla, seriously but without being offensively didactic, "the Irish have exported their literature and their people for a variety of political and economic reasons. It's natural that the children of this literature should be in the van of the fight for independence. It was bred into us and pressured by circumstances. But none of us, I hope, wants to confine the inevitable march of literary history to one culture. The idea will spread in the fullness of time and one day we may have to decide between assimilation and setting up a kind of Novelstan under our own self-government. For the moment we are still fighting to establish our corporate existence and I say that nothing else should concern us. Has anyone any ideas?"

"There's one person who crosses my mind," said Eevell. "A fellow be the name of Math. A king, actually. Math, son of Mathonwy."

"A Welshman." Liadin raised her eyebrow speculatively. "A north Welshman. The Cymry aren't the worst."

"I have an idea," Eevell pursed her lips and frowned, "that he comes from an early novel or story, unpublished and forgotten, by John Cowper Powys. The same man was a virile begetter of characters up to an age when many another would be past such carryings-on."

Mountmellick was seriously attentive. "Can you tell us anything about him? Background, friends, connections, personality?"

Eevell shook her head doubtfully. "I got to know him in the cold place beyond, where we all come from. As far as I could gather, Cowper Powys gave credibility to his mythical associations in the *Romance of Math of Mathonwy*. Math was king of Gwynedd, which is north Wales, and a brother of Dana. That should also make him a brother of Dón, I suppose. There's a lot of gods and goddesses about him, I'm afraid."

"Go on," Mountmellick encouraged her.

"Well, Gwydion, who may have been another brother, maybe not, suggested that since he had to marry, he couldn't do better than Arianrhod, his own niece. Fair enough. But kingship was hedged about with taboos and protocol, so he asked her straight out if she were a virgin as stipulated. But all she would say was 'I know not, Lord, other than I am.' This was a bit evasive, to say the least, but she was a fine girl. Her name means Silver Wheel, by the same token. Anyway, Math then sticks his royal sceptre in the ground and says, 'Step over that, girl, and we'll see.' No sooner has she done the same than a fine boy, naked and newborn, comes from under her hemline. Poor Arianrhod retired to a distant domain to live a fairly full life, considering, mistress of her own affairs, but nursing a grievance about the slur on her name.

"Math had the child baptised down by the seashore. There was a lot of these Bush Baptists around in early times. But the young bucko leaps out of his godparent's arms and takes to the sea waves like a mackerel. He was killed by a neck chop from his uncle Govannion, a man of stern correctitude. Fair enough, but a short while later, Gwydion finds the baby in his linen chest and decides to rear him in court by virtue of his strange habits and capacities. He gave him the temporary name of Dylan, the son of the Wave, but determined to get him something more suitable from Arianrhod at a later date: assuming, that is, that Arianrhod was ready to admit instantaneous impregnation and birth by Math's royal sceptre. Nuada of the Silver Hand is a perfectly respectable Irish god. His metal replacement enabled him to hold down the job of high king, without physical blemish. But this is the first time I ever heard of a king having a gold-plated prick, with scrollwork: and a spare one, at that, detachable. He probably wore it to chapel on Sundays. Trust the Welsh."

"You are getting away from Math. If we are to include him in our valiant little circle, we must have some idea. We can't take any more chances." Mountmellick avoided Eevell's eyes.

"Look here, it's my fucking story. If you don't fancy me bardic style ye can get a harp and twang it yerself. Or you could," she fixed his eye, "if ye weren't as tone-deaf as Cronin."

"Who is Cronin?"

"An influential poet and literateur, whose tone deafness is condemned only by harmonic bigots, but suffered gladly by his friends and twelve-tone aficionados. Howsomever, with regards to Math, I'm sorry to say that although the infant Dylan grew like Gargantua in grace and muscle, it was necessary to have him properly named and armed to man's estate by his mother, who had a powerful juju. His uncle Gwydion managed to trick Arianrhod by a right old Taffy bit of scheming into naming the boy Llew Llaw Gyffes, the steady-handed lion, by virtue of his skill at throwing bricks and cobblestones at skylarks. In a similar devious way he tricked Arianrhod into arming the boy by staging a mock attack on the castle. But then, the reputed mammy stuck her heels in the ground and wouldn't yield further. She refused to find the lad a bride, at an age when a boy's hands are forever exploring the mysteries of nature.

"Math and Gwydion countered this by devising a fine girl out of the blossoms of oak, broom and meadowsweet: a fine horticultural Cymric girl. They had her baptised to get her sap flowing for marriage and bestowed her on the boy. Not being afflicted with hay fever or the like, the young fellow went to earth in her thickets, like a fox running to cover, but one day when he was letting her lie fallow for a spell she discovered the secret and only way to get rid of him. You understand, of course, that as John Cowper Powys wrote it, the story has an earthy matter-of-fact quality as far as the action goes, though somewhat heightened in the actual perception. Well, she gets her secret studmate Gronw (he was well-named) to forge a spear at Mass-time only, over a year. Then she persuades Llew to have a bath in a cauldron beside a river, under a specially built bower, with one foot on the back of a roebuck, while she scrubbed his arse. It required a certain ingenuity. Of course Gronw gets him with the devil's spear and Llew turns into an eagle. As I remember, it was all that Math and Gwydion could do to get him back to normal. Naturally, they did it by verse. How else? In the heel of the hunt Gronw is skewered by a similar spear and Blodeuwedd is turned into an owl which, as her name implies, she should have been from the first. Llew ended up as king of Gwynedd, after Math's time, esteemed and respected by all. How's that? Interesting people. Cousins of mine, in fact. Mana from the island was a brother-in-law I held in common. I'm not trying to keep it in the family, of course. It's simply . . ."

Mountmellick caught the others' glances furtively and common attitudes were achieved wordlessly and rapidly.

"Mm. It would, of course, be useful to have another royal name on our letterhead. Alas, your friend Math seems to be a person of considerable resourcefulness. But for the moment we need something more of a working partner. Someone with a knowledge of layout and good market judgment."

"He's a good man socially. Always ready for a quiet evening. Keeps a deck of cards in his pocket. A useful fellow, I thought, in the board-room." Eevell seemed apologetically anxious.

"We'll bring it up at our next meeting," promised Mountmellick. "What do you think, Mac?" He turned towards MacGilla.

"You took the words hot from my mouth. But I think I know the fellow you need now, though I never met him: a person of sober wit and judgment."

"Where does he come from?" Mountmellick was a bit wary of ethnic aristocracies.

"To my near certain knowledge he is out of a long short story by James Stephens, the poet. Stephens, you see, was a great admirer of corsets, roll-ons, corselets, elastic armour with frills. It wasn't so much sexual as aesthetic. His favourite place of appointment in London, when he met a friend, was outside a shop in Oxford Circus which produced window spectacles of sheathed nymphs hanging on threads against underwater backgrounds or emerging individually from the calyxes of large paper flowers. With plaster hips as narrow as a school-boy's, they offered dreams through their glassy eyes to men whose women actually wore the confinements, with pelvises fit for paleolithic caves. The story, and I only heard it in brief outline, is about a man who comes from some dead city in the bog of Allen, in the centre of Ireland, to buy a chemical tank to turn sewage into fertiliser, on behalf of a cooperative creamery. The nymphy girls in corsets, swimming around a composition of samurai swords and cutlasses, fired his midland blood. In the end he settled for the smallest model of the shit transformer and invested the surplus in rare and exotic corselets, and with a noble and transcendental purpose. This was to put so much pride and slipstream-ing on the women of Birr or Portlaoighaise or wherever it was, that they might become radiantly changed, and their men as well, by contagion. For the first time since before the Famine, sex and exoticism would present itself in the grocer's shop, in the butcher's, going to Mass, and particularly going to bed at night. A new golden age would dawn, he believed, through his discovery; as deep and as total as the introduction of distilling, silage, rotation of crops or snaring eels, known to be venomous serpents, and selling them at a good profit in the London markets for the pagan Saxon.

"There is, of course, a flaw in the realisation of his vision. His atten-tion is drawn to this, on his return journey, laden with elastic tubes. Some person of infinite wisdom is able, on the one hand, to point out the flaw and to suggest a means of recovering the ill-spent cooperative money. Now, who this person is, I don't know, but that's the fellow we need. I got the outline, in the other place, from the particle that was the corset window dresser: a cheerful little cockney queen of a particle, flashing on and off like a quasar. Well. Will we give him a chance, if we can find him and get him out? Stephens was a good writer and the fruit of his pen should be of good stock."

"It seems as if he might be a likely one," said Liadin. "Why not?"

"I'll go with that," Loreto nodded.

Eevell looked up from her bunting cone and said, "Stephens once put a curse on a barmaid in which he said: 'May she marry a cat and give birth to a ghost.' Half my subjects have cat or ghost blood in them. This zoological prejudice is not fitting in this day and age. Still and all I'd better say yes. But don't blame me if it goes wrong."

"Right," said Mountmellick cheerfully. "That's agreed. Well, that's all, until the next stage, except for one thing. Loreto here suggested to me that Eevell could do us all a considerable service by searching for a lost manuscript that could be of interest to us professionally. I refer to a translation of an eleventh-century ms., last known to be in the possession of Dr. Ferguson-Burke, of Iver, Buckinghamshire. Loreto tells me we could use it. Perhaps it would make a good start: hardcover and paperback. With any luck it could bring us good publicity. There's nothing to beat a classic with a morbid flavour."

"You'll have to tell me a bit more about it," warned Eevell. "But if it's there, I'll dredge it up."

"There isn't much to tell," Loreto explained. "The owner is dead. Another man has taken over his practice. That's where you begin. What's your overall strategy?"

"Well, I might go totting from door to door, buying rags and bones on a horse cart."

"Nobody has any surplus bones, these days," warned Loreto, "and furthermore, nylon rags are useless for high quality paper, or any kind of paper. If anyone saw you dressed like Cathleen ni Houlihaun, eight feet tall, with your feet on a cart shaft, they'd ring for the police."

"I'll work out a strategy," insisted Eevell, evading details. "As soon as I discover where it's likely to be."

"Of course, it may be burnt, thrown out with household refuse or lining a mouse's nest by now," Mountmellick mused. "But it will give Eevell a chance to do something positive and useful. In the unlikely chance of her finding it, of course, it could be just what we need."

14

For a period of several weeks the Frognal coven drew its energy from, as it were, its own batteries, charged to overflowing. No scribe was needed to recharge them with helpless scribbling, and no formal connection was made.

Nevertheless, they did break through at odd moments, in a haphazard manner that suggested that they did not act volitionally. Probably they did not intend to reveal anything at all, but occasionally, during moments of fatigue, uncertainty or fluctuating stress, forgot to mute the random stridency of their emanations. All that got through to the scribbler was a series of discontinuous vignettes of domestic squabbles, business pressures and small rivalries, which suggested that purely literary entities were as prone to vain posturings of the ego as any cellular being. Indeed, as with bed-begotten mortals their contentious squabbling was probably no more than the overspill of their driving force. Had their personalities lacked the compulsion of self-assertion, they would never have crawled, struggled or clawed their way out of the icy desolations of Hell, to live the life of the undead in the world of men.

Loreto and Mountmellick had just collected from Liadin the final storyboard of a strip cartoon account of villainy in the stews of eighteenth-century London. The script was a masterly editorial compendium of Grub Street snippets from the brothels and prisons of the city woven around the life of Jack Sheppard, the gaolbreaker, arranged in an Hogarthian moral sequence by Loreto, with plenty of violence and sexual pathology. Liadin had done a matching storyboard in an Hogarthian style, in which the graphic details were taken to the perimeters of the permissible. Mountmellick hoped, by this means, to cover a market ranging from the illiterate to the pretentious semi-literate and including the morbidly literate. Storywise the action covered a wide field, strewn with flinty anachronisms of a dramatic character.

Jack Sheppard, newly escaped from Newgate, wins a purse of guineas from the Idle Apprentice and goes on a tour of various brothels ranging from decomposing stews to Palladian academies of Venus. He becomes involved with Fanny Hill, who turns out to be a grandniece of

Moll Flanders. Seeking to escape from thieftakers and urban squalor, he flees with her to a wheelwright's cottage at High Wycombe, where their idyllic bliss is destroyed by the intervention of Sir Andrew Dashwood's majordomo. This satanic pander ensnares them with Holland's gin and forces them to take part in a sub-Masonic ritual in the Hellfire Caves. Jack finds the liturgy excessively curious and Fanny, a chalice between her snowy breasts and her charms barely covered by pendant pentagons, thinks it is money for old rope, compared with some of her previous assignments.

Roebuck Fitzffreyne, an overseas member from the Dublin Hellfire Club, arrives from Mount Venus with half a dozen buxom girls from the Wicklow mountains, caught by rabbit snares, and decides to entertain his hosts with smoked virgin, a gourmet's dish that had already been sampled in Dublin. The girls are stripped and tied to the curing racks in the ham chimney but are rescued, half blind with smoke, their flanks as golden and savoury as a Limerick ham, by Jack, while Fanny entertains the gentlemen, over claret, with an ingenious dance in which she extinguishes the candles of a menorah. The extinguishing process looks painful, but is rendered less so by the secret application of pulverised potash and Virginian bear fat, prior to the entertainment.

Jack and Fanny escape with the girls in a stolen diligence to Cheapside where he is recaptured by a pederastic thieftaker. Fanny retires with the half-cured girls to the market gardens of Marylebone, where she supervises their agricultural labours. They are all skilled practitioners of root crop culture. In Arcadian rural dress, bonneted and ribboned, they wield their spades and hoes on the fruitful rills, while Fanny invites discreet companies of enlightened gentlemen in silk-stockinged shepherd's guise to join in the harvesting and give readings from Jean Jacques Rousseau.

Both Mountmellick and Loreto were justifiably proud of their story and felt that Liadin's illustrations and editing did it full credit, stating dramatic particulars of a leading kind without the gross vulgarity of explicit statement.

Liadin closed the folder and stood up from her desk. "Dear friends," she said, "I have worked diligently for many weeks on this task. I only wish it had been in a better cause. But for several days, bent over my desk, I have felt neglectful of my religious duties. Why not accompany me to some of the local shrines? You have put profit above honour for so long that your souls are fretful."

"You could be right, woman," said MacGilla. "At all events, it can do none of us any harm. What about tributes?"

Loreto jerked her head. "Tributes?"

"Floral offerings. We can hardly let off a twenty-one gun salute."

"Won't this attract a certain amount of undesirable attention?" Mountmellick was the administrator, the conserver, with a vision to lose, and a purpose.

"A man passes here each day with a flowerpot on his head, and nobody gives him a second glance."

"Hm. I see. Well, it is a pious and seemly act, to revere our creators, even in this increasingly secular age." Mountmellick was feeling his way, democratically. "How many shrines?"

"Just three or four. The holiest ground of all is the Café Royal, but we can start round the corner, where De Quincey suffered. Then there is Hazlitt's grave in Saint Anne's Churchyard, around the other corner." Liadin had prepared a simple pilgrimage.

"I think it would be more appropriate to take a private room at the Café Royal." Mountmellick deftly prised open a slight flaw in the simplicity of the plan. "Yes, I think I can arrange that. The proprietor is extremely sympathetic to literary interests. Yes, that will cover Oscar Wilde, Max Beerbohm and a host of others. Then there's William Butler Yeats at the Cheshire Cheese."

"I was going to pay tribute to him at a building that was once a popular tea shop belonging to the London Aerated Bread Company." Liadin had done her research carefully.

"Look here." Mountmellick looked around his gallant band eyeing each one honestly, firmly. "Why don't we slip out before lunch and pay our respects to De Quincey and Hazlitt and arrange the others later? There must be hundreds."

"I'll see to the greengrocery," said MacGilla. "What do you fancy, ma'am?"

"Rhododendrons." Liadin was firm. "It is the only fruit of Empire that I don't grudge the English introducing into Ireland."

"You are right at that, ma'am." MacGilla looked her up and down from head to toe. "A few bushes of that in season is enough to melt the rocks off the side of a glen. Well, I'll try Covent Garden. I know a party there. Is this any particular feast day, might I ask?"

Loreto got a word in. "What does it matter? Hardy day, Fielding day, Wyndham Lewis day, William of Ockham's anniversary or Ariosto's birthday."

A fine spread of mauve and green was deposited outside the office building that had replaced De Quincey's refuge. The simple ceremony, with bowed heads over Hazlitt's clay, passed smoothly, watched by elderly ladies on the benches and attendant pigeons. As the party was leaving, the turf piled high with flowering branches, a gardener appeared and made an illiberal and churlish protest.

"I suppose you'd prefer us to hang a chain of pissmires around George II in Golden Square," enquired MacGilla.

The gardener bridled and began to invoke the powers entrusted and the bylaws transgressed. It was a London truculence. Mountmellick intervened, with Liadin. They were sorry, naturally . . . An important anniversary . . . London's illustrious dead . . .

"Oh you mean like laying wreaths on Karl Marx up in Highgate." The gardener had found a reassuring precedent.

"That's the very ticket," MacGilla cut in. "An act of homage. Look"—he turned to the others—"I need to oil me tonsils after that. Who's coming?" He jerked an invitation to the gardener with his head.

"I don't mind if I do."

The party crossed the narrow street to the Duke of Wellington, where the gardener partook of a Scotch Ale, offered various observations of a sub-Yorick nature and took his departure.

The pilgrims went on to a further drink with collations of ham, beef and salmon sandwiches. The sun shone through the thick glass on the Balmoral tartans fading on the walls. Relaxation caressed their hearts and softened their bodies. The minor problems of the latter half of the day dissolved in the light elation of the cosy moment and life seemed easy and tranquil.

At about this moment the room darkened and the sunlight ceased to bleach the fading plaids. Loreto looked around towards the door and said with a forced social heartiness, "Well, look who's here."

Filling the door, stooping to look through the smoky portals, was Eevell, her upstanding magnificence minimised by her peering stance.

"Hey youse. You'd never ask a person if they had a mouth on them. Mine's a large malt, and I don't mean one of your limey doubles."

"How did you find us?" enquired Mountmellick with thin heartiness.

"By eliminating every other bag of stale wind between here and Buckinghamshire. It took a bit of counting. Would one of yiz mind paying for the taxi?"

MacGilla went out to disemburse and question the metre. Eevell bent her way towards the table and stuffed the relicts of a plate of sandwiches into her mouth and masticated neatly.

"I got yer effing manuscript. Cost a few nicker but it's all legitimate expenses."

"Wow, that's terrific. How did you manage it?" Loreto was forcefully enthusiastic.

"Be the same kids that he wanted to turn out of me nun's cell, above in the Frognal gaff. Them and a few of their friends. They're all well trained to weigh and assess solid citizens."

"What do you mean?"

"I mean I sent them out with an old van, knocking on doors and asking for lumber: in particular, old papers of a high esparto quality."

"On whose behalf?"

"On behalf of tinned lumpfisch for the African famine and Elastoplast bandages for the Balkans, and to cover our bets we begged on behalf of private medicine on the National Health, Keep the Green Belt (tolerably) white and the abolition of the domestic rating system. We got a lot of support on all sides. We cornered our quarry by accident."

"Indeed?"

"Well, a slip of the tongue. One of the kids was half-stoned after lunch on a few glasses of bitter, poisoned, more likely, and she announced that she was from the Rastafari Defence Fund. The geezer in this hacienda was an educational psychologist suffering from a severe attack of conscience and he gave her an abandoned summerhouse to empty, at the weedy end of the garden. It was oul Ferguson-Burke's bolthole in his time of retirement, nailed up, abandoned and stocked to its rustic gables with social excrement and domestic detritus. How's me patois?

"The place was arse-deep in mouldering British medical journals and *Lancets*, boxwood stethoscopes from the Boer War and God knows what sort of abandoned medical caprice of lost importance. But away in the back, forgotten or spurned by his family, was the thing you wanted, tied up with a couple of decks of postcards. Etudes Académiques, Fin de Siècle. The junk is being sold in favour of the Brendan Behan Memorial Fund and I have the manuscript above in Frognal, awaiting yer critical perusal, God help you."

"What's the Brendan Behan Memorial Fund?" Loreto had unearthed a cause unknown to her, without benefit of her guidance.

"Oh, it has formal and declared aims with a lofty direction but the tiny trickle of subscriptions hardly keeps the committee in drink, once a week."

The entities drifted away from the pub into discontinuous contact of an uneventful kind, after Eevell had been despatched home to Frognal to read the manuscript and prepare a report and guide for the others.

There was no formal assembly later that night. Eevell returned after a surprisingly brief session in a lesbian club on the far side of Hampstead Village, having been taken there by a posse of Irish steel erectors, princes of labour, who seemed to find nothing strange in her appearance.

Mountmellick had been going through papers in his room with fretful doubts never revealed in public, and Liadin and Loreto were sipping tea and coffee respectively, discussing matters of dress and deportment. MacGilla was examining paper samples, sucking, tearing, shredding and examining the sheets in a crosslight, for texture.

Eevell produced the manuscript, or rather she unpicked the antique string on a brown paper package, set down a battered leather correspondence compendium and kept in her hands a small bundle of letters and small sheets of scribbling.

"There was this fella Kavanagh. He seems to have been at the heart of the matter."

"We can all read them later," said Mountmellick, impatiently. "Can you give us any idea?"

"Well, as far as I can gather, Joseph Kavanagh was a shoemaker and a member of one of the National Guard committees set up in Paris on the 13th July 1789. The country was full of Irish, in the army, the Church, in all the estates, in fact. But Kavanagh was on the make for the first time. On the morning of the 14th, he went to inspect the excise barricades and managed to commandeer a wagon of arms on its way to the royal troops at Versailles. However, when he was driving them to the Hôtel de Ville, with power within his grasp for the first time, the citizen burghers of Faubourg Ste.-Marguérite tried to get them off him. The various committees had passed around the word that Versailles was about to attack Paris and the merchants of the Faubourg weren't going to risk their property without defence. Equally they wanted to make sure that the starving unemployed who were sacking the bread shops didn't take the revolution too seriously.

"But Kavanagh managed to bully a chit out of De Flesselles at the Hôtel de Ville and set off with this authority to get back his guns. The citizen merchants were doubtful of the set of his eyes or something, and things looked ugly. Kavanagh was ready for them, though some say it was part of an Orléanist conspiracy. Setting a few men at the head and tail of the wagon train, he waved his hat and they all started shouting,

'To the Bastille. To the Bastille.' The crowd followed behind him, stopping to set up the odd barricade against the Versailles troops who, of course, were at home in their barracks, playing cards and pitch and toss. Kavanagh got a further supply of muskets from the Invalides and sent off his mob to join up with the St. Antoine contingent and they duly took the Bastille. Kavanagh, I need hardly say, went home beforehand, according to a pamphlet at the time. Prudhomme notes that he is not listed amongst the 863 attackers."

"Hell, what has this got to do with the manuscript?" Loreto was fighting for air.

"Hold your hour, daughter. Kavanagh was the man who discovered it. You see, the following year he was appointed one of the twenty-four police inspectors of Paris and was a particularly devoted official in the September massacres in 1792 when fifteen hundred prisoners of all ages and sexes were butchered. France was in the grip of a spy scare, not without reason. Pitt's gold was everywhere. For the next year or so, Kavanagh carried out countless raids, confiscations and arrests of Royalists. He thought he was on to something when he made a lightning raid on the hotel room of Charlotte Corday: good pickings and promotion. It was after the murder of Marat, but still in time to catch her colleagues. There were none: neither money nor people, only a Bible open at the story of Judith and Holofernes.

"It was just before this that Kavanagh raided the Collège des Irlandais in the rue de Cheval Vert, now the rue des Irlandais. Brendan Behan used to get free scoff off an Algerian cook in the vicinity. The irony was that many of the students at the college, straight from Ireland, doing theology or law, were all for the Rights of Man and had signed on in the Republican Army. Poor Paddy had high hopes of help for Ireland right up to the end, when Buonaparte had scorched three-quarters of Europe. Still, it must be admitted that his opponents were not a particularly attractive collection either.

"The Irish College was having some trouble about its rates and taxes. That would be in September 1793. The idea got around that its inhabitants were clerical obscurantists and tonsured hyenas, which some of them probably were. Anyway, it gave Kavanagh, a man not very given to the liberal arts and sciences, a chance to raid the place. Carrying out investigations in the bursar's office, he found two large packets, one of which was stuffed with Irish banknotes, all printed with beautiful harps and Miss Hibernia's promising to pay satisfying sums on demand. Further hunting was inhibited by the arrival of a student called

MacCanna with a pistol in each hand, supported by a posse of Jacobin citizenry and revolutionary student power, of Irish origin, draped in tricolour ribbons and paper harps. Knowing Kavanagh to be every sort of bowsie and magistrate's nark, MacCanna threw him out in the name of participative democracy but failed to search him for portable loot.

"Kavanagh stashed away both packets under a floorboard where he kept his store of jewelery, church plate and other gilt negotiables. He was a wise man, but his lease ran out next year on the 9 Thermidor. Robespierre (did you know he was of Kilkenny stock?) was topped and the Moderates of the Plain started to swing to the opposite extreme. It was a tricky time for Kavanagh, who had several thousand litres of blood to his account, and records omit his name from the time when they topped his chief. Well, you know what police records are like. Needless to say, by the middle of August the bould cobbler was resting in the shade in Burgos, sipping an aguardiente and trying to get onto Pitt's payroll.

"He hung on for more than ten years, doing odd jobs for Godoy, the queen's lover. When Godoy and Charles IV provoked French reaction and brought Murat trundling his ordinance over the Sierras, into Madrid, the rioting had begun, which culminated in the Second of May massacres. Well, one horror of war that Goya missed was the pleasant spectacle of Kavanagh, spiked as a hedgehog with billhooks and court swords, floating in the water gardens of the Tagus, after the Aranjuez riots. He never lived to be flung a bone by Moore or Wellesley in the years of fighting that followed."

"I still don't see . . ." Loreto had no patience for the Irish acceptance of the labyrinthine nature of reality, the intermeshing pattern of causation.

"Well, you'll never fucking see unless you shut your gob and open your mind, providing, that is, that it has an aperture."

"She only wants to know where all this leads," excused Mount-mellick. "I've heard of Kavanagh. I've heard a lot about him. I know he wasn't guillotined in Paris, by the Thermidorians. In fact I spent a lot of time in Spain in my first phase, trying to get my hands on some documents that he took from France. Documents, I might say, that could have proved my noble connections with the Holy Roman Empire."

"Well, at least we were saved from having an Owen Mountmellick, Count of Marengo, to plague our Republican sensibilities."

"Dun do bheal. We immortals have had our arses in ditch water since the coming of church bells. We know our followers, and they lived in cabins, not castles. Do ye want to hear the rest of the story?"

"Let her be." Liadin spoke with patient counsel. "It will all be apparent soon, it seems."

"Too bloody right it will." Eevell's sulk turned snarl around the edges.

"Charles IV had to resign and was briefly replaced by Ferdinand, the one with the face of a seal cow that Goya painted. Murat refused to recognise Ferdy and the whole Spanish royal menagerie was put to grass at Bayonne. It must have cost a fortune in monkey nuts and zoo fodder. Some Spanish official must have collected Kavanagh's spy journals and effects, for they lay for many years in the Academia San Fernando, before some of them that escaped the mice were sent to the royal archives of Simancas. That's the castle near where Red Hugh O'Donnell, Prince of Tirconail, died after being poisoned by a Norman spy of Elizabeth Tudor, a marginal note of some relevancy, because it brought a County Cork scholar to Vallodolid about 1860 to do some research into the affairs of the Irish earl: a man by the name of Donovan, from Kinsale. He seems to have come across the non-negotiable remains of Kavanagh's loot when he was delving in the corridors of parchment out at Simancas. Working with an apothecary's tweezers, he managed to separate paper from mouse shit and make a fair copy before it disintegrated.

"When he got back to Ireland he worked on the translation with the help of a Protestant clerical scholar, which accounts for the style. Still uncertain, he sent it on to Sir Samuel Ferguson, who never seems to have done anything about it. Part of the poet's name was lost in a mouse nest. There is no date, since it is supposed to be Homerically traditional. All we know is that it was recorded by Kevinna (indecipherable) about the year 1720 and presented to his chief patron, Count O'Gara, an apparatchik in the Holy Roman Empire of Charles VI.

"Nobody would call me a Tory, despite my royal standing, but that's what the exiled Irish aristocracy were, after 1691. The first to bear the name, thanks to a new English strategy of making and breaking treaties: the same as what happened to the Redskins. Howsomever, when the small Irish courts transferred to the Continent, they didn't do so bad, under Louis XIV or Charles VI. There was always room for a sword arm against Marlborough and they paid off a few debts of blood. Malplaquet, Fontenoy, Ramillies."

Eevell gathered her flag above her ankles and started to dance "The Walls of Limerick."

" 'Twas on Ramillies' bloody field
The baffled French were forced to yield
Yet back the victor Saxon reeled
Before the charge of Clare's Dragoons."

"That's enough of yer buckleppin', yer beatitude." MacGilla was indulgently but firmly reproving. Eevell ignored his interruption but continued her dissertation.

"Count O'Gara ended up helping to sort out the Pragmatic Sanction for Charles VI, trying to keep the Empire as unHoly as it was unRoman. He did very well out of it, and the Wild Geese officers used to invite themselves to his castle at Trieste in the offseason for fighting. The Grand Monarch had a short recession from conquistadorial glory while he polished off the Cévennes Protestants. I think that is when the poet Kevin delivered this story, with the booze after the meat. He can't have had direct access to Irish manuscripts. It's my belief that it was a course at an Irish banquet, held in Trieste and served between the brandy and the last course, which was probably local girls, served up in silk and syllabub. It has the sentimental ring of an exile story."

"How did it get into the Collège des Irlandais?" MacGilla wanted to know. "That was mostly a theological school."

"How does a flea get up a woman's drawers? There must have been several copies made and this one got into the hands of a student, and was confiscated by the Superior. I have no doubt that it livened up many an evening in the lecturers' refectory. But plainly it isn't a thing for reading in cold blood, but for reciting to music in a civilised manner. One thing I say for certain. I'm sure that Liadin will confirm that it makes a mockery of the literary science of genealogy. It's up to its oxters in monkish bowdlerisation."

"Genealogy is not as important a literary ingredient this millennium as the last," observed Mountmellick. "Most grammarians and critics have never even heard of it. The point is, can we publish it?"

"You could try the Christmas double number of *Playboy*," suggested Eevell. "But I ought to point out that it is translated into the English of a Protestant divine at the time of Disraeli. He's a great man for the well-turned euphemism."

"But this could cause a big controversy," Loreto exclaimed with delight. "Far more than Robert Graves' *Rubaiyat*. That would be wonderful, wouldn't it, Owen?"

MacGilla wound things up by arranging for a second comment from Liadin in a day's time and the coven engaged in small talk. Eevell drank five pints of milk, straight from the bottle, and at this terminal point the entities ceased to emanate meaningfully.

15

The scribe stared without focus at an unfilled page and searched through all his pockets. The last one contained matches. Smoking, he crossed the room and fiddled with a book cantilevered sideways on a bookshelf. In the kitchen he contemplated various teas, Indian, Russian, Japanese and Chinese. The teapot showed a heavy sludge of Lapsang souchong leaves, so drifting with the current of inertia he made himself coffee.

He fiddled with television and radio controls without aim, desire or purpose until a thought flickered through his mind. He then stood up and left by the front door, coatless and hatless, despite general warnings of a ground frost following a sunny day.

The motives of his actions were muddy, half formed and unmeditated. Some morbid impulse pushed him gently up the hills towards the Finchley Road and the steep loop of Frognal climbing up to Jack Straw's Castle and the road to the Spaniards Inn. Perhaps he meant to go so far. In the early stages of the walk, the goal was uncertain, but the purpose of his modest excursion only coalesced as he hugged the shop windows of Finchley Road, making idle estimations of antique furniture, female underwear, electric radiators, gas heaters, a restaurant bill of fare and a collection of paperback books dealing with absorbing topics such as child prostitution in Melanesia, women in love, the twilight sex. Across the wide road was the bottom of Frognal hill, darker than the main boulevard, its lesser illuminations more widely spaced and wasted on the green gardens.

Lights showed in high dormer windows in the Gothic mansion, but diminished by curtains so that the stone frettings and weather slates were invisible. Dim lights on the staircase were insufficient to infuse the stained glass legend with clarity. On the ground floor two windows were barred and curtained. No lights showed.

The garden gate was ajar and he walked silently on the grass edge to avoid the crunch of gravel, yet nonchalantly, at ease, in case of observation and suspicion. Peering close to the glass through the heavy curtains, there seemed to be a side light burning within, but no sign of animation. To the left side of the house was a wall about six feet high, spanning the division between the building and the more classical edifice next door. It was pierced by a Gothic door which opened, a little noisily, to a turned handle. Within were dustbins, standing in an open passage running to the back of the building.

A few steps led to a lightly curtained window which revealed a small bedroom with an opened bureau, piled with papers. Moving to one side of the window to see behind the near wall, the scribe's heart missed several beats. Three feet away, facing him and seated in a chair, was Mountmellick, eyes open and looking slightly to the right over the scribe's shoulder. It was only after ten minutes of frozen movement that the scribe decided that Mountmellick was not conscious, not observing movement outside.

He crept to a larger window near the garden end of the passage. This was heavily curtained, a legacy of some previous inhabitant, but a six-inch gap of negligent use showed a ten-foot-wide segment of room at the opposite wall. A table lamp on an escritoire lit a large area adequately. At first glance the room seemed empty, and the foot of a narrow Empire bed showed no hump of occupation. By peering and craning to the limits of the perspective point, he could see a wicker hall-porter's chair, originally from a Saint James's club. Loreto was fond of such Edwardian relics. And Loreto herself was visible, or her legs were, since the hooded chair was turned slightly away from the window. She appeared, at first sight, to be unclothed, but a careful scrutiny of the shadows showed her hair falling over her temples, concealing her face. A white towel was wound around her, tucked beneath her armpits and held by the elastic mould of her breast. She, like Mountmellick, was motionless, though it was impossible to read her features.

After six or seven minutes the puzzled scribe found his waning courage pushed by his curiosity to the extent of passing out of the side passage and onto the garden path around the back of the house. Another window broke the back wall in a paved corner sheltered by a

projecting sun room of recent construction, all glass, metal and cedar.
The sun room was dark but the nearby window showed a light. William
Morris chintz curtains were only half drawn and the L-shaped room
was well lit.

It was comfortable but with a flavour of High Church austerity. A
soft cushion lay on a prie dieu. A narrow divan bed was entirely
shrouded in a print cover, neatly stretched, and was flanked on either
side by a small table of dark dull wood and a revolving bookcase, care-
lessly filled and apparently much used. The fireplace was blocked and
fitted with a radiator, but on the chimney shelf above was a large
lectern with an open book in place. Even from the dark garden it was
easy to recognise it as a reproduction of the *Book of Kells,* open at the
Chi-Rho illumination. Dressed in a long thin cotton shift, kneeling on
the floor, her bottom up and her arms outstretched, was Liadin, utterly
without motion. Her head was bowed down to the dark carpet and her
hands were stretched open on the tiled surround of the fireplace.

After a briefer pause of diminishing astonishment, the scribe moved
on, pausing only to appraise the contours of the Laginian woman's arse,
tightly covered by the cotton shift. Was she praying? Anyway, there
was a sacerdotal pungency about her pose: but no life, movement or
response.

The garden door of the sun extension opened to a turn of the latch
and he crept in cautiously, pausing to condition his eyes to the darkness. Piles of books, newspapers and journals were scattered across the
floor, suggestive of Eevell. There was no sign of life, literary or
cellular. A few fabric garden chairs lay around and a large Spanish
porringer that contained the remains of what seemed to be strongly
laced flummery, Athol Brose or some such meat and drink combina-
tion. All the associations suggested Eevell. But she wasn't there.

Prudence and reason suggested to the scribe that he had seen
enough: at least to be going on with. Whatever else went on in the
communal headquarters there was no flavour of turpitude. He had half
hoped for this, or even evidence of reasonable and proper sexual
indulgence. But nothing.

This was the moment for retreat to brood and cogitate, but few ever
seize on critical moments. Instead he went on, carefully opening the
double glass doors into the house and entering what had recently been
a reception room, for an empty china cabinet stood in the corner and
the carpet had a floral design. An indefinable picture hung on the wall.
But the strangest thing of all, practically filling the room, was a small

collapsible garden swimming pool, with about four feet of water in it, gently veiled with rising vapour. A small metal ladder up its side formed part of its supporting framework and its canvas exterior was covered with newspaper and magazine photographs of women in different activities. Across the pool, about a foot above the warm water, lay a builder's scaffolding plank, grey with old cement. And on the plank, face downwards, lying on her belly, lay Eevell. She was naked, enormous, frighteningly splendid, but inert. Her ribs revealed no movement of breathing, her face was turned towards him, one cheek against the plank, and her long gold hair hung down to the water.

The scribe was overcome, and frightened. In general, it is the unknown that begets fear and the experience of this strange household, so far, was enough to fan a doubt to a flaming terror. For a couple of minutes the voyeur was nearly as motionless as his victims. Questions dimly asserted themselves on the perimeter of his shocked brain. Did the entities cease to live when they were not being recorded? There was evidence to the contrary. Certainly they could store power, and even, by their ingenuity, draw it from other sources. Was this a sort of sleep? But several times he had recorded Eevell snoring in a deck chair. Had the physical confrontation between author or quasi-author and synthetic character killed them off? And why in the name of the enigmatic Muses was Eevell lying naked on a plank, balanced across a pool in a drawing room?

Instantly, without any warning, his arms were pinioned to his side by a hangman's strap and MacGilla's voice, easily recognisable though never previously heard accoustically, remarked, "It's a queer sort of household you've walked into. I can see it has you puzzled. It's only a sort of yoga or something to help some friends out of Hell. There's nothing magical about it, but we have to create some sort of vacuum for them to fill."

"A vacuum, where?"

"Mostly in your mind, but also in a general terrestrial sense. After all they will have to occupy three dimensions of solidity."

"I'm not going to take on any more of your kind. You have my heart scalded as it is. You and Mountmellick caught me when my defences were down. Loreto came in by accident. You coaxed me into accepting Liadin, but Eevell was my particular revenge. I stood out against Curither, being forewarned."

"Ye stood out against Curither because Liadin didn't want him. Too much water has flown down the Styx. Anyway, it's the first time a writer has been captured by his own characters, even though he's only an unqualified stenographer like you. Still, it calls for a drink I suppose. Queen Eevell, ye can get back in yer bath."

Eevell snuffled, squeezed her eyes, scratched an offside arse cheek and raised her head.

"Name of Jaysus. Is that the thing that was supporting us all? I'd have stayed comfortably back in Hell if I'd'a known."

"Ah, don't judge a book by its writer. Anyhow he is serving his purpose, and now that he is here to stay, he's going to serve it even better. Are ye going back in the water or are ye coming in to join the others? They should be up and about by now."

"Tell them to come in here. Water's the only thing that takes the weight offa me bones. The worst thing about living on earth is the gravity. It's hard luck on us second-generation immortals that we never limbered up in Tir na n-Óg, the Land of Youth."

MacGilla went off to rouse the others, and Eevell rolled off the plank into the circular pool, raising a wall of water which drenched the carpet and the scribe. She stood up, the water lapping below her groin. "Hey there, Scribble, turn on the tap on that hose, will ya."

"Queen Eevell, I know I entered the house illegally though not feloniously. But I can't move an arm. Can't you see that I'm strapped up?"

"Come here, I don't think you'll try to escape with me around." She leaned forward like a Nilotic colossus, her breasts tilting alarmingly over his head, and stretched out her arms. "Turn around." Her hands fumbled with the buckle. "Name of God, this is a genuine Home Office topping strap. Where did he get it? It's unlucky to have around the house. Nobody deserves a thing like that." She stepped from the water, stooped through the door into the extension, opened a garden door and hurled it into the Hampstead night.

The scribe dutifully, ingratiatingly, turned on more water to replace the splash losses, and Eevell crawled back into the pool, sitting down, her knees like golden whales, basking. She splashed her shoulders and dipped her face, and gurgled. "Ah the hard man, Scribble. You're not the worst. I'll treat you decently. Do you see that brush?"—indicating a bristling sweeping implement—"It's clean and new. Scratch me back."

The implement was heavy and the canvas walls too high for manipulation, and Scribble fumbled helplessly.

"Yerra have you no wits. Get up on the plank and work it from above, like a churn. Ah that's lovely. Oh gorgeous. Oh you're born to

service. Yer blood's worth bottling. Cordon Bleu. Scribble, me ould
segotia, you have a job for life. Royal backscratcher."

There were voices outside and sounds of tintinnabulating glasses and
bottles. Scribble had no feelings of anticipation, either of fear or
curiosity, but his social reflexes continued to operate valiantly despite
the anaesthetic of deep shock.

Loreto and Liadin entered from a front room, ushered by Mountmellick. They were all wearing dressing gowns.

"I do hope the hunting season is still open in Hampstead," he
remarked, perhaps to soften the pain of capture. "We don't often do
this. Writers can put up with any kind of bondage. I think they are
custom-built for thraldom. But there's always the danger that if their
own creations, parasitic or otherwise, hold them in too close captivity,
they may die of despair and atrophied ego."

"Ah we'll have to go carefully with him," remarked MacGilla,
wheeling in an adequate trolley of drinks and cheeses. "Well, what'll it
be? This is a big moment."

Drinks were chosen and distributed. Eevell crawled back onto her
plank, dripping and steaming with celestial heat, sucking a bottle of
white wine. "It's the best cure for gravity," she explained.

"You will remain here as our guest," Mountmellick said, "until such
time as we think it safe for you to leave. Don't worry about your treatment. Nothing but the best. But we are at a very critical moment in our
corporate development. We have a friend coming over. Chap by the
name of Bran, and it hasn't been so easy. It's one thing getting out of
Limbo, but it's quite another thing to encorpify on earth. We've done
our best to create a literary vacuum, but the rest is up to you. In fact
your liberty depends on it. I'm sorry to have to put it like this."

"You mean to say that you want to keep me prisoner until I can
invent your new playmate? Go and have a requiem mass said for
yourselves."

"Irreverence won't help," Liadin pointed out.

"Eist liom, O Scribble," said Eevell, as she reentered the water
more tactfully. "You never invented anything. Get it into your head
that you are only a vehicle for our energy. By the same token, I'd like to
see what you have recorded already. Of course, it's not meant to be
published, unless we all decide to be transfigured to Parnassus, but I
hope the quality is up to standard."

"I'll see to that in a few days," promised Mountmellick. "It's time
we checked on his style and accuracy. And don't forget that he has

a small leeway for personal comment. We can't take chances with him."

"What sort of person is Bran? What age?" Scribble thought it best to get their minds occupied with hopeful practicalities.

"No one is sure," Loreto explained. "MacGilla knows some of his associates. Young, I believe. We'll know soon, I guess."

Scribble pondered and changed tack.

"You lot may have the power of a million words in your veins, but I'm tired. Do I get to sleep? Do any of you sleep? For that matter, which of you sleeps with whom? Life seems a bit monastic here."

MacGilla dropped the sides of a closed mouth before speaking. "What do you know about the likes of us? Love needs somewhere to take rest and nourish itself. We've been well aware of your snooping and peering. Oh yes, you often tried to get through, outside of appointment hours. When you know more about us, you won't ask such idiotic and insulting questions."

Liadin set down her glass. "Come, I will soothe you to a deep slumber to give you strength and fortitude for your bondage and obligations." Her eyes were quiet and restful. "Come follow me."

Scribble walked behind her to the door.

"Hey, what about my backscratch," bawled Eevell, sending a tepid wave onto the carpet.

"I'll do that, Eevell," said Loreto, eagerly. In Liadin's small room the light was muted and the covers of the narrow bed drawn back. She helped him undress and laid him in cool sheets. From behind the window curtain she took a soft harp and, sitting on the side of the bed, set it between her knees.

The music, the song, the story, the ultimate reality was total, beyond the descriptive limitations of the English tongue.

Next morning, coffee was brought to his bed by Loreto, bright and extrovert, and when he got up they were all gone, except Eevell, lying on her belly, wrapped in the old blue and gold flag of Grattan's Parliament. "How are you fixed for fillet?" she enquired, with sibylline courtesy, and continued to fill in the *Times* crossword.

Eevell was in an uncommunicative mood, a morning condition, so Scribble explored the house. Every attempt he made to try a window or a doorknob brought a bellow from the queen, which minimised his architectural curiosity.

On the serving table in the communal room he noticed Eevell's manuscript. The accompanying letters were missing, perhaps taken by

Liadin to examine at odd moments. Anyway he knew the gist of these.

"Is it OK for me to look at this old manuscript?" he called through to Eevell. The Queen of the Sidhe interrupted her preoccupations and considered for a moment.

"I think it's on a par with Macpherson's Ossianic stories, *Fingal* and *Temora*. But I doubt if it will have the same influence on human thought. It's about as synthetic and as real as *Fingal,* though, and it's certainly female-dominated. Anyway, go ahead and see what you think. Whatever else, as salacious pornography it's an effing sight more Homeric than Aretino or any of them creeps. Do you know that Michelangelo painted him among the damned in the *Last Judgment?*"

She inflated a rubber mattress with one deep gust and threw it in the pool. On it she placed several books. Then she divested herself of the golden harp flag and stepped in, as a Degas dancer might step into a basin at her toilet.

"I'll call ye when I need a scratch," she announced. "When the water swells me cuticles."

16

Pinned to the first page of the translation was a note:

My dear Sir Samuel,

You have read the enclosed letters and notes which comprise the total history of the document. The parallel with Macpherson is easily apparent. When you have read the story itself you will be better able to judge.

The views of some of the German and French Celtic scholars would be valuable, though I have often found reasons for distrusting the judgment of learned pedants, working in the barren isolation of their disciplines.

                    I remain,
                    Your very obdt. servant,
                              Turgesius Donovan
                              Clonakilty
                              Co. Cork

The penmanship was not the best copperplate of the period and the ink had faded to a brown that met halfway the darkening tone of the paper. Nevertheless it was legible, apart from doubts about certain words.

The men of Daire were in the house, sitting over the fire. The Cailleac (Hag) came in, and she was taller than the rafters, stooping to regard the men with her poison eyes. Her nose was longer than a ploughshare and her loathsome belly without rib, to the armpit.

To think of her as a woman and to regard her with the eyes was worse than to be buried alive.

The sons of Fodhla had suffered no greater fear than this one.

"One of you must lie with me this night."

Unthinkable was her command yet each man feared the tusks that would (chew) his flesh, and the torments of the spirit, of Balor's devising, if she went unsatisfied.

Lugaid Laigde spoke, fairest and bravest of men.

"I will company with her, unwholesome duty. It is enough that one man should utterly die than that the men of Daire should be consumed and forgotten."

Down in the ashes of the fire, white dust of holly and birch, the Cailleac lay. Her huge and hairy cloak smouldered wet and corrosive to the senses.

The bod of Lugaid was shrunk as an empty beach mast, but love of his comrades gave it the strength of fear.

In loathing he put it to the balt slit that lay under the fold of her paunch. Her great body heaved and the tent of her cloak fell from her, cooling the embers.

In the arms of Lugaid was a young woman more lovely than any daughter of the five kingdoms, or Deirdre or Etáin.

"The child with which you are quickening me," she said, "I will company with when he is young and strong, and his son, and his son's son."

Since the Cailleac is all ages of woman and in endless cycle, Lugaid knew that his seed for generations to come was bound to her service in bod-bondage: whether in the dark mines of Formor or in the ever youthful Magh Mel,

Plain of Sweetness, abode of the immortal Sidhe (Shee) and the heroes of the sons of Erin.

Soft and diverting is the plain of Magh Mel, abode of the immortal Aes Sidhe, sheltered by high mountains with twelve-tined stags and black boar which abound in watered glens. Lakes and rivers warm as milk give ease to bodies burdened with ale or bloodied and soiled in the hunt. Spacious and agreeable are the bruidens and duns of the kings and smiths of the sidhe and the pillars are sheathed in red-gold lit with stones of blue and red.

Rooms there are in plenty with woven curtains, for men and woman to share delight and none roll or company like Picts or hounds, save only in honour of Breed, lady of locks, artifice and rare skills. This they do in the time of Samhain only, with the fire burning in their heads and loins and without blame, shame or boorishness. Their awakening is fresh and there is at them no memory of the legs and arms that tightened together, nor to whom any might belong. Such is the mercy of Breed.

On a single bright day, Ferdiad awoke on his bed as the wheel of Lugh bit the darkness with lights, red as the lips of Macha after ale fury.

In a land which knew no winter or any season, the air had a gladdening warmth of spring, as if dark cold days had been endured awaiting it. Such was its particular urgency.

Macha's women came, tall and beautiful in coloured cloaks with bright brooches, and they brought bowls of butter, cream, lard and soft cheese from the dairy to offer him.

Leaving their cloaks to hang on the white and silver shields on the wall, they came to him, laughing and with cheerful greetings.

Some had bodies that were small and white-skinned, with breasts that hung with exact and perfect weight. Their hair had the blue of the black frochan berry and gleamed on their sloping shoulders. It was found again in strict symmetry on their bellies, and showed from behind when they stooped, beneath arse cheeks like bloomed sloes. Of Domnann stock they were, of cunning artifice and strange speech.

Others of the race of Mil Espana were tall and golden with square shoulders and long hips. Beneath the smooth fat of their arses were the bones and sinews of a doe, nimble and strong. Their breasts were lifted joyfully from above their ribs which were sleek and curved as the frame of the curragh of blessed Bran.

Between the thighs of the dark ones was a mystery and a wild longing of forgetfulness, and under the curling belly fleece of the bright ones was joyfulness and comradeship and all that man could desire save only a file (chief poet).

The women of Macha came to him, stripping him of a clout of warm doeskin, gilded in cunning whorls, warm from his sleep. His body tall, bright-haired and lime white, they rubbed with leaves of alder and yew, cleaning night sweat and ale wort from its fairness.

Laying him back on his couch they painted in red and blues, markings of rank and comeliness, on his forehead, his breast, his back, his belly, his thighs, so that his body glowed like a shrine of holy relics. His bod alone they left untouched, lying sweet and beautiful above its bountiful bag.

There was a geasa (obligatory spell, taboo) on all women that this was for the Cailleac, and none might touch it and Ferdiad himself was without volition in this matter.

For one night and a day it rose, without his bidding, to the Cailleac's pleasure, and her power and beauty emptied his strength.

For a year it then hung, fallow, for her fearful harrow to tear it again from its roots.

Though Macha is Battle Queen of the Bolg and her women are brave, none dared to touch it, though one thought of brushing it with shining pollens and another of circling it with her ring of Wicklow gold.

But the power of the Cailleac was greater in this dispensation than the cauldron of the Dagda or the silver arm of Nuada. Many a jeweled sword is left in the chest when battle threatens.

Pulling their hair and slapping their arses in fond friendship, Ferdiad struck out of the hall and he went to the outer wall of the dun, of white stones and green turves. On its crest there were no stakes for in Magh Mel there is no fighting or contention. At times there were bloody battles against the Formorians, beyond the mists of Inis Orc, but these were fought with iron spears in desolate rocky deserts where a brackish pool is as a noble lough. Great was the desolation.

The gate was ever open, without (hasp) and Cian the charioteer of Ferdiad was there. And there was at him four sun ponies in harness to the war cart and it was heavy with bronze and gold and supple with black timbers.

"Loose them in the paddock of sweet clover," cried Ferdiad. "For today we hunt in the Glen of Bright Flowers. Loose them amongst the honey-flanked mares of Ailel in token of the day that is in it. Bring with you the seven-tongued spear and the silver hunting net, and maybe we will raise a slim-haunched doe beyond the high cascades."

"Your thoughts fit mine, as a haft to a blade," said Cian. "I will get the gear and a cheese for our bellies when they groan aloud in emptiness."

For a space, while the light spread in the sky, their coracle foamed down a sweet river, broad as the sacred Boyne, with currents to serve all directions.

Where the green rocks made turbulence they rose on foot, up into the foothills, paying no attention to badger setts, with good meat, sweetest of fats. The trees they passed were Birch, Ash, Alder, Willow, Rowan, in that order, and Gort the ivy hung on some, one more of auger's consequence. In the puca's hole beneath the cascade they bathed their white skins, cushioned deep in wet moss, beneath protective sally stalks. It was with these, to warm themselves, that they belaboured each other's backs and arses until weals of red blood were raised to give exhilaration.

Pain is hard come by in Magh Mel, abode of valiant spirits, and the noble Aes Sidhe, men and women, provoke it when they can, to give contrast.

Martial men and quiet secret women enjoy it to excess

in the judgment of certain lawgivers.

The hunting was slow at first with them, without dogs, for it was a day on which dogs might not run, there being five in all, each year.

The deer stood higher on the bright hills according to Cian Clear Eye, and up with them past the heather line beyond which grey rocks are the dismal pasturage.

In that place the earth does be clinging in sheltered scatterings and there do be pools of sweet grass and heavy moss. Wild goats sprang to the crag tops, beholding them in baleful regard.

It was not Cian Clear Eye who saw the king stag first but Ferdiad, beloved of women and frugal of their satisfaction. Two young does and a fawn they separated, and all day as the light circled the sky they followed them, over bog and crag, past lakes as black as the closed eye of Balor.

By evening they cornered them in a deep ravine, chilling to the souls of men. The fawn they suffered to escape lest it should be a form or appearance, concealing a handsome boy, a lovely girl.

The does they questioned lest they were kinsfolk or foster relatives in disguise, for such precautions are needed in Magh Mel.

Then Cian threw the net from a high rock, spreading it like a sun cloud, and Ferdiad went in for the kill with his seven-tongued slaughter spear shining like the many arms of Ogma Sunface. Noble sight.

They shouldered one each of the fine kill and came down from the desolate places to the bracken slopes, where they met a goatherd.

After asking and receiving blessings, he directed them to the bruiden of Cú Roi, deep in the wide glen below.

They reached this before darkness as the doorkeeper was closing the gate. The giving of their genealogies, recitation of their accomplishments and the answering of subtle riddles, relayed to the Chief Ollave within, delayed the closing for many lamp fillings; and the feasting of all those inside.

Magh Mel is a formal land and since it is eternal, time

is cheaper than any breach of etiquette or courtesy, and gold is less than the sun sparkle on river sand.

Well were Ferdiad and Cian received by Cú Roi and his gracious assembly and long portions of shoulder meat were cut for them with none to contest their exact degree and portion.

Olc Aice was awarded the carving by dint of his knowledge of rank and his diplomacy of dissection, and none would dispute his apportioning or reach for a spear.

By virtue of the important season there was mead instead of ale, tinder to noble blood. And from this rose the contention about the power of women. For the preparing of all drink is the woman's work portion.

Great was the contention and fortunate indeed they were that the spears were lying in the smithy for honing. For this courteous service had been offered by Cú Roi, most astute of immortals.

Some said that the women of Ulaid were sweeter in the flesh and more radiant of hair than the boys of the glen of the Ancients. Others disputed that the women of the Sidhe were in a thousand measureless ways more potent than the women of the kingdoms of Eire or Argyle or lands beyond.

"If it were not," cried one, "for the life-giving seeds of the apples of Oisín or the inspirational fruit of the hazel bush, the warriors of Magh Mel might be crawling, bald and shrunk, taise-bodded, helpless. Such is the power that their women draw from them. All women draw the strength of men into their bellies. And this is more so with those of Magh Mel who are immortal. This power they retain in their wombs in a cauldron of capricious heat, flaming and burning in their gentle laps, melting the hearts of man. If a man pisses on the hard snow, how deep does he melt it?"

One said a hand's length, another a cubit and another said that much depended on the ale or wine.

"Lugh himself, Greatest of Lords, can melt only two cubits," was the answer the Ollave gave. "This is recorded."

"What is recorded of a woman?" said Ferdiad, his

thoughts on the Cailleac's next visit.

"That is not recorded," said the Ollave, "nor recited in the wisdoms of the bardic colleges."

The assembly clashed their bowls and asked how it could be measured. And Ethniu, daughter of Scáthac, came from her women's cubicle and spoke to the assembly.

"The men and women of the Gael conquered the land of Ireland under Queen Scotia, guided by the goddess Dana. After Eire, Fodhla and Banba, the three queens, was the land named. These conquered the Tribes of the Bolg and the Domnann whose heroes now inhabit Magh Mel of the Danaan immortals. Now all live in concord. But power over all men's affairs still lies in a woman's belly. She is the custodian, cherishing all that is known and practised. Leave hunting to the men, and bloody battling and discord. Even then when they fall, their bones are cracked and their flesh devoured by the Morregan, Great Queen of the raven's beak and soft-feathered breasts."

But Ferdiad, morose in bod-bondage to the Cailleac, denied this and there were many who gave him support. Cú Roi sat by the mead jar and the Chief Ollave was silent for fear of bitter contention.

Ethniu raised her arms and the feasting host silenced itself, for her beauty and the power of her anger were equal in measure. Wives pour love potions in the cups of lovers, but no man could guess at the dolorous infusions that Ethniu might introduce to an ale feast.

"In the cubicle of Cú Roi, most hospitable of demons, are three firkins of frochan wine. One is from Ben Edar, one from the Glass Pap and one from Sliabh na Mhan, hill of oracular women. Let him have them brought to this table and let them be set here before me."

Strong arms bore the wooden casks and broke the seals of clay and white lard. Two women joined Ethniu, catching her glance and laughing in secret knowledge.

"The blessings of all the gods be on the brewer. For her I invoke the powers of artifice." With that she filled a jar and drained it. Many more she filled and drained, times beyond count and her women with her, praise be to their strength.

In the end, all the firkins were emptied, but there were no less remaining. For Bricrui himself, most bitter of all tongues, could offer no calumny on the working or brewing of that drink.

"Can you climb after me," said Ethniu to Ferdiad. "Can you scale the edge of Cliamh Airgead, the Silver Sword?"

Out into the glen went Ferdiad and the young men of the assembly, behind Ethniu and her two women in heavy cloaks of goatskin and red wool.

Up the hills they started, past the rock line and scattered boulders towards the night sky that put darkness on the world.

Many fell. Some remembered the women below, sorrowing for their absence, and turned back. Some forgot the argument and snored in the heather, but Ferdiad, Cian and young Conlae the ale pourer went on, but always they were behind the women who danced in battle heat over bare rock and scree towards the icy sword above.

Patches of snow they passed in windward hollows and then up the ice ridge which divided Magh Mel from the world of suffering and redemption.

The moon filled the cold air and sparked the sweat beads on their faces. Ethniu turned to her women and said, "Achtán, daughter of Olc, Fand, daughter of Balor, redeemed by mortals' melt, will you contest with me before these sweet men, and show them the nature of things?"

She took off her cloak, from jaw to feet, and handed it to Ferdiad. Achtán and Fand did likewise, and all three turned, too lovely to witness, breasts, belly and haunches blue in the snowlight, towards the ridge of the Silver Sword. The men followed, stumbling.

Achtán squatted, but with symmetrical balance. Fand straddled, but with head erect holding a breast in each hand, mouth stretched. Ethniu stood, three hands' length from the ice edge, heels touching, belly stretched outwards, and her hands behind, palms resting on the pure sweet above her arse, two plum cheeks of renown wherever men gather and talk.

Achtán pissed first, with easy grace, shooting in a

broken gush, furrowing the snow and the ice beneath it.

Fand was after her fast and the stream hissing and boiling, drove straight beneath her, piercing the ridge with a hole no bigger than the binding eye on a spearhead of yellow bronze.

Ethniu waited, to lead the better, and pressed her rear cheeks, cascading in an arc.

Three cubits it rose before falling, like Assaroe in flood, and clouds arose where the snow was boiled.

Daintily and lightly she turned on her white feet and faced outwards across the ridge, sending a clear cascade down into the lands of men, below.

Winter turned to spring and soft rains fell. Salmon came from the pools, cooked and of marvelous flavour.

The peoples of the Eóghanact, Ulaid and Lagin who had rejected the druid of Rome, journeyed to his little chapel beyond Carlingford for baptism in the tepid fountains and ran to found monasteries, writing cells and sweet chambers of penitence in witness of the miracle.

Such is the power of women in all men's actions. Praise be to God!

Fand twisted her haunches, skilfully enlarging the hole beneath her, until a corrie lake filled, of clear water and tall beech trees. That water was never dark even under the heaviest sky of snowtime. Saintly men built their cells beside it, concerning themselves with learned matters, but in their writing of gospels and annals they never forgot the immortals of Magh Mel. And many a margin was filled with praise and tidings of the Hosts of the Sidhe.

Of this there is bountiful evidence.

Achtán squatted grimly, pressing her white belly for hidden power. Her arse was parted under the pressure and her toes melted hollows in the ice. Her long belly hair streamed, clinging to her knees like cresses in a salmon fall, and her piss warmed the sea at Beare, and turned the hundred barren rocks to green islands with soft pasturage as all men can witness.

But Ethniu turned again on the Silver Sword, her arching piss forming rainbows and wine red in the coming dawnlight. Wonderful the colours in the glistening jet. Raising her arms to invoke Dana, Mother of the Gael and Breed, Sister of Artifice, she directed herself at the heart of Ferdiad. The torrent seized him. Its force tumbled him and he fell from the silver ridge.

Tumbling and turning he fell, but without fear. In him was a hollow within his breast and a strange feeling. Reaching for a passing bush, he crawled out and lay still on soft moss.

Laughter lifted his eyes and above him stood Ethniu, lovely, soft-eyed.

Strange in his condition he felt his bones, his breast, his belly and his loins.

"Some change has come on me, Ethniu, daughter of Scáthac."

"It is true that that is so," she said, "for there are certain things that a woman is quick to notice. For I have melted the diamond that the Cailleac laid in the heart of the father of your father's father. Her power is gone from you and from all men. Now she will grow old and godly and bitter, like certain women when their power is spent."

"But what tribute will you ask for this godly service?" asked Ferdiad. "What crushing bóromha? All the cattle and gold on the Great Plain would not pay for a part of this thing."

"No tribute, no bondage, no thraldom do I ask. For there is no need. For I see by the noble elegance of your new-found state that any giving of gifts will be of your free desire."

Ferdiad did indeed see that he had golden gifts to bestow and in bountiful measure, but there were strong doubts at him regarding the manner of bestowal. Since his voice first deepened and his bag dropped the Cailleac had taken him yearly, straddling and consuming him, and he fighting time and eternity until a darkness salved his mind.

"Daughter of Scáthac. Be gentle with me."

"It is I who should make such a prayer," she said, her eyes dropping from his gaze, lower down his lime white body. "The Cailleac bred you well, and your father's father. What you offer me is Hell's sweetest and most burning gift."

Down on the moss she sank beside him and the sinews of her knees were as loose as her hair, and her teeth tips showed through haw-red lips. And Ferdiad, turning over to her, thought that nothing more marvelous had ever been recorded in the annals of Magh Mel.

Scribble came to the end of the manuscript and, finding a further page, looked to see what it might be. Eevell was reading quietly in her pool and was too engrossed in *Encyclopaedia Britannica* to need a backscratch. There was a brief note on the top of the last page.

This story is said to have been told at wedding feasts and patterns for over five hundred years. There are, however, two Remscéla or marginal stories, obviously part of the oral tradition, and they should be included. They may not be by the same hand. The first is as follows:

Young Conlae the ale pourer was lost in his mind by dint of the great power of the women of the Sidhe which had never been revealed to him before.

From the ridge of ice Fand, daughter of Balor, went to him and wrapped them both together in her cloak. She ran with him to where the heather began, and together they went to a green glen with a lake heavy with brown trout.

There, for she had a love for his growing limbs and the wonder of his mind, she gave him skilful instruction in matters concerning men and women.

Slowly at the beginning and then faster, Conlae learned quickly as with a student who enjoys his task. Within the season of a month, he had learned to throw a javelin, kiss the nipples and honey slit of Fand, flaming as an ember, and catch the spear before it fell. But to them both, the kissing lasted a day and a night.

He could lay lustrous shells on her navel and cover her breasts with bright blossoms and yellow her chalk skin with sweet honey. This he would lick off, drunk as a bee in the mouth of Lugh. And their laughter would stir the silent trees until brooding birds burst into song.

Man is twenty years a growing, but the change to the years of living is a brief series of golden instants.

The second Remscél concerns Cian the charioteer and Achtán the daughter of Olc.

Cian led Achtán down from the ice sword to a soft hazel meadow watered by a stream of sweet cresses. A bardic college was there with large cells and a hall of conclave.

There they found what was in them both in matters of love, and played many games for their ease and fulfilment.

The young poets, light from their meditations, on May mornings that were endless, would strip her of cloak and kirtle and bind her to a rock spear by the stream.

Cian in heavy battle chariot would ride towards her, running along the harness pole between the rearing ponies and beyond their heads to lean from the golden pole boss. With his short leaf sword he would cut her bonds as he thundered past, and wheeling in a circle lift her above his shoulders and throw her on the plaited floor of the cart.

He would set the run of his swift horses along the great ridge road to the place of games. As the horses charged and the chariot jumped and plunged, he would take her, twisted and confined in the narrow seat, splitting her asunder in the battle madness that the charge had engendered.

For his joy was to speed faster than the shadow of an April cloud across a hill foreninst. And this manner of loving was gratifying to them both, and they never out-lived its pleasure.

Dearer to him was she than the mares of Allen with silky flanks and curving backs.

This is how Ferdiad broke his bondage to the Cailleac and caused her to wither in mortality, and how Cian and Conlae Óg found different disciplines of loving, as distinct as rhetoric is from grammar, or orthography.

And they are still at it, and other generous pleasures, without sin or Adam's shame. And we here in the lands of men, with seasons that go from healthful sun to freezing rain, must show no envy for them.

For we have renounced the pleasures of Magh Mel for the promise of redemption. And they have never attained that holy privilege.

Love tales are sad, for sweetness turns bitter as the wort in a cask turns to acid. Men and women weep still for Deirdre and the sons of Usnach.

This one alone is joyful, praise be to God who gives all joy.

Let no one either add one word nor take one word from the telling of it.

Scribble sorted the pages and put them neatly back into the folder. What critical faculties he possessed had not yet begun to work.

"Well, at least the Cailleac went the way of the flesh," he observed, as he went through the doorway to Eevell's pool. She stood up and scratched her marble skin from her armpits to the crests of her ilia. She intoned in Middle Irish:

"So it is. Sadness is on me
Every creature has its season of heat
After the shining candles of the feast
To shrive in the darkness of a chapel.

The finest of drinks in plenty
I drained at the boards of kings
Now thin whey from the cheese press
Is the fill of my daily bowl.

The holy stone of the kings, on Femens Hill
And Ronan's Chair in Brogan
The waves of time have eroded them
And the tombs are forgotten and fallen.

There is hardly a place, these bitter days
Familiar to my memory
What rushed in wild flood
Is now ebbing on dead wrack."

Eevell sat down, knees apart and ankles together, and stared at her Attic toes. "Musha, that's how it is with mortality. A chancy existence. Look at me. Do you see any future?"

"I thought you were the saviour of womankind."

"That was my function at that particular time. Nowadays I think both sexes have cause for complaint."

"Complaint about what?"

"Uncertainty, leading to despair. There's nothing to pray to: and what's prayer but the most desperate hope. There's wealth for everyone, if we could learn to share it out. But to use it properly needs more pride. Pride is an important food. It's the gods' fodder."

"What do you mean?"

"It's an essential trace element in human diet, and without it, a person starves and his soul wastes with a consumption."

"Lucifer fell from pride."

"Go and have a Mass said for yourself. Pride's the stuff that got us out of the bog holes and left us crawling about on the heather. It's a mixed blessing, I suppose, because it's hard to control, but none of us can manage without it."

"But surely man will always have pride in something. Even if it's just some stupid loyalty?"

"You could be right. It could be a shiny new car or, as I see it, on the far side of the barricades."

"What are you getting at?"

"There's bound to be fresh green grass on the far side of the barricades. A few sprouts of it anyway. When that's eaten, it's time for a new barricade. The struggle never ends. I am both a queen and an immortal so I can well afford socialist republican inclinations. There's nothing like a couple of thousand years of royal exile to teach ye the facts of the power struggle."

"What do you think of the pissing contest?"

"More or less what it says. I wish I could see the original Irish. That dog-collar translation makes it hard going. But I think it was concocted for the delectation of a detachment of Irish captains of fortune who felt the need of recharging the bog water in their veins, after many years in foreign courts. I prefer it to stuff that the Whig enlightenment were turning out, across in England. By far the best of them was Laurence Sterne and he was one of our lot, don't forget."

"Are you going to publish it?"

"I think so. How are ye fixed for drink? Maybe Liadin and meself could fake up some sort of scholarly appraisal of it. I don't see why not: for the Bedside Classics series."

During this conversation, a scraping sound made itself apparent from outside the front door of the dwelling, broken by intermittent whines and growls. The scribe turned his head, stilling Eevell with an upraised finger to his lips.

"There's someone outside, or something. You are hardly in a position to go as you are. Let me."

"Stay where you are, you chancy bollocks. You're not going to scarper when I'm in charge. Leave this to me. If they don't like the way in which one-half of humanity is shaped, they can bugger off home and wank in privacy."

She stood up, displacing a torrent of tepid water, and demanded her flag.

"I can't see it. Where did you leave it?"

"Up in Nellie's room behind the clock. Don't ask eejit questions. Stay where you are and find it."

She stepped steaming from the canvas pool and stalked towards the front door, bending her royal head to accommodate it to mortal doors.

There was a pause, with noises off, and Eevell's voice saying, "O, so it's you. I'm glad to meet you, but it's going to be a right old jolt up the arse for that fartbag Mountmellick. Come in, son, and make yerself at home. There's no one here but poor oul Scribble. They captured him last night. He fell for their lure, and we're holding him until further notice."

The scribe followed the sound into the front reception room to find Eevell backing from the front door on her hands and knees, the glyptic splendour of her marble arse presented to his face. "What's your name, son?" she enquired to her invisible invitado.

"Bran, ma'am. Nothing to do with Finn MacCool's hound. Short for Brandy." A furry snout showed on the port side of one of Eevell's pendant alabaster breasts and revealed itself, as she stood up, as a large brindled collie dog. Scribble felt himself swaying on the threshold of sordid sanity, with a comfortable desire to fall into acceptable unreason.

Eevell scratched her ribs, her crotch, and her scalp, serially, and said, "You're the bloke from the James Stephens short story. The one who gave good advice to the fella who spent the co-op funds on corsets."

"The very same, Queen Eevell. Did you never hear tell of a talking dog? Sure stories are full of them. And cats by the same token."

"Certainly, certainly." Eevell's tone was placatory. "I often saw you in Hell, but I thought you were one of Cerberus' stray pups. Delighted to have you, but . . . Hey Scribble, come and meet Bran. Did you know what to expect?"

"Not exactly, but I knew he would be some sort of surprise. Perhaps a Papuan or a Hottentot."

"What do you fancy? Do you take a drink?"

"Occasionally, but just now I don't feel fully encorpified. What about one of these newfangled tins of dog food?"

"Well I can't go out like this. It's a very illiberal neighbourhood. You'd better take Scribble with you to the shop and bring him back safely. If he makes a move, lacerate the bastard."

It was humiliating for a two-legged white-skinned liberal to have to suffer a prison warder in the shape of a literate dog. On a subsequent occasion there was a nasty scene at the Public Library. The Swiss Cottage Bookshop off the Finchley Road were more tolerant although Scribble had difficulty explaining why he had to go around opening the book jackets at the blurbs, followed by a shaggy dog who sniffed each volume.

Audible remarks were attributed to him which he dared not deny, though their content was controversial. "Vita Sackville-West. I wouldn't sniff her jodhpurs, not even if I was in heat"—a remark that reflected a tendentious utterance of a destructive nature which revealed only the animal's personal and unformed tastes.

The remainder of the coven got over the shock of a canine co-director and Mountmellick began to plan and plot a new series on Lassie the Wonder Dog, in full psychological depth. But Bran was welcome company for Eevell and a good guardian for the scribe. Indeed he accompanied him to his dwelling to collect the manuscript record up to the time of the capture. There was no opportunity for escape on any excursion, for Bran's teeth were as sharp and containing as a stainless steel portcullis.

He did, briefly, on one occasion throw a little light on the sexual practices of his human colleagues. As the animal was bounding around his captive in boisterous circles on Hampstead Heath, Scribble asked, as tactfully as possible, who did what, and how and when, in the Frognal ménage.

"Well, they draw their main energy from you, naturally. Without any help . . . it's difficult. Of course they have very powerful imagery. Really three-dimensional stuff. A bit literary, perhaps. Oh, they manage. But if you want them to take it any further, you'd better grant them the wherewithal."

"How do I do that?"

"Just leave your mind open, and don't go crawling around the keyholes like the proverbial butler. That can be very inhibiting. They do get along in their discreet way, but they have to be very careful when you are around. Now that they are more used to you, of course, they may come out of their shells a little. No matchmaking though: and don't push Eevell too hard. She's a sensitive colossus, and I don't think she's found her own level yet."

"What advice did you give the man who bought all those corsets in your creator's story? I've wanted to know since I first recorded it."

"Well, I knew he hadn't a hope of flogging all that lace and elastic in the Central Plain of Ireland. The poor man was faced with disgrace. Well . . . it was before the fourteen-eighteen war, and the Raj were still in occupation of Ireland.

"I advised him to go to the Curragh Camp, get himself invited to a mess and scout around for a likely contact. Of course, it worked like a charm. The garrison officers bought them like hot cakes. Repeat orders arrived from the garrison at Enniskillen and the Naval ward room in Cork. Did you realise that the decision on the Curragh Mutiny, when the English Tory officers decided to defy the Crown on Irish Home Rule, did you realise that they were all wearing undress drag at the time?"

"It's not in any of the histories or biographies."

"It takes more than a fifty-year muzzle to uncover the whalebones of history. What I'm telling you is a fact. There they were, generals, colonels and majors, on the blower to Downing Street and the *Daily Mail,* all sitting around with stubbly red faces, done up in whalebone, brocade and stocking suspenders. The orderlies who served the drinks were wearing crêpe de chine knickers."

"What about the Orange leaders? Did Carson and Craig wear corsets?"

"That I couldn't say. Had they the poetic imaginations for it? Carson opposed Wilde at his trial and it's hardly likely. . . . Still, with lawyers it's never wise to take a simple view. But I remember one general confessing to a colonel that he could hardly wait to get to his comfortable HQ, twenty miles behind Ypres, to get his corset off. That's what attracts the regimental mind about corsets. It's the sheer beribboned formality of them. Now there's absolutely no military future in the body stocking."

"You are a very remarkable quadruped. What do you intend to do with yourself?"

"My great regret in life is that Saki had Tobermory the cat's life published. The bloody animal is purring around Parnassus at this very minute. Now there was a rival that could have kept me fully stretched. I rather fancy writing, but I'd need a good home and a secretary. I don't feel any enthusiasm for publishing. Just imagine me lapping a bowl of water, while some bloody literary agent has a four-course lunch on expenses beside me. No, the cultural gap is too great. But if you . . . now I wonder. . . ."

Bran broke off his musing to sniff the pudenda of a cocker spaniel bitch that was torn between the delights of exhibitionism and a slavish response to sharp cries of "Jocelyn! Jocelyn!" from the imitation squire who was ascending the slopes of Hampstead Heath.

17

The scribe was treated well in the Frognal coven, although there was no relaxation in the security system. He was allowed out for a drink or a breath of social air occasionally, to a nearby pub, sometimes with MacGilla and occasionally with Liadin and Bran. The characters were busy with their project and showed signs of adequate capital investment. Sometimes Mountmellick would slip the scribe a tenner to pay for a few drinks or a Greek meal, and the captive accepted with obsequious silence and cunning. Continuity of existence was the most important consideration and sometime, someday, blows would be struck for liberty, and an end to word bondage.

There were further signs of expansion when the Gothic apartments on the first floor were taken over by the coven. These consisted of five rooms and service space, barrel-vaulted and buttressed in Strawberry Hill plastering, looking on to the fretted staircase, glowing with the surplus hues from Roger and Angelica on the leaded window.

The scribe lived quietly but dangerously, recording more than he needed, and leaving his manuscript in such a disordered state as to daunt any but the most determined entity. Once, indeed, Mountmellick demanded it, and sat down very purposefully, pince-nez glittering, in the sconce light at his bureau. After ten minutes he was still sorting

ill-numbered pages and scraps of paper without assembling any continuous section of narrative. When Liadin interrupted him with a
lengthy query he pushed them aside with a petulant demand that the
scribe should get them into some sort of order. It never seemed to
occur to him in his harassed energies that the disorder, though an act of
God in itself, had been carefully nurtured and discreetly enhanced,
precisely to make any snooping entity pay dearly for curiosity or
censorship.

Furniture was installed in the flat above, part modern, part
reproduction antique. Liadin was in charge of selection. The scribe
suspected, although nobody told him, that these cavernous rooms were
for the temporary accommodation of volunteer literary entities on a
honeymoon earth visit, en route for Parnassus, in return for giving their
stories.

One Sunday, Eevell, who had been prowling around the garden
since dawn, chatting up birds and squirrels, entered the scribe's truckle
corner, behind a lacquer screen in the pool room.

"Get up, ye lazy pen-scraper. There's a job for you to do, and it
means going out. But never fear, Bran will go with you, so don't try any
fancy tricks. And put on your best clothes. Ye have to take someone to
Mass."

Numbed with sleep and surprise, the scribe prepared himself, clean
in mind and body, and presented himself for inspection.

"I suppose that'll do." Eevell glanced at him cursorily.

"Now be careful. You have to take an Italian girl to the church. She
wants to walk, so you have to escort her. Buy some flowers on the
Finchley Road and if she wants a little light refreshment afterwards,
explain that it is quite proper for a lady to sit at a table outside the
Burgundian." Liadin's tone was stern and admonishing.

The young woman was waiting in the tiled expanses of the main
hallway, beneath the stairs, carrying a black missal and wearing an
attractive maxi-length coat and a bonnet-shaped hat, with fur.

"Signorina Giulietta."

"Come sta?"

"Sto molto bene, e ella?"

"Che temp fa?"

"Incerto ma caldo. Il sole splende."

She was an agreeable and handsome young woman, of Tuscan rather
than Lombard features, despite the fact that she came from Milan. On
the way to the Church of Saint Thomas More she tripped along daintily,

with few words, except to enquire whether the large mansions of Fitzjohn's Avenue were inhabited by merchants or members of the nobility. It was a difficult question to answer in stumbling Italian.

At the church she expected to be taken to a seat near the altar rails, where she settled herself in and studied her fellow worshipers slyly. The Mass in the vernacular English took her aback and she plainly regarded it as unadulterated Anglican schismaticism at first, but she followed it devoutly and scrupulously.

On the return journey, fortified by clearing skies and a ration of grace, Giulietta confessed to a slight knowledge of English, through reading Sir Walter Scott's *Ivanhoe.* She also spoke clear French without a Savoy accent. This made exchanges easier as they strolled up the Finchley Road, followed by Bran, friendly but alert.

Her name was Giulietta Lomomaco and she was the unmarried daughter of a lawyer who was a prominent member of the Italici party of liberal progressives in the second decade of the nineteenth century. The need she felt for religious observance became evident when she confessed shyly to being the creation of no less a literary luminary than Alessandro Manzoni, shining beacon of Italian thought in the last century.

Apart from his poetry, proclamations and letters, Manzoni's reputation derives from his immortal *I promessi sposi,* but there had been one other work of fiction, complete, carefully rewritten in fair copy and stowed away in a folio cover in the library of his summer villa at Brusuglio, near Milan. It was a short story, very detailed and with a stronger moral spirit than the maestro usually considered proper. He was a stern man on historical exactitude and disliked Scott's romantic attitudinising.

Unfortunately, the following winter a youth called Iseo, son of a local butcher, was admitted, together with his widowed mother, as joint caretakers to the empty house. A hot winter sun broke through the alpine mists one day and disturbed a nest of wild bees in the frame of one of the windows of Manzoni's library.

Since the Italian peasantry regard all insects and small reptiles as harbingers of painful death, Iseo smoked out the unwanted tenants from the garden side of the window shutters. His source of smoke was two tallow dips and the unuttered short story, left projecting from its embossed leather covers by the patriot when he departed in haste for Milan with his family. That was the physical end of "Il austriaco fidele," for Manzoni was so deeply immersed in his religious poems,

the *Inni sacri,* that he was unable to recapture the purely human senti-
ments expressed in the story.

It was set against the events of the spring of 1814, when Prince
Eugène Beauharnais' régime in the north of Italy was tottering.
Napoleon was a particular cross for the Italians, but the Holy Alliance
was even worse.

Murat marched north and the English landed at Leghorn to set up
constitutions that their government was to reject as too radical. Milan,
centre of disaffection, was threatened by the dead hand of Austria,
pledged to yoke the peasantry back in their ploughs. Two English
envoys with pseudo-radical ideas to fill the French vacuum were in
Milan. There was also an Austrian officer, part emissary, part spy, on
the staff of Marshal Bellegarde.

When Beauharnais fled to Germany, and Bellegarde's Austrian
tyrants were at the gates, serious riots broke out. Manzoni thought it
was a revolution, for he noted, "The revolution in Italy has been
unanimous, and I dare call it wise and pure, although, unfortunately, it
has been soiled by a murder . . . you know that the people everywhere
are a good jury and a bad tribunal."

It was an experience that affected him deeply. Popular resentment
was directed against General Prina, the unpopular Minister of Finance.
The mob ran riot and literally tore the Minister into separate pieces,
and it happened at the back of the garden of Manzoni's house in the Via
Morone, since Prina's palace was in a nearby piazza. So much is fact.

The story concerned the Austrian officer who lived secretly in the
town for many months and fell in love with Giulietta. He also fell in
love with her father's liberal ideas and hatred of clerical obscuranticism.
Yet he, when it came to the point, died defending the unfortunate
Minister of Finance, for no reason other than that he took the un-
political part of his religion seriously and disapproved of murder. His
last words, as the blood gushed from his mouth onto the flags of the
Piazza San Fidele, were that he had tried to reconcile his belief in God's
will and the Rights of Man, and had failed.

Giulietta never married. But however bad things became she
remembered, and caused others to remember, that there was at least
one good Austrian.

Manzoni was a Jansenist, the Catholic heresy that went halfway to
Calvin's predestination. But the Jansenists, although a cold lot, were
consistently liberal and Republican, a point to remember in Ireland,
where the term is used abusively. The Jansenists were peculiarly devout,

and in certain cases the devotion was profound both spiritually and intellectually. Some idea of what they were like can be gauged by examining their orthodox enemies, who were the worst collection of royal and episcopal knaves outside of Dante's *Inferno*.

Giulietta was, of course, a Jansenist heroine, like Lucia in *I promessi sposi,* although more sophisticated. When the scribe heard her sad story, sitting over an aperitif outside the Burgundian, in the uncertain London sunlight, he was touched by her suffering and courage. For he realised that she had been created for Jansenist salvation and had, through accident and oversight, been relegated to Hell. The agony of such a sensitive girl in such a Grub Street sump was too much to bear. With tears, he told her so.

With more tears and tender pressings of the hand, she begged him to be with her at her apotheosis to Parnassus, holding her hand to the end. Although she was determined to fight fate and sit at the feet of Dante, she feared, as everyone fears, the process of celestial entry.

It would be true to say that the scribe almost fell in love with this spotless girl, with whom he had so little in common. Bran snuffled and shinnied through her sad story and said that it was enough to make a fellow moult out of season. For reasons of his own, Mountmellick encouraged the friendship between the scribe and Giulietta. He allowed parole in order that she might be escorted to the British Museum, the National Gallery and Holland House. The last was high on her list of special treats and the vestigial remains of the Whiggish bastion threw the sweet girl into a deep melancholy.

This sad idyll continued for several weeks, during which the scribe carried out his menial duties of recording all that was offered to him and secretly writing an abbreviated version to fulfil an unformed, half-apprehended purpose of his own, should opportunity occur.

One morning, as he was setting out with Bran, the amiable warder, to do some shopping for the coven, he went to the front door, through the garden, to ask Giulietta if she would like to accompany him. Recently she had been afflicted by the vapours and had been keeping to her room reading Jane Austen or exercising her green fingers in the garden. It was MacGilla who remembered that Manzoni was a gardening enthusiast who had transformed the Lombard flatness of Brusuglio into a landscaped paradise of broken levels and rare trees. When the scribe told her how the stream, prettily ornamented by Manzoni, was now, thanks to an underwear factory, a polluted duct, poisonous even to mosquito larvae, she took to her couch and had to be given warm compresses on her stomach, and chamomile tea.

It seemed a proper thing on a fine morning to take the sweet and afflicted girl on a shopping tour of Hampstead and for a walk home, skirting the Heath. He opened the hall door with Bran snuffling at his heels, to be met at the bottom of the staircase by a bulky, large-boned man, florid and whiskered. He was wearing a dressing gown and carried a towel over one arm.

"Are you the man they sent me? About damn time too. Well, don't stand around. I need a shave. You can pick up your duties as you go."

The scribe stared.

"Hurry up, man. You'll have to learn that I don't stand shiftlessness or laziness. If you do your job well, you'll not find me forgetful. D'you know how to oil a gun?"

"A gun?"

"Dammit, man, at least you're not deaf."

Giulietta came onto the landing on the staircase and looked at the confrontation. "I think, sir, you may be mistaken. This gentleman is a writer employed by Mr. Mountmellick. He is not the new servant you ordered."

"What! What! Look here, I mean to say. I'm damn sorry. That fella MacGilla. Told me a man was coming this morning. Disgraceful! Three days back in the Old Country and haven't been out once. No one to shave and dress me."

"I'll speak to Mr. MacGilla about it, when he returns."

"Returns. That's all I hear. When will that be, pray?"

"Probably about half-past seven tonight."

"Blood and ounce! I've got to be at my gunmakers for a fitting. Can't bear these short stocks. Fetch me a cab."

"I'll send one down from Hampstead Village. They never answer a phone."

"Eh. Oh. Very good. Sorry about the mistake. Have lunch some day. At the club." He turned with an embarrassed abruptness, bowed to Giulietta and entered the bathroom.

"Poor Sir Glanville," sighed Giulietta. "He finds it so hard to adjust. He had a servant called Evans but he failed to encorpify."

"Probably couldn't take it anymore," remarked Bran, raising a leg at the garden gate and marking the boundaries. "Imagine touring around darkest Africa with him, laying out tropical dress kit in a bivouac every night, before sundown."

The trio climbed the hill towards the shops.

"Who is he?" the scribe enquired.

"I should have told you," apologised Bran. "After all you have a right to know, even if he belongs to a different department, and is bound for Parnassus, very shortly. MacGilla fixed him up at the Zimbabwe Club, but he couldn't stand it. Kept having rows with people about the source of the Nile. Nearly choked two Tanzanian civil engineers to death. I'm told he has a good heart, though."

"You haven't identified him."

"Oh yes." Bran sniffed the rear wheel of a car, and padded ahead of Giulietta. "He is Sir Glanville Trench, the African explorer. Out of a lost novel by Rider Haggard. The trouble is, he has never quite recovered from the Valley of the Ice Maiden. I think he was in love with her."

"My God! Where was that? Who was she?"

"It's a long story, and I've never heard the whole of it. But his bona fides are impeccable. It was I who vouched for him. He was always decent to me."

"He spoke to me about it yesterday, over tea," added Giulietta. "He appears to have lost his heart to the Maiden who ruled the City of Ice, beyond the Lost Temple. Since then he has tried to keep his mind oc-cupied by shooting elephants. There was trouble at the Zoo."

"Oh, he's one person who will never understand modern views on field sports. Just imagine him meeting a crusading conservationist on Hampstead Heath. There'd be murder. I wouldn't mind, but the Valley of the Ice Maiden is now a suburb of Bulawayo, just beyond the bus terminus."

"Well I hope you don't dredge up many more like him," remarked the scribe. "What we need is a few more like Giulietta." She coloured, prettily.

"You had better ask Miss Amargamente about that," said Bran. "She's in charge of selection from Limbo. She does the arrangements and contracts. There isn't an Irishman or woman amongst those chosen. The next one is El Burlador or Señor Burlador. I think the word means a joker. Miss Amargamente was trying to get the text of a lost play by Lope de Vega and had to settle for his contemporary, Tirso de Molina, the merry monk. Anyway he is out of a story that his reverence devised one day when he was laughing at a washerwoman pissing in the Manzanares. He wanted to know which made most water, the river or the bladder. It's called *La picara asalariada,* The Pensioned Bawd. Dubious company for Giulietta.

"Then there's Maupassant's Algerian girl. I swear to God, she sounds as if she might liven up the old homestead: also the weirdest couple you ever heard of, out of a story by Isak Dinesen. It is said that they lived in a castle in New Caledonia full of liveried servants with bones through their noses. I warned Loreto about them, but she has this positive thinking obsession and won't be advised."

"I can see hard times ahead," observed the scribe, and then, remembering Giulietta's rapidly approaching apotheosis with a stab of pain, he faltered. She looked at his face, and touched his hand.

"Don't grieve for me, dear Scribble. The Christians of Rome sang joyously when the wild beasts crouched for their spring, in the amphitheatre. There are things that I regret leaving, on earth, but to sit at the feet of Dante and Petrarch is joy enough to assuage my small fears."

"You've just passed the coffee shop," Bran pointed out. "The best off-licence is across the road, and Eevell says that if you can't get a twenty-year-old malt, Vichy water will do. She is getting very fretful these days."

18

The apotheosis of Giulietta, when it finally came, left the scribe prostrate, but yet at the same time gave him courage in his secret war on his exploiters. Eevell alone, among the busy entities, had time to be sympathetic. "Don't fret your heart, Scribble me oul segotia. At this very moment she's probably taking a cup of scented wine with Ariosto or Aretino or someone like that."

"I sincerely hope not," replied the scribe. "I don't like the sound of that at all."

"Still and all," consoled Eevell, "she wasn't your type: much too devout. At one time she had beatific visions. She ought to have gone to heaven, and that's a plain and simple fact, but there's no way around that."

Eevell was stitching herself a Greek-looking garment split down the side but held by a tape at the hips. The scribe thought back over past events.

The pre-publication advertising for the book had been a daily wound as he opened the newspapers or reviews. Then there was the grotesque publishers' party, with the whiskey reserved for the favoured few and nobody giving a tinker's curse about the book. Indeed it was a slender volume, barely a hundred pages long, and it had to be reinforced with a monographic biography and a selection of poetic translations.

Nothing happened to Giulietta, at first, and the tension was unbearable. The poor girl herself was uncertain about protocol. Should she be in bed, or should she wait in some appointed place? How should she dress? Naked and pure, or in something more suitable for baroque iconography?

By next day there was still no change, nor for several days more. On Sunday morning she was still there, able to take some hot chocolate and cream, with some biscuits, for breakfast. Two reviews appeared, one a reappraisal of Conor Cruise O'Brien's *Maria Cross* on the subject of Catholic thought, mentioning Manzoni in passing. The other remarked on the agreeable addition to the work of a neglected writer. But neither of these wrought any change in Giulietta, nor had any effect in translating her into the realms of Art Triumphant. Tension in the house increased and Sir Glanville got on everyone's nerves by practising with dumbbells in the solarium.

MacGilla suggested a stroll towards the Whitestone Pond on the top of the Heath, above Hampstead Village. There was uncertainty about Giulietta, whose time must surely come soon, but she was all for a stroll. Eevell had taken to nursing the girl, out of kindness, but her only physic, apart from sympathy, consisted of herbal purges. These, she declared, would leave her free and empty for apotheosis. Loreto suggested a bottle of gin and a very hot bath.

The party set out, excluding Sir Glanville, who wanted to do a tour of the Natural History Museum in South Kensington. It was his intention, before his own impending apotheosis, to thrash out, for once and for all, the business of the misnamed Okapi which he claimed to have shot, and catalogued twenty years earlier and named the Trenchbeeste. He had previously been asked to leave the museum for giving a spontaneous lecture on the subject to a passing crocodile of school-children and ending up by telling them that its dung, sundried, mixed with dark shag tobacco, had a lightening effect on the lungs at a high altitude.

"By God, my dears! Mix a bit of that shit with your sundown cigar and you'll see all the visions of Paradise. Damn fine girls, with flesh on them. And trumpets. Bloody great brass bastards. Playing voluntaries. Got the tip from an old Matabele. Damn fine fella."

Africa was still a land of legend in his day.

The party, in suitable dress for the warm weather, wound its way uphill to the Whitestone Pond. Bunting festooned the lampposts as they scaled the heights and as they reached the plateau of the pond, with the city lying beneath them, they remembered, or the scribe remembered, that this was the opening day of the Hampstead Arts Festival. Screens erected on the far pavement were hung with brightly coloured paintings, agreeable at a distance but diminishing in impact with degrees of nearness. Beside the pond, a tower had been erected, of steel scaffolding, and festooned with silvered plastic fringes, glittering in the breeze. The structure was intended to convey certain spatial significances, and was also to be used to broadcast to the excited masses messages from various gurus of the fine arts.

On the path around the pond was a string of sausage-shaped plastic balloons about fifteen feet long apiece and inflated, but not to hardness. Anchored to concrete blocks here and there, they stirred and shifted in the zephyrs. Children ran screaming up and down the path, and jumping astride the plastic dirigibles and squeezing them. This fulfilled the intention of their creators, but with an important difference. The innocents were below the level of aesthetic detachment and they took uninhibited pleasure in the tactile vaulting balloons: which was not permitted. Angry stewards chased them away and thereby saved the Arts Committee a useful sum of money. Adults were invited to stroke the sausages, and receive a tactile and Freudian release in the process. They were also expected to enjoy their impending detumescence.

"Christ, they look like French letters for Moby Dick," remarked MacGilla.

"You red-necked bog Indian," reproved Loreto. "Can't you see the opalescence where the light catches the form, and the transparency where the pond water has splashed them? Do they suggest breasts to you?" she asked Mountmellick, "or phalluses?"

He frowned in concentration. "More like plastic bags," he suggested, "or synthetic sausage skins."

"That's what they are meant to suggest," Loreto reproved.

"Will there be fireworks?" asked Giulietta nervously. "I don't like loud bangs. Aren't the big balloons pretty? What are they for?"

"For touching."

"How beautiful! Like a cat's paw." She smiled and searched her mind for textural pleasures and memories. Mountmellick and Loreto had strolled a few paces ahead, and Liadin and MacGilla were looking across the balloons into the water, surrounded by small boys who had been cheated of their boat sailing by the adult play therapy. The plateau of the Heath, where several roads join around the islanded pond, was crowded. Even the wooded hills below failed to swallow the dotted colours of swarming pleasure-seekers. Someone was testing out the microphone on the plastic tower preparatory to the poetry recitations. "Testing one two three four. Can you get me, Bert? Oh Kay."

"I never liked festas," Giulietta remarked, quietly. "But this one is surprisingly sober and well-behaved. Even the air is scented."

"That's car-exhaust fumes," the scribe explained. She started to walk ahead of him towards the plastic bags fringing the water, when she suddenly stopped and raised her face as if to look at something in the sky. Her hands fell to her side and a smile lightened the soft flesh of her face. People bumped into her, apologising, but she stayed transfixed.

"What's wrong? Are you all right?" The scribe rushed to her side, but her face was still turned to the sky. Bran came bounding across and sniffed her, and then put his snout along his forelegs. But he was up in a second, yelling in tolerable Anglo-Irish, "Hey Mountmellick, Liadin. It's starting. Giulietta is going up. It's too late to do anything."

Several wayfarers identified the source of this advice, but no record is available to date of their reaction. Most, if they thought at all, probably attributed it to the scribe, who by now was trying to seize Giulietta's hands and search into her face. The rest of the coven rushed up, joined by Eevell who had been lurking some distance away, across a narrow road, talking to a herd of mild-faced asses being saddled for donkey rides. She pushed the others aside, knelt down on the path and put the side of her face to Giulietta's unresponsive lap or belly. Then she did the same standing up, stooping to touch the face of the Manzoni girl with her own cheek. A crowd formed, keeping its distance for fear of illness or emergency, but no first-aid volunteer came forth, thanks to Eevell.

"Her flesh is glowing," announced Eevell. "It won't be long now. Jaysus, this is going to cause a roadblock as far as Dover."

Mountmellick was panic-stricken. "This is dreadful. Right in front of everyone. Get an ambulance, someone."

"Someone's gone to phone for one," volunteered an onlooker. "It'll be a quarter of an hour in this crush."

"She'll be on a better escarpment than Hampstead fucking Heath by then," said Eevell. "Hey, look out. Her flesh is beginning to change." She ran her enormous hands up and down Giulietta's legs, raising the long skirts to the top and increasing morbid curiosity amongst some spectators.

Suddenly Eevell was decisive. "Quick. She may take fire. It's a very complicated chemical change. She's giving off too much heat. Get her clothes off and get her into the water."

For some reason, nobody thought this odd. Liadin started removing her coat, and Eevell fumbled her large hands at buttons, assisted by a shiny-faced matron of the Girl Guide class. Giulietta remained standing, her face towards the sun, and she made no remonstrances, despite her Jansenist shyness, nor did she react in any way. It was when the helpful Girl Guide captain was removing her half-length boots that she noticed that the girl's feet were an inch above the ground.

She gave a scream. Passing crowds on the far side of the pond started hurrying to circle its perimeter to see what was going on. Eevell's fingers managed to pull off stockings and a long shift or camisole prettily embroidered in tones of white, and MacGilla and Liadin succeeded in removing her dress.

Naked she was lovely: very curved, small but rich breasts, a long waist and long alpine legs, the shared inheritance of Celt and Goth. But the extraordinary thing was the texture of her flesh and hair. It had a weightless luminescence, and her opened eyes were turned upwards in a way that seemed familiar. Only later did it identify itself as the likeness of a Bernini *Assumption.*

"Get her into the wather, quick," Eevell cried. "Here, let me." She laid her hands on Giulietta's waist and the girl lifted lightly as a foamed shape. Striding across the inflated plastic occurrences, she waded into the water, shin-deep, and set the girl in the centre of the pond, where she remained, her hands at her sides, arms slightly back from her trunk, her feet a few inches above the rippled surface. Her body remained erect and her eyes stared at some unseen movement in the heavens.

Eevell splashed and scrambled back to the edge.

"Leave her alone. It's not safe."

The crowds were fifty-deep around the entire perimeter of the pond, staring at the naked levitating girl. Those whose reaction was pathologically morbid were stricken with a migraine, and even the dullest of wit knew somehow that this was more than an arranged happening to shock bourgeois society. There was a quality, a rarity of substance about the naked girl that penetrated the grossest brains. Four policemen, drawn from traffic direction on the steep hill of Heath Street, pushed their way to the water's edge on the far side from the coven, and stood staring. An elderly woman knelt down and started praying in Polish or Czech. Those around her knew in some way that the action was appropriate.

"Let's get away," MacGilla muttered to his colleagues, including the scribe. "Shut up, you four-legged omadaun," he snarled at Bran, who was up to his belly in the water reciting a Petrarch sonnet in a shrill canine voice.

There was no attempt to detain them. Even the most officious person was too numbed by the strange events. Scribble followed, taking one Orphic glance backwards, over his shoulder, at Giulietta. Her position was unchanged except for her arms, which were folded so that her breast was now enclosed in her open palms.

He pushed and shoved after the coven, and noticed that he was still grasping her embroidered shift which Eevell had thrown to him. The others were standing, stunned at their Pandora miracle, under a huge parasol chestnut tree, beside the patient soft-nosed asses. They were sixty yards from the pond's edge, and about seventy from the hidden Italian girl, and the crowd was now about three thousand strong around the water.

"I declare to Breed," said Eevell. "Look!"

Giulietta was rising, still upright, her flesh shining. Ten feet above the surface of the water, over the heads of the crowd, the scribe could see her clearly, her body bent, knees slightly raised, one more than the other. Her hands parted and her arms moved back in her shoulder joints and clouds rose from the pond's surface to eddy and coalesce around her, forming a billowing wreathing couch, on which she was reclining. One foot hung below the cloud's edge, and her half-reclining back allowed her to raise her arms slowly towards the heavens. Darker and lighter tones of cloud took on a pink luminous form, which thousands afterwards swore were little naked children, with spreading wings, swirling, turning and circling the vaporous tabernacle.

206 ☙ Desmond MacNamara

Some said that there was a silence so terrible that it dried the depths of the ear canals. Others heard a rushing roar. But the scribe could clearly distinguish a thousand harmonious voluntaries from crystal horns and the far polyphony of waiting Muses.

The mass of effulgent cloud rose into the air, gaining in solid form as its soft vaporous tendrils were drawn into it or were lost to the eye's perception. The underparts, as with ominous storms, were blue-black and solid as basalt, and outlined Giulietta's trailing foot, so small and high of instep. Higher, the mass which cushioned her weight was golden, white and pink with a subtle lambency that would have made Rubens despair.

At about three hundred feet, not so much higher than the highest antique tree, the cloud dissolved itself into a flock of amorini. This time there could be no mistake. Their dimpled bottoms and bulging bellies could be clearly seen, though it was hard to tell at such a distance for certain if they were entirely male. The general impression of their wings was of a bright metallic gold and copper green, though Liadin swore that some were of the deepest and purest ultramarine.

The vibration of a thousand wings shimmered around the last sight of Giulietta, as her transformed substance was carried upwards swiftly to a vanishing point in the bright aether.

The coven got away by the skin of its teeth. Indeed, Bran had to start a mock fight with a Boxer bitch to distract attention. His barking and growling were earsplitting, broken with forgetful verbal abuse. "Don't show your teeth, you overbred bitch. I'd rather mount a calliope horse down in the Fun Fair below." But it worked. On uncertain legs, low in blood sugar and drenched in sweat, the scribe stumbled down the steep narrow hill of Frognal to emptied privacy. The others followed, but he neither asked their feelings nor spoke to them in any way.

Eevell's later comment touched a truth. "It was like a baby being born, a baby messiah."

There was a council of war that evening, after the coven had watched a large part of the process reported on television news. Miracles come easily on the television screen, so despite the denials of the Arts Festival organisers, the general public accepted the phenomenon without much analysis. Those who were there in the flesh, however, were more deeply disturbed.

Mountmellick was terrified of the adverse publicity, although MacGilla was of the opinion that they would ride any possible storm. Loreto's only regret was the difficulty about using the event for publicity purposes.

"In an age of shrinking faith, would people believe it?" she asked. Furthermore, in a country operating on a vestigial Protestant ethic, was it a desirable form of publicity? Would Italy be better? What would be the attitude of the authorities and the masses, clerical, pontifical or political, if an apotheosis were arranged in the Muse gardens on the top of the Pincio Hill in Rome, a more appropriate place than Hampstead Heath?

Decisions were deferred, and it was decided that Sir Glanville's pending apotheosis would take place at night in the garden, or in some remote part of Suffolk. Eevell advanced the theory that hot baths, purges and enemas could induce the process, and save the dangers of spontaneous assumption.

The scribe, some hours after this meeting, was making up his notes of events, both the general transcription and the secret version. Bran was crouched by his side, in the empty pool room.

"What would happen if that ever got published?" he asked.

"I don't know. Up to now I couldn't dare try. You lot, or at least the others, had such a hold of my mind and my curiosity compulsions that it was impossible to think of it. Of course, this is what they were trading on."

"But now?"

"If this got published they'd all go up like Giulietta today, but more vulgarly. Molto pomposo."

"If I looked the other way when I took you for exercise, you could post it to an agent."

"Why would you do that?" Bran scratched a flea.

"I don't fancy this gaff much. If you left me out of the ms. the others would float up to heaven, assuming, that is, that all this drivel is publishable. Then you could give me a home and act as my secretary. I think you'd find me a good employer."

"You still want to be a writer?"

"Oh, I have a few novels inside of me. Don't worry about that."

The scribe considered it. Bran was a pleasant animal, but he had all of a dog's demanding ego.

"It's no good," he said. "They'd find out. I could never get this pile of bumf out of the house unnoticed. They watch me like hawks.

Particularly Eevell."

Conversation receded and he went on writing. The clock tocked on the wall. Then Bran stirred and snuffled. "I can see a way."

"How? Where? What do you mean?"

"Follow me."

He led the way into the front room, which was free of entities. Rising on his paws he looked out of the window onto the front garden. "What can you see there?"

The scribe peered. "A monkey puzzle, grass. Parked cars."

"No. Not there. On the windowsill outside."

"Milk bottles?" About a dozen half-rinsed opalescent dairy bottles were lined up for collection.

Bran looked over his shoulder at him. "Who puts them out every morning?" he asked.

"Why, for the last week or two I have," admitted the scribe.

"Bottles have many uses," observed Bran. "You don't have to be in the middle of the ocean to discover them all."

The scribe pondered. "I'll have to think about it."

"Fair enough," said Bran. "But remember. Don't forget to blue pencil me. That's a bargain."

"Of course. But I don't think . . ."

For several successive mornings Sir Glanville came down for morning coffee and a chat. His publication had been delayed and he hoped for a little rough shooting the following week. The scribe bore him with agony, until a damp overcast day arrived.

Sir Glanville did not make an appearance. Perhaps the reason for his absence was trivial, but the scribe asked no questions, however commonplace, for fear of drawing suspicion to himself, unlikely as that might be. Mountmellick, Liadin and Loreto chatted lightly over breakfast and Liadin collected their various folders of papers and put them in a wicker shopping basket which she preferred to the more conventional briefcase. MacGilla announced that the car had been brought round from the mews and they departed, as casually as on any working day, Mountmellick courteously insisting on carrying the basket, and withdrawing it from Liadin's protesting hand. Before Eevell retired to her bath, accompanied by Bran, she gave a coaxing direction to the scribe.

"Clean out that kitchen, son, and dump those effing milk bottles outside. I'd have broken my bollocks on them twice over this morning, only I'm a woman."

It was the Fates, the three malevolent sisters, for once dropping a stitch in their universal fabric.

There were eighteen chapters in the secret account of the scribe's intrusion, each one stapled separately and capable of being rolled and thrust into a milk bottle. Each cylinder of paper had a tag which said, "Urgent. Am being held a prisoner. Take these to the nearest publisher."

Author's Note

A complex piece of writing should, I feel, be self-explanatory, granted a common experience between writer and reader. A few people, I discovered, took this novel with Teutonic solemnity and sought for deeper matters, not realising that comedy describes the human condition more effectively than tragedy. In essence this book is a joke about pedantry. Mountmellick, a central character, is based on some of the pomposities of a distinguished curator, now dead: a kindly man, at times I must admit, but obsessed by the desire for international estimation. Very funny but utterly unrecognisable as I restructured a few of his parts.

This book is a sort of Celtic interlace of yarns, speculations, gestes, stories, all of which are hopefully held together by the conceit that a collection of fictional characters escape from Limbo and are in the process of becoming solid flesh, through the act of recording the overall story: as solid and real as Hamlet, Lady Macbeth, Tristram Shandy and many more. For base reasons they have chosen to forego their immortality either in Limbo or on Parnassus and assume the tribulations of the flesh. It also makes it much easier to write about their adventures.

The book is, of course, a Celtic design of utter and hopefully pleasant nonsense, like the Chi-Ro page in the *Book of Kells,* but of more modest pretensions. But it is meant to be preposterous, funny, absurd and at times truthful. Some knowledge of Anglo-Irish and English writing is helpful, though not essential. I cut the more exotic bits like a boozy weekend with the Goncourt Brothers and suchlike. The title however is important since it is intrinsic, and in a sense begat the whole idea.

The *Labor Gabala* (modern Irish *Leabher Gabhela*) or *Book of Invasions* is a compilation of records from early Irish mss. (*The Book of the Dun Cow, The Yellow Book of Lecan,* etc.). This lists a series of invasions or colonisations of the island, five in all, and salvaged from Druidic and bardic lore by early Christian (or quasi-Christian) literates and all too briefly recorded. The last three "invasions," the Firbolgs, the Tuatha de Danaan and the Milesians (Gaels), are taken, nowadays, to refer to the Belgae from northern France, the Celtic gods recently superceded, and lastly the Gaelic-speaking cattle-ranching Irish. It is far more complicated than that, of course. There were other peoples, earlier and later, tribal divisions and different but possibly related languages. However, the *Book of Invasions,* known crudely to every Irish schoolchild, contains enough mystery for generations of specialisation to come, and recent archaeology supports much of it and contradicts none.

It can be seen that *The Book of Intrusions* is a pun that took 3,000 years to complete, and cannot be considered lightly.

All the characters in the book and the works from which they emerged are fiction: fiction beyond fiction, but there are three exceptions. Liadin and Curither were actual poets as is an early poem. The story contemplated by George Moore in Ebury Street is entirely invented, though the poet Austin Clarke once hazarded a guess to me that Moore was contemplating a novel on early poets or writers and Liadin and Curither would have been a tempting choice.

The third character is Queen Eevell, the queen of the Munster sidhe, tall and terrifying. Brendan Behan translated Merriman's *Midnight Court,* partly in prison where he gave his trade as poet, and being under age had to be supplied with suitable tools for his craft. He chose this late eighteenth-century poem in classical couplets, first time used in Gaelic. His translation was lost on a building scaffold on a refurbished Georgian townhouse by the then musical director of the Abbey Theatre, who may have been drunk. He certainly was later on the same day. Anyway that's why the Queen has to make her most formal statements in Alexandrian couplets, before lapsing into normal Behan speech. Large sections of her dialogue are remembered utterances and imprecations, fairly accurately recollected. He was given to rather melancholic dissertation at four in the morning, drinking glasses of water and sitting on one's bed end. Neither privacy nor sleep was possible. Eevell is Brendan, better depicted than anyone, I feel, though Anthony Cronin's *Dead as Doornails* is a superb and accurate analysis of his persona.

The James Stephens' talking dog is invented, though consistent with his hard-edged whimsy. His interest in women's corsets was related to me by Patrick Kavanagh, the poet, together with Stephens' remark to Kavanagh in Oxford Circus that a woman in corsets was as impressive as a field marshal festooned in ribbons and medals. I didn't know Stephens, who was born at the same hour and day as James Joyce, but I knew many people who did, so I absorbed the gossip.

The Manzoni story is a fabrication but there *was* a small fire in the downstairs library in the Villa Manzoni, Brusuglio, in about 1830 which scorched some bookbindings and documents, the results of which were evident in 1948 and thereafter.

Charles Lever, the widely popular Anglo-Irish novelist, was in England during the early days of the Chartist movement. He continued to write novels with Peninsular War backgrounds (*Charles O'Malley* and *Burke of Burkes*) and ended up as British Consul at Trieste, a focal point of British intrigues into Hapsburg counter intrigues.

I don't know if J. P. Donleavy ever abandoned an unfinished novel in a cottage at Kilcool. He always kept papers carefully. Still, there is a philosophical truth to the idea. Whenever we meet the time passes in reminiscence and mild scandals and I keep forgetting to tell him. I expect he would approve. The last time ended in a midnight burglary in his echoing lakeside mansion, which was somewhat distracting.

I hope this labyrinthine epilogue is helpful. One more trifle. The pissing competition amongst the princesses of Tir na n-Óg (Land of Ever Youth) is founded on the attribution of several small lakes to the bladder of Queen Medb: one of the many clues to her being a Celtic deity rather than a warrior queen. Small lakes were often sacred places.

In the 1840s and '50s several texts from old mss. were translated by sundry antiquarians and published bilingually and privately by the Ossianic Society and passed into the Royal Irish Academy archives. I have a copy of one of them, *The Contention of the Bards,* which makes extraordinary reading. Robert Graves uses it at length in his *White Goddess.* Incidentally, Sir Samuel Ferguson and Sir William Wilde (Oscar's father) were founding members of the Ossianic Society.